PENGUIN BOOKS

The Inner Darkness

Having worked as a police officer and head of investigations before becoming a full-time writer, Jørn Lier Horst has established himself as one of the most successful authors to come out of Scandinavia. His books have sold over two million copies in his native Norway alone and he's published in twenty-six languages. The Wisting series, produced by the team behind *Wallander* and *The Girl with the Dragon Tattoo*, was a hit BBC series in 2019.

The Inner Darkness

JØRN LIER HORST

translated by Anne Bruce

PENGUIN BOOKS

PENGUIN BOOKS

UK | USA | Canada | Ireland | Australia
India | New Zealand | South Africa

Penguin Books is part of the Penguin Random House group of companies
whose addresses can be found at global.penguinrandomhouse.com

First published in the UK by Michael Joseph, 2020
This paperback edition published by Penguin Books, 2021

001

Copyright © Jørn Lier Horst, 2020
English translation copyright © Anne Bruce, 2020

The moral right of the author has been asserted

Typeset by Jouve (UK), Milton Keynes
Printed and bound in Italy by Grafica Veneta S.p.A.

The authorized representative in the EEA is Penguin Random House Ireland,
Morrison Chambers, 32 Nassau Street, Dublin D02 YH68

A CIP catalogue record for this book is available from the British Library

ISBN: 978-1-405-94163-1

Line raised her head to peer through the door's wire-mesh window. She could see him at the end of the corridor. Tom Kerr, walking towards her, escorted by prison wardens in front and behind.

He had changed.

Immediately after his arrest and during his trial four years earlier, his face had been splashed across all the media. Smooth shaven and with dark eyes and thick, cropped hair. Well groomed, in an effort to create a good impression. Now he looked more like the man he really was, someone capable of the crimes for which he was behind bars. His shoulders were broader, his chest thrust further forward. A curtain of hair hung over his forehead and his pale complexion was flawed. His angry eyes stared straight ahead as he chewed gum with his mouth open, a froth of saliva collecting in one corner of his mouth.

When he reached the door separating him from the waiting police officers, keys rattled while Tom Kerr moved his head from side to side, hoisted his shoulders and rolled them, as if to loosen stiff muscles.

Line glanced across at Adrian Stiller, who nodded in response.

She lifted her camera and took a step back, ready to film.

The prison warden opened the door, sending a cold draught into the room. Tom Kerr's mouth stretched into a smile, as if someone had said something that amused him. As he crossed the threshold, Line caught him in her lens and started recording. He was wearing blue jeans, a grey T-shirt and a dark training jacket.

Adrian Stiller stepped forward to enter the picture. Half a head shorter than the man facing him, he held a folder in one hand and a radio transmitter in the other, making it impossible to shake hands.

'Tom Kerr,' Stiller said in an artificial, formal tone. 'You've agreed to take part in a crime-related site visit.' He glanced at the camera. 'Everything you say will be recorded and form part of your legal statement. However, you can seek assistance from, and confer with, your lawyer as we progress, without that being recorded.'

Line zoomed out to include Claes Thancke in the picture. The defence lawyer, dressed in a dark suit, wore a pair of black shoes hardly suitable for the forthcoming expedition.

He had been involved in many controversial cases and his clients were among the most notorious of criminals, the ones from whom society needed protection. He was known as a capable advocate, but Line had never liked the way he trivialized his cases to the media.

'I'm the lead officer for the site visit,' Stiller went on. 'We'll both be equipped with a microphone and transmitter to secure a recording of your statement.'

He gestured with the hand holding the transmitter. 'I'm going to attach it to you now.'

Tom Kerr answered with a nod. Stiller handed him the tiny microphone so that he could tuck it beneath his T-shirt and fasten it to the neckband. Then he walked around him and spent some time attaching the transmitter to his belt at the back.

'Can you say something so we know that it's working?'

'Test, test,' Kerr complied, speaking in a rough, gravelly voice.

Line checked the sound input levels on her camera and nodded to Stiller. She had prepared twelve hours' battery and recording capacity, longer than she had arranged for a babysitter.

'Do you have anything with you?' Stiller demanded.

'What do you mean?' Kerr asked.

'Do you have anything on you? In your pockets?'

'No.'

Stiller produced a pair of latex gloves from his back pocket. 'I have to check,' he insisted.

Kerr reached his hands above his head, clearly a well-practised move. Stiller ran his hands over the prisoner's pockets and the outside of his jeans.

'Open up!'

Tom Kerr stuck out his tongue and raised it to the roof of his mouth to demonstrate that he had nothing hidden in there.

'Take off your shoes,' Stiller continued.

Kerr placed the toe of one trainer on the heel of the other and flipped it off.

'I've been inside for four years,' he said, stepping out of the other shoe. 'Do you really think I've found something in here I'd want to smuggle out?'

Without answering, Stiller picked up the shoe and stood with his back turned slightly from the camera as he examined it.

Line looked up, her eyes on Stiller's back and the taut muscles beneath his thin shirt.

'OK,' he said, placing the shoes in front of the prisoner. 'Not counting the driver and camerawoman, we'll be six persons in the minibus, in addition to you.'

Wrenching off the latex gloves, he cast around for a rubbish bin, but found none.

'Sergeant Gram will be responsible for security during the operation,' he said, pointing at a police officer in a protective suit.

Line brought him into the picture.

Gram stood ready with handcuffs and leg irons, an additional precaution when transporting prisoners. He approached Kerr and indicated that he should hold out his hands.

Kerr turned to speak to Stiller. 'Do I need to have leg irons as well?' he asked, sounding dismayed.

'He's the one to decide,' Stiller replied, gesturing towards Gram.

This seemed to be a normal division of roles, with the uniformed officer taking charge of any confrontational aspects.

'You've been assessed as an escape risk,' he stated brusquely.

The defence lawyer intervened: 'You're eight against one, and that's only in the vehicle.' He argued further: 'Probably even more of you on site. Is this really necessary?'

'It's not up for discussion,' Gram answered. 'You submitted a letter of complaint to the National Police Directorate and received approval for this site visit to go ahead without our officers being armed.'

'You know very well why that's the case,' the lawyer went on. 'Two officers fired shots during his arrest, entirely without justification. It was sheer chance that he wasn't wounded.'

Ignoring him, Gram eyeballed Tom Kerr. 'Loosen your belt,' he said.

Kerr complied. Line held her focus on the image, documenting how Gram led a chain with a ring attached down the inside of one trouser leg and locked it around his ankle. The other end was fastened securely to the handcuffs.

There was a real danger that Tom Kerr would attempt to escape. He had been sentenced to twenty-one years in custody with a minimum term of fifteen years. This meant that after this period had elapsed, his sentence could be extended by up to five years at a time for as long as the law believed there was considerable risk that he would commit further crimes upon release. In reality this sentence could entail a lifetime in custody. He had nothing to lose by trying to escape.

'Are we ready?' Stiller asked.

With a nod, Gram barked an order over the police radio. One of the waiting prison wardens unlocked the next security door, letting them through to the minibus parked outside.

Line had kept her distance, approaching Tom Kerr only by means of her camera lens. Now he walked towards her. The handcuffs and leg irons caused him to take short steps and slowed his gait. As he passed Line, he turned and looked straight into the camera, so close that she could smell him. A dank, stale odour reminiscent of the interior of a house left empty for a long time.

2

'Over there,' Hammer said, pointing.

A police car blocked the gravel track. Slowing down, William Wisting switched on his indicator and pulled up at the verge.

The other vehicle reversed out to make room. A side window rolled down and a young policewoman stuck her head out. She was one of the new recruits in the patrol section, but he could not recall her name.

Driving forward, Wisting stopped alongside and lowered his own side window. It came to him that her name was Marlene. Marlene Koht.

'They haven't arrived yet,' she told him.

'We're a bit early,' he said. 'Has there been any traffic?'

Marlene Koht shook her head.

'We've been parked here for three hours,' she replied, lifting a clipboard from her lap. A sheet of paper with a short list of names of those who had driven in or out was attached with a steel clip.

'We're only talking about a handful of locals,' she explained.

Hammer leaned forward from the passenger seat and looked across. 'No press?' he asked.

'No press,' Marlene Koht assured him.

Wisting thanked her. A scatter of pebbles struck the wheel arches as he started up and drove on.

The black fields flanking the car were freshly ploughed and the bumpy track eventually led into dense deciduous forest. At this point in the middle of September, some of the trees had already begun to shed their yellowing leaves.

The track followed a low dry-stone wall. Here and there, narrow access tracks led to the occasional summer cabin. After driving for a couple of minutes, they arrived at an open space where the ruins of an old sawmill stood beside a meadow.

Wisting turned and parked the car, making sure not to block access for the others when they arrived.

It was 10.50 a.m.

Pushing open the car door, he grabbed the frame with both hands to haul himself up and out. It was a mild autumn day with full sun. For a moment or two he stood listening to birds chirping somewhere nearby. Then he closed the door behind him, moved round to the front of the car and leaned back on the bonnet.

Hammer stood beside him with his hands deep inside his trouser pockets.

'What do you think?' he asked.

'It's possible,' Wisting replied, squinting at the woods on the far side of the meadow.

He and Hammer had been here four days earlier and walked along many of these narrow tracks. They were familiar with the terrain. Eftangland was a peninsula comprising almost 1,250 acres of rolling countryside filled with forest and agricultural land. To the east lay a marshy area before the road at Ulaveien formed a natural border. In every other direction the landscape ended at a coastline that alternated between smooth rocks and shallow sandy coves.

She could be lying somewhere out here.

Taran Norum.

The young woman had been nineteen years old when she disappeared on her way home from a party with some classmates at Bekkelaget, less than six hundred metres from her own neighbourhood. The search had started at around 2 p.m.

the following day. All that had been found was her phone and one shoe.

Nothing connected Tom Kerr to her disappearance, but two months earlier, Thea Polden had gone missing in the same way from a residential area at Stovner. Someone had pointed out the similarities, but serious speculation had not begun until Salwa Haddad had vanished on her way home from her boyfriend's house in Hellerud. Three girls of the same age had disappeared in similar circumstances. The badly beaten corpses of Thea Polden and Salwa Haddad were later found near Nøklevann lake. Taran Norum was the second girl to disappear, but as the case unfolded and subsequently in court, she was referred to as 'the third victim', the one who had never been found.

'But the dogs should have detected something when they were here,' Wisting pointed out.

Removing a sachet of snuff from beneath his lip, Hammer tossed it on a heap of grey sawdust.

'It was nearly five years ago,' he said. 'I don't know how efficient they are, really. Anyway, it's not certain that her whole body is in one place. After all, the others were dismembered.'

Deep in thought, Wisting drew the toe of his shoe across the ground. It was five days since they had been informed that Tom Kerr's third victim might be hidden in their police district. A fellow prisoner had contacted the prison authorities and told them that Kerr had confessed to him that he had murdered Taran Norum. Confronted with this allegation, Kerr had surprisingly admitted this to the investigators in the Cold Cases Group at Kripos, the National Criminal Investigation Service, and expressed his willingness to show them where he had buried her.

'I don't know what Tom Kerr is up to,' Hammer went on.

'But I don't entirely believe that he wants to cooperate with the police.'

'Strategy,' Wisting said.

Kerr had requested a move from the penal institution where he was currently held to the less draconian conditions at Halden Prison in return for his confession. This would mean that he would be spared contact with prisoners with mental illnesses and give him greater educational opportunities. A full confession would be regarded as settling up with the past and also demonstrate the kind of changed behaviour deemed necessary for later assessment of parole.

Wisting had no confidence that, in the long run, this would help Kerr leave prison. The man's crimes were so brutal and so permeated with evil intent that it would take far more than this to warrant releasing him back into society.

The negotiations with Kerr had involved both the Director General of Public Prosecution and the National Police Directorate and had continued for several weeks. Wisting himself had never had any dealings with Kerr, as Oslo Police District had investigated the killings. Kerr had no connection to Wisting's police district, but now he had pointed out Refsholt sawmill as the most appropriate assembly point for him to show them the burial site of his third victim.

He had obviously been there, as he had given a detailed description of the meadow, the old sawmill and the remnants of machinery left there, but he had failed to explain why he had chosen that particular spot.

The police radio on Hammer's belt crackled into life. The prison transport with Kerr in custody announced its arrival on the main road.

When Kerr had designated an assembly point, the area surrounding the sawmill had been searched with cadaver dogs in the hope of beating him to it. This had failed to yield results, reinforcing the arguments of those who felt that the site visit itself was being arranged as cover for an escape attempt. In the early hours of morning, a checkpoint had been set up at the end of the approach road and several undercover vehicles had been placed at strategic intervals on all the surrounding roads. They had taken every precaution.

3

The black minibus was escorted by two uniformed patrols. Behind them, the lawyer followed in a Mercedes with tinted windows.

A caged police dog began to bark as the vehicles drew to a halt.

Adrian Stiller was first to step out. There had been no active investigation of Taran Norum's disappearance in the past four years. All stones had been turned. The trail had gone cold and the documents transferred to the Kripos Cold Cases Group as a matter of routine, giving Stiller responsibility for the new investigation.

Wisting and Stiller shook hands.

'Helicopter?' Stiller asked, lifting his eyes to the blue autumn sky.

'The new helicopter has been redirected to a search operation in Kongsvinger,' Hammer explained. 'A nine-year-old has gone missing. They can be here in thirty-five minutes, though. The old one's in for overhaul. Gram has been informed.'

Hammer nodded in the direction of the burly policeman who stood at the open sliding door of the minibus, talking on the phone. Kittil Gram had attended the preparatory meetings at which the various responsibilities had been divvied up. On the actual expedition, Wisting and Hammer's only role would be as observers.

'I would have organized a flyover and heat-seeking camera to see if there's anyone in the area,' Stiller said.

He approached Gram and, after a cursory consultation, it appeared that they had decided to go ahead. Once Gram had issued a few brief orders, the sniffer dog was brought out and the minibus began to empty. Two policemen stepped out first, followed by a policewoman. Wisting gave the female officer a passing nod. Maren Dokken. When she had served a probationary period in the Criminal Investigation Department, she had proved impressive. Possessing the analytical eye needed to pick up on crucial little details, she would one day make a fine detective, but at present she was working in the patrol section.

Line emerged with her cine-camera. Wisting, who abhorred the idea of her involvement and disapproved strongly of Stiller employing her for this purpose, folded his arms across his chest.

Their professional paths had crossed before: she as a journalist and he as a detective. They had both been clear about their individual roles and retained their individual integrity, but he did not take kindly to her coming so close to a man like Tom Kerr, so near to such evil.

Line, more far-sighted, saw the bigger picture. She had secured first refusal on the rights to use the recordings later in a documentary film and had been in contact with a production company interested in her idea. That was not difficult to understand. The crimes Tom Kerr had committed were unusually bestial and his trial had failed to elicit all the answers. Far from it: Tom Kerr had undoubtedly had an unknown collaborator, someone the media had dubbed 'the Other One'.

Wisting's main objection had been that there was too much scope for roles to be at cross-purposes in such a project. Line could not work on a documentary at the same time as working for the police. Although aware that her employment with

12

Kripos had to end formally before she could proceed with the documentary, she felt that her presence during the site visit would provide a unique narrative approach. Anyway, that was all in the future. First Taran Norum's murder had to be cleared up and Tom Kerr found guilty in a court of law. Which could take years, but it was a process Line was keen to follow.

Wisting drew back to join the others, who were huddled in a semicircle around the minibus. Tom Kerr appeared in the doorway and his leg irons jingled as he took a final step down from the running board to the ground.

Pausing for a moment, he first raised his head to gaze at the sky before scanning all the individuals whose presence this operation necessitated. His eyes finally rested on his lawyer.

'We need to talk,' he said.

Claes Thancke stepped forward and glanced across at Stiller.

'Where can we do that, undisturbed?' he asked.

'You can go back into the minibus,' Stiller suggested.

Thancke's features took on a sceptical cast, as if he suspected the vehicle might be bugged.

'Can't we do it in my car?' he queried.

Stiller looked at Gram, who responded: 'If I can have the car keys.'

Digging them out from his pocket, Thancke tossed them to the policeman.

'Take off the recorder,' Tom Kerr insisted.

Adrian Stiller moved forward to remove the microphone lead and transmitter while Kittil Gram examined the interior of the lawyer's car.

'Into the back seat,' he said, holding the door open.

Once the lawyer and his client were seated inside, the uniformed officers moved to stand guard around the vehicle.

Claes Thancke was his family's third generation of defence lawyers and one of the country's most controversial advocates. Wisting had met him in connection with a number of cases and held him in some regard. Controversial and much criticized, he had been provocative in expressing his support for legalizing narcotics, for example, introducing euthanasia, permitting prostitution and removing the minimum age of sexual consent. These were challenging opinions that offended many. He had been forced to endure being called a male chauvinist pig and a misogynist, but Wisting respected him as a custodian of minority views and considered him a valuable asset to the rule of law. A distinguished, fearless spokesperson, he stood up for the weakest outcasts in society and took on the least popular cases. Always unbiased, he showed his clients a great deal of care and concern. Many of them were offenders who were despised and held in contempt: paedophile molesters, rapists, killers, racists and wife abusers.

Tom Kerr was one of these. Now forty-three years old, Thancke had defended him for the first time twenty-five years ago. At that time he had been found guilty of seven counts of voyeurism and slaughtering pet animals belonging to several of his neighbours. Wisting had read up on it: in court his explanation had been that he found an outlet for his anger by torturing and killing animals.

Wisting could just make out the contours of the two men behind the tinted car windows. Now and again he could discern some movement, as if one of them was pointing or clarifying something.

'What on earth do they have to talk about?' Hammer asked, sounding agitated. 'Good God, they spent an hour together in the prison before they left.'

Wisting wondered whether he should have a word with Line, but at that moment the car doors burst open again. Claes

Thancke smoothed down his suit jacket as Tom Kerr stood waiting. Stiller approached to reattach the microphone and transmitter and Line put on her earphones.

'Are you ready?' Stiller asked.

Nodding, Kerr spat on the ground before raising his hands as far as the handcuffs would allow and pointing to a track on the other side of the meadow.

'We go that way,' he said.

4

The track was little used. Line, number five in the procession, immediately behind Stiller, was continually forced to grasp the branches of nearby trees as they sprang back after the others had passed by.

She had become acquainted with Adrian Stiller through two previous cases. The first had been when she was still working for the *Verdens Gang* newspaper, making a podcast about an unsolved kidnapping case from the eighties. The other was the previous year when she had been appointed to a special investigation team tasked with tracing the origins of a considerable sum of money found in the summer cabin belonging to a recently deceased politician. She had contributed to the resolution of both cases.

Stiller had turned out to be a meticulous investigator, but she also found that he always harboured an ulterior motive in everything he did.

This was the third assignment she had carried out for him and the Cold Cases Group. The first of these had involved producing illustrations for an internal publication. The second had required her to document a reconstruction during which a man had confessed to a murder committed almost twelve years ago.

This, however, was different.

When he'd phoned her a week earlier, she had thought it had been to ask her out at first. The question had hung in the air somehow, and she had already rehearsed how she would turn him down. Although he was attractive and the difference in their ages was not so significant – he was only six years older – she would prefer to maintain the professional relationship they had developed.

The long procession moved slowly along the track, with no one uttering a word.

Line had no idea what Tom Kerr had said about Taran Norum's murder, but she was well aware of what he had done to the other two victims.

They had been callous and sadistic crimes, with both girls held captive for several days, subjected to sexual torture and in the end suffering harrowing deaths. They had been raped repeatedly, including with various implements, and some of these had been heated before being rammed into them. In each case, the intestines and urinary tract were internally torn and damaged, and the post-mortems showed that the nipples had been ripped off with pliers while the victims were still alive. After they were killed, their bodies had been dismembered, and the head, arms and legs separated from the rest of their bodies, probably to facilitate disposal of the corpses.

She turned round without deflecting the camera and noticed that her father was one of the last in line. He looked old, she thought, his movements sluggish. If it had not been for Tom Kerr being slowed down by the leg irons, he would most likely be trailing behind.

A windblown tree blocked the track and Kerr needed assistance to step over it.

'Stiller!'

Her father was shouting.

'Yes?'

'A word before we move on?'

Adrian Stiller ordered the procession to a halt as Wisting approached. Line heard their murmured conversation through her headphones, transmitted via Stiller's microphone.

'I don't like this,' her father said. 'We're more than a hundred metres along this track already. There's no logic to it.'

'What's your thinking?' Stiller asked.

'The other burial sites were less than twenty metres from where he parked his car. Why on earth would he have carried this body so far?'

Stiller glanced back along the track before turning and gazing ahead.

'Is there far to go?' he asked, now addressing Kerr.

Line zoomed in on the prisoner and listened through her earphones as he smacked his lips and spat on the ground again.

'No,' he answered.

'How far is it, then?'

Kerr shrugged and gave a languid reply: 'A couple of hundred metres. We come to an old sheep enclosure on the right-hand side, with an opening in it. Then we'll be right there.'

Stiller took a few paces towards him.

'Why did you bring her so far from the road?' he asked.

'So that she wouldn't be found,' Kerr replied. 'It worked, didn't it?'

'I know what enclosure he's talking about,' Line heard her father say. 'It's at least three hundred metres further on.'

Gram had come to join them. 'What's up?' he asked.

Stiller had no chance to answer before Claes Thancke intervened: 'Sorry it's so far for you to walk, but he really must be allowed to show us the exact location where she can be found,' he said in an ironic tone.

'This should have been made clear earlier,' Gram said.

'He refused to give us that information until we were here, on the spot,' Stiller explained. 'He wouldn't specify the direction we would take or how far it would be.'

Chains rattled further ahead along the track. The leg irons

meant that Tom Kerr had to dip his head in order to scratch his forehead.

'We'll go on,' Stiller decided.

Kittil Gram sent the dog handler on ahead with instructions to walk as far as the sheep enclosure. The others continued at Tom Kerr's pace. After a few metres, he tripped on a tree root. He fell forward and tried to throw out his hands, but the leg irons held him back. He managed to twist on to his side so that his right shoulder took the impact when he hit the ground.

Two men had to haul him up again.

'Are you OK?' Adrian Stiller demanded.

Kerr did not answer – he was busy shaking his body in an attempt to dislodge the dust and dirt he had picked up in the fall.

'These leg irons are not really suitable for a ramble through the woods,' Claes Thancke protested. 'It's surely unnecessary to expose my client to danger. He's cooperating and is here to help the police.'

'This is part of the cooperation,' Kittil Gram commented, checking that the cuffs were still in place. 'Continue.'

They walked on, Tom Kerr still determining their speed and last year's dry leaves rustling under their feet. Line shifted the camera to her other hand and now carried it at hip height. Despite weighing no more than a couple of kilos, it was awkward to hold aloft and felt heavy and cumbersome.

As the track widened and turned north, the surrounding forest changed character and the dense deciduous trees were replaced by taller trees with crooked, rough trunks and twisted, warped branches.

When Tom Kerr turned and looked back, Line could hear his breathing through her earphones: ragged and winded.

As he turned round again, he lost his balance, and though the nearest policeman tried to grab him, he fell heavily.

Line zoomed in. When he was dragged up again, she noticed that a small cut on his cheek was bleeding.

'You've got a scratch,' Kittil Gram pointed out. 'Do you want something done about that, or should we move on?'

Claes Thancke protested again about the use of handcuffs and leg irons, but received no response.

'Let's go,' Kerr replied.

After two minutes, an old barbed-wire fence could be seen on the right of the track. The pasture on the other side was overgrown and some of the posts had rotted away. Broken fragments of fencing lay in the tall grass.

The dog handler who had been sent ahead stood waiting beside the remnants of a gate. From there the ground sloped down towards a stream.

The procession stopped.

'We go down that way,' Kerr told them, jerking his head to one side.

'That's far more difficult terrain than we've been walking so far,' Claes Thancke pointed out. 'It's hardly advisable to head off down there in chains. You're risking my client sustaining a serious injury.'

As Kittil Gram and Adrian Stiller conferred with Wisting, Line adjusted her earphones. Wearing them made her feel sweaty, but she kept them on to listen in on their conversation.

'He does have a point,' her father said.

Stiller agreed.

Wisting looked across at the prisoner and then back at Gram. 'Are you comfortable with us removing the leg irons?' he asked.

Gram nodded his grudging agreement. 'As long as we keep the handcuffs.'

'Then we'll do as you both ask,' Stiller said.

Tom Kerr had to loosen his belt and Gram unlocked the clamp around his ankle and drew the chain up through his trouser leg. Then he unhooked the leg irons from the handcuffs and handed them to a policeman wearing a rucksack.

Raising his hands to his face, Kerr rubbed his fingers over the wound on his cheek. He got blood on two of his fingers and stood for a moment staring at them before putting them into his mouth and licking them clean.

The sniffer dog barked impatiently as Kittil Gram gave the order to continue.

It was now easier for Kerr to walk, but he did not move any faster. He edged diagonally down through the old pasture towards the point where the stream emerged from the trees. There appeared to be an opening in the fence there and a cart track on the other side.

The uniformed officers followed, fanning out in his wake, as if no one wanted to move too close to the prisoner. Line looked around for her father and saw that he and Nils Hammer were bringing up the rear. The lawyer with the slippery soles was also lagging behind.

All of a sudden Tom Kerr's movement altered. He flexed his knees and thrust his body forward. Line heard a deep indrawn breath in her ear. Then he broke into a run.

5

The shouts alerted Wisting, who was walking at the very back of the procession of fourteen people, his thoughts drifting to the next phase of the operation. If Tom Kerr could identify the spot where Taran Norum was buried, he would be responsible for digging up the remains and arranging the forensic examinations. They would have to clear the track in order to drive up in a four-wheel drive vehicle with all the necessary equipment.

When he heard the cries, Tom Kerr was racing towards the cart track that led through the woods on the other side of the field. Somehow he had managed to loosen one cuff and it dangled from the other wrist as he ran. He already had a good head start of almost ten metres when he passed through the opening in the fence.

Suddenly there was an ear-splitting boom. Wisting was blinded by a coruscating flash of light and thrown to the ground. Colours in grotesque patterns whirled in front of his eyes and a cacophony of screams and shouts filled the air. A shower of soil and sand rained down around him after he was buffeted in every direction.

With ears ringing, he fought to breathe and had to force each breath down into his lungs.

Hauling himself on to his elbows and then all fours in an effort to recover, he was struggling to comprehend what had happened. A young policeman was crawling in panic along the ground, making unintelligible noises. Wisting scrambled up, stumbling over his own feet, and scrabbled onwards. Another officer was staggering about, his arms held out stiffly from his body, his clothes in rags, his face covered in dust and blood. Unrecognizable. He lifted his head and looked up before falling to his knees and bursting into uncontrollable sobs.

Wisting opened his mouth wide to clear his ears. Someone called out, a high-pitched shriek, and he turned to the source of the noise. Maren Dokken was already on her way to a colleague of her own age lying on the ground contorted in pain. Her uniform was ripped to shreds and she was bleeding from several gashes on her face. Her left arm hung stiff and bloodied at her side.

Taking a few tentative initial steps, Wisting surveyed the scene and caught sight of Line sprawled on the ground. He rushed forward but she was already casting around for her camera as she struggled to her feet.

'Stay here!' he said, placing a restraining hand on her shoulder. 'Don't go anywhere.'

He remained in that position as he tried to gain an overview of events. Every muscle was tensed and adrenaline was pumping through his bloodstream. His pulse hammered in his temple and the smell of dynamite stung his nose.

At the entrance to the woods, a crater had opened up in the ground, with the remains of the sheep enclosure blasted away. Two policemen were sprawled on the ground, writhing and screaming in pain and shock.

'Stay here!' he repeated to Line.

The dog handler shouted a command and sent the barking Alsatian in the direction Tom Kerr had fled, before following himself. Kittil Gram tried to call them back.

'The track could be mined!' he warned.

At that moment two rapid pistol shots were heard from among the trees and the dog's barking was cut off immediately.

Wisting concentrated on the injured police officers. One of them had struggled into a sitting position and was coughing up clots of blood. The other seemed to have one foot almost torn off. He was no longer screaming but lay pale and unconscious in the long grass. Hammer arrived and checked his breathing and pulse. Wisting raised the leg with the damaged foot to reduce the flow of blood. As he unlaced the man's boot, mangled tendons and muscles hung from the open wound.

Hammer shrugged off his jacket and wrenched off his shirt, tearing it into strips, which he handed over. Wisting pushed a couple of these into the open wound before wrapping the others around the officer's leg and pulling them tight.

'I need urgent medical assistance,' he heard Gram relay over his walkie-talkie. 'There's been a grenade explosion. Three colleagues are seriously wounded and at least four others have minor injuries.'

The switchboard was aware of the nature of this operation and the operator acknowledged the message without asking any additional questions. Several of the other police officers in the entourage had received minor cuts to their faces and noses and their ears were bleeding. Gram ordered two of them back to the minibus to fetch a first-aid kit and to remove the weapons stored there. Another took Wisting's place.

The police radio sparked into life again and another, more authoritative voice requested a situation report.

Kittil Gram gazed along the cart track where Tom Kerr had disappeared.

'We no longer have custody of the prisoner,' Gram advised. 'He is armed and moving on foot in a south-easterly direction.'

'We need roadblocks set up,' Wisting said. 'And the helicopter.'

Gram lifted the walkie-talkie again and, using his local knowledge, asked for checkpoints to be set up at intersections and other strategic locations.

'We also require support from Heli 3-0 and for Uniform 3-0 to be manned,' he continued.

Uniform 3-0 was the police boat, usually berthed at this time of year.

'Copy,' was the response from the other end.

Stiller, his face speckled with earth and sand, had been on his phone. He rounded off the conversation and came to join them.

'I've an undercover team taking care of the nearest roads,' he told them. 'Four units.'

A radio transmitter crackled. 'Ambulance helicopter on its way,' the switchboard operator announced. 'The emergency medical team is turning out with a doctor and five vehicles.'

Gram acknowledged receipt of the information.

Further calls were transmitted over the airwaves. Units en route, reporting positions and estimating time of arrival. Gram responded and directed the crews.

The situation around them became clearer. Injured officers were taken care of and there was little else they could do other than wait for medical assistance.

Wisting peered down at the unconscious policeman. The shirt material around his ankle was saturated with blood, but the blood flow appeared to be stanched. He looked to be in his mid-twenties. His uniform was in rags and his face splattered with blood.

'He'll be OK,' Hammer reassured him. 'He doesn't have any other serious external injuries, apart from his foot.'

'I'm more worried that the blast may have inflicted internal injuries,' Stiller said, glancing at a policeman who sat coughing up blood. 'That it's damaged his lungs.'

Hammer picked up his jacket and put it on. 'What actually happened?' he asked, glancing around.

Walking around the crater, Wisting studied the ground

and found what he was searching for: a fishing line stretched across the grass.

'A tripwire,' Hammer commented. He grabbed the line and pulled it up to reveal the safety lever from a hand grenade dangling from one end.

'He triggered it when he ran through the opening in the fence,' he said, pointing.

Wisting looked along the cart track where Tom Kerr had made his escape. The dog handler was walking towards them, his hands and uniform soaked in blood from the dog that lay somewhere behind him.

The sound of sirens could be heard in the distance.

The dog handler turned down the sound on the radio handset attached to his breast pocket and looked around angrily. His eyes fixed on Claes Thancke, as if all this was the lawyer's fault.

'He had a fucking pistol,' he said, holding up his bloodied hands. 'Someone had planted a gun here for him.'

The men Kittil Gram had sent back to the vehicles for first-aid kits and weapons had now returned. One of them also had a map, which he now spread out. Wisting stood slightly on the fringes of the circle that formed around it, but managed to find his bearings. He could identify the stream and the dotted line that showed the cart track Tom Kerr had run along. It led to a private road that accessed a cluster of summer cabins on the shore and adjacent skerries.

'OK,' Gram said, straightening up. 'Three men.'

He pointed to the dog handler and two of the oldest and most experienced officers who were still fit for active duty.

'I want a search along that track, all the way to the water's edge.'

The three entrusted with the task armed themselves with guns and the dog handler was appointed leader.

Gram was about to add something further but was interrupted by a call from the switchboard: 'The Police Chief has called an emergency meeting of key personnel. She has given the following preliminary orders: Tom Kerr must not be allowed to leave the area. He must be stopped by all necessary means.'

'Copy,' Gram answered, scanning the faces around him to ensure they had all caught the same message.

Claes Thancke, who had remained quiet in the background, now spoke up. 'By all necessary means,' he reiterated, his voice unsteadier than usual. 'What does she mean by that?'

No answer was forthcoming.

Metal struck metal as the dog handler pulled back the slide and prepared his gun for firing. The two men at his side followed suit and they marched off.

6

The camera had been running the entire time.

The first paramedics, with kit on their backs, came charging along the track. One was carrying a stretcher. Line followed them with the camera all the way to the scene of the incident.

It was impressive how speedily and efficiently the situation was brought under control. In the first few minutes after the explosion, total chaos had reigned. The cries of pain from the policeman whose foot had been shattered by the blast had been agonizing. One man with an injured arm had seemed completely dazed.

The task of taking charge had fallen to Kittil Gram. The circumstances had been complex and confusing, but he had quickly gained an oversight of the extent of the damage and shared out the assignments and arranged for the necessary first aid. After that, he had concentrated on the escaped prisoner.

It was a vast area in which to hide. Ten years earlier, when Line had worked as a reporter on the local newspaper, she had been here in connection with a search operation for a lost six-year-old. Volunteers and Red Cross personnel had combed the terrain, also using dogs and a helicopter. Nevertheless, it had taken more than twenty-four hours to find the boy. Exhausted and chilled to the bone, but in relatively good shape, he had crawled out from under a cabin when he heard voices in the vicinity.

She zoomed in on her father, who stood about fifteen metres away from her. His face was tense. The gravity of the situation was clear to see in the lines etched around his dark eyes and above the bridge of his nose. Through Stiller's micro-phone, she could hear him talking about the surrounding area.

Around three hundred permanent residents had homes here. In summer, the population increased many times over with holidaymakers, but few of them were here now, so late in the season. Hundreds of holiday cabins lay empty, if Tom Kerr was looking for a place to find cover, but most likely he would try to get hold of a car or boat in order to make good his escape. This meant that everyone living in the area was in danger. Tom Kerr had led the police into a trap and was on the run, armed with a pistol. Pursuing him could easily pro-voke situations in which he used threats to acquire a vehicle or even, as a last resort, took hostages.

Turning towards her, Wisting looked straight into the camera, as if he had only just realized that she was filming. Stiller did likewise. They exchanged glances before approach-ing her.

Line lowered the camera but let the recording continue.

'Did you manage to film what happened?' her father asked.

'I think so,' Line replied. 'I was trying to keep Kerr in the centre of the camera lens the whole time, but I don't know what actually went on. I'll need to watch it to see what I've got.'

'When can you send me the file?' Stiller queried.

'As soon as I get home,' Line told him.

Stiller gave her a nod. 'You can put the camera away now.'

'Isn't it OK for me to go on filming?' Line asked.

Stiller seemed to give this some thought before pointing at the camera. 'Just remember that all the film is owned by the police,' he said. 'You can't use any of it without our approval.'

'Sure,' Line answered, raising the camera once more.

7

The rumble of a helicopter could be heard in the east. Wisting checked the time. It was too early to be the police helicopter and, anyway, it was approaching from the wrong side. This must be the ambulance helicopter. He gazed up into the treetops but failed to catch sight of it.

Stiller's phone rang. He listened to a short message before removing the tiny microphone and tugging the cable from under his shirt.

'You'll have to come with me,' he told Wisting.

'Where are you going?'

Stiller did not answer. Unfastening the transmitter from his belt, he handed it and the microphone to Line.

'Don't follow me,' he said.

'Where are you off to?' Line asked.

Giving no response, Stiller turned to Wisting again.

'I need your local knowledge,' he said, using his head to indicate the direction of the parked vehicles.

The ambulance helicopter now appeared above their heads. As it approached low above the trees, it hovered in the air as the grass flattened out beneath it. Then it landed cautiously on a level patch beside the stream. The rotor system slowed down and a door slid open. Two men in red overalls clambered out and crept, doubled over, beneath the rotor blades.

Wisting made eye contact with Hammer, gesturing to inform him of his departure with Stiller.

'What are you doing?' he asked, turning back to Stiller.

'He's here somewhere,' Stiller said. His subdued voice

could only just be heard above the roar of the helicopter. 'This could be our chance to find him.'

Wisting scanned their surroundings. He was not talking about Tom Kerr but about 'the Other One', Kerr's accomplice.

They encountered several paramedics on their way back to the cars. On the open space beside the old sawmill, their vehicles had been driven as close to the track as possible.

A grimy white delivery van was parked behind the minibus in which Tom Kerr had arrived. Wisting recognized it at once as a van used for special operations. The last time he had sat inside it, it had been fitted with Lithuanian number plates and the advertising logo of a fictitious construction company. Now it was completely anonymous.

Stiller slid the doors open and let Wisting enter ahead of him. A man, seated in front of a wall of computer screens, reached his hand out to Wisting.

'Ove Hidle,' he introduced himself, without mentioning his professional title or place of work.

Stiller drew the door closed behind him.

Ove Hidle came straight to the point. 'I followed him through the woods and out on to the gravel track,' he said, pointing at a map on the largest screen.

Wisting had no difficulty finding his bearings. He recognized the pasture that sloped down to the stream and the spot where the grenade had exploded.

Ove Hidle checked the time. 'He was on the move until fourteen minutes ago,' he said.

'Where is he now?'

'Here.'

Hidle pointed at a cluster of buildings at the end of a track, almost at the water's edge. A red pin symbol rested above one of them.

'I planted a transmitter in his shoes before we left the prison,' Stiller explained. 'To be on the safe side.'

'So that's where Tom Kerr is, then?' Wisting said, pointing at the screen.

Ove Hidle handed him a pack of disinfectant wipes.

'We have him under strict supervision,' he assured them, shifting from the map to a satellite image of the same area, and then zoomed in.

Wisting studied the picture while he rubbed the bloodstains off his hands. There were six summer cabins with outhouses and adjoining buildings, twelve units in all. The red dot indicated that Tom Kerr was inside an extension to a white-painted sea captain's house. Fifty metres below, there was a jetty with a sailing boat alongside.

'He's been there for quarter of an hour now,' Hidle added.

Wisting sat down in a spare seat. He estimated that thirty-three minutes had elapsed since the explosion. Kerr had taken eighteen minutes to reach the nearest cabins. After that he had been lying low.

'You both think he's waiting for someone, then,' Wisting said, turning to face Stiller. 'That he's waiting for the Other One.'

'He's going to sit tight until everything calms down,' Stiller said. 'Until the police pull out. Then his accomplice will come and pick him up.'

'But surely the police won't pull out of the area until all the properties have been searched,' Wisting objected.

'I know that,' Stiller agreed. 'I need your help to persuade the Chief of Police and the top brass to call off the operation out here.'

A sceptical Wisting chewed his lip. Messages continually streamed in on Stiller's walkie-talkie radio. A breathless voice announced that a pair of handcuffs had been found at the spot where the cart track ended at a road leading to the cabins where Tom Kerr was now located.

'We can choose to take him now, right away. Or we can wait until the Other One comes and catch them both,' Stiller went on. 'But a decision has to be taken before the search parties find him.'

'I'll phone Kiil,' Wisting said, producing his mobile phone.

Agnes Kiil had been appointed Chief of Police for the new, enlarged police district following the reorganization incorporating Telemark, Vestfold and Buskerud regions. Wisting was happy with the choice and the appointment. She had both insight and a good understanding of the role of the professional investigator.

'Wisting,' she said as she took the call. 'I'm in an emergency meeting with my colleagues. What can you tell us?'

In his mind's eye, Wisting pictured the various section leaders assembled to advise her on the strategic decisions that had to be taken in exceptional cases such as this.

'The escape was carefully planned,' Wisting began. 'Everything suggests that Kerr received help. We have reason to believe that the so-called Other One is the person who has provided him with assistance.'

'I'm switching you to loudspeaker,' Kiil informed him.

What Wisting was about to suggest was extremely delicate.

'Who is there with you?' he asked to make sure that no outsiders were present.

Agnes Kiil rattled off the names of the established members of the emergency committee and Wisting continued.

'We've located Tom Kerr by use of an electronic tracker,' he said, explaining how that had been accomplished.

No one at the other end made any comment on what, strictly speaking, was an example of illegal surveillance.

33

'We believe he's waiting for further assistance in order to leave the area,' Wisting went on.

'What do you mean?'

'That he's waiting for the police to withdraw from the area so that the accomplice who organized his escape can come and pick him up.'

'What are you really suggesting?' Agnes Kiil asked.

'That we alter this from a search operation to a surveillance assignment. We know where Tom Kerr is located. We can wait until his visitor turns up.'

The police officer in charge of operative details of the action broke in: 'Where exactly is Tom Kerr, then?' he asked.

'In a summer cabin,' Wisting clarified. 'It's in a fairly open position, but the surrounding land and vegetation make it possible to observe it from concealed positions. There's a road leading up to it, but the most effective approach would be from the sea. It's about fifty metres down to a jetty from the cabin. I can send you the coordinates.'

Outside, a helicopter passed over the van roof. The most critically injured policeman was on his way to hospital.

'What you're suggesting will require a cover operation,' the officer in charge said. 'We can't just pull out without doing anything. We must be able to demonstrate some activity in the area for the next few hours.'

'This also implies that we will, in effect, deliberately mislead the media,' another voice interjected. Wisting assumed that this belonged to the officer responsible for information and communication.

The Police Chief took over again. 'Give us some time to discuss this further,' she said. 'I'll call you back.'

8

Wisting stared at the red marker on the screen, expecting it to move at any minute.

'There will be an investigation into this,' he said. 'An internal inquiry.'

'It was your lot's responsibility,' Stiller said.

Wisting looked at him. He was not interested in doling out blame but knew that Stiller was right. His police district had been given responsibility for the security arrangements with respect to the conduct of the site visit. The practical details had been assigned to Kittil Gram, who had prepared a comprehensive plan, but the use of weapons had not been approved.

'I'm not blaming anyone,' Stiller went on. 'I'm just telling you who Internal Affairs will go after.'

'We'll have to cross that bridge when we come to it,' Wisting replied. 'But in actual fact, this should never have been possible. From the moment it was decided to take Tom Kerr out of prison, you should have been checking all of his communications. He should never have been able to discover what day you intended to move him. Then he wouldn't have had the opportunity to plan anything.'

'That wasn't feasible,' Stiller explained. 'We had to arrive at a day that also suited his lawyer.'

'But phone calls and letters should have been monitored, making it impossible for him to communicate with anyone on the outside without it being intercepted.'

'We *did* do that,' Stiller assured him. 'But we weren't able to supervise his visitors.'

'Who has visited him?'

'A woman he writes to, his brother and a befriender from the Red Cross.'

'A woman?' Wisting repeated. 'An admirer of some sort?'

'It seems so from their letters,' Stiller replied. 'She could have been the one who smuggled information and instructions in and out of jail for him.'

'Who is she?'

Ove Hidle took out a folder.

'Lone Mellberg,' he said, without opening it. 'Forty-three years of age. Lives in a basement apartment in Hokksund. Divorced, with a daughter of eighteen, but she doesn't have custody. She works in a grocery shop. Spotless record.'

'How long has this exchange of letters been going on?' Wisting queried.

'For nearly three years.'

'Did they know each other previously?'

'No.'

'When did she last visit him?'

'Yesterday.'

Running a hand through his hair, Wisting realized it was full of soil and sand from the explosion.

'He should have been denied visits until the site visit was over and done with,' he commented.

Stiller shrugged in such a way as to suggest that it was easy to be wise after the event.

'This doesn't necessarily have anything to do with the Other One,' Wisting added. 'He could have persuaded her to help him. Instructed her to obtain a gun and hand grenade and how to lay a tripwire.'

'Maybe,' Stiller conceded, motioning to Ove Hidle.

Ove Hidle changed the onscreen map image. 'We have her under surveillance,' he said.

A satellite photo from Hokksund showed a mix of houses and industrial areas beside the River Drammen. A red marker was visible in the middle of a large car park.

'She's at work,' Hidle clarified, moving closer in on the screen image. 'This is the Kiwi supermarket. We have a tracker on her car. It's in the customer car park.'

'In addition, we have visual surveillance on her,' Stiller added. 'An unmarked car with two undercover officers.'

'How long have you been watching her?' Wisting asked.

'Since early this morning.'

'So she could have been here yesterday or last night and made preparations for the escape?'

'That's theoretically possible,' Stiller admitted. 'We're waiting for information from Autopass about vehicles transiting the toll stations.'

'Do you have surveillance on his brother and the befriender as well?' Wisting asked.

Shaking his head, Stiller explained that this had not been possible due to lack of resources.

'We chose to home in on Lone Mellberg. She seems the most susceptible to influence. Someone easily persuaded, but it's entirely possible that Tom Kerr's been communicating with someone on the outside by smuggling letters in and out via a fellow prisoner's visitor, or even via an employee. It's happened before, and he's had plenty of time to make plans.'

Outside, they heard the rumble of a heavy vehicle and then car doors slamming. Shouted commands reached in to them. The cargo space in which they were sitting had no windows, but a screen showed what was going on through external cameras. A group of eight police officers from the Emergency Squad was in the process of unloading equipment and getting kitted up.

Wisting's phone rang, but he let it rest in his hand.

'You anticipated that something would happen,' he said, fixing his eyes on Stiller. 'That he would plan to escape with outside help. This was never about finding Taran Norum. It was always about luring the Other One out.'

Stiller refrained from replying but darted a glance at Wisting's phone as it continued to ring. The display showed that the call was from Police Chief Kiil.

Wisting answered without taking his eyes off Stiller.

'We'll do as you suggest,' Kiil advised in a steely voice. 'We'll catch them both.'

9

The police helicopter had arrived and now circled the meadow before landing on the south side of the old sawmill.

Wisting stood ready to greet them. The roar of the rotor blades vibrated through his whole body as the downwash caused the trees to sway and the rippling grass to flatten out.

The cockpit door opened. The leader of Oslo's Emergency Squad took off his set of headphones and laid them down on the seat before striding towards Wisting. Behind him, the crew jumped out and organized their equipment.

'Stenberg,' he said, taking Wisting's proffered hand. 'I've been told you have information for me.'

'Come with me,' Wisting said, nodding.

He ushered the officer into the delivery van where Stiller was tracking Tom Kerr's movements. The leader of the local squad, Robert Vinje, was also waiting there. He had been given charge of the operation, taking over from Kittil Gram. Wisting briefly introduced them before cutting to the chase.

'Before Tom Kerr was taken from the prison, a concealed electronic tracker was placed inside one of his shoes,' he explained. 'That means we now know he's located in a summer cabin about 1.7 kilometres from here.'

He gave the new arrivals time to study the onscreen satellite images.

'He's had assistance to escape,' Wisting went on. 'Maybe from the same guy who helped him to commit the murders of which he was convicted.'

'The Other One,' Robert Vinje said.

Wisting nodded in reply.

'Our assessment is that Kerr is hiding in the expectation of help later on,' Wisting added. 'In other words, the person who helped him with the preparations for his escape is going to come to pick him up. The Police Chief and her emergency team want us to conduct a mock retreat by pulling out of the area in the course of the afternoon, following what will appear to be a fruitless search operation.'

The Emergency Squad leader moved closer to the screen with the satellite picture and nodded, as if approving the plan.

'We've three officers who have advanced into the vicinity,' Wisting continued. 'They've been ordered to keep their distance from the building.'

'Could he have found the tracker?' Stenberg asked, without taking his eyes from the screen. 'Could that be a false signal?'

Wisting left Stiller to answer. 'He has two devices on him,' Stiller explained, giving information that was new to Wisting. 'One in his right shoe, and the other inside the back waistband of his trousers.'

'How did you manage to plant them without him noticing anything?'

'At the body search prior to leaving the prison,' Stiller said. 'In order to record whatever he said during the site visit he was equipped with a microphone and transmitter on a belt clip on his back. The second tracker unit was attached then. They're no larger than the head of a drawing pin.'

Ove Hidle launched another screen image, identical to the last one. The transmitter in the waistband and the tracker inside the shoe were both located in the same place.

'We must secure the prisoner,' the local operation leader said.

Hidle moved to make room for the two men with responsibility for the practical implementation of the operation in front of the screens. They both discussed the terrain, alternative strategic moves, places where they could establish observation posts and possibilities of intercepting any further escape, whether by car or by boat from the jetty.

Stenberg issued a number of instructions on his walkie-talkie and received answers via an earpiece. Every move he made and every word he uttered were imbued with authority.

It took them less than five minutes to agree a plan of action.

'OK,' Stenberg said, heading for the sliding door. 'We'll set up a command post outside here. Vinje is going to stay there.' He looked across at his colleague before turning to face Stiller. 'You'll all have to be accessible to him.'

Adrian Stiller nodded.

'The helicopter is going to return to refuel in half an hour or so,' Stenberg went on. 'It will return and stay here for another two hours. The most important thing is that the police boat remains on standby until all this is over. Our crew will be fully informed but, apart from that, we'll keep this on a need-to-know basis.'

'Good,' Wisting agreed.

'Then we'll get a move on,' Stenberg said, rounding off the conversation as he slid the door open.

He and Robert Vinje stepped out. Their crew stood ready and waiting, and two dog patrols had also arrived. Wisting looked around for Nils Hammer, but he was probably still down at the sheep run with Line. Hammer was his second in command, and he was keen for him to be fully apprised of the situation. He took out his phone to call him, but waited before keying in his number. Something about Stiller told him that he hadn't learned everything yet.

'Is there more I ought to know?' he asked.

Adrian Stiller hesitated. 'Not as far as this is concerned,' he eventually replied.

'Let me be the judge of that,' Wisting said.

Stiller slid the van door closed and hesitated again before launching into an explanation: 'We believe that the sidekick has begun to operate off his own bat,' he confided.

As Wisting sat down again, Adrian Stiller gave him a name. 'Nanna Thomle.'

Wisting recognized the name from the media. The case was under the jurisdiction of the Øst Police District. She had disappeared one Saturday evening in the middle of July after a night out in Oslo city centre. She had taken the train home to Lillestrøm and the last confirmed sighting of her was from a CCTV image taken at the railway station. She lived about five hundred metres from there, and somewhere along that stretch she had gone missing. Three weeks later, a hiker had found her right arm in the forest at Svartskog, south of Oslo. A search in the area had led to the rest of her body being found in a shallow grave. Animals had been digging around and unearthed several body parts.

This was the same modus operandi that Tom Kerr and his accomplice had used. Abducting young women out alone late at night. They dismembered the bodies before they disposed of them.

'Her body parts had been soaked in bleach,' Stiller added.

This was also Tom Kerr's favoured method. He had dismembered his victims to make room for the bodies in a bathtub that he filled with a solution of liquid chlorine. Some of the injuries to intestines and urinary tracts occurred when he used the same solution to clean the victims internally. This was done prior to dismemberment, while the victims were still alive.

'It was an effective method of removing biological evidence,' Wisting commented. 'Another perpetrator could have adopted the same MO.'

'She was mistreated in the same way,' Stiller countered. 'Her nipples were torn off with pliers. The same knots were used to tie her wrists and ankles.'

Kerr's victims had been tied to a bed in his home while the abuse took place. In all probability, they were not cut loose until after they were dead.

'A bowline knot with a clove hitch as a securing loop,' Stiller elaborated.

This was a detail in the case that Wisting could not recall. 'I see,' he said.

'The Other One has now operated single-handedly on one occasion,' Stiller went on. 'We think it's only a matter of time before it happens again. Two months elapsed from when they took Thea Polden until Taran Norum disappeared, but only four weeks until Salwa Haddad was abducted.'

'So you set up the opportunity for Tom Kerr to make an attempt to escape?' Wisting asked. 'To lure the Other One out?'

'We considered it a possibility,' Stiller conceded.

'It almost cost the lives of three police officers.'

'None of our projected scenarios took into account the idea that anything like that might happen,' Stiller said. 'We thought perhaps he might turn up in a car. That was why we had unmarked vehicles on all the surrounding roads. We never envisaged anything like this.'

Wisting was not sure how far Stiller would have been willing to go. As the situation now stood, it might appear that everything had gone according to plan.

'The stakes are high,' Stiller continued. 'Hopefully, the plan will still yield results.'

Wisting glanced across at the red onscreen marker again. While he was staring at it, it made an almost imperceptible movement, as if Tom Kerr was walking from one side of the house to the other.

He lifted his phone and called Hammer. 'I need to talk to you,' he said.

Line, following Hammer, had returned to the open area beside the old sawmill. It had become a gathering point for both the rescue services and response teams. En route, she had encountered the specially trained crews from the Emergency Squad and the dog handlers with their barking hounds. The police helicopter looped above her head in ever-increasing circles.

The injured police officers were brought out and driven off, while three ambulances stood by in readiness out on the summer pasture along with other emergency vehicles. The air was filled with the crackle of walkie-talkie radios, the buzz of conversation and the ringtones of mobile phones. She raised her camera to capture the desolation, anxiety and bewilderment.

One hour and seventeen minutes had passed since the explosion. The first journalists had appeared and now stood in a huddle out on the road. They were escorted away from the outer-perimeter barrier. The alternative would probably have been that the most eager of them would have made their way independently through the woods. Line recognized several of them. These were the ones with the shortest distance to travel, representing the local newspapers in Sandefjord and Larvik, in addition to a reporter and cameraman from *NRK*'s provincial office in Tønsberg. She also spotted a couple of photographers she presumed to be freelancers.

She took out her phone to check what kind of information had filtered out. The story was the headline item in her former newspaper, *VG*. At least three police officers had sustained injuries in connection with an operation. One of the leaders on the ground confirmed that there had been an explosion but could not say anything further about what had happened. A map segment illustrated approximately where the explosion had occurred. *VG* had also been able to report that there was major police activity in the area and that a number of roadblocks had been set up. All traffic out of the locality was being checked and all incoming traffic had been stopped.

Morten Pludowski turned up among the other journalists, with his *VG* press pass slung around his neck. He was one of the colleagues she had learned most from and worked best with when she had been employed at *VG*, but also one of the ones she had most often disagreed with and caused her temper to flare.

She was reluctant to let him see her, as this would place her in a difficult position. He would be desperate to know what had taken place, but she had signed a declaration of confidentiality and could not breathe a word.

However, it was too late. He waved her across. Any attempt to avoid him now would be foolish.

Striding towards him, she gave him a friendly hug and nodded to the other members of the press corps.

'You got here fast,' she said.

'I was lucky,' Morten P replied with a smile. 'I was in Tønsberg on another assignment when this message came in.'

He walked a few paces away from the others, with Line tagging along.

'What are you doing here?' he asked.

'Freelancing,' Line replied. 'Some documentation work for the police.'

'What do you mean?' Morten P queried. 'What's really going on here?'

'My lips are sealed,' Line answered. 'If I tell you anything, that'll be the end of any further work for them.'

Morten P nodded his understanding. He was a skinny, ungainly man of around forty, but his eyes were alert and inquisitive.

'I see,' he said. 'We've been promised a press briefing at one o'clock.'

Line glanced at her watch. More than a quarter of an hour until then.

'But an explosion,' Morten P ploughed on, taking a step back to study her closely. 'Were you there when it happened?'

Line looked down at her clothes, spattered with earth and smeared with grass stains. Her left arm was smudged with blood from her father after he had helped one of the wounded police officers.

'I have it all on tape,' she replied, gesturing towards her camera. 'The recording belongs to the police, though,' she added, realizing she had already said too much. Once the newspaper knew that a recording existed, the editor and his legal team would argue relentlessly for the opportunity to use it.

Line lingered there with the other journalists but stood her ground inside the crime scene tape that was stretched out around an extensive area. If she crossed it, she would probably find it difficult to get back in again.

Unable to see either her father or Adrian Stiller, she concluded that they were probably inside the white delivery van she had seen Nils Hammer disappear into.

The *NRK* reporter was relaying a live broadcast. He described the police cordon through which they had had to pass in order to reach his present location but had nothing new to add about the actual incident. *Dagbladet* and TV2 appeared on the scene, followed soon after by a radio reporter from channel P4.

The police helicopter that had occasionally hovered above them moved off in a northerly direction. It was now almost 1 p.m. A few more journalists arrived. Line wondered who would be the police spokesperson; it would surely be Stiller, since the entire operation had been his initiative.

However, it was her father who stepped forward.

He trudged towards the assembled press corps. Somehow he had managed to get hold of a shirt and jacket that were not soiled with blood and dirt. Both the shirt and jacket were one size too small and he seemed uncomfortable with the task that had fallen to him, but Line knew that deep down he felt that informing the press was tantamount to informing the public. And the public always had a right to know, at least about events such as this.

Line detached herself from the press pack and filmed the journalists instead of her father. She could always access a recording of her father's statement later. What she wanted was the reaction when he began to speak about Tom Kerr.

She was standing on her own. This was not like an American press conference, in which all the relevant authorities bunched together behind a spokesperson, as if to ensure visible documentation of being part of an important news story or dramatic incident.

'I'm going to keep this short.' Her father began to speak, without referring to any notes. 'We are still involved in an ongoing operation.'

The journalists took their places in almost drill-like fashion. The camera crews and those transmitting live images took up the best positions and were then surrounded by the rest of the press members with various kinds of recording devices. The photographers with the longest lenses remained in the background.

Line checked her battery. She could keep going for another half-hour before she would have to replace it.

'My name is William Wisting,' her father continued. 'I'm here in my capacity as Chief Inspector in the Criminal Investigation Department at Larvik police station.'

He paused briefly before going on. 'The Kripos Cold Cases Group had intended today to take fresh measures in the investigation of a missing person from a five-year-old case. Convicted killer Tom Kerr had expressed his willingness to point out where he had buried Taran Norum.'

Camera shutters clicked incessantly.

'During this site visit, Tom Kerr managed to evade the security arrangements that had been put in place. He is armed and must be regarded as dangerous.'

One of the journalists interrupted the briefing. 'Has Tom Kerr escaped, then?'

'He fled from here at 11.23,' her father confirmed. 'He was wearing a grey T-shirt, a dark Adidas jacket, blue jeans and grey trainers. Photographs taken of him last week will be circulated.'

Morten P was the loudest voice in the crowd facing him: 'The messages we received said that a number of police officers were injured in an explosion.'

Line's father nodded. 'Explosives were used in the course of the escape,' he admitted. 'Three police officers have been taken to hospital. Several others have been treated at the scene for minor injuries.'

He ignored the questions that began to rain down on him.

'We must be permitted to postpone publicizing any further details about what has happened. Just let me repeat in conclusion that Tom Kerr is dangerous and armed. The residents of the local area should remain indoors and keep their doors locked. If anyone catches sight of Tom Kerr, we ask that he is not approached or tackled but that the police are notified immediately. Thank you.'

He turned on his heel and retraced his steps, finally taking cover behind the parked police cars.

Line kept her camera focused on the group of journalists. She felt rather cynical: this was something that had often haunted her when she worked as a journalist and her only task in an accident or tragedy was to provide reportage. She had completed her assignment for Stiller and was now filming merely with the idea of using the recordings in a documentary about Tom Kerr and the Other One. The already bizarre story had just taken a dramatic twist and she had unique material in her possession.

She let the camera sweep slowly across the surrounding area.

Claes Thancke, the lawyer, stood conversing with Stiller and her father beyond the view of the reporters. He shook his head almost melodramatically before marching across to his car. Some of the journalists caught sight of him and shouted his name. Thancke held up a dismissive hand as he clambered into the vehicle and drove off while the cameras followed him.

Line approached Stiller and her father.

'Where's your car?' he asked.

'It's at Kripos headquarters in Oslo,' Line replied, gesturing with her head towards Stiller. 'I was supposed to go back there once Kerr was safely returned to prison.'

'Take mine,' her father told her, taking out his keys. 'We need to see the footage of what happened.'

Line was keen to stay. 'You can look at it on the camera,' she offered. 'Right now.'

Stiller shook his head. 'We're not the only ones who are interested in it,' he said. 'You'll have to transfer it on to a server or something, so that the Police Chief and Kripos top brass can also have a look at it.'

Line sighed. If she had thought to bring her laptop, she could have done this now, here on the spot.

'I'd like to stay here until it's all over,' she said.

'Nothing's going to happen here in the next few hours,' Stiller told her.

'How can you be so sure about that?' Line asked. 'Have you caught him already?'

Stiller made no response. 'Will you let me know as soon as you have a link for the video recordings?' he asked instead.

Line nodded.

'Don't give them to anyone other than me,' he insisted. 'I'll distribute them further.'

He turned on his heel and walked towards the delivery van. Her father took his car key off his key ring and handed it to her.

'He's right,' he said. 'There's no point in staying here. We're going to have to sit tight for a while yet.'

Line took the key with an expression that made clear how unhappy she was with the situation.

'OK,' she said, adding in a defiant tone: 'He went off with my microphone and transmitter. Let me know if you find them. They were expensive.'

Heading for the car, she turned off the camera before settling into the driver's seat. A branch scraped the side of the car as she drove out along the track. The radio was tuned to P2, not her choice of station. She switched it off and looked in the mirror. Dust from the track whirled up behind her.

The stretch through the woods was really nothing but a pair of bumpy wheel tracks with thick foliage on either side.

At one point she noticed some kind of rusty agricultural tool on the verge.

Line slowed down and stopped. She lifted her camera from the passenger seat and turned on the power again, ready to film the police barriers out on the main road.

She noticed a shadow in the mirror, as if someone was moving behind the car. When she turned round in her seat, all she could see was a bird taking off from a branch, as if something had frightened it off.

An unpleasant feeling stirred inside her. There was nothing outside the car, but a sudden irrational fear made her lock the doors. The tyres spun on the ground when she drove on again.

Soon the landscape opened out before her and freshly ploughed fields replaced the woods. Out on the main road, two police cars were parked, one of them with a blue flashing light. An old blue Ford had been stopped and the police had opened the boot.

Line drew to a halt again and raised her camera. The boot lid was slammed shut again and the Ford sent on its way. Another car arrived, this time a small Toyota. Through the camera lens she could see two women seated inside it. The vehicle was stopped and the police checked the driver's documents, opened the rear doors and checked the boot before the car was allowed to move off.

A policewoman had spotted Line, and now her colleague turned around too. The woman kept a tighter grip on the gun suspended from a strap across her chest. Line put down her camera and drove towards them. She stopped at their signal, wound down the side window and took out her driving licence. The policewoman positioned herself by the door.

'We're searching for this man,' she said, holding out a phone with a photo of Tom Kerr on the display. 'Have you seen him?'

There was no need for Line to explain her involvement. 'Tom Kerr,' was all she said. 'No.'

'Can you open your boot?'

A policeman checked that it was empty and closed the lid again. The female officer handed back her driving licence.

'Don't stop if you see him,' she warned. 'Drive safely.'

Her eyes scoured the terrain on either side of the road as she drove. She kept her speed down. A dog barked at her when she drove past a house on the roadside. She saw some horses in a field and an elderly woman in a farmyard, taking in washing.

Out on the main road there was another checkpoint. Line placed her camera on the dashboard and let the film run.

A number of vehicles were permitted to drive into the controlled area, while others were held back. Probably rub-berneckers and others who had no good reason to be there or who did not live locally.

The car ahead of her was checked in the same way as at the previous checkpoint. Line wound down the side window in readiness for her turn.

Once again she was shown the picture of Tom Kerr before being asked to open the boot, and her car was examined.

Twenty-five minutes later, she let herself into her home in Stavern. She walked straight through the house and down to the basement, where she had a home office installed. She switched on the TV. The last channel she had been watching was CNN and she changed to the Norwegian news channel. Commercials.

Removing the memory card from the camera, she down-loaded the recordings. The camera had more or less been running the entire time. She had only stopped and restarted to avoid having files that were too large and inconvenient to move around.

It was tricky transferring the files to an encrypted server so that she could share them. Stiller would want the raw material. There was no need to edit anything. She sent him an email with a link to the files and an automatically generated password. One of the files was a recording that began just as the minibus parked at the old sawmill and lasted until half an hour or so after the explosion and escape. She let Stiller know the file name and sat down to watch it.

There was a great deal of milling around before the procession began to move off. In addition to the footage, she had a sound recording of the conversation between Stiller and Hammer about the helicopter that had failed to appear. They waited for the dog handler, and Kerr and his lawyer had a chat inside the car before they got started.

She glanced up at the TV on the wall. The news channel was broadcasting direct from Eftang. It did not look as if there had been any developments. She turned down the sound and concentrated on her computer screen, where Tom Kerr and his entourage were making their way through the woods. She had caught the moment when he stumbled and fell. Line stopped the recording, spooled back a little and played it again. Kerr groaned as he hit the ground. He was hauled up and told to walk on, while his lawyer made loud protests. It was after the next fall that they had removed his leg irons, but this was part of the reason.

She replayed the sequence one more time at reduced speed. There was no obvious reason for him to take a tumble. Admittedly, one of his feet caught a tree root on the path, but the actual fall looked contrived.

The recording rolled on. The next time Kerr took a nose-dive, the fall was more dramatic. His feet were not included in the camera image, so it was impossible to see what he had tripped over, but once you were aware that it must also be part of the plan to make the police remove his leg irons, this fall also looked artificial.

The chain meant that Kerr's ability to save himself by putting out his hands was considerably restricted. When he was lifted up again, he had scraped his cheek.

The procession moved on. When it reached the slope at the pasture, Claes Thancke protested and the discussion that ensued ended in agreement to remove the leg irons.

As the clamp around his ankle was unlocked and the chain removed, Kerr stared straight into the camera. Once it was off, he lifted his hands to his face and wiped the blood from the gash on his cheek. Then he said something before putting his bloodied fingers into his mouth and licking them clean.

Line wound back, turned up the volume and concentrated on hearing what he had said. It was only a low whisper. She had to play the recording again with the sound turned up.

'See you later,' was what it sounded like.

She played it again. Kerr was staring directly into the camera as he spoke, as if he wanted to transmit a message. This time it sounded even more like 'See you later', his intent to depart wrapped in a threat.

I2

The computer screens and all the technical equipment crammed into the back of the van made the air close and stuffy. Wisting was still wearing Ove Hidle's shirt and the flimsy fabric was sticking to his back.

The largest monitor was displaying the recordings Line had made, with Tom Kerr on his way down the sloping field. All of a sudden he broke into a run and shouts were heard from the police officers surrounding him.

Taking a deep breath, Wisting waited for what was to come. The explosion filled the screen with a bright, white light and the loudspeakers roared. The camera ended up lying on its side in the tall grass, but they could see and hear the earth and pebbles that rained down in all directions.

No one said anything.

The camera resumed its normal position and swept over the area, taking in the wounded, bleeding police officers as they heard Wisting make sure that his daughter was unhurt. Then the video focused on the track where Tom Kerr had run off. The dog handler sent the dog after him and followed with a younger officer. The camera rotated again, watching as the most severely injured police officers were given first aid. Two loud pistol shots were heard on the audio track and the camera quickly pivoted back again.

Nils Hammer turned away from the screen with a loud groan and used the back of his hand to wipe a bead of perspiration from his forehead.

'What a fucking gamble that was,' he said, making no attempt to hide his irritation and anger.

'It was never the plan for it to turn out like that,' Stiller tried to explain.

'Your lot set it up, and it's all gone to hell,' Hammer snarled. A few drops of spit landed on Stiller.

'The plan was for him to show us the place where he had hidden Taran Norum,' Stiller said, unruffled. 'But of course we had a back-up plan. We tried to take all eventualities into consideration.'

Hammer was shaking his head. 'You never believed that Taran Norum was here,' he muttered.

'It had to be checked out,' Stiller objected.

'A young police officer could have lost his leg,' Hammer reminded him.

'It wasn't our task to secure the area,' Stiller pointed out, turning his head slightly in Wisting's direction.

As Hammer stood up, he bumped his head on the roof.

'Christ, don't you dare try that move,' he said, pointing his finger. 'Don't shift the blame on to us. This whole operation was organized to provoke an escape attempt. The responsibility is yours and yours alone.'

'Who should I talk to about the Other One?' Wisting asked, in an effort to draw a line under the discussion. 'Who knows most about him?'

'Idar Semmelmann,' Stiller replied. 'He was the chief investigator.'

Wisting could not recall the name from the case notes.

'He was brought in after Kerr was arrested,' Stiller explained, 'and appointed to lead the group tasked with trying to find the accomplice. Now he's the only one left of that team.'

'Have you spoken to him?'

'Not about what's happened today, but he's been informed that we were taking Kerr on a site visit.'

'Do you have his number?'

With a nod, Stiller produced his phone and read it out. Wisting keyed in each separate digit, craning forward in his chair and staring at the floor as he waited for an answer.

'Semmelmann.'

'William Wisting, Larvik. Have you heard what's happened down here?'

'I heard you on the news,' the former chief investigator confirmed. 'Have you found him yet?'

'We've a lot of men out in the field,' Wisting replied. 'It will be difficult for him to slip through the net.'

'You mustn't let him,' Semmelmann warned. 'He'll do it again. Without a doubt, he'll kill again.'

Wisting straightened his back. 'How far did you get in your pursuit of the Other One?' he asked.

There was a prolonged silence at the other end before he answered. 'You're familiar with the Thomle girl?'

'Nanna Thomle,' Wisting said. 'The new girl who disappeared this summer. Stiller has filled me in.'

'I had to take out what I had on the Other One when they found her body parts,' Semmelmann continued. 'But we know as little now as we did then.'

'No suspects?'

Another silence.

'The simplest thing would be for me to take what I have and come down to you.'

'When can you be here?'

'Let's say seven o'clock.'

'Fine,' Wisting replied. 'My office, then.'

Someone tugged at the door, but it was locked. Wisting was nearest, so he pushed it open a crack and saw Stenberg from the Emergency Squad, holding out a pair of handcuffs in a plastic evidence bag.

Wisting slid the door open wide and made room for him.

'A dog handler found them about fifty metres from the spot where the dog was shot.'

He held the bag out to Wisting, who noticed a key in the lock before passing the bag on to Hammer.

'Where did he get the key from?' he asked.

'It's a standard key,' Stiller pointed out. 'All handcuffs used by the Norwegian police force can be unlocked with the same key. It's probably the same supplier in many other countries too. There are no restrictions on their purchase and sale. No doubt they can also be ordered on the Internet.'

'Fair enough,' Hammer grumbled. 'But where did Tom Kerr get the key from? After all, you body-searched him before he left the prison, didn't you?'

'The same place as the gun?' Stenberg suggested. 'Someone had probably left it out there somewhere for him.'

Wisting shook his head. 'He had unlocked the handcuff before he took off,' he said, pointing at the monitor on which the footage from the explosion was still running. 'It was dangling from one wrist.'

'He tripped and fell,' Stiller reminded them. 'Twice. That was part of the plan to persuade us to remove the leg irons. The key may have been left lying somewhere along the track. He could have picked it up when he fell.'

With a sigh, Hammer cursed the whole situation again.

'Movement,' Ove Hidle suddenly announced from his seat in front of the bank of computer screens.

Wisting peered at the screen. The marker showing the location of Lone Mellberg's car was on the move. It had left the car park outside the Kiwi supermarket in Hokksund and was travelling east, towards Drammen.

'It's five past three,' Stiller commented. 'She's finished work.'

Stenberg took a phone call. He answered briefly, received a message and hung up. 'The undercover guys are in pursuit,' he told them.

They all followed the movements on the screen. After six minutes, the car turned off the main road into a residential area.

'She's going home,' Stiller decided, pointing out where she lived.

The movement stopped.

'Anyway, it's too early for any action,' Stenberg commented. 'It won't be dark for another five hours.'

13

Line had played the video of the moments before the grenade explosion three times and seen how Kerr suddenly broke into a run and quickly gained a lead of ten metres. One of his hands was released from the handcuffs, and his arms were in motion as he ran, like a sprinter.

When Line was little, she used to play with her father's handcuffs, and she knew that if they weren't tightened firmly enough they could be yanked off if she bent her hand and jiggled it slightly.

She spooled back in an attempt to see how the handcuffs were fastened and froze the image where he was holding his hands up to his face, licking the blood from his fingers. His hands were big and rough and the handcuffs were tight, with only a few millimetres of clearance. Like a wristwatch.

'See you later,' Line said, repeating the words Tom Kerr had used.

Still images taken from video film were rarely good, but the quality of these was excellent and they contained many elements that made them iconic portraits of the criminal. The blood, the handcuffs, his grin and the darkness in his eyes.

It looked as if he had something in his mouth too. Something shiny.

She moved the recording a few frames forward to the point where Tom Kerr's mouth was open at its widest. Freezing the image, she zoomed in, tilted her head and shouted when she caught sight of it.

It was a key. A handcuff key.

Where had that come from?

She forwarded the photo to her own phone, scribbled a message about the discovery and forwarded it to Stiller and her father.

Everything else about the escape seemed planned in minute detail, so it was no surprise to her that Kerr had also managed to get hold of a handcuff key. But where had it come from?

Of course, he could have brought it with him from the prison. Someone who had paid a visit could have smuggled it in, but Stiller had body-searched him before he left and even asked him to open his mouth and stick out his tongue.

She let the video run on and tried to find the place where Kerr had unlocked the handcuffs, but it was difficult to work that out, since he was walking with his back to the camera.

She received a message on her phone – Stiller acknowledging receipt of the photograph.

The video ran on. The sound of the actual explosion became distorted through the mini-loudspeakers. Shouts of bewilderment and cries of pain followed. The camera fell to the ground. A bleeding policewoman hared past once it was righted again, hurrying to the aid of a wounded colleague.

It was not difficult to understand what had happened. Someone had laid a booby trap by attaching a string to the safety lever on the grenade and stretched the string across the path so that Tom Kerr dragged it with him and set off the explosion as he ran.

On the news channel, the presenter in the studio reviewed the main points of the investigation into the killings of which Tom Kerr had been found guilty. They showed pictures taken in connection with his dramatic arrest.

Freja Bengtson had narrowly missed being Tom Kerr's fourth victim. Six weeks after Salwa Haddad disappeared in

Hellerud, an attempt was made to haul Freja into a van by a man wearing a motorcycle helmet.

For years, Freja Bengtson had actively trained as a kickboxer in Gøteborg. She had been runner-up in the Swedish National Championships but had been forced by injury to give up a professional career. She had moved to Oslo and worked there as a bartender. The attack had taken place when she was on her way home to her apartment in Lambertseter. She had struggled furiously and managed to break free but had been caught and dragged towards the vehicle.

A taxi driver, spotting what was going on, had sounded his horn and flashed his lights. However, this had not deterred the perpetrator from continuing. Just as Freja Bengtson was about to be thrown into the back of the vehicle, the taxi driver had accelerated and crashed into the back of the van. Freja was left sprawled on the ground. The man in the motorbike helmet had tried to get back into the van, but one of the passengers in the taxi had leapt out and attempted to restrain him. Another passenger in the back seat had filmed all this on his mobile phone. Now the news channel was showing the old footage again. The man in the motorbike helmet was Tom Kerr.

He had fled into a garden, over a hedge and continued along through the neighbourhood. The van had driven off at top speed. The driver was the Other One, the unknown accomplice who had never been found.

The next images showed the major police presence that had been summoned and the police helicopter circling above the area with a powerful searchlight.

The taxi, damaged in the collision, remained at the crime scene, and a white scarf lay on the pavement. During the trial, it emerged that it had been dipped in a home-made solution of acetone and chlorine, a combination that produced an anaesthetic effect that had not had time to work on Freja Bengtson.

The archive pictures were good. The case was recent enough for the recordings to be HD quality. The production company Line was working with had some of the same photographs. She was not the only one who had expressed interest in making a documentary film recounting the case of Tom Kerr and the Other One. In order to succeed with the project, it would naturally be crucial to have good images. If she got the opportunity to use that day's recording as well, she would have an exceptional starting point. But the most important aspect of all in order to bring her plans to fruition would be to have the approval of the relatives and survivors, and this was something she had managed to obtain. Freja Bengtson had also signed a contract agreeing to cooperate with her and the production company in an effort to track down the Other One. The only person who had not agreed to take part was Johannes Norum, Taran Norum's father.

New pictures appeared on the TV screen. The reporter told how Tom Kerr had broken into a house, found some car keys and stolen a car but had been discovered just as he sat down in the driver's seat. Footage existed of the dramatic car chase. Kerr had been forced off the road and had driven into a ditch. When he attempted to flee on foot, a police officer had fired a warning shot. This had not prevented Kerr from running on, and two officers had fired shots at him but had missed. After that, Kerr vanished into a grove of trees. In the end a sniffer dog found him and pounced, pinning him to the ground. With that, the police could concentrate on searching for the Other One, a pursuit that had proved futile.

Tom Kerr had kept his silence and no forensic evidence had ever been uncovered.

The news report now showed two buildings ablaze. A farmhouse and a barn – the property, east of Oslo, owned by Tom Kerr.

The report of the fire had come in less than an hour after Kerr had been apprehended. At this point, Kerr had not even given his name. His identity was first brought to light through a fingerprint analysis.

Inside the burnt-out barn, the investigators had found the remains of the escape vehicle in which the Other One had fled the scene of the crime. The fire had obviously been set in order to remove all traces of Thea Polden, Salwa Haddad and Taran Norum being held captive and killed there, and evidence that might enable the investigators to identify the Other One.

One week after the fire, the police had found the first grave. In the forest, almost six hundred metres from the smallholding, a sniffer dog had indicated a spot in a marshy area where it looked as if the top layer of turf had been removed and replaced. The dismembered body beneath the earth had been that of Salwa Haddad. The next day, Thea Polden was found in similar circumstances.

The TV news item went on to show pictures of Tom Kerr's workplace while the reporter told how his job in a firm that designed, manufactured and delivered products for the operation and maintenance of swimming pools gave him easy access to large quantities of liquid chlorine, used to disinfect and eliminate all trace of biological evidence from the corpses.

The news anchor in the studio returned to the screen and now handed over to the reporter on the ground in Eftang, inquiring if there was any news.

'The search for convicted killer Tom Kerr continues with considerable forces deployed here,' he began, going on to explain that the assembled journalists had been promised a new press briefing at 5 p.m.

Line looked at the time. Another hour and a half until then. She should really go up to her father's house, find him a clean shirt and drive out there with it.

14

A black bird with a yellow beak was pecking at something on the track. It took off and flew away as soon as Wisting approached.

He was filled with a restlessness so severe that it felt almost painful. The disquiet that raged through his body made him irritable and he felt an urge to slip away from the stuffy space in the back of the command vehicle.

The crime scene technicians had been working at the explosion site for a couple of hours now. They must soon be able to say something about whether there was any forensic evidence. Whether they could find out what type of grenade had been used, and where it might have come from. Or whether anything else had been found to indicate who had helped Tom Kerr to escape.

In the course of the last few hours the track had been well trodden. Wisting made his way to the spot where Tom Kerr had stumbled the first time. Parts of a twisted tree root protruded slightly from the hard-packed earth. Wisting kicked it. It would be easy to trip over, but it was also so conspicuous that if you wanted to choose a place to pretend to fall, then it would be here.

He walked on and located the second spot where Kerr had taken a tumble. Here too a root protruded slightly from the otherwise level ground.

All around him the foliage was dense on both sides. Wisting put his head back and caught sight of blue sky above the leafy trees. A few birds sang somewhere in the treetops, but all sound of the ongoing police activity was shut out.

One of the trees closest to the path had lost some of its bark. It looked as if it had been scraped off, like when a forest owner marks out the trees he wants the loggers to fell.

Wisting moved closer. There was a rectangular area, about three centimetres broad and ten centimetres long. A few drops of fresh sap lay within the cut, and on the grass at the foot of the tree he could see the strip of bark that had curled up and lay in a little ball.

Taking out his phone, he took a photo of both the gash in the tree and the grey bark lying on the ground. Then he walked along the path again. Two metres beyond the root that had tripped Kerr up there lay a flat stone about the same shape and size as the mobile phone he held in his hand, with some pale green moss growing on it.

Wisting flipped it around with his foot. There was nothing underneath it. No creepy crawlies or mould to indicate that it had lain there for a long time.

The stone could be part of the carefully planned escape. Tom Kerr's task had been to look out for a marked tree. He had to stumble there and find a key for the handcuffs under a flat stone. It would have been a simple matter to take it out and hide it in his hand without anyone noticing.

Before he walked on, Wisting took a photo of the stone, but he would have to get one of the technicians to secure both it and the sliver of bark.

At the explosion site, three men in white overalls were busy working. Wisting approached the one he knew best, Espen Mortensen. Previously, his permanent office and small laboratory had been located at the local police station in Larvik. However, as a result of the reorganization of police districts, all the crime scene technicians had now been brought together in a single unit further north in the region. This meant they no longer had daily contact with the investigators, but it provided an improved professional environment and sharpened their expertise.

Mortensen pulled down his face mask and gave Wisting a nod.

'What have you got?' Wisting asked.

Mortensen took Wisting aside to a portable workbench set up on site. The items found by the crime scene examiners were laid out in transparent evidence bags.

'We've found fragments of the grenade,' Mortensen told him. He held up a bag containing a black sliver about the size of the nail on a little finger. 'There's no doubt it was a high-explosive stun grenade,' he continued, handing the bag to Wisting. 'This here is part of the asphalt-impregnated material in the container.'

Several bags with similar contents were arrayed on the bench. Some of these particles had traces of yellow writing.

'A stun grenade?' Wisting repeated.

'It contains only explosives, not splinters,' Mortensen went on. 'Injuries occur when you're hit by other loose objects propelled by the blast. In this instance: twigs and stones. In addition, the pressure of the blast itself can damage internal organs. But first and foremost it's intended to paralyse your opponent.'

Wisting put the bag back. 'Where does it come from?'

'It's too early to say. I don't know what kind of grenade it is yet, but there have been a number of thefts from military warehouses.'

'Anything else?' Wisting asked, looking beyond the workbench.

'We've found two empty cartridge cases,' Mortensen

answered, locating the appropriate evidence bag. 'Nine millimetre.'

'The most common calibre in the world,' Wisting commented.

Mortensen turned away slightly, towards the edge of the woods behind them.

'They were lying on the path,' he said. 'The handcuffs were also found there, but I think they've already been brought to you, right?'

Wisting nodded. 'What about footprints?' he asked.

'We haven't found any yet,' Mortensen replied. 'Whoever has been here would probably have parked his car in the same place that you all did, and walked along the same track. It was most likely no more than twenty-four hours ago, but it would be futile to search for car tracks or footprints now. The earth on the path is not soft enough, anyway, to provide suitable prints.'

'I see,' Wisting answered, moving towards the path where Tom Kerr had disappeared. 'Can you come with me partway along the track?'

'What do you have in mind?' Mortensen asked, wrenching off his latex gloves.

'The pistol must have been left out for him,' Wisting replied. 'Have you found the exact spot?'

Mortensen shook his head.

As they walked together, side by side, Mortensen pointed out the place where the tripwire for the grenade had been stretched out.

'There's a time delay in the trigger mechanism of two to three seconds,' he explained. 'This meant that Kerr could advance to a safe distance while those who came after him were hit with full force.'

Wisting cast a backward glance before they moved on.

Just over fifty metres further on he found what he was looking for: a grey tree trunk with a sliver of bark missing.

He told Mortensen about the tree on the other side of the sheep pasture that was marked in the same way.

'That sounds about right,' Mortensen said. 'The empty cartridges were found about a hundred metres further on.'

Wisting retraced his steps to the tree. At the foot of the trunk there were two leafy branches that had been torn from a bush. Although not large, they could easily have concealed a handgun.

'I'll go and get the camera,' Mortensen said, turning round.

Wisting followed him. The restlessness had returned. For hours to come they would fail to do anything other than wait for the right moment to capture Tom Kerr and his accomplice. Something within him strongly resisted this waiting game as a strategy for handling the case. The trail was already going cold.

15

Line chose the blue shirt she had given him for Christmas. It would look nice with his dark casual jacket with the honey-comb pattern.

The shirt was freshly laundered and hung in the ward-robe, but it was creased. She set up the ironing board in front of the TV in the living room so that she could watch the news. While she waited for the iron to heat up, she phoned Sofie to find out how her daughter, Amalie, was doing.

Sofie was the one she turned to whenever she needed a babysitter. She had a daughter only a few months older than Amalie. They played well together and attended the same nursery. They had arranged for Sofie to take both girls home with her today.

They were in a shop when Line called.

'We're having fish for dinner,' Sofie explained. 'Creamed pasta with salmon and peas. It was a recipe I found in a booklet.'

'Sounds good,' Line said.

The iron was hot now and she began to iron the shirt while they exchanged a few words about the children.

'I'm not sure when I can pick her up,' Line said. 'You've heard that Tom Kerr has escaped?'

'Yes.'

'That was the assignment I was out on,' Line explained.

'No! What really happened, then?'

'I can tell you all about it when I come for Amalie, but I don't know when that'll be. I've just popped home to transfer all the recordings, but I have to go straight out again. My car's parked in Oslo, of all places.'

'Did you film it?' Sofie asked.

'I'll tell you later,' Line promised.

'Amalie can stay the night here if it gets too late,' Sofie assured her.

'Thanks. You're a star.'

She hung her father's shirt on a clothes hanger and fetched some other clothes to iron while she had the iron out. The news channel had obtained an interview with Johannes Norum, the father of the victim whose grave Tom Kerr had promised to show the police.

Line put down the iron and gazed at him. He had travelled down to Larvik and was standing in front of the outer-perimeter cordon with his arms crossed. She had met him a fortnight earlier to let him know about the documentary project. He had been convinced that Kerr had murdered his daughter and extremely critical of the police investigation but had not been willing to participate in the documentary. Line suspected this had something to do with his past, which included a conviction for rape and a spell in prison. His daughter had distanced herself completely from him. Nevertheless, here he was, turning up on TV.

'Were you aware that Tom Kerr had admitted killing your daughter?' the reporter asked.

'They phoned from Kripos to tell me that,' Johannes Norum confirmed. 'I said I wanted to be present when they came for her, but I wasn't allowed to do that.'

He nodded towards the barrier behind him.

'If I'd been with them today, this would never have happened,' he said. 'He wouldn't have got away.'

He came out with some heavy-handed statements that

would not normally have been sanctioned in the editing process – the interview seemed totally unedited.

'What do you think of what has happened?' the reporter asked.

'It's a scandal,' Norum replied. 'The whole case has been a scandal.'

'In what way?'

Johannes Norum's eyes flickered and he seemed uncertain now that he was put on the spot and asked for further clarification.

'Well, he got away last time,' he retorted. 'You see, they never got him convicted for what he did to Taran. Now he's slipped through the net again. Now, just as we were about to get some answers.'

The reporter had a few more questions about how things had been in the time that had elapsed from when his daughter was murdered until the present day. Norum's reply emphasized how difficult it had been, and his answer gave the impression that he and Taran's mother were still a couple. In reality, they had divorced when Taran was only two years old and he had been absent for most of her upbringing.

The news item was over. Line switched off the TV and took her father's clothes with her out to the car. In all honesty, this was simply an excuse for returning to the scene.

There was a queue in front of the roadblock. Two of the vehicles ahead of her were forced to go back. Line took out the vehicle registration document and her driving licence and kept them ready for her turn.

'My father is William Wisting,' she said, showing her licence. 'This is his car. I've brought him some clean clothes for the next press briefing.'

That did the trick. The officer at the roadblock nodded her through. 'Keep your doors locked,' he told her, waving her past. 'Don't make any unnecessary stops.'

Line locked the doors and drove on. She encountered a search party, but apart from that there was no other traffic on the road.

The guards at the inner roadblock had changed shift. Line showed her documentation and recited her explanation once again.

At the entrance to the woods, she met a police car and had to reverse into a layby along the track to let it pass.

The car was only a few years old and had reversing sensors that were set off by the vegetation along the verges of the track as she manoeuvred backwards. They beeped at increasingly frequent intervals, but she had to bring the car as far into the edge as possible so that the larger police vehicle was able to pass. She heard the bushes rustle along the side of the car until the sickening sound of metal on metal assaulted her ears.

Line stamped on the brake pedal as the police car slipped past. She waited until it had gone before driving forward a little and going out to investigate what she had backed into.

The car had a scratch along the rear wing. An iron bar projected from the bushes. It looked like the remains of an old irrigator.

Swearing, she kicked it and used her foot to push it further out on to the verge. Then she hunkered down and inspected the damage to the car more closely. She ran her thumb over it. The scratch, too deep to be buffed off, was scored right through to the metal and would cost a few thousand kroner to have repaired.

She got to her feet, put her hands on her hips and stood

with her back to the trees, staring at the scratch. She couldn't tell her father. Not today.

A gust of wind rustled through the surrounding trees. Line looked around. Her irritation at what had happened was abruptly replaced by a sense of unease. The engine was still idling and she hurried back to sit behind the wheel. Distinctly unsettled, she locked the doors and drove on.

16

The weather was changing: it had clouded over and the wind had picked up.

Wisting knocked on the sliding door of the white delivery van. Adrian Stiller pushed it open and let him in.

'Any news?' he asked, glancing at the computer screen, where nothing seemed to have changed.

'We've surveillance on the house from four different angles,' Stenberg explained, holding up his phone with photos taken from one of the observation posts.

'Any movement?'

'No. All the curtains are drawn.'

'Do we know how he gained entry? Any sign of a break-in?'

Stenberg nodded, thumbing through the photographs on the phone, and showed him one taken from the rear of the cabin.

'There are recent signs of forced entry at the kitchen door,' he said.

The marks on the door and its frame were barely visible.

'It's an old cabin,' Stenberg explained. 'It wouldn't take much to create some play between the door and frame so that you could get in.'

Stenberg showed another picture of a spade, suitable for forcing the door open, propped up on the wall beside the steps.

'He's locked the door behind him,' Stenberg went on. 'The damage isn't bad enough to prevent the door and lock from working normally.'

'Have you had people advance all the way up to the cabin?'

'We've a patrol going from door to door. It would seem conspicuous to the guy inside if we didn't check.'

'Who owns the cabin?'

'A car dealer from Drammen,' Stenberg said. 'The road-block crews have been informed to make sure they don't let him into the area if he has a sudden notion to take a trip out here.'

Wisting took a seat and told them about the marks made in the places where the pistol and key had been left out.

'He could've got hold of a phone as well,' Nils Hammer pointed out. He asked Stiller: 'Is it possible to trace tele-comms in the area?'

'Hidle is on it,' Stiller replied, nodding to his colleague at the computer screens.

'We're getting data for the last seventy-two hours,' Hidle told them. 'It might be interesting to see who was in the area last night. Real-time data is a bit more difficult to access when we don't have a specific number to trace, though.'

Wisting received a message. Line had texted to say that she'd come back with clothes for him. The phone rang while he still held it in his hand, this time Torunn Borg. Based in the police station, she was handling tip-offs and inquiries about Tom Kerr and had not been apprised of the current situation.

'Do you have anything for us?' Wisting asked.

'Nothing specific. We've checked out a few addresses and have just taken action on a bus on the E18 after someone insisted that Tom Kerr was on it, but it led nowhere.'

Wisting ran his hand through his hair. This waiting strat-egy had consequences, putting an additional load on both the police force and the public.

'There's one thing you should maybe take a look at,' Torunn

Borg continued. 'We've received two independent observations of a boat travelling at full pelt in a northerly direction. Of course, there's always some traffic on the water, but the time and place do match.'

'When was this?'

'Between 12.15 and 12.45. I don't have a detailed description, but it was an open boat with a central console, about sixteen foot.'

'I see,' Wisting said.

He rang off and turned to the others to relay Torunn Borg's information.

'We can use that,' Stiller suggested. 'We can mention it at the press briefing and say that Tom Kerr has probably left the area. It might well hurry things along.'

'Shouldn't we consider the possibility that Tom Kerr has actually left the area?' Hammer interrupted. 'Everything else connected to his escape has been carefully planned. He could have seen through you and got rid of the trackers and transmitters.'

Wisting felt nauseous. This was certainly an unwelcome thought.

'We've seen minute movements that suggest he's walking from one room to another,' Hidle reassured them. 'He's in there. We're on top of things.'

There was a knock at the side door.

'I need to go out,' Wisting said, grabbing the handle. 'It's Line. She's brought me some clean clothes.'

17

'Strip off,' Line said, draping the clean shirt over one of the seat backs in the minibus.

'You didn't need to do this,' her father protested. 'I could have made do with this one.'

He seemed uncomfortable that she had returned.

'Well, I'm here now,' she said.

Wisting cast a glance out of the windows before he began to undress.

'Any news?' Line asked.

'Not really,' her father answered, struggling to wriggle out of his jacket between the rows of seats. 'Mortensen has found projectiles and remains of the grenade. But we're not publicizing that yet.'

'But what was that you said about nothing happening for a few hours?' she quizzed him. 'How can you be so sure of that?'

His smile creased his forehead and the corners of his eyes. 'I'll tell you later,' he replied. 'When this is all over.'

Line refused to budge. 'Is this about the Other One?' she demanded.

Wisting, bare-chested, now stood in front of her. His skin hung loose on his body and she was suddenly struck by the thought that he had grown old.

'Right now this is all about Tom Kerr,' he answered, reaching out for his clean shirt.

His mouth puckered as he dressed, and there was no point in trying to persuade him to say anything further.

'Can I go back to the explosion site?' she asked.

Her father shook his head. 'Your job is over,' he said. 'I can't let you wander around here.'

He headed for the minibus door. 'Sorry,' he added. 'It's best if you just go home.'

She adjusted his shirt collar and stood watching as he walked away. There was something about that white delivery van in which he and Stiller spent so much time that made her curious. It had not been here when they had arrived with Tom Kerr.

When she looked up the registration number, she learned that the owner information was unavailable.

Taking out her camera, she approached the old ruined saw-mill and sat down on one of the rusty rollers. A couple of paramedics on standby stood chatting outside their vehicles. A short distance away from them, three police officers were cooling their heels. No one noticed as she pointed the camera lens at the van's side door and zoomed in. It was quarter of an hour until the next press briefing. The sliding doors would soon open, affording her a glimpse of what was going on inside.

The camera was running and she covered the red light with the palm of her hand. To everyone else, it would appear that she was looking through the footage from earlier that day.

After ten minutes, the door slid open and her father stepped out, along with Nils Hammer and Adrian Stiller. Their bulk filled most of the door opening. The camera display was too small anyway for her to make out any details, but what she could see reminded her of the interior of a TV station's outside-broadcast vehicle.

Then the door slid shut again. The three men stood talking in hushed tones before her father moved off to meet the press.

18

It began to rain during the second press briefing. A fine drizzle that soaked the sheet of paper on which Wisting had jotted down a few key words about what he wanted to convey.

He started by announcing that the hunt for Tom Kerr was still in progress, gave a few numbers and facts about the forces and units taking part and imparted some information about the condition of the injured police officers.

'It's evident that Tom Kerr has received help in his escape,' he continued. 'The operation was well planned: for example, a gun was left on the ground here in advance. We therefore urge anyone who observed anything out of the ordinary in this vicinity during the past forty-eight hours to contact the police.'

'Are you searching for the Other One, then?' one of the journalists broke in.

'That's a natural question to ask,' Wisting replied. 'But so far we have no concrete information about who has assisted with the preparations for the escape.'

He gave the phone number the public should use to make contact and quickly moved on to avoid detailed questioning.

'The search will continue for a few hours longer, and will be extended. However, Tom Kerr may have already left the area. We've had reports of a number of sightings of small boats nearby, and we request everyone who has been along the coast outside Eftangland today to get in touch.'

He rounded off by repeating his appeal that anyone who caught sight of Tom Kerr should not approach him but instead make contact on the police emergency phone line.

Hands shot in the air. The questions were mainly about the Other One and how it had been possible to plan the escape and put it into action. Wisting avoided them by pointing out that he had not participated in the original investigation into Tom Kerr and his accomplice and could not answer about anything other than the current operation.

As the rain increased in intensity, Wisting ended the session and returned to Stiller and the others. Line had taken refuge in the passenger seat of his car. The windows were gradually misting with condensation. He strode past without stopping to chat to her.

'Excellent,' Stiller said as he entered the van.

One of the screens on the wall showed footage from the news channel that had broadcast his briefing live.

'You shouldn't have used Line in this,' Wisting said, taking a seat.

'She's smart,' Stiller objected. 'We've used her before. She knows what we need.'

'You knew what might happen,' Wisting insisted. 'Not a civilian freelancer. It's not so fucking difficult to film a guy who's going to point out a grave.'

'She has a special interest of her own in this, though,' Stiller reminded him. 'She needs the footage for a documentary film.'

Wisting sighed. 'You could go now and send her home.' He nodded at the door. 'She's sitting in the car waiting for something to happen. Tell her that her assignment is over.'

There was reluctance in Stiller's gaze. 'I was just trying to help her,' he said, getting to his feet.

Wisting remained silent and looked straight past him. The red marker on the map of Hokksund disappeared. It vanished for less than a second before reappearing out on the motorway.

'She's out driving,' he said, pointing at the screen. The marker moved along the main road, down towards Drammen. Tom Kerr's prison pen pal was on the move and heading in their direction.

Ove Hidle's phone rang. 'We've noted that,' he confirmed after a brief exchange of words. The conversation ended and Hidle fired up a computer screen that had been unused until now.

'The IP transmission is turned on,' he explained, keying his user name and password into a dialogue box.

A busy street appeared on screen. 'From the dash camera in the undercover vehicle,' Stenberg clarified. 'Live images.'

'Are we recording this too?' Stiller asked.

'As long as the image is moving, it's being saved,' Stenberg confirmed.

Wisting sat upright in his seat. He had never been involved in a direct broadcast undercover operation before. He was used to the undercover officers relaying their positions over the police radio and having to sit with a map following their moves. In the past few years, technological developments in police methodology had advanced at breakneck speed. The entire force was being transformed. In many ways, they had become an improved and more modern police force, but in the areas of openness, transparency and public scrutiny little progress had been made.

'She's two cars ahead,' Stenberg said, pointing at an old grey Ford.

The images were so sharp that Wisting could read the registration plate on the nearest car.

Stenberg tapped on the keyboard to open a loudspeaker output. They could now hear music playing on the car radio and the regular buzz of traffic in the background.

'Come in, please,' he asked.

The music on the car radio disappeared. 'We're here,' a woman's voice said.

'Anything to report?'

'We've received information from Autopass,' the under-cover detective replied. 'The car hasn't passed any toll stations in your neck of the woods in the past week or so.'

Stenberg turned to face Wisting. 'She doesn't have her own car,' he said. 'The one she's driving now is registered to her father. We don't know if she has access to any other vehicles.'

'But there's nothing to suggest she came here last night to set things up?' Wisting said.

Stiller agreed.

'She's the last person to visit Tom Kerr in prison,' he reminded them all. 'She could easily be a go-between for Kerr and the Other One and have smuggled information in and out of the jail. She doesn't even need to have known what she was involved in.'

The undercover car traversed a roundabout and passed the district boundary into Nedre Eiker.

'If she's heading over here, then she'll arrive in an hour and a half,' Wisting estimated. 'When it gets dark.'

They remained seated, watching the live footage. It felt unproductive, and Wisting's restlessness had returned. He needed to go to the police station so that he could sit down at a desk, gain an oversight of the situation and make inroads into the tactical work.

The journey continued along the River Drammen, through Møndalen and into the Strømsås tunnel. After just over quarter of an hour, the retinue turned out on to the E18, moving in a southerly direction.

'This way,' Stiller commented.

Wisting checked the time. The former chief investigator

86

in the case against Tom Kerr would soon arrive and, anyway, he had another task to perform.

'I'm heading back to the police station,' he said, glancing at Stiller. 'Semmelmann will soon be here. I need all the info you have about Tom Kerr's prison visitors.'

Stiller handed him a folder. Wisting got up and pushed open the sliding door.

'We'll do the next press briefing at the station,' he said. 'That'll shift the journalists out of this area.'

'I'm coming with you,' Hammer said.

Stiller nodded. 'What about Line?'

As Wisting stepped out, the rain buffeted his face. 'Don't give her another thought,' he said. 'I'll drive her home.'

19

The raindrops had settled on the windscreen, obscuring everything outside. Line stretched over to the driver's seat, fired up the engine and switched on the windscreen wipers and heater. The radio came on automatically.

Nothing was happening around her, and the lack of activity was making her impatient.

Fifteen minutes ago, a car had arrived with food and flasks of hot drinks. Apart from that, there had been no movement whatsoever.

She spent these idle moments on the phone, but the online news pages also contained nothing to move the case on.

The restlessness she felt made her tap her feet. In around an hour it would be dark. She wondered whether to drive around to find a police patrol and film their search for Tom Kerr. *VG* had just published a photo of two police officers beside a boathouse at Viksfjord. She could find her way there easily enough.

As she was on her way out of the car to move to the driver's seat, the white van's door slid open and her father and Nils Hammer emerged. They approached and clambered into the car, Wisting in the driver's seat.

'Any news?' she asked, for the umpteenth time.

Her father shook his head. 'Hammer and I are going back to the station to work from there,' he said. 'I'll drive you home first.'

The car juddered over tussocks of grass when he drove forward.

'We can pick up your car from Kripos HQ tomorrow,' Wisting continued. 'I have to go to Ila anyway, to search Kerr's cell and talk to the staff there.'

Line fastened her seatbelt. 'Fine,' she answered.

No one spoke on the way out of the woods. The car was waved through the two barriers without the boot being checked.

'Do you think he could have got away?' Line asked as they approached the town.

Glancing in the mirror, her father met Hammer's gaze.

'After all, everything else was so well planned,' she added. 'Surely it wouldn't be too far-fetched to think that there was a car or a boat ready and waiting for him?'

'That's mere speculation,' her father replied.

Line shifted slightly in her seat. 'What would he do if that were the case?' she continued to quiz him. 'Where would he go? Where could he hide?'

'I've no idea,' her father admitted. 'I don't know yet.'

'Did the police never have any suspicions about the identity of the Other One?'

Her father was breathing heavily now. 'I'm going to meet the former chief investigator later on today,' he answered. 'But I don't think he'll have any names for me.'

She received a text message from Adrian Stiller.

Apologies for the sudden end to your assignment today and that we didn't get time to discuss your documentary project, he wrote. *We'll have to do that another time. Will see if I can help you with further material.*

It felt as though something lay behind the simple sentences, some sort of invitation.

What's really going on? she wrote, trying to fish for information in her return message, but she received no answer.

The car drew to a halt in the street outside her house.

'What about Amalie?' her father asked.

'I'll sort that,' Line replied. 'Thanks for the lift.'

Hammer moved to sit in the front seat as Line turned and headed towards the house before her father drove on. She should have collected Amalie. It wasn't too late now to cycle down to Sofie's, but she needed to gather her thoughts first. She felt compelled to go down to her workroom, sit in front of her preparatory research material and try to find a fresh angle on it.

20

It was surprisingly quiet in the hospital corridor. The harsh ceiling light reflected on the freshly waxed linoleum floor. An elderly patient in a pale blue gown was hunched over a walking frame. Outside the duty room, a man in uniform was seated. Frank Kvastmo. He was in charge of what had been named the Patrol Section following the most recent reforms, and was the line manager for the wounded officers.

He scrambled to his feet when he caught sight of Wisting and Hammer.

'How are they doing?' Wisting asked.

'Tore Bergstrand is at Ullevål Hospital in Oslo,' Kvastmo answered. 'He's being operated on as we speak. They think they can save his leg. I'm going there tomorrow.'

'What about the others?'

'Jensen, Ranvik, Otnes and Ramsland have been discharged with minor injuries. There'll be a debrief this evening, so they should be back at work tomorrow. Emil Soffer and Maren Dokken are here. Soffer's wife is visiting just now. I'm waiting for her to come out. He has internal injuries and they're going to keep him in for a few days.'

'What about Maren Dokken?'

'She's torn some ligaments in her shoulder,' Kvastmo explained. 'They've already operated and sewn them together again, but she's facing a long period of physiotherapy.'

'Where is she?' Wisting queried, peering down the corridor.

'In the recovery room. They think she can be discharged as early as tomorrow.'

'I knew her grandfather, you know,' Wisting said. 'Ove Dokken. He was Chief Inspector here when I began in the police.'

'I've heard the name,' Kvastmo replied.

'Does she have any family here now?'

'Her parents are listed as her next of kin. They've been informed, but they've two days left of a holiday in Singapore. They're staying on there to finish their holiday.'

A nurse emerged from a side room and hurried past them.

'Is there any news of Kerr?' Kvastmo asked. 'Or about the accomplice?'

When Wisting shook his head Kvastmo glanced in the direction of the nearest patient's room. 'Nothing I can pass on?' he asked.

'Not yet,' Wisting replied.

21

A man in his early fifties, with thick grey hair and beard, stood outside the police station, a cigarette in his mouth.

Wisting turned in and parked next to an old Passat covered in dents and scratches: an undercover police car.

The man took out his cigarette and pinched the glowing tip between his thumb and forefinger. 'Are you closed?' he asked.

'The public entrance closes at three o'clock,' Wisting told him, stretching out his hand to shake. 'Semmelmann?'

The stranger nodded.

'Come with me round this way,' Wisting said, pointing out the route to the service entrance at the side of the building.

Opening the boot of his car, Idar Semmelmann slung a computer bag over his shoulder and drew out a cardboard box. A long roll of paper jutted out at the corners. He carried these items with him into the police station and up to the spacious conference room.

Wisting switched on the coffee machine while he gave a rapid summary of how Tom Kerr had managed to escape. Moving to the door, he scanned the corridor before closing it.

'Kripos placed two concealed transmitters on him prior to the site visit,' he added. 'One in his shoe and another on his belt. We know where he is.'

Semmelmann raised an eyebrow.

'In a cabin on the other side of the peninsula,' Wisting explained. 'He's had help to escape, and we believe he's waiting for help to leave the area.'

'You think he's waiting for the Other One, then,' Semmelmann surmised.

Wisting poured coffee into a cup and handed it to him. 'I don't like waiting,' he said, gesturing towards the box of case documents that Semmelmann had set down on the table. 'I'm keen to know who the accomplice is,' he added. 'I want to know his identity now.'

Nils Hammer had logged on to the computer in the room, which was linked up to a large TV screen. Having obtained the IP address of the camera in the surveillance vehicle, he keyed in the password to allow them access to the encrypted transmission.

'Is Lone Mellberg a name familiar to you from the case files?' he asked.

Semmelmann shook his head as he squinted at the large flatscreen. 'Who's that?' he asked.

'The last person to visit Tom Kerr in prison,' Wisting clarified.

He recognized the footage on the TV. The undercover team had now passed Tønsberg.

'She's on her way over here,' Hammer said, indicating Lone Mellberg's grey Ford. 'We're following her.'

'It's not a name I recall,' Semmelmann commented.

Taking the roll of paper from the box, he spread it out and placed leftover coffee cups, one in each corner, to keep it flat.

In the centre of the chart was a picture of Tom Kerr with smaller photos with names underneath arranged around him. This was a relationship chart, in which all the people who had any kind of link to Tom Kerr were sketched in, almost like asteroids in orbit around a planet. Those nearest to Tom Kerr's picture were the ones with closest contact. Those placed furthest out on the periphery lacked photos and were simply names in small print.

'This was drawn up almost four years ago,' Semmelmann told them. 'It contains around seven hundred names of people with some kind of relationship to Tom Kerr. Family, all previous workmates, neighbours in places where he's lived, people he went to school with, childhood friends, other criminals he's spent time with in prison. All the ones we've been able to track down are mentioned here.'

He pulled out a laptop computer. 'We have them all in a database,' he added. 'I'll search for her there.'

Wisting studied the relationship chart, pondering how many people he had crossed paths with or had some kind of relationship with and whether it would be possible to create a comprehensive reconstruction in his case. Probably not.

The nearest photo to Tom Kerr was that of his brother, Jon Kerr. Beside him was a picture of a bald man called Stig Skarven.

'Who's that?' Wisting asked, tapping his finger on the image.

'A workmate at Pool Partner,' Semmelmann replied. 'They worked together on servicing and maintenance of swimming pools. For a long time, he was our main focus. Before he started working for Pool Partner he'd worked as the maintenance manager of three public swimming pools in Bærum but had to leave because of indecent behaviour. He kept finding excuses to visit the women's changing rooms when they were in use. We managed to confirm an alibi for him on the night Tom Kerr was arrested and his farmhouse burned down. The data log from his router showed that he had been at home in Asker.'

'So all these folk have been checked out?' Wisting asked, sweeping his hand across the relationship chart.

'That proved impossible, but we've spoken to them all,'

Semmelmann answered. 'Though it didn't bring us any closer to the Other One.'

He concentrated on the laptop screen. 'Lone Mellberg isn't in here,' he said.

'They began to exchange letters around three years ago,' Hammer pointed out. 'After you'd drawn up this chart.'

Semmelmann nodded. He added her name to the database and allocated an index number, locating her in Kerr's innermost circle.

'Is there anyone else called Mellberg there?' Wisting asked.

The database returned a negative response.

'We've one person who lives in the same town as her,' Semmelmann continued. 'Rune Ness of Hokksund. He and Kerr were in the same class at primary school. You'll find him on the outer edge of the chart.'

Wisting took out the folder of case papers he had received from Stiller. 'I have another name here,' he said, leafing through the documents. 'Floyd Thue, a visitor from the Red Cross. Only he, Kerr's brother and Lone Mellberg have visited him in prison.'

Semmelmann keyed in the name. 'I do have someone called Floyd, but his surname's not Thue.'

Wisting sat down and glanced at the TV screen. The undercover detectives' car was now passing the exit for Sandefjord.

'They're getting closer,' Hammer commented.

22

Semmelmann laid four ring binders on the table, one for each of Tom Kerr's victims. The two murders of which he was convicted: Thea Polden and Salwa Haddad; one for the victim who had never been found, Taran Norum; and another for the one who had got away, Freja Bengtson. Each of them was marked with the date and time of the crime.

'The way we worked was to chart Tom Kerr's movements in advance of each crime to find out where he'd been and who he could have been in contact with,' the former chief investigator explained. 'Somewhere or other there had to be a point of intersection with the accomplice. That gave us lots of names, but no link.'

'What about phone contacts?' Hammer queried.

'Phone, email and other electronic communications were of course included in this exercise,' Semmelmann said. 'There was nothing of note.'

'He could have had a special phone for that type of use,' Hammer suggested.

Semmelmann agreed. 'We assumed that the communication between Kerr and his sidekick took place on separate phones,' he said. 'Kerr lived in a fairly isolated spot, you see. In principle, there were only two base stations that conversations from his smallholding could go through. We conducted a mass download of all conversations on the three days prior to each abduction.' He tapped his finger on the laptop, as if to indicate that the information was held in there. 'The data was analysed, but we didn't manage to find out which service he subscribed to, if that was how they kept in touch.'

'Can I have access?' Wisting asked, pointing to his laptop.

'I'll send you a link and password.'

'She's turning off,' Hammer alerted them.

Wisting looked across at the TV screen. Lone Mellberg's car was diverging from the E18, down towards Larvik. The undercover detectives in pursuit followed as the first car behind her. Mellberg was driving as if she knew where she was going, through two roundabouts and out along Elveveien towards Lågen.

Hammer turned to face the other two. 'She's going down to him,' he said.

Wisting phoned Stiller. 'Do you see the same as us?' he asked.

'She's on her way down here,' Stiller confirmed.

'How do you intend to handle it?'

'The roadblock officers have been instructed to quiz her if she appears,' Stiller said. 'They'll let her know that the road will be closed until 9 p.m. Until then, we'll just have to follow her and see what she's up to.'

They discussed a few practical considerations in connection with the next press briefing while Wisting followed the live transmission of the surveillance footage. After Lågen the journey continued over the Gloppe bridge and then east towards Sandefjord and Eftang.

He wrapped up the conversation and turned to Semmelmann again. 'What about the car they used?' he asked. 'The one they tried to drag Freja Bengtson into?'

'Totally burnt out,' Semmelmann said, fishing out a folder of photographs. 'The vehicle was included when Tom Kerr inherited the smallholding from his uncle. It was never reregistered, but plates stolen from another, similar vehicle were attached to it.'

He produced another folder and riffled through the contents to find a printout.

'We've information from Autopass about the various toll stations it passed through. It's likely they put on new plates every time they were out and about. We had an entire project looking into that. Plates from the same kind of vehicle were stolen in two instances from locations near where Tom Kerr had worked on swimming pools.'

The undercover detectives had let one car move between them and Lone Mellberg and were now continuing along the old coast road towards Sandefjord.

'She'll be at the outer barrier in five minutes,' Wisting said.

Semmelmann sat down again. No one in the room said a word. All eyes were fixed on the TV footage.

There was now a queue of traffic. The grey Ford turned off from the coast road to arrive in front of the roadblock. With one car between it and the surveillance car, their view was obstructed. When Mellberg's turn came, she spent far longer than the car in front of her in conversation with the police officers before she finally turned her car around. As she passed the surveillance vehicle, they caught a glimpse of her behind the wheel. A round face with a full fringe.

'Are they letting her go?' Semmelmann asked when the undercover car continued to sit in the queue.

'They also have an electronic tracker on her car,' Hammer explained. 'They'll pick her up again.'

Wisting stooped over the impressive relationship chart once more. 'Which of these is your preferred candidate?' he asked.

Semmelmann moved his head from side to side. 'There are no obvious candidates, really,' he replied. 'But there is one person of interest who isn't included.'

'What do you mean?'

'When Tom Kerr took over the smallholding it seems there was an Eastern European living there. Admittedly, it's quite a while back, but we have that intel from three different sources. The last sighting of him was about eighteen months before Thea Polden went missing, when a new electricity meter was installed in the main building. It was a foreign guy who opened the door to the installer.'

'You haven't publicized his details?'

'We considered that. We tried to have an identikit sketch drawn, but the descriptions were too vague. None of the three people who saw him thought they would recognize him again. We don't even know what nationality we're talking about.'

'Are there no Eastern Europeans here?' Wisting asked, looking at the chart.

'There are twenty-two, actually,' Semmelmann answered. 'Mainly men he met in prison. They've all been checked out. None of them fits the timeline as Kerr's collaborator. They were either still in jail, abroad or have some other alibi. And none of them has ever visited Kerr's home.'

'What does he say about it himself? During interview?'

'He dismisses it. Claims it's not true.'

Wisting's phone rang. It was Stiller again. 'Lone Mellberg was just stopped at the roadblock,' he said.

Wisting peered at the TV screen. The surveillance footage was on the move, but he could no longer see Lone Mellberg's grey Ford.

'She had no plausible reason for being there,' Stiller went on. 'Just said she'd gone out for a drive, so she was turned back. Denied any relationship to or knowledge of Tom Kerr when questioned and shown a photograph of him.'

'So she lied, then?'

'She at least avoided telling them that she visited him in prison.'

'Where is she now?'

'At a petrol station on the Sandefjord district border. She was told that the road will re-open for free passage at nine o'clock tonight.'

Wisting turned back to the ring binders that Semmelmann had brought. The most interesting one was the case of the girl who had got away, Freja Bengtson. This had led to Tom Kerr's arrest. In a separate folder, there was a collection of information about his smallholding in Østmarka: maps, plans and pictures of the fire in which the barn and farmhouse were totally destroyed.

The flames had had plenty of time to do their worst. The fire was reported late and a missing cattle grid that normally straddled the narrow farm track hampered the arrival of the fire crew. Instead, they were met with a deep ditch the fire tenders could not cross until wooden planks were laid to allow them to drive on. The photos showed how a chain had been attached to one of the metal bars on the grid and it had been dragged for more than two hundred metres, all the way into the barn.

'It looks carefully thought out,' Wisting said. 'Well planned, in fact, just like today's escape.'

'The remains of twelve petrol cans were found in the ruins after the fire,' Semmelmann agreed. 'In addition, dynamite was stashed in several places in both the house and the barn. The arsonist had obviously thought the time would come when it would be necessary to remove all traces.'

He drew the folder towards him and flipped through to a page of photographs of a burnt-out room in the farmhouse cellar that looked as if it had originally been used as a laundry. Now it was crammed with roof tiles and other leftover building materials. A cast-iron wood-burning stove had also fallen down from the floor above.

'We think this is where the kidnapped girls were held captive,' Semmelmann said, leafing through to the next page.

The cellar space had been cleared. A washing machine in one corner and the skeleton of an iron bedstead were all that was left. In the next photographs, there were segments of handcuffs, chains and padlocks, all burnt black. Saws, knives and other cutting tools were scattered around.

'Was everything destroyed in the fire?' Wisting asked. 'Were there no traces left at all?'

'There was evidence of the victims' blood,' Semmelmann replied, thumbing through to a picture that showed a drain on the cellar floor.

'But nothing pointing to the Other One?'

'He could have left the smallholding by motorbike,' Semmelmann explained. 'Tyre tracks were discovered on a route he must have used to avoid the cattle grid.'

He tried in vain to find the appropriate pictures. 'Everything's in the project database,' he said, pointing at his laptop. 'You'll see it in there.'

They discussed various aspects of the case – theories, possibilities, analyses and hypotheses were all tested.

'I believe you also tried getting a psychiatrist to produce a criminal profile?' Hammer asked.

'Yes, we did try that too,' Semmelmann admitted. 'Nothing came of it, apart from the obvious – a man with extremely high self-esteem and lack of empathy. That sort of thing.'

'A psychopath, in other words?' Hammer suggested.

Semmelmann shook his head. 'No, the opposite, in fact. A psychopath is governed by impulse. Their actions are motivated by sudden ideas and whims. They see only the immediate benefit or gratification in what they do. In contrast, the psychiatrists considered the accomplice to be strategic and creative with a high level of intelligence that gives him the ability to take the long-term consequences into consideration.'

'And there's no one like that on here?' Wisting asked, looking at the relationship chart.

'I guess there are a few,' Semmelmann replied. 'The most interesting one is someone Kerr grew up with. Reino Lystad.' He leaned over the chart to search for the name in the middle section, but failed to find it. 'Reino Lystad was once the national chess champion,' he went on. 'But the relationship between them was never positive. Tom Kerr tortured and killed his cat when he was twelve years old.'

Wisting located the name. Reino Lystad was now a grown man with a receding hairline and thinning hair. The photo looked as if it had been taken at a chess tournament.

Getting to his feet, he checked the time. 'I have to phone the Chief of Police,' he said, excusing himself. He headed for his own office, called Agnes Kiil and gave her the latest update.

'We've just received a briefing from Stenberg of the Emergency Squad,' she said. 'If there are no developments overnight, his crew will move in at dawn.'

'At 6 a.m., then,' Wisting said.

'Most likely something will have happened long before that, but we need to set a time frame for ending this. Our officers need to rest and change shift.'

'What about Lone Mellberg?'

'We'll bring her in at the same time.'

They agreed on the aspects he should emphasize at the next press conference. Wisting was to head that up too. It was a matter of continuity, the Police Chief insisted. In reality, it was a matter of apportioning blame and responsibility. A mistake had been made. Tom Kerr had succeeded in escaping. This was a case about which no one from the prosecuting authorities wanted to face the press and talk about. However, if Kerr had already been recaptured, it would in all likelihood have been one of the police lawyers who stood up in front of the cameras. If they were successful in apprehending the Other One, probably the Chief of Police would come forward to make the announcement to the media.

At 21.30 Wisting descended the stairs to the police station foyer to meet the journalists. He spotted some of the same faces he had addressed out at Eftang, but also a few newcomers.

Ten hours had passed since Tom Kerr's escape. Wisting began by announcing that the prisoner had still not been recaptured.

'We are about to end the manhunt in what has been our primary search area until now,' he continued. 'It's terrain that is naturally circumscribed by the sea in the north, south and west, and by the main trunk road in the east. We have examined all the garages, outhouses, boathouses and other buildings, spoken to all the permanent residents and used heat-seeking camera equipment. This work has not yielded any results, unfortunately. We have reason to believe that Tom Kerr may have left the area even before the comprehensive police effort was launched. The roadblocks and police barriers have now been lifted, and we are now entering a new and less intensive phase in our operations.'

He had never before had to mislead the press in such a way, and this bothered him, but he continued with the agreed statement. He intimated that they were now following an intelligence and investigative route, explained that a high-explosive stun grenade had been used to facilitate the escape, and rounded off by repeating the warning that Tom Kerr was dangerous and armed.

The first few questions concerned the location of the search for Tom Kerr. Wisting asked for understanding as this was information that could not be divulged to the media. Instead, he provided further information about how the grenade explosion had been rigged up and stated that they were receiving assistance from the group that had originally pursued the Other One. Then he thanked them for attending and left the foyer.

Now it was just a waiting game.

23

Midnight came and went. Three hours had passed since the police had officially withdrawn from the area. The specially equipped surveillance vehicle was parked in the back yard and Adrian Stiller and Ove Hidle had come inside.

The last hour had been spent watching Lone Mellberg's progress. The marker on the computer screen was moving around continuously, in a peculiar pattern – back and forth on the same stretch of road.

Wisting's restlessness forced him to pace the floor a couple of times. The adrenaline had drained from his body and his thoughts were sluggish. He knew he should grab a few hours' shut-eye, as tomorrow would be long and arduous, regardless of tonight's outcome.

Yet another hour passed without any action. Semmelmann had spent it arranging a hotel room for himself, and Hammer had dozed off in a chair. When it was past 2 a.m., Wisting announced that he was going to try to catch some sleep. He walked along the corridor and let himself into the office allocated to Christine Thiis. Police prosecutors' offices were larger than those of investigators and furnished with a modest seating area. He had used this before and knew how to make the most of the space on the small settees.

But sleep eluded him. He lay listening out for any activity in the nearby room. At some point, however, he must have fallen asleep and, when he woke, his body felt stiff and he took some time hauling himself on to his feet.

It was still dark outside and just past 6 a.m. He heard voices from the conference room and went to join the others.

Stiller turned towards him. 'She's driven into the area,' he said, pointing at the screen.

There were now three red markers on the same map: a double marker for the two transmitters on Tom Kerr and another for the car belonging to his prison pen pal. The latter was on the move, following a narrow, delineated strip: the gravel track that ended at the cluster of holiday cabins on the south side of Eftangland, where Kerr was waiting.

'Are Stenberg's people ready?' Wisting asked.

'Yes,' Stiller said. 'We'll get a visual soon.'

Lone Mellberg's car would soon pass the expanse of land beside the old sawmill. After that, the track divided in two, with the track on the right leading straight to Kerr.

No one in the room spoke a word. The marker stopped at the intersection and hovered there for half a minute before continuing to the right.

Stiller called Stenberg. 'You'll soon have visual contact,' he said.

'*Copy*,' was the reply, followed by orders about radio silence.

Hidle called up a new computer program and split the screen in two. On the right-hand side, two indistinct camera images appeared. All Wisting could see were shadows and various shades of grey and black.

'Bodycam,' Hidle explained, touching his chest to demonstrate where the cameras were mounted.

Soon two headlights appeared in one of the pictures. Vegetation obscured parts of the camera lens, but everything else grew sharper as the vehicle approached. Wild rose bushes along the way were highlighted as the man wearing the camera moved and vision improved. They could now see a white picket fence and a scatter of buildings.

Wisting checked the map to find his bearings. Hidle had zoomed in now. Lone Mellberg's car passed the holiday cabin where Kerr was ensconced. The red dots inside flickered slightly.

The live footage showed the car driving down to the jetty and turning. Then it remained at a standstill with the engine running and the headlights shining along the track.

'When will they make their move?' Wisting asked.

'As soon as they establish contact,' Stiller answered.

'What if they make their getaway in the car?'

'There's a vehicle on its way in. They won't get past that.'

Wisting rubbed something from the corner of his eye. As he stared at the screen, his mouth became dry.

The car's interior light came on as the driver's door opened. The distance was too great to make out anything other than the contours of a face. The person got out and was enveloped by darkness.

'What's going on?' Hammer asked from behind him.

A tiny glimmer of light appeared. 'Looks as if she's having a smoke,' Hidle commented.

Almost two minutes went by before the car door opened again and the old grey Ford rolled slowly forward.

Radio silence was broken: '*Object Bravo on the move.*'

The car's marker advanced while the two red dots inside the cabin stayed put.

'*Alone?*' was the next question.

'*Object Bravo is alone,*' was confirmed.

The vehicle passed the summer cabin and continued on. Once again, a minuscule movement was detected inside, but nothing more.

Stiller called the surveillance car. It was ready to move in after her once she had turned on to the main road, but at the point where the track divided in two when she drove in, she took a sharp right turn and followed the alternative route.

She drove all the way to the end of the track, turned, drove back and found another side track. She continued in this pattern, criss-crossing all the tracks in the area the police had scoured in their search for Tom Kerr.

'Maybe she's looking for him,' Hammer suggested.

Wisting moved to the window. 'It'll be light soon,' he said. 'We'll drive out there.'

24

Wisting and Stiller sat in the back of the specially equipped delivery van while Hammer drove. They could see Lone Mellberg moving further and further away from Tom Kerr's hiding place until, in the end, she was out on the main road again.

'We're going to meet her,' Hidle said. 'She's on her way home.'

Stiller drank from a bottle of water. 'I don't get it,' he said. 'If the arrangement was that she should pick him up, then something must have gone wrong with their communication.'

'Do we know anything about the phone traffic in the area?' Wisting asked.

'We'll receive an analysis in a few hours,' Hidle replied. 'But we haven't been able to monitor real-time conversations.'

A hatch in the dividing wall between the cargo hold and the driver's cabin meant they could see out on to the road, where there were few vehicles. They encountered a lorry and a taxi before passing the little grey Ford that Lone Mellberg was driving. Two hundred metres further back, they spotted the car with the undercover officers. Stiller rang them and gave instructions to follow her.

'She's to be brought in as soon as we've arrested Tom Kerr,' he concluded.

Their vehicle began to rock from side to side when they drove on to the gravel track. The surrounding landscape was coloured ash grey by the early-morning light. The weather was fine, but there had been some rain overnight. The bumps in the track had been filled with brown water.

They stopped at the last turn, out of sight of the house where Tom Kerr was hiding. The leader of the Emergency Squad emerged from behind a summer cabin. When Stiller pushed open the side door, Stenberg stood in the opening.

'What's the plan?' Wisting asked.

'We want him to come out so that we can apprehend him in the open,' Stenberg replied.

'How will you coax him out?'

'The usual way. We'll use a loudhailer and, if that doesn't work, we'll use tear gas to force him out.'

'When will that happen?' Stiller demanded.

'We're ready now,' Stenberg said. 'We're going into action as soon as we get the command vehicle in.'

'Where can we park?' Wisting queried.

'You can take over the observation post on the north side,' Stenberg answered, pointing towards a hill with a flagpole.

The sound of a heavy vehicle approaching made them turn and gaze back along the track. The Emergency Squad's armoured vehicle came rolling towards them, followed by the dog patrol and an ambulance with a crew of paramedics warned to be ready for action.

Stenberg gave the order for his squad to move into position. Ove Hidle stayed inside the van. Wisting, Stiller and Hammer ascended on foot to the outlook point Stenberg had indicated. They lay flat on the bare hillside and peered over the edge. The distance down to the cabin where Tom Kerr was located was around forty metres. It was surrounded by a large garden and a white picket fence. The track ran past it down to the little jetty beside the water.

The tang of the sea drifted in on the gentle breeze. Wisting took a deep breath of the salty air as he surveyed the sea beyond. It was grey, with dark patches where clouds hid the sun. Towards the shore, foaming waves rolled in over the smooth coastal rocks.

This was an expensive property, with a hot tub on one of the terraces and a barbecue area equipped with pizza oven and seating to accommodate a large group. There was a trampoline in the garden and a swing hung from one of the old fruit trees. A few branches obscured some of their view, but they could see the main entrance at the front and parts of the walls with the side door through which Kerr had entered.

As the armoured vehicle drove forward, three heavily armed officers moved under cover of its flank. Three men with bulletproof shields emerged from the other side and took up position near the side door.

Adrian Stiller took out a video camera, small enough to carry in his jacket pocket, of the type normally used by extreme-sports enthusiasts. He triggered the recording function and placed the camera on the smooth base of the flagpole.

A faint whistling came from the external loudhailer on the command vehicle. An authoritative voice addressed Tom Kerr, announcing that armed police had surrounded the property and ordering him to come out. The words ricocheted back from the nearby rocky outcrops, but they produced no immediate reaction.

Half a minute passed.

'Tom Kerr!' the loudhailer called out once again.

The command was repeated, now with a warning that if he did not follow the order, tear gas would be deployed.

The police radio crackled. Stenberg wanted to know if there was any sign of activity at the windows of the cabin. The various observation posts answered in the negative.

'*Do we have any digital movement?*' he asked.

'*A very slight internal shift,*' was Ove Hidle's response.

Kerr was called out for a third time and warned that the tear gas would be fired in just two minutes' time.

A grey-speckled gull came gliding above their heads on outstretched wings. It hovered for a moment before landing on the roof ridge.

The warning about the imminent use of tear gas was re-iterated after one minute, followed by a final warning that there were only thirty seconds left.

The seagull took off and flew away.

An abrupt message was relayed over the police radio: '*Fire!*'

They heard a muffled bang, and then the sound of shattering glass. Three tear gas grenades were fired in from three different locations.

Fifteen seconds went by. Stiller checked that his camera was still operating.

'*No movement*,' Hidle reported.

Stiller shifted uneasily. Another fifteen seconds passed before Stenberg repeated the order to fire. Three more grenades were fired in. The policemen behind the barrier of shields pulled on their gas masks. Soon after this, Wisting noticed that the wind carried a whiff of chemicals that stung his nose and eyes.

'Some individuals don't react to tear gas,' Hammer remarked.

Almost five minutes passed without any perceptible activity. Then orders were shouted from the area below them in front of the cabin. A team of six officers advanced to the front door, armed with machine pistols and equipped with heavy bulletproof vests, gas masks and helmets with visors. One of them was carrying a crowbar. He inserted it into the crack between the door and its frame and forced the door open. A stun grenade was tossed inside before the specially trained officers entered the cabin.

The shouted commands inside were audible. The officers who had lain undercover in the vicinity moved forward to the cabin and assumed positions at the wall beside the windows.

'Something's wrong,' Hammer said. 'There's something out of kilter here.'

They could still smell the reek of tear gas as they lay watching. Wisting's eyes began to stream. He blinked tears away but did not take his eyes off the cabin.

'*All clear*,' was announced over the police radio.

Two of the officers emerged from the cabin and wrenched off their gas masks.

'*Object apprehended?*' Stenberg asked.

'*Negative*,' was the reply. '*He's not here. The cabin is empty.*'

Wisting struggled to his feet, brushed down his trouser legs and drew himself up to his full height. Stiller remained outstretched on the bare ground. His plan had backfired. He needed time to digest this.

25

There was a noticeable change in the air: it had grown colder and sharper. The temperature had dropped and grey mist, damp and chilly, drifted in from the sea.

Wisting scrambled down from the hilltop. Stiller and Hammer followed in his wake all the way down to the cabin. The lingering tear gas still stung his eyes.

Ove Hidle had driven the van with the surveillance equipment up to meet them. 'Something here doesn't add up,' he said. 'We're still picking up signals from inside.'

Stenberg gave orders for the squad members positioned around the cabin to stay at their posts and sent in a new team to search the cabin one more time.

'Inside cupboards and underneath beds this time,' he commanded.

All doors and windows were opened to disperse the tear gas. A dog handler arrived with a growling Alsatian but was told to wait outside until the manual search had been completed.

Hammer spat and swore furiously. 'You've been conned,' he said, directing his ire at Stiller. 'Right from the start when you attached those transmitters to him and convinced yourself that he didn't notice anything. He's not here. The whole time we've been waiting to go into action, he's been moving even further away.'

Stiller did not reply. He strode up to the door and into the cabin.

'Kerr's plan was better than yours!' Hammer yelled after him before turning to speak to Hidle: 'You've let a dangerous criminal give you the slip,' he said. 'Let him back into society again.'

Wisting took a few steps towards the cabin and the terrace laid out in front of the entrance. 'It looks as if there's a basement somewhere here,' he said, tilting his head. 'A crawl space, at least.'

He turned to face Stenberg. 'Have you searched it?'

Stenberg relayed the question onwards. Two replies came simultaneously, but Wisting could understand that no one had looked under the floorboards.

'It's located in the foundations,' Stenberg said. 'But there's no access, and no guarantee that there's anything down there at all.'

Hammer began to circumnavigate the cabin. 'There's always a hatch of some kind,' he said. 'These spaces are needed for ventilation. Also, there are water and drainage pipes that require access.'

The hatch was in the middle of the east-facing wall, partly concealed behind a climbing rose bush. The trap door in front of the hatch was painted the same grey colour as the wall. The soil in the flowerbed beside it was damp and filled with a variety of weeds: nothing indicated that the hatch had been used any time recently.

Hammer kicked it open without waiting for the go-ahead. A blast of stagnant air wafted towards them, redolent with mould or damp. A man arrived with a powerful flashlight and handed it to Hammer as he aimed his gun at the opening.

Dust motes whirled up and danced in front of the beam of light. There was half a metre or so between the ground and the under-floor beams. Insulation mats had been fixed between the rows of beams, with an electric cable looped around them and water pipes criss-crossed beneath them. A number of supporting walls made it impossible to view the space in its entirety.

Stenberg summoned the dog patrol. The large Alsatian lay flat in front of the hatch, thumping its tail on the grass in anticipation of a command.

The man with the gun aimed at the opening shouted a warning and challenged Tom Kerr to show himself.

Wisting shook his head. He did not believe for a minute that Tom Kerr was in there. 'At the very least he didn't go in that way,' he said, thinking of the grey layer of ancient dirt and dust that now carpeted the ground.

The dog was sent in, leaving behind distinct marks in the soil. It ran around the basement in a clockwise direction and disappeared behind a brick wall but soon reappeared on the other side.

Adrian Stiller had joined them to watch the futile search.

'Let me borrow the torch,' Wisting said.

Hammer handed it to him.

Wisting directed the beam at the brick wall, approximately in the centre of the cramped space. Something loosened and drizzled down from the dry wooden beams and he heard the boards above him creak as someone walked across the floor.

'This was originally a sea captain's house,' he said, casting a glance up at the white-painted walls. 'It was usual to have your own kitchen cellar.'

He straightened up again and let his gaze take in the others around him before he turned on his heel and walked round to the kitchen door at the other side of the cabin. His colleagues followed him in. The chemical fumes from the tear gas still hanging in the air made him cough and splutter.

The blue-painted kitchen was kitted out with an extensive worktop, plate racks and a corner fireplace. In the centre of the room there was a lime-washed long table with a bench along the wall and high-backed chairs with cushions set out around it. Two colourful rag rugs lay on the floor, one with a crease in the middle.

The floorboards sagged slightly beneath him as Wisting crossed to the other side of the room. He used the toe of his shoe to push the rag rug aside. Underneath was an unmistakeable square on the floor, a trap door.

Stenberg moved the rug away to expose a metal ring at one edge of the hatch.

It would in fact be possible to climb down through the hatch in the floor and hold both the trap door and the ring handle at the same time, so that the rug would still cover the hatch when it was closed from below.

Stenberg nodded to the men armed with guns and protective equipment. Wisting moved back a few paces and Hammer did likewise. Stiller switched on his camera again.

A man flipped open the hatch while two others stood by with guns cocked. It banged loudly as it hit the floor, but there was no response from the cellar below.

The man who had opened the trap door used a telescopic rod with a mirror and light to look down into the cellar without exposing himself to danger. He twisted it and turned it to take in the whole cellar space. In the end he shook his head and snapped the rod shut again.

'Empty,' he declared.

Wisting, still with the flashlight in his hand, approached the opening in the floor. A ladder led down into a cold stone cellar, an open space of about three square metres. The walls were lined with shelves of empty glass jars and bottles, all coated in dust. In the middle of the floor was a pile of clothes and a pair of shoes, as if they had been tossed down there.

He handed the flashlight to Stiller and stepped aside to let his colleagues see.

'Those are his clothes,' Hammer concluded, turning to face Stiller. 'Your transmitters are lying down there too. They've been there the entire time. Kerr just changed his clothes and moved on.'

One of the Emergency Squad crew took off his helmet, set down his machine pistol and yanked off his heavy protective gear before climbing down into the kitchen cellar and gathering up the clothes, dropping them into a variety of plastic evidence bags.

Stiller called Ove Hidle, who was still sitting in the surveillance van, and asked him to come inside. Then he turned to the leader of the Emergency Squad. 'Could he have got away in Lone Mellberg's car? When she was here last night? Under cover of darkness?'

Stenberg shook his head. 'We set up the observation posts at 12.45 p.m.,' he said. 'Kerr must have left the building prior to that.'

When Hidle appeared, he was brought up to date. The officer who had been down in the cellar now emerged with the clothes and put the bags on the kitchen table. One of them contained the microphone and transmitter belonging to Line that Kerr had been wearing.

Stiller checked the shoe and found the wireless transmitter. The tiny device was no larger than a fingernail.

'The transmitter was moving inside the cabin, though,' Wisting said. 'I saw it for myself.'

'There were only minute deviations,' Hidle said quietly. 'We interpreted them as him walking around inside the cabin. But I've checked it out and it seems that could have been changes of satellite, or interference from other electronic signals. There have been a lot of different police radios in use in the area.'

Cursing, Hammer left the room. Wisting shut his eyes in

an effort to compose himself. 'Where is Lone Mellberg now?' he asked.

'Still in her car, on her way home,' Hidle replied. 'She's already passed Drammen.'

'Bring her in,' Wisting said.

Stiller called the undercover detectives and passed on the message.

Hammer came in from the living room and threw a framed picture on to the table. It had been taken down by the jetty and showed a man in his forties with a teenage boy on board a boat.

'He took the boat,' he said. 'That was how he got away. He found the keys in here.'

'It doesn't need to . . .' Stiller began.

Hammer cut him off. 'There's no boat berthed there now,' he said, flinging his hand out in the direction of the jetty. 'We got a tip-off about it. We even mentioned two boats. All the same, we just sat on our arses, waiting.'

Wisting's phone vibrated in his trouser pocket. When he dug it out, he saw that the call was from the Chief of Police. He walked outside and stood with his face to the sea before answering. He was the one who had proposed the waiting strategy to her. Now he had to tell her that it had all gone wrong.

26

A sudden noise woke Line, but she was unsure whether it had come from outside or somewhere inside the house.

She lay listening. The house moved constantly, and she had grown used to the different creaking and cracking sounds, but this was different. She had installed an alarm a year ago but was far from conscientious about turning it on. Even when she went out.

Her pangs of conscience grew stronger as she lay there under the quilt. She should have collected Amalie the night before and brought her home to her own bed. Instead, she had sat engrossed in work and taken a break only in order to watch the late news.

Picking up her phone from the bedside table, she saw that it was nearly half past seven. This forced her up. She wanted to hear the latest news and see if there had been any further developments in the search for Tom Kerr.

The clothes she had been wearing the previous night were lying in a heap beside the bed. She pulled on her T-shirt and padded barefoot into the living room to switch on the TV. Then she headed for the kitchen and inserted a capsule in the coffee machine. From the window she could see her father's house, but his car was not there. If he had been home at all last night, he had already gone out again.

She cleared the worktop a little and picked up some toys from the floor while she waited for the coffee machine to finish its work.

Amalie had slept elsewhere before. She and Maja had

occasional sleepovers. The last time, it had been Maja who had slept at Amalie's house, and Line had taken them to nursery the next day, just as Sofie was doing today.

She and Sofie had so many things in common. They were both single mothers and had both lived in Oslo but had broken away from their former friends and colleagues. Now Line regarded Sofie as her closest friend, the person she shared everything with.

Once the last few drops had trickled out of the coffee machine, she brought her cup into the living room and stood in front of the TV. Tom Kerr's face flashed up at the start of the news broadcast.

'The police report that they implemented a major operation in the early hours of this morning in the area searched yesterday in the hunt for the escaped prisoner, but Tom Kerr has still not been apprehended.'

The news item was illustrated with images from the day before. Line changed channel, but NRK had no new footage either, and only the same information accompanying the police appeal, pleading for citizens to make contact if anyone spotted the missing prisoner.

Line sipped her coffee. She had to make sure she was present when Tom Kerr was apprehended. She wanted photos of him in handcuffs.

27

'What about the helicopter?' Hammer asked as he flopped down on a chair at the conference table. 'It flew over the cabin with a heat-seeking camera. Surely they should have picked up that it was empty?'

'The thermal imaging doesn't penetrate through walls and roofs,' Hidle explained. 'There was no reason to believe he wasn't there.'

Torunn Borg entered the room and sorted through some papers. She still seemed indignant that she had not been informed about the covert operation.

'I've spoken to the owner of the summer cabin and told him about the police activity,' she said. 'He's a business lawyer in an investment company and he's coming down to take a look at the damage.'

She sat down. 'He told me that the family own a sixteen-foot Yamarin powerboat that is normally berthed at the jetty. The key is left hanging on a hook in the hallway.'

'That fits with the observation reported from Kjerringvik,' Hammer volunteered. 'An open boat with a centre console.'

'He was able to tell me more than that,' Torunn Borg continued. 'Something that's been a source of a lot of discussion in the family.'

'What's that?'

Torunn Borg gave a resigned sigh. 'Almost five years ago, they had an outdoor jacuzzi installed,' she said. 'It was supplied by Pool Partner.'

'Tom Kerr's employer,' Hammer broke in. 'He's been out there before, then. He knows the area.'

'He was there a week before he was arrested,' Torunn Borg agreed. 'When Tom Kerr was apprehended and his photos appeared in the media, they recognized him. Later, Pool Partner was also mentioned in the press accounts of how he removed all evidence from the bodies with liquid chlorine from his workplace.'

'What's the cabin-owner's name?' Idar Semmelmann asked.

'Frank Lewy,' Torunn Borg replied.

Semmelmann keyed this in and got a hit. 'It's in the database,' he said. 'Kerr was there with Stig Skarven. It was one of the last jobs he worked on before his arrest.'

He stood up and leaned over the enormous relationship chart still spread out on the conference table. 'Here,' he said, pointing to a man in the fifth circle around Tom Kerr.

Wisting peered at the photograph: a man in a collar and tie with close-cropped hair.

'Why is he placed so close to the centre?' he asked. 'Did they have more than a client–customer relationship?'

Semmelmann turned back to his computer. 'He was in court twice for sexual harassment,' he clarified. 'Anyone who has shown any kind of sexually deviant conduct was automatically given a higher score on our index.'

'So Lewy could well be the Other One?' Hammer asked.

Semmelmann shook his head. 'There's nothing to suggest that. They don't have any other connection.'

Torunn Borg spoke up again. 'I've reported the boat missing,' she went on. 'It has a forty-horsepower outboard motor. The fuel tank is a twenty-five-litre one and was apparently almost full. He could have gone pretty far out into the Oslo Fjord, or even across to Østfold.'

'But it's not likely that he's crossed the Oslo Fjord,' Semmelmann commented. 'Kerr doesn't have much experience with boats.'

'The police boat has gone out to search for it,' Torunn Borg told them. 'They're receiving assistance from two rescue vessels, but it's an area with a long coastline.'

Stiller's phone rang. He exchanged a few words with the caller, said thank you and hung up. 'That was the surveillance team,' he said. 'We've located the brother, Jon Kerr. He lives in Jessheim and works in a concrete plant at Skedsmo.'

'What sort of surveillance are they using?' Hammer queried.

'We've set up some undercover monitoring,' Stiller explained. 'Other family members are being tracked down too.'

'Who else might Tom Kerr think of turning to for help?' Wisting asked.

'Stig Skarven,' Semmelmann suggested. 'His workmate at the pool company.'

'He's on the list of people we've been in contact with,' Hidle added. 'The same applies to his befriender from the Red Cross, Floyd Thue.'

There was a knock at the door, and a young uniformed policeman put his head round and made eye contact with Wisting.

'They're bringing in Lone Mellberg now,' he said.

28

The new interview room was simply furnished: two chairs with a small table between them and a camera on the wall.

Wisting drew his chair closer to the table. 'Tell me about Tom Kerr,' he said.

'I don't know where he is,' the woman opposite replied.

The overweight woman's face was pale and pasty. She looked both confused and scared as her eyes flitted around the room.

'How do you know him?' Wisting asked.

'I don't know him,' Lone Mellberg protested. 'Not really.'

Wisting was searching for the right words to get the conversation moving. 'How did you make contact, then?' he persevered.

The woman opposite hesitated. 'I wrote to him,' she explained.

'In prison?'

She nodded. 'Everyone needs somebody,' she answered. 'Somebody who won't condemn you for what you've done. I offered to be there for him, as a friend.'

'But you didn't know him from earlier?'

'No.'

Wisting had no desire to provoke her and refrained from asking for any further explanation as to why she had made contact. He knew of other prisoners convicted of murder who had received flattering attention from unknown women. The reasons could be complicated and convoluted. Some were Christians keen to cure or convert, others women who wanted to play the role of mother, and some few others even wrote what could only be described as love letters. The sender usually had an unbalanced emotional life but the total focus they might receive from a long-term prisoner gave them a feeling of much-sought control.

'You also visited him,' he pointed out.

The woman nodded.

'When did you last visit him?' Wisting probed, even though he knew the answer.

'On Monday.'

'Two days ago, in other words?'

Lone Mellberg nodded again.

'Tell me about that visit,' Wisting said.

She shrugged. 'It was just the same as usual.'

'What does that mean?'

'He asked me how I was. What I'd been doing since the last time.'

Wisting remained silent while he waited for her to say more.

'He was interested in that sort of thing. He showed concern. Always asked how my father was, and how my daughter was getting on. My father had a stroke this summer. He's gone into a care home.'

'You told him about your daughter?' Wisting asked, feeling a tinge of annoyance.

'She's in the last year of high school,' Lone Mellberg answered. 'It's not been so easy with friends, and so on. He's been concerned about her. I have too, and it's nice to be able to talk to someone you know won't pass things on.'

Wisting decided against pursuing this. 'Did he tell you anything about himself?' he asked, changing tack.

'We just talked about day-to-day things. About a TV

series we were both following, and about a book he had read.'

'Did he tell you he's also confessed to killing Taran Norum?' Wisting ploughed on.

Lone Mellberg swallowed hard as she curled one hand around the glass of water on the table, but she did not take a drink. 'No,' she replied.

'Did you know he was coming out of prison for a site visit yesterday?'

'We never spoke about things like that,' Mellberg answered.

Wisting continued along these lines, unearthing further details about their conversations and meetings in prison. Nothing of what Lone Mellberg told him had any relevance for the case and he decided to move on.

'What were you doing in Larvik last night?' he asked, in a slightly sharper tone of voice.

'What do you mean?'

'You left home at 17.23 yesterday,' Wisting spelled out to her. 'At 18.56, you tried to drive into the area where Tom Kerr was last seen, but you were turned back at the barrier. You drove around all night in the locality where we had reason to believe he was hiding.'

He used these exact timings to create the impression that they had more detailed knowledge than was actually the case. This would make it more difficult for Lone Mellberg to give an evasive answer.

'I was looking for him,' she admitted.

'What do you mean?'

'I heard it on the news, that he'd escaped. So I went down to the place where it had happened.'

'Why did you do that?'

'To look for him,' Lone Mellberg repeated. 'The police . . .

128

you see, you had tried to shoot him before. I don't know . . .
I thought that if I found him and managed to talk to him,
then it would work out. Then it would be OK.'

'Have you been in this area before?' Wisting asked her.

She shook her head.

'No. I used my phone to find my way around.'

Wisting got her to repeat all of this again. About how she
had heard on the radio about Tom Kerr's escape, that she had
made up her mind to try to help him, and how she had driven
around all night long. She seemed so naïve that her explanation might just be credible. He put pressure on her until she
found herself backed into a corner, just where he wanted her
to be when he came out with the crucial questions.

'Has Tom Kerr ever asked you to do any favours for him?'

'What sort of favours?'

'Have you ever brought letters or any other kind of message in or out of the jail for him?'

Lone Mellberg did not answer and Wisting took this as an
admission of sorts. 'What type of message?' he asked.

'Only once,' she replied.

'What was it about?'

'A letter.'

'When was this?'

She did not answer his direct question. 'It was a private
letter,' she said instead. 'He didn't want the wardens or any-
body else to read it.'

'Who was it addressed to?'

'A friend.' She swallowed audibly. 'Someone who'd been a
good friend of his a long time ago. He was hoping that he'd
come and visit him. It was a thick letter. He had written a
number of pages.'

'Do you remember what he was called?'

Lone Mellberg nodded. 'It happened twice,' she said in an

undertone. 'The first time a month ago, and then again last week.'

'And you remember the name?'

She nodded.

'His name was Theo. I wrote down his name and address before I posted it. I have it at home. I thought I could get in touch with him and tell him how Tom was. That he needed a visit.'

'Theo,' Wisting repeated. 'What else?'

'It wasn't a Norwegian name,' Lone Mellberg explained. 'It sounded German. But he lives in Oslo. I have a note of it in my kitchen.'

29

A number of them sat around the conference table after watching the video of Lone Mellberg's interview. Wisting sat at the head of the table. The Kerr inquiry crossed the borders of several police districts, but he had been allocated the task of coordinating and leading the work of finding him. Tom Kerr had escaped on his watch.

'There's no one called Theo or Teo in the database,' Semmelmann said. 'I've tried different ways of spelling it.'

'She said his surname sounded German or something,' Hammer pointed out. 'That could be your suspect. The Eastern European you never managed to track down.'

Wisting scanned the comprehensive relationship chart. 'We'll soon have his full name and address,' he said. 'We should get ourselves ready for that.'

He turned to face Christine Thiis. 'We'll need a decision about moving in there.'

The police lawyer agreed. 'That won't be a problem.'

Wisting took out his phone to give advance warning to headquarters in Oslo.

'How far have the undercover detectives got?' he asked as he searched for the number.

The undercover officers who had followed Lone Mellberg's movements in the past twenty-four hours were now on their way back to Hokksund to enter her apartment and find the note she had written with the name and address of the person with whom Tom Kerr had communicated.

'They can't be far away now,' Stiller said.

He sat with his phone in his hand, as if waiting for an answer at any second.

Pushing his chair away from the table, Wisting moved off from the others so that he could speak to the person in charge in Oslo. He introduced himself briefly, explained the situation and was given the direct number of the team leader who would provide assistance when they were ready to enter the apartment.

Torunn Borg slipped into the conference room and closed the door behind her. 'They've found the boat,' she announced. 'It was lying under water near Ringhaugstranda, outside Tønsberg.'

'He's sunk it, then,' Hammer said.

'It was one of the rescue boats that located it,' Torunn Borg went on. 'The police boat is on its way now. I have the coordinates.'

Ove Hidle, already logged on to the large-screen computer, took the note and keyed in the position. It took them to the western side of the Oslo Fjord, between Tønsberg and Åsgård-strand. The map itself told them nothing, and Hidle changed to a satellite image of the same area. This showed what looked like a rocky shoreline and dense forest further inland.

'No buildings,' Stiller commented.

'He must have driven on to the pebbles and knocked a hole in the bottom of the boat,' Hammer said.

Ove Hidle moved the cursor on the screen. 'There's a track here,' he said, drawing a line through the trees. 'Almost all the way down to the fjord.'

'He could have had a car waiting there, or been picked up,' Stiller suggested. 'We can get the data from nearby toll stations.'

Wisting nodded. 'Zoom out,' he said, in order to pick out the discovery site in relation to Eftang.

Hidle did as requested, and they saw that the site was a few kilometres south of the oil refinery at Slagentangen. Hammer reckoned it was thirty nautical miles from there down to Eftang.

'It's taken him about an hour and a half,' he calculated.

Adrian Stiller's phone buzzed. 'Theo Dermann,' he read aloud.

He held up the phone screen showing a picture of the Post-it note on which Lone Mellberg had written the name and address:

Theo Dermann
Anton Brekkes vei 72
0041 OSLO

Hidle shifted the screen to criminal records and keyed in the name, but it brought zero results. He opened the population register, but the name was not listed there either.

'Foreigner,' Hammer commented. 'Clean sheet, in Norway at least.'

Hidle tried the intelligence register, but that was equally unsuccessful.

Semmelmann tried the surname in the database: 'No Dermann in here,' he said.

'Check the address,' Wisting requested. 'Find out who else lives there.'

'That 0041 postcode must be somewhere in Sagene,' Semmelmann said. 'There are a lot of high-rise blocks there.'

The address yielded no results.

'Postcode 0041 is not in use,' Hidle informed them as he tapped a few more keys: 'There's an Anton Brekkes vei in Fredrikstad. That's the only place in Norway where one exists, but the house numbers don't go as high as that.'

'What a fucking shambles!' Hammer said. 'Try to google him, or try Facebook.'

Ove Hidle copied the name from the screen and pasted it into Google. The highest-ranked result was for a German children's book called *Theo und der Mann im Ohr. Theo and the Man in His Ear.*

Hammer groaned. 'What the hell is this? Is there no one in the whole world whose name is Theo Dermann?'

'Check with the postal service,' Wisting said. 'They must have a listing. After all, they've delivered two letters to him.'

Nodding, Hammer took note of this assignment. 'If Lone Mellberg's to be believed,' he added.

They rattled through a number of tasks and shared out other assignments before Wisting closed the meeting.

Chairs scraped on the floor as they all got to their feet and went about their business. Adrian Stiller packed away his papers and laptop in a case, slung it over his shoulder and approached Wisting. 'I'll come with you to the prison,' he said.

Wisting accepted his offer. 'I just have to go home and get Line first,' he said. 'I have to give her a lift. Her car is parked at your place, remember.'

30

It had started raining again, and Line was sitting in her basement workroom, listening to the water gurgling in the downpipes from the roof.

It occurred to her that Amalie needed new wellington boots. She had outgrown the ones she had, and her puddle suit was also getting too tight for her.

A car tooted outside and she knew it must be her father. A quarter of an hour ago, he had sent her a message asking her to get ready to leave.

She logged off, got to her feet and checked the kitchen window. She saw that Adrian Stiller was also in the car.

Her father tooted his horn again impatiently.

Shrugging on her jacket, Line went out and clambered into the back seat. 'Hi!' she greeted the two men in front.

Stiller turned around to face her and smiled. Her father cast a glance in the rear-view mirror. 'Have you remembered to bring your car keys?' he asked.

She nodded but checked in her bag to be on the safe side. 'Is there any news?' she asked.

Wisting shook his head.

'What was that I heard about an action that took place this morning?'

'We went into a summer cabin on the south side of Eftangland,' her father explained. 'But he wasn't there.'

'We found your sound equipment, though,' Stiller added. 'Your mic and transmitter. You'll get them back soon.'

'So he was hiding in a cabin down there,' Line said. 'For how long?'

'Not long at all.'

'What does that mean?'

'He got away in a stolen boat, probably even before the helicopter was brought in,' Stiller replied. 'The boat's been found outside Tønsberg. All trace of him ends there.'

Stiller was more willing to talk than her father. She liked that. It made her feel included. 'So what are you going to do now?' she asked.

'Follow up tip-offs,' was her father's answer.

Line looked away and out of the window. His response annoyed her. It told her nothing and was of the type that journalists in the front row of a press conference were used to receiving.

'Have you checked the people he had contact with in prison?' she asked after a pause. 'Visitors and suchlike?'

'We're working on that,' he said.

Line shifted in her seat. 'Did you manage to speak to the chief investigator yesterday, then?' she asked.

'Yes.'

'What did he say?'

Wisting drove out on to the E18 and accelerated. 'He told me about the work they'd done in the search for the accomplice,' he replied.

'Do they have any suspects?'

Her father met her eye in the mirror again. 'We're in the middle of an active case, Line,' he answered. 'You'll just have to cool your jets and wait until it's all over.'

With a sigh, Line put her hand to her forehead. 'I'm no longer a journalist,' she said, leaning forward. 'I'm asking because it affects me. I was there when Tom Kerr did a runner. I still have a sore head from the explosion. I can't just wait until it's over. I won't be able to rest until he's safely back in jail.'

Neither of the men said anything further, and her father turned up the volume on the car radio. As the wipers scraped across the windscreen, Line shook her head and flopped back in the seat.

'Where is this cabin you're investigating, then?' she asked. 'Surely that can't be a secret. What's the owner's name?'

Adrian Stiller turned halfway round towards her. 'We have pictures from the operation this morning,' he replied. 'I can try to get them released.'

He smiled. 'When this is over and done with,' he added.

31

The lock buzzed. Wisting pushed the grated door open and walked through the outer perimeter of the prison all the way up to the massive brick building.

Someone shouted something from one of the windows on the second floor, some sort of confused message about rights and justice.

The prison governor stood at the top of the steep stone stairs, waiting to greet them. A prison guard recorded their names and they handed over their police ID badges in exchange for visitor passes. They then headed for the prison governor's office.

'We closed down the whole section when we learned that Kerr had escaped,' he told them. 'Of course, the inmates have found out about it through TV and radio broadcasts, but they haven't had the chance to talk to one another about it.'

'Is there anyone who might know something?'

'Tommy Hornland is still here,' the prison governor replied. 'He was the one who started the ball rolling, if you remember.'

'The informant?'

'Yes. He's probably the one most likely to have something to say. Have you spoken to him previously?'

Wisting shook his head. Stiller had not met him either, only read the reports in which he recounted what Tom Kerr had confided to him about the killing of Taran Norum.

'Don't worry about his eye, by the way,' the prison governor warned them. 'There's more wrong on the inside of his head than outside it.'

'What's wrong with his eye?'

'He was born with an empty eye socket. He used to use a glass eye, but not any more.'

'We need to talk to Kerr's contact warden too,' Wisting said.

'Molander. He's been off sick for a few days, but he's back at work now. He's here today.'

The prison governor leaned over the intercom system to request Fredrik Molander's presence at a meeting in his office.

'Molander can accompany you,' the prison governor said.

A man in his thirties wearing a crumpled uniform shirt appeared at the door. The prison governor introduced Wisting and Stiller and asked him to answer any questions they might have.

'They want to see Kerr's cell,' he rounded off. 'Can you take them there, please?'

'Of course.'

The guard produced a bunch of keys and led the way to the custodial section.

Wisting could feel a strong sense of the deprivation of liberty as they walked. Metal doors that were unlocked and relocked, pale fluorescent-light tubes and long, grey corridors.

'How long have you been Tom Kerr's contact warden?' Wisting asked.

Molander turned his head and cast a glance behind him. 'Ever since he came here,' he answered. 'More than four years.'

'You know each other well, then?'

'That's the idea,' Molander replied. 'Good relations between inmates and wardens have a positive effect when it comes to security, and reduce the level of conflict.'

They moved through a common room with sitting areas and a kitchenette and on into another corridor.

'It's intended as a stable point of contact for prisoners throughout their stay here,' Molander went on. 'To be a support and someone to talk to.'

There was a sermonizing tone in his manner of speaking, but Wisting ignored that. 'What did you talk about?' he asked instead.

'Mostly practical details about being here. Guidance and orientation. Helping with various applications. Getting him on to a number of courses and programmes. Planning for his future.'

'And what plans did Kerr have for his future?'

Fredrik Molander stopped at an unmarked cell door. 'No matter what they're convicted of, or how long it is until their release, we have to work towards rehabilitation and transformation,' he said as he inserted the key in the lock.

Somewhere further along the corridor, someone shouted something from one of the cells, but it was impossible to decipher what was said.

'My most important job is to be present,' Molander continued, turning the key slowly. 'To try to be a positive factor in their daily life.'

The door bolt shot back and the massive metal door swung open..

The room inside measured about two by five metres and contained a bed, desk, shelves crammed with ring binders, a cupboard, a wash basin, a TV and a cork noticeboard.

Stepping inside, Wisting walked to the window and peered out between the bars. The deserted exercise yard was surrounded by a seven-metre-high perimeter wall, behind which spread out a fertile forest landscape beneath a blue-grey sky.

Stiller read a quote from one of the notes on the

noticeboard: *'Laws are like telegraph poles; you can't jump over them, but you can get round them.'*

Wisting approached the desk. A pile of different textbooks sat on it: philosophy, psychology, a book of facts about criminal law and a couple of self-help books.

He sat down and pulled on a pair of latex gloves before opening the top drawer. It contained a few CDs, writing materials, envelopes and stamps. A folder contained a letter from the Norwegian Correctional Service in connection with his prison sentence, while another folder held correspondence with other public bodies.

Wisting put back the folders and lifted the writing pad. There was nothing on it, but he could make out the outlines of what had been written on the previous sheet. He held the pad up at an angle towards the light from the window to see more clearly. It looked like a formal letter layout. He saw the impression of a sender and recipient address, and the name Tom Kerr was clear to see. The recipient appeared to be Ila Prison. The letter itself began with a heading that had been underlined forcefully.

He laid the writing pad aside to take with him.

In the next drawer there was a bundle of letters held together with an elastic band. He pulled it off and peered at the letter on top. It was from Lone Mellberg and dated three weeks previously. She thanked him for the visit and wrote that she understood how difficult it could be to open up about your feelings.

For most of my life I haven't been emotionally present [she wrote in round letters]. *So I know how it is for you. I wasn't brought up to show my feelings either. But when you hold your feelings in check for long enough, in the end they overflow. I hope I can be the one to make your dam burst . . .*

It continued in a similar vein. Nothing in the correspondence between Tom Kerr and Lone Mellberg could be interpreted as preparation for an escape attempt.

'Here!' Adrian Stiller exclaimed. He was rummaging through the cupboard and had found a note. '*Theo Dermann*,' he read out as he held it up to Wisting.

This was the same name and address as on the letters Lone Mellberg had talked about having smuggled out.

Wisting turned to the contact warden, who was leaning against the doorframe. 'Is that a name you recognize?' he asked. 'Theo Dermann?'

Fredrik Molander shook his head. Wisting peered into the cupboard where the note had been found. 'Anything else?' he asked.

'Only this,' Stiller replied, placing the note in an evidence bag.

Wisting concentrated on the desk again and dropped the bundle of letters from Lone Mellberg into a similar bag.

The third drawer contained items bought in the prison shop: bags of boiled sweets, packets of biscuits, potato crisps, chocolate, peanuts and cocoa powder.

The shelf above the desk was filled with ring binders stuffed with documents from the criminal cases brought against Kerr and letters from his lawyer. The last one was a copy of a letter to an insurance company about their failure to pay compensation for the fire at his smallholding in Østmarka.

The rubbish bin beneath the desk was empty. There was nothing behind the cork noticeboard on the wall or the mirror above the washbasin. They upended the bed, leafed through magazines and browsed through the books. The search was fruitless.

Wisting turned to face Molander. 'Was there anything he said or did that, in hindsight, might be relevant to his escape?'

Molander shook his head. 'Not really. We discussed the possibility of day release and parole when his minimum sentence period is over. I was honest with him, spoke my mind and said that if he didn't demonstrate personal change, he would probably have his sentence extended. I think that made him believe he ought to confess to the third murder. That it would be important for him to be able to move on.'

Wisting crouched down and looked under the bed. All he could see was a pair of slippers. He pulled them out and checked that there was nothing in them. Then he rose to his full height again and looked at Molander.

'Tell me about the telephone routines,' he said.

'What do you mean?'

'If Tom Kerr wanted to make a phone call to someone on the outside, how would that happen?'

'He can phone out to anyone he likes, but he has only twenty minutes of phone time a week, Monday to Friday. He has to use a wall-mounted phone beside the guard room. All private conversations are monitored. There was also surveillance on his letters.'

Wisting nodded. 'All the guards knew about that?' he asked.

'Of course,' Molander replied in a self-assured, almost disdainful voice.

'What about this phone regime?' Stiller asked. 'Was it followed strictly?'

Fredrik Molander avoided the question: 'Conversations with the police or his lawyer are not included in his phone-time allowance,' he explained instead, 'and they're not tapped either.'

'But is it possible for inmates to obtain extra phone time, for example when he's meeting a social worker or a care worker? Would he be able to get permission to use their office phone, for example?'

Molander shook his head. 'Not for personal conversations, no.'

'But the escape was well planned,' Stiller interjected. 'He must have communicated with someone about it.'

'Visitors,' Molander suggested. 'Either directly, or by someone carrying messages in and out.'

Wisting approached the window again. The rain had formed puddles outside in the exercise yard.

They knew that Lone Mellberg had smuggled out two letters, but the level of detail in the escape plan demanded two-way communication. So far, she had denied bringing anything in for him.

'The one you should check is that lawyer of his,' Molander went on.

'Claes Thancke?'

'It wouldn't be the first time he moved beyond his role as a defence counsel,' Molander said.

Wisting did not pass comment on this rejoinder. If the defence lawyer had operated as a courier, then Tom Kerr would not have needed to use Lone Mellberg to post letters for him.

'We're done,' he said, taking one last look around the cell. 'Can we have a chat with the informant?'

'Tommy Hornland,' Molander replied, nodding his head. 'He's going through a bad patch.'

Wisting left the cell with Stiller following at his heels. 'How do you mean?'

'He's borderline psychotic, but the doctor is reluctant to increase his medication. Not yet, at least.'

He closed the cell door and locked it carefully. 'You can wait in the visitors' room.'

32

It felt like a waste of time to travel into Oslo merely to pick up her car and drive home again. As Line drove out of the back yard at the Kripos building, she looked up Ingar Holm's number. He was the development manager at Septemberfilm and her contact person for the documentary project. They had spoken several times the previous evening. He had gained access to her film footage but was eager to meet her in person. He cancelled another appointment and arranged access to an editing suite so that they could watch the recording together.

A quarter of an hour later, Line was parking in Nydalen. Holm met her in reception. He was about ten years older than her and had worked on numerous TV productions, everything from reality shows to major drama series.

'Nina Gullow will join us,' he said, ushering her into a corridor. 'She hasn't seen the footage.'

Line had only said hello to Nina Gullow once in the past. She was the person at Septemberfilm who would have administrative responsibility once a final decision had been made about the production. She was already seated in the editing suite and leapt up from her chair when they came in.

'Quite a development,' she said, shaking Line's hand. Her voice was husky and hoarse but carried authority. 'When can we have official access to the material?'

'That might take a long time,' Line said as she sat down. 'The arrangement was that it would happen once a legal judgment is in place against Tom Kerr. That could take a while yet. First, they have to find him.'

Nina Gullow looked unhappy with the answer.

'I've got a good relationship with the leader of the investigation from Kripos,' Line went on. 'Adrian Stiller. He has promised me pictures from the unsuccessful operation in the early hours of this morning.'

Ingar Holm played the recording from their arrival at Eftang. This would be the sixth time Line had viewed it.

'Will there be a problem with impartiality regarding your father?' Gullow asked. 'After all, he's heavily involved in the case.'

Line shook her head emphatically. 'The problem is that he doesn't tell me anything,' she answered. 'I think there's a lot more going on than what's emerging from the news reports.'

'Like what?'

'Something to do with the Other One. He must be the person behind it all who has organized the whole escape.'

Gullow nodded thoughtfully.

'Tom Kerr acted as a decoy,' Line went on. 'Bringing him out of prison might well have coaxed out the Other One. I don't know if the police included that idea in their calculations, but there's definitely something going on behind the scenes here.'

Onscreen, they watched as Tom Kerr fell for the first time. None of them spoke as he got to his feet and walked on. When he fell again, Line asked for the footage to be replayed in slow motion. They saw Kerr wipe the blood from a cut on his face and lick it from his fingers.

'There!' she said, pointing to the tiny key inside his mouth.

'Fucking brilliant!' Gullow commented. 'What are the police doing today? Is there any news?'

'They've brought in the chief investigator from the two cases Kerr was already convicted of,' Line replied. 'Right now they're at the prison talking to the wardens and other inmates.'

'It's crucial that you stay close,' Gullow said. 'Document everything and gather as much information as possible.'

'Here it comes!' Ingar Holm prompted them.

Tom Kerr had started to run. Nina Gullow focused on the TV screen, waiting for the explosion. The flash of light made her swear again.

The camera fell to the ground as soil and sand drizzled down. The blonde policewoman appeared in the picture. They heard Wisting's voice ask her if she was uninjured before ordering her to remain on the spot, while the camera showed the obviously wounded policewoman assist a colleague.

'Who's the girl?' Nina Gullow demanded.

'I don't know,' Line replied. 'She hasn't had a permanent job for long. I spoke to her in the minibus on our way from the prison.'

Onscreen now, the police dog was following Tom Kerr into the woods.

'Rewind!' Nina Gullow asked. 'To the girl.'

Ingar Holm complied and froze the image when the policewoman was closest to the camera. Her long hair was tied back in a thick plait over one shoulder. Her face was grubby and speckled with cuts and grazes.

'She's attractive,' Nina Gullow commented. 'Find out who she is. If anyone is going to talk to camera about what happened, then it should be her.'

33

Wisting stood at the window in the visitors' room and looked out at the rain. A crow strutted around in the exercise yard, pecking at the ground. They had been waiting for Tommy Hornland for the past ten minutes. Wisting's phone was still with the guard in the lobby. If there were to be a development in the case, they would not learn about it until they came out again.

The door opened and Wisting turned round. Tommy Hornland was a tall, thin man with a sharp nose and tousled hair. He had stabbed his mother to death and had also been found guilty of the attempted murder of his father and sister.

Fredrik Molander sat down on a wooden chair beside the door while the prisoner plumped down on the settee. He scowled at them with his one eye and there was something distrustful, but at the same time distant, in his gaze. In the space where his other eye should have been his eyelid hung down and the surrounding skin was wrinkled.

'It's OK,' Wisting said, addressing the prison guard. 'You can wait outside.'

It looked as if he was thinking of protesting, but then he stood up and made his exit.

Wisting explained who they were. The leather settee squeaked as Hornland twisted and turned. 'I knew it,' he said, and began to rock back and forth.

Wisting glanced across at Stiller, who shrugged. Tommy Hornland was clearly in a different mental state now than when the investigators from the Cold Cases Group had spoken to him.

'Knew it the whole time,' he added.

'What did you know?' Stiller asked.

'You should have realized that he was going to do a runner,' he said with a noise that sounded like a sniff. 'Everybody knew it.'

'We took every precaution,' Stiller commented.

'Everybody knows that a hungry lion is going to attack,' Hornland said. 'Everybody knew that Tom Kerr was going to escape.'

'It was very well planned,' Stiller continued. 'He must have received help.'

Tommy Hornland crossed his arms on his chest. 'Yes, from the Other One,' he said. 'The guy who has always helped him.'

'Did he ever talk to you about his sidekick?'

'No one knows who he is,' Hornland said, without actually answering Wisting's question. He placed one leg over the other and leaned to one side on the settee. 'He's used you, just like he used me,' he said, swinging his foot. 'I should have cottoned on to it before. His confession was false. Not false in the sense of not being true, because he did murder that girl, but the reason he started running off at the mouth to me about it was that he wanted to break out.'

Tommy Hornland tapped his finger on his forehead, as if to say that he had worked out how it all fitted together. 'He didn't only talk to me about it, but to quite a few folk in here. Everybody, to be honest. He reckoned that someone would eventually go to the guards with it. I just happened to be the one. You wouldn't have gone along with it if he'd approached you directly and suddenly confessed, so he used me. And you snatched at the bait. You took him out of here on a wild-goose chase.'

Even though he was talking breathlessly, there was something rational and logical about his reasoning. Stiller said something about it being easy to be wise after the event and repeated his mantra that the escape was well planned.

'He spent a long time on it,' Hornland said. 'Years, in fact.'

'How can he have done that from inside prison?' Wisting asked. 'He must have talked to someone on the outside. Received help.'

Tommy Hornland glowered at the door with his one eye. 'The Other One,' he repeated. 'His pal, who has always helped him. With everything.'

'How would you have gone about it, if you wanted to communicate with someone on the outside?' Stiller asked. 'Without the wardens finding out?'

'Send messages,' Hornland replied, glancing at the door again, as if desperate to leave the room. 'It's easier for some people than for others. Much easier.'

'Who is it easier for?'

'Loads of people.'

'Who, then?'

Tommy Hornland rolled his head and fixed his one eye on Wisting. 'It's easier for the ones who have a lawyer,' he answered. 'Lawyers come and go without hindrance. In and out all the time. I don't have a lawyer. I haven't had one for twelve years. I don't have a girlfriend either, or a brother. I do have a sister, but she doesn't come here.'

Wisting adopted a thoughtful expression. He nodded sympathetically and tried to steer the conversation on to something that might provide them with relevant information, but Tommy Hornland's responses grew increasingly vague. In the end, Wisting got to his feet and knocked on the door to indicate that the interview was over.

Tommy Hornland stayed behind in the visitors' room while

Wisting and Stiller were escorted back to the main entrance, where they retrieved their police badges and mobile phones.

Wisting had eleven missed calls, two of them from Semmelmann and two from the Chief of Police. The rest were numbers he had not stored: most likely from journalists.

He called the Police Chief as they walked through the heavy rain to their car. 'Any news?' she asked.

'No,' he replied, going on to explain that he had just left the prison.

'Internal Affairs want to speak to you,' the Police Chief said. 'They're sending an investigator down to Larvik. You must make yourself accessible to them.'

34

'We should talk to Floyd Thue,' Stiller said as soon as they were seated in the car. 'The befriender from the Red Cross. He lives near Bekkestua.'

Wisting glanced up at the imposing prison building before driving out of the car park. 'Do you think he'll be at home now?' he asked.

'According to the paperwork, he's an investor and works from home. Draws up financial analyses. Buys and sells shares on the net. We can but try.'

He found the address and typed it into the satnav. It was almost on their way back to Vestfold.

They drove south, skirting a golf course. The houses were scattered but gradually grew more numerous, and soon they found themselves in a residential area of large villas with extensive gardens. The GPS led them into a cul-de-sac.

'Number 32,' Stiller said, pointing at a white-painted detached house with glazed roof tiles.

The curved wrought-iron gate was open wide and Wisting turned into the paved courtyard. There was no car parked outside, but it looked as if there was a large garage beneath the house.

'He lives alone,' Stiller said. 'Never been married. No children.'

Wisting remained seated behind the steering wheel as he gazed at the grand residence. Tall, round pillars loomed on either side of the entrance.

'Why on earth would someone who lives here visit a convicted killer in prison?' he wondered.

'Let's go and ask,' Stiller suggested, stepping out.

The double entrance doors were painted black and looked impressive. The doorbell sounded like a clock chime, and Wisting almost expected a maid or a butler to open the door.

The man who did materialize was in his thirties, and his clothes and appearance were not entirely in keeping with the style of the house. His thin, stringy hair lay flat on his head above his pale complexion, his pointed chin was slightly lopsided, and he had one large and two smaller warts on his left cheek.

'Floyd Thue?' Wisting inquired.

'Yes, that's me.'

Wisting had envisaged a man in a suit, but Floyd Thue was dressed in well-worn joggers and a T-shirt spattered with coffee stains.

'We're from the police,' Stiller explained. 'It's about Tom Kerr.'

'I see,' Thue replied, and went on to mention that he had seen Wisting on the TV news. 'I've been expecting you, really.'

They were led through to a workroom on the opposite side of the house. A huge horseshoe-shaped desk was covered in computers, two of which were in use, the screens showing constantly changing stock exchange figures. A glimmer of daylight spilled through a gap in the curtains.

There were no chairs for visitors beside the desk so Thue had to go into an adjacent room to fetch a couple of dining chairs.

'You featured on the list of Tom Kerr's visitors,' Wisting began. 'How often do you visit him?'

'Once or twice a month,' Thue replied.

'How long has that been going on?'

'For nearly five years. I have three prisoners I visit regularly. It takes me quarter of an hour to drive over there.'

Stiller leaned forward a little. 'Can I ask why you do that?' he queried.

Tilting back in his chair, Floyd Thue picked absentmindedly at the largest of the three warts on his cheek. 'The intention is to do something useful to society,' he replied. 'What I do here is just about numbers and money.'

He waved his hand towards the computer screens. 'The people I meet are all in the same profession. We talk about the same things. As a befriender, I'm exposed to different ideas. A completely different perspective on life.'

'What do you talk about?'

'It varies, but often about philosophy and ethical questions. About freedom, for example.'

'Freedom?'

Thue smiled. 'In the beginning, human beings are free to choose,' he replied. 'We can even choose to commit illegal acts that break the norms and rules of society, but then we must also take the consequences of the choices we've made. And we can't avoid those consequences. Many of the prisoners in Ila are there because they've made the wrong choices, but do human beings really have free will?'

He left the question hanging in the air, as if he wanted to hear the two police officers' opinions on this. Then he shook his head and let them know what he himself thought about it.

'What we may believe to be independent choices are really the unavoidable results of previous events,' he said. 'Just as you can predict that a hungry lion is going to hunt his prey, you can also predict what a human being will choose if you're familiar with the whole of his previous history.'

Wisting recognized the reference to the lion. 'Do you also visit Tommy Hornland?' he asked.

'So you've spoken to him too?' Thue said, smiling.

'We've just been to Ila,' Wisting answered.

'Freedom can be regarded from various aspects,' Thue went on. 'Freedom of action is usually regarded as the opportunity to do whatever we want. But the greater our freedom of action, the greater responsibility we also have to take. Therefore, it's possible to turn this on its head and say that absolute freedom means being totally devoid of responsibility, incapacitated. Viewed from that perspective, freedom can also be experienced even when strapped to a restraint bed in Ila. Whoever is lying there, tied up, has no opportunity to choose. He has no responsibility to take. He can only lie there, restrained. He is completely submissive. For Tommy Hornland, that is the best form of freedom.'

The thought of how Tom Kerr and his accomplice had chained up their victims crossed Wisting's mind, but he passed no comment.

'The inmates, of course, will never have the same economic freedom or freedom of action as me. But their experience of freedom will be different and far greater than anything I can ever experience, a kind of freedom that only people who have been held captive can experience. In that respect, you might even envy them.'

It appeared to dawn on him that his ideas were badly expressed. He smiled and tried to put things right: 'The more you think of freedom as a term, the more difficult it becomes,' he said. 'In our thoughts it can be very far-reaching, because our thoughts are free, aren't they? Even if all religions insist that we should avoid sinful thoughts. That makes it easy to restrict your freedom. We create our own prison. I try to let my thoughts float freely, to be a free-thinker in every possible way. It often ends up with clumsy statements, though.'

'Did you and Kerr talk about what he'd done?' Stiller asked.

'No, but it wasn't as if I didn't know about it. After all, I followed the court case.'

He looked from Stiller to Wisting. 'It was sheer chance that I was the one assigned to Kerr as a befriender,' he explained. 'It wasn't by my request, just to make that clear. As a befriender, you have to be of spotless character. No doubt you've already checked me out. You probably also know about my father.'

Wisting shook his head.

'My father was a prisoner in Ila,' Thue explained. 'I was never allowed to visit him when I was little. You might think it odd that I visit other inmates there now. I can see that, but that's just how it is.'

Straightening up, he darted a glance at some red figures on one of the computer screens. 'What I *can* say is that Kerr and I have had some interesting conversations, but he never spoke to me about trying to escape.'

'When were you there last?'

'Last week.'

'What did you talk about then?'

'Well, we spoke about atonement and reconciliation, among other things, but nothing of what he said gave any indication of his plans for escape.'

'Did he ever ask you to do any favours for him?'

'Not Kerr. Other prisoners I visit have asked me to bring in food from McDonald's or Peppe's Pizza. That's about the only thing that's allowed. But Kerr has never asked me for anything.'

'Has he never asked you to take anything out of prison for him?'

'No.'

'Has the name Theo Dermann ever been mentioned?'

Thue rubbed the warts on his cheek again, but this could scarcely be interpreted as recognition of the name. In the end, he shook his head. 'Who is that?' he asked.

'Just a name that's cropped up.'

'I see . . . no one I know, anyway.'

They posed a number of further questions before asking Thue to go through his own movements in the past few days. He had mainly been at home: he had had a cleaning firm in the house and had received a few food deliveries at the door but, apart from that, only his computers could provide him with an alibi.

'Sorry I can't help you,' he said, getting to his feet. 'I hope you find him.'

He walked them to the door. It was still raining. A fine mist of condensation covered the inside of the windscreen on their return to the car, and Wisting turned the fan on full blast, wrenching off his jacket as he settled in the driver's seat.

'What do you think?' he asked, glancing up at the man who stood at the top of the steps.

'I think we should put surveillance on him.'

35

The phone rang on the hands-free set. The caller gave a long-winded preamble before introducing himself as Terje Nordbo, Chief Inspector in Internal Affairs.

Wisting knew who he was. They had met in unfavourable circumstances several years earlier when Wisting had been accused of fabricating evidence in a homicide case. At that time, it had seemed as if Nordbo had decided in advance that Wisting was guilty, but Wisting had been the one who had emerged from the case with his head held high.

'It concerns Tom Kerr's evasion of justice and a possible case of police misconduct,' the internal investigator continued in a formal tone. 'I understand from your Chief of Police that you'll make yourself available for interview.'

Wisting glanced across at Stiller but did not reveal that he was not alone in the vehicle. 'Fine,' he replied. 'I might be able to see you at the end of the week.'

'We're in Larvik now and would prefer this to be expedited today,' Nordbo said. 'I thought your Police Chief had acquainted you with the matter?'

'I see,' Wisting replied.

He could be back in Larvik in an hour and a half, but had no wish to hurry as he had other priorities. 'I'm in Bærum now, busy with various matters, but should be able to be with you at four o'clock.'

That gave him a few hours' breathing space.

'Then we'll make that an appointment,' Nordbo replied. 'We're staying at the Hotel Farris Bad.'

He ended the conversation and looked over at Stiller again. 'Have you heard anything from them?' he asked.

'No, but I'm probably the one they should blame,' Stiller answered. 'They'll gather other statements first and take me last. Standard police tactics.'

The phone rang again. This time it was Semmelmann. 'I'm on my way to a meeting with the investigation group that has responsibility for Nanna Thomle's murder,' he said. 'I think it would be useful all round if you're in on it.'

'Where and when?' Wisting asked.

'The police station in Lillestrøm,' Semmelmann replied. 'Two p.m.'

Wisting glanced quizzically at Stiller. He nodded, indicating that he was keen to attend too. 'Then we'll see you there,' he said, wrapping up the call.

They had to drive through Oslo to the other side of the city and there were queues of traffic before Wisting emerged on to the ring road. By the time they had parked in front of the police station, they were quarter of an hour late. A police officer at the front desk escorted them to one of the upper floors, where six investigators sat around a massive conference table waiting for them. A woman in her forties rose from a chair at the end of the table.

'Reidun Koksvik,' she said, introducing herself as the leader of the investigation.

Wisting sat down on a spare seat beside Semmelmann and Stiller installed himself on the opposite side. They conducted a brief round of introductions before Wisting gave an account of his case. He avoided mentioning the abortive surveillance on Tom Kerr and merely stated that they had found a summer cabin where he had changed clothes and stolen the keys to a boat.

'Do you have anything to suggest who has helped him?' Koksvik asked.

Wisting explained about the letters that Lone Mellberg had smuggled out.

'Theo Dermann,' one of the investigators repeated. 'That sounds like a false name.'

Wisting cocked his head. 'What did you say?' he asked.

The young investigator had a west Norwegian accent. Wisting had actually caught what he had said, but it contained something that resonated with him.

'That it must be some kind of alias,' the investigator explained. 'Even if the name isn't listed in the population register, it may well be on a mailbox somewhere.'

'The address isn't genuine either,' Wisting said. 'There is no Anton Brekkes vei in Oslo.'

He made a note to check with Hammer about how far they had reached with their inquiries at the postal service.

Reidun Koksvik thanked him for his report and launched into an account of the Nanna Thomle murder case. 'It has significant similarities with the murders of which Kerr was convicted, and to some extent Taran Norum's disappearance also,' she said. 'That has led us to consider the possibility that the Other One is behind it.'

She called up a picture of the murder victim on the large screen on the wall. Wisting recognized it from the extensive media coverage: blonde hair surrounding an oval face with blue eyes, freckles and full lips.

'Nanna Thomle, twenty-two years of age,' Koksvik announced. 'She worked at a café bar in Universitetsgata in Oslo. Lived with her mother.'

The next image was taken from a CCTV camera at the railway station. The time given in the corner indicated that it was taken on 14 July at 01.47. 'This is the last picture we have of her,' Koksvik said.

She left this hanging for a moment as she changed to a

satellite photograph. Nanna Thomle's apartment was marked, and a dotted line showed her most likely walking route. The distance from the railway station was given as 732 metres, but as the crow flies it was shorter.

'We've no sightings after this of relevance to the case,' Koksvik went on. 'We've charted movements and vehicle traffic in the area, analysed phone traffic and collected whatever CCTV footage was available. It hasn't brought us any further forward.'

She gazed at her colleagues around the table as if to check whether any of her investigators had any comments to make.

'Six weeks ago, a severed right arm was found in a forest in Oppegård, between Gjersjø lake and Bunnefjord.'

Her account was illustrated with a map on the screen.

'Further searches were initiated and more body parts were found, and eventually also the place where the body parts had been buried. Some had been damaged by having been dug up and dragged away by animals.'

A number of photographs followed, including of fragments of rope around ankles and wrists. Close-ups showed the same knot used on all the ropes.

'Rope with identical knots was found on the two bodies in the woods behind Tom Kerr's property,' Reidun Koksvik continued. 'No biological traces were found. The body parts had been cleaned with liquid chlorine. Internally and externally.'

Stiller had already imparted all the information given by the investigation leader to Wisting. However, Wisting had never seen these photographs before. 'What are those marks on the thigh?' he asked, pointing at the onscreen image.

Along one thigh, two faint diagonal lines were visible where the skin was darker than the rest.

Reidun Koksvik nodded, as if to acknowledge his

observation. 'There are similar marks on other body parts,' she replied. 'The technicians believe that, after dismemberment, the body parts were placed in plastic storage boxes with grooves on the base that were then filled with chlorine. The parts that lay on the bottom have various impressions from those grooves.'

'Have you managed to trace the kind of storage boxes that were used?'

'They're most likely from a Swedish manufacturer called Smartstore,' Koksvik replied. 'In Norway, they're sold at Europris discount stores as well as other outlets. The distance between the grooves suggests that seventy-litre boxes were used.'

'He must have used two or three at least,' the investigator with the west Norwegian accent added. 'We have an ongoing project in which we're tracing everyone who has bought these containers in the past twelve months, but that depends on them being members of a customer loyalty scheme or paying by bank card.'

Wisting nodded as he leafed through his notes.

'There's one thing about this discovery site that's different from the way Thea Polden and Salwa Haddad were buried,' Semmelmann commented. 'They were buried deep in the ground, almost a metre down in boggy land. In this case, the body parts were buried in such a shallow grave that animals have been able to drag them out.'

One of the investigators, previously silent, now spoke up: 'The earth here is much harder than in Svartskog,' he explained, 'with a lot of roots. It's far more difficult to dig a deep grave, and he was on his own this time. Besides, there was minimal risk even if she was found. He knew the chlorine treatment worked. There was no reason to fear that the police would isolate DNA if the body was found.'

'Did you search for other bodies in the area?' Wisting asked.

Reidun Koksvik gave him a questioning look.

'I'm thinking of Taran Norum,' Wisting explained. 'She's never been found,' he reminded them. 'If it's the same killer, he may well have hidden her in the same area.'

'A search for trace evidence was conducted with sniffer dogs in the land around the discovery site, but it didn't uncover anything.'

The discussion around the table continued, the investigators talking enthusiastically and coming up with varied suggestions. Wisting was watching the clock. He would have to drop Stiller off at Kripos headquarters before driving back to Larvik and his appointment with Internal Affairs.

The meeting was brought to a close with an agreement to share any information and progress made.

The rain had stopped by the time they moved outside, but grey clouds still hung low in the sky.

'You won't make your appointment with Internal Affairs,' Stiller pointed out when they took their seats in the car.

'They can wait,' was Wisting's terse reply.

36

The main item on the radio news was that Tom Kerr was still at large. One of the injured police officers was still in hospital, but the others had been discharged.

Line dropped her speed. A car drove past in the rain as she turned off the motorway into a picnic area.

She needed a source inside the police, someone other than her father, someone who could speak a bit more openly. Not Adrian Stiller either. Someone like the injured policewoman, in fact.

She did not know her name. Adrian Stiller had introduced Line to the other police officers and explained her role to them, but they had not introduced themselves to her. She did not think the name had cropped up in the minibus yesterday either. She could look through all the video footage to listen out for it, but another idea had occurred to her.

The unknown policewoman had mentioned a previous placement in Larvik during her practice year. When her studies were over, she had worked in the north of Norway for a couple of years. Now she had a temporary post back in Larvik.

Line took out her phone and ran a search in the *Østlands-Posten* newspaper. Every autumn, the local paper ran a story about the new intake of student police officers, usually assembled for a group photograph in front of the police station.

When she found the photo she was looking for, she enlarged each face in all the rows of students. In the third row, number four from the left, she found the face she was looking for. It was a few years ago now, but the young recruit was unmistakeable all the same. The caption gave her name as Maren Dokken.

A further search, this time in the phone book, produced one result: Maren Dokken, resident in Hammerdalen. Line was familiar with the address, an apartment block only a few hundred metres from the police station.

Line sent her a text message, explaining who she was and hoping that she was making a good recovery, before going on to say that she had video footage of what had happened. If Maren was amenable, Line could call in on her to let her view it.

There was no answer.

Line fired up the engine and drove out on to the road again. The rain was pouring down now, pelting the wind-screen and reducing visibility. As she turned off the motorway down towards Larvik, her phone beeped. Glancing at it, she saw there was a message from Maren Dokken, short and succinct. *I'm on sick leave. You're welcome to drop by.* She had added her address.

Ten minutes, Line replied.

The apartment block was five storeys high and the display on the door entry system said that Maren Dokken lived on the third floor. The lock gave an electronic buzz as she was allowed in. Maren stood at her door, waiting. She seemed exhausted. Her pale face had two sticking plasters on it and was covered in tiny scabs. She hugged her left arm close to her body.

'How are you?' Line asked.

'I was lucky,' the young policewoman answered. 'Tore some tendons in my shoulder, but they've patched me up. I was discharged this morning.'

'I was even luckier,' Line said. 'Just a few bruises.'

She peered into the apartment. Although it was small, the furnishings were practical.

'Are you on your own?'

'For the moment,' Maren replied, showing her in.

There were fresh flowers in a vase, and a bar of chocolate and an as yet unwrapped bouquet lay on the worktop. Line regretted having neglected to bring anything.

'Mum and Dad are abroad,' Maren continued. 'They won't be home for a few days. I just had a visit from some colleagues.'

'Did they say anything about Kerr?' Line asked.

'Only that everybody's looking for him.'

'He got away in a boat,' Line said. 'They found it over in Tønsberg.'

'I heard that,' Maren replied. 'William Wisting's your father, isn't he?'

'That's right,' Line said. 'I should have mentioned that in the minibus.'

'Can I offer you anything?' Maren asked, suggesting tea or coffee.

'No, thank you, please don't trouble yourself,' Line replied.

They sat down on a settee and Line took out her laptop.

'Have you seen anything?' she asked. 'I've sent the files over to the police.'

Maren shook her head. 'There's to be another press conference on Friday,' she answered. 'Maybe they'll show some of it then.'

Line put her laptop on the coffee table and explained about the documentary film project. 'The arrangement is that I can use the footage when the court case is over,' she said.

'Of me too?'

'We'll edit out anyone who doesn't want to be included,'

Line went on, but held back from asking Maren if she would consider taking part. It was too early for that. 'Are you ready?' she asked instead as she pushed the cursor over to the 'play' icon.

Maren grabbed a cushion with her uninjured hand, placed it on her lap and responded with a nod.

The recording started with Tom Kerr emerging from the hired minibus with his hands and feet shackled.

'I wrote my dissertation on people like him,' Maren said. 'Criminals driven by evil. Sadists who take pleasure in the pain they inflict on others.'

She drew a curtain to avoid a reflection on the screen. They saw Tom Kerr raise his chin and squint up at the sky.

'There aren't many like him,' Maren Dokken continued. 'People who lack any kind of conscience.'

'Are you familiar with his case?' Line asked.

'I followed the trial,' Maren replied. 'When I was writing my dissertation, I got in touch with one of the forensic psychiatrists who examined him.'

'*We have to talk,*' they heard Kerr say to his lawyer.

A discussion followed that ended up with Tom Kerr and his lawyer sitting in the back seat of the lawyer's Mercedes.

'I was allowed to read his report,' Maren went on. 'It contains a lot more than what emerged in the course of the trial. He once tied up a girl who was a neighbour, when they were ten or twelve years old, stripped off her clothes, pulled a bag over her head and did all sorts of perverted things to her.'

Line had heard how Tom Kerr had plagued and tormented pet animals in his neighbourhood, but this story was new to her.

'There were also other signs that there was something seriously wrong with him, but nobody did anything about it,' Maren added.

'Such as?'

'At junior high school, he sent photos of himself naked to some of the girls in his class, with his face obscured.'

'Dick-pics,' Line commented.

Maren nodded. 'Of course, it was before everyone had mobile phones, so they were developed photos, printed on paper. Photos of him slashing his foreskin with a sharp knife, or burning himself with a lighter. He sent them along with clandestine pictures he had taken of the girls.'

Line pulled a face. 'Creepy.'

'He should have been checked out when he was still a youngster,' Maren Dokken said. 'Received treatment from the child and adolescent mental health unit. The need for early diagnosis and intervention in developmental problems was one of the things I wrote about.'

'Which forensic psychiatrist was it that helped you with your dissertation?' Line probed.

'Elias Wallberg. He's based in Tønsberg.'

Line jotted down the name. Maren was watching the screen. 'I wonder what they were talking about,' she said.

The recording showed Claes Thancke's Mercedes, with him and Tom Kerr sitting in the back, chatting behind the tinted windows. Uniformed officers surrounded the vehicle. Maren Dokken was standing in front of the car and could see them through the windscreen.

'What did you see?' Line asked.

'It wasn't easy to make anything out,' Maren replied. 'They were sitting in the back seat, you see. Kerr was thumbing through some papers that his lawyer had produced from an envelope. The lawyer was looking away, as if it was something private. Afterwards, Thancke showed him something on his phone.'

Line's interest grew. 'Did Kerr *use* his lawyer's phone?'

Maren shook her head. 'I would have intervened if he had,' she said. 'They were just looking at something.'

On the laptop screen, the car doors swung open and Kerr stepped out. He soon had the transmitter attached again and they could hear his laboured breath as he began to walk.

They saw him stumble. The second time he fell, Line stopped the playback and explained how Kerr had the key for the handcuffs concealed inside his mouth.

'Rewind a little,' Maren requested.

Line did as asked and played it again. The camera image wobbled as she changed her grip and moved it from one shoulder to the other.

'There!' Maren said. Line froze the image. 'Look at that tree,' Maren said, pointing. 'It looks as if some of the bark has been scraped off.'

Line had watched the footage many times now. She had not noticed this before but had to agree that Maren was right.

'It could be a sign,' she said. 'A marker.'

'So he would know where to fall and pick up the key,' Maren concluded.

Line looked at her. The inference was quick and well thought out. She wondered whether Adrian Stiller and her father had spotted the same thing and made a note of the playback time to send them a screenshot.

The recording moved on. From the camera angle, it was impossible to see whether Kerr had picked up something.

Maren's breathing quickened as the procession reached the sheep enclosure and the pasture. She sat motionless, watching intently, and gave a start only when the explosion occurred. She made no comment when she saw herself on the screen.

The footage lasted another twenty-three minutes. Line had several recordings of the chaos following the explosion, including some of Maren Dokken being laid on a stretcher and carried away, but did not offer to show them. She had to pick up Amalie from nursery soon and had intended to do some shopping first.

'Thanks,' Maren said. 'It was helpful to see that. I had so many fuzzy images in my head. Now I know exactly what it was like.'

Line packed away her laptop and prepared to leave. She could not bring herself to ask Maren if she would take part in the documentary. The time was not right. It was just like an interview, or an interrogation – there was a right time for everything.

'Could I read your dissertation?' she asked instead.

Maren smiled. 'I can send it to you,' she said. 'I got an A for it.'

Line stood up and handed over a business card with her phone number and email address. 'I hope they catch him,' she said. 'Asap.'

Maren Dokken moved to the kitchen worktop and shook a painkiller out of a box. A gust of wind hurled a sheet of rain at the window.

'Me too,' she said, moving across to look outside. 'I don't like the thought of him being out there.'

37

The phone rang as soon as Wisting parked outside the hotel, an unknown number, and he reckoned it would be Internal Affairs. He was almost an hour late for his appointment.

'Wisting here,' he answered, staying inside the car to shelter from the rain.

'It's Tim Skage,' the caller said. 'CID, Oslo Vest. Have you got five minutes?'

Wisting leaned forward, anticipating that the call had to do with Tom Kerr. 'What can you tell me?' he asked.

'I have a suspicious death here,' the investigator said. 'Chris Paust Backe, thirty-seven years old, found dead in a burnt-out apartment three weeks ago.'

'Homicide?'

'Well, neither the cause of the fire nor the cause of death is clear. Carbon monoxide was found in his trachea and lungs, and it's obvious he died from smoke inhalation, but the toxicology report has just come in. Traces of acetone and other solvents have been detected in his blood.'

'Substance abuser?'

'Yes. Of long standing, with a lot of other things on his record. Of course, he could have sniffed it himself, to get high,' Skage said. 'In any case, it points to him being unconscious when the fire broke out.'

He paused for a beat and Wisting glanced across at the hotel entrance.

'To begin with, it was regarded as a classic outbreak of

fire,' Skage continued. 'He had an old-fashioned cooker with ceramic hotplates. The fire investigation indicated that one of the switches was on full and there was a frying pan on the hotplate. At any rate, the fire spread extremely fast. Now it's been shown that there were traces of flammable liquid in several places on the scene, and the technicians are about to conclude that the fire was a case of arson. You can put two and two together and get it to add up to murder.'

'But why are you phoning me?'

'When we couldn't file the case as an accident we began to talk to people who knew the victim,' Skage explained. 'There are two witness statements of particular interest. They both say the same thing: in the days before Chris Paust Backe died, he tried to get hold of a handgun and a hand grenade.'

Wisting raised his eyebrows and looked at his reflection in the rear-view mirror.

'What happened in your neck of the woods yesterday has turned our case upside down,' Skage went on. 'All of a sudden, the killer we're looking for could be the person who helped Tom Kerr to escape. We could have common interests here.'

'What else do you know?' Wisting asked. 'Is there anyone who can say what he had in mind to do with a hand grenade? And did he manage to get hold of one?'

'Well, there aren't many of Backe's crowd who are willing to talk, but apparently it wasn't for his own use. Neither the grenade nor the pistol. He was to get hold of them for someone else.'

'You don't know who?'

'No, but we know that he *did* get hold of them. A girl-friend saw the hand grenade in his home, and we have some information about where he got it.'

'Where, then?'

'We have a name. Tallak Gleich. Known criminal in these parts. Lives in Billingstad. We're preparing a raid and plan to have him in custody sometime this evening. You might be interested in coming along?'

As Wisting closed his eyes, he felt a nerve in his forehead start to pulse.

He had driven past Billingstad an hour earlier and it would take the same amount of time to drive back. The meeting with Internal Affairs should not last more than an hour, anyway.

'I can be with you in two hours,' he replied as he opened the car door to step outside.

'See you then,' Skage replied.

38

Internal Affairs were installed in a conference room in the hotel basement. Wisting stood at the door rounding off a phone conversation with Nils Hammer. He informed him about the man with the grenade and asked him to accompany him to Billingstad.

'Can you be ready in an hour?' he asked, closing the door behind him.

'Yes,' Hammer confirmed.

Terje Nordbo looked up from his large-screen laptop.

'Apologies,' Wisting said, making an apologetic gesture with his phone before tucking it inside his pocket.

Nordbo stood up. He was wearing a new suit with a sharper cut but otherwise had not changed much since the last time they had met, five years earlier. Nordbo had led the investigation against Wisting when he was charged with planting false evidence in a murder case. He had discovered that, even before their interview, Nordbo had already arrived at the conclusion that Wisting was guilty. The entire Internal Affairs inquiry had worked on confirming that theory. They had been like hunting dogs, with one aim in sight: catching him. During the investigation he had been suspended and had been compelled to prove his own innocence from outside the police force.

They shook hands. A video camera was pointing at an empty chair and Nordbo invited Wisting to sit down.

'I was thinking of phoning your Police Chief,' he said.

Wisting drew his chair up to the table. He could feel the

hostility coming in waves from the man on the opposite side.

'Why is that?' he asked.

Nordbo checked the camera angle. 'It's unfortunate, to say the least, that you've tried to delay our meeting,' he replied. 'It's vital that we have clarity about what actually took place yesterday.'

Wisting shook his head, as if to say that there had been no intention of delaying matters. 'Something cropped up, that's all,' he said as the camera light flashed on. 'I'm afraid I'll have to leave soon.'

Nordbo looked at him appraisingly before taking plenty of time to go through the formalities concerning the making of a statement to Internal Affairs. Then Wisting was asked to relate the previous day's course of events and went through them in broad outline. Nordbo did not take notes but occasionally cast a glance at the camera, checking that it was functioning properly.

'Everything was filmed,' Wisting said in conclusion. 'The video footage gives a good understanding of what happened. Have you seen it?'

Nordbo did not answer. 'Who led the site visit?' he asked instead.

'The responsibility was shared,' Wisting replied. 'The aim of the site visit was for Tom Kerr to show us where Taran Norum's body is buried. Formally, it's still a missing-person case under Oslo police district's jurisdiction, but this was transferred to Kripos's Cold Cases Group. Adrian Stiller led on the tactical aspects. He was the one who had the dialogue with Kerr. However, the site visit was to take place in the south-east police district, so I had the local knowledge and appointed Sergeant Kittil Gram as operative leader on the day.'

'You appointed an operative leader,' Nordbo repeated. 'That is to say, you delegated that task.'

Wisting nodded. 'I assigned it to someone more competent than me,' he replied.

'But when you're in a position in which you delegate something, does that not imply that you had the senior responsibility?' Nordbo queried.

'Yes,' Wisting responded. 'I had responsibility for the local aspects on the ground.'

'What did that entail?'

'Well, I was assigned to make preparations and organize the site visit,' Wisting explained.

'What did that involve, more specifically?'

'As I said, to appoint an operative leader, but also to allocate the manpower he felt necessary. In addition, I was in discussion with Kripos and conducted the reconnaissance and survey of the area in question.'

One corner of Nordbo's mouth puckered into a smile, making Wisting feel that he had been lured into a trap.

'When did you conduct this reconnaissance?' Nordbo asked.

'Friday,' he replied.

Nordbo checked his notes. 'Friday 11 September,' he said. 'Four days prior to the site visit.'

Wisting realized where he was going with this. 'That's right,' he answered.

'Would it not have been more appropriate to do this the day before?' Nordbo asked. 'Four days is a long time. Plenty of time to lay out a gun and a hand grenade.'

'The purpose of the reconnaissance was to acquaint ourselves with the area, not to uncover a possible escape attempt. In principle, no one should have known where or when the site visit was to take place. There was no one who should have been able to plan an escape.'

'The facts speak for themselves,' Terje Nordbo interjected.

Wisting left that unchallenged as Nordbo leafed through to another page of notes. 'What measures were taken to prevent an escape?' he asked.

'We were superior in numbers,' Wisting replied. 'And also Kerr's movements were restricted. He was wearing handcuffs and leg irons.'

'So an escape was not just a hypothetical possibility?' Nordbo asked. 'Even though no one knew of the operation, you still took a number of precautions?'

'Of course,' Wisting agreed. 'You take out an insurance policy, but you don't expect the house to burn down.'

'Why weren't you armed?'

Wisting leaned back in his chair and glanced at the time. 'That was a precondition laid down by Kerr and his lawyer,' he answered, explaining how the question had been referred to the Police Directorate for a formal decision.

'But you accepted it?' Nordbo asked.

'In consultation with Stiller and the operative leader,' Wisting agreed.

'Would it have been within your sphere of responsibility to have the final word on that?'

'It would, yes,' Wisting replied. 'But the guidance from the directorate was clear. Kerr was shot during his previous arrest. If we had insisted on being armed, the site visit would not have gone ahead.'

'So it was a chance you took?'

Wisting sat bolt upright in his chair. 'I'm happy to give a statement about the course of events and respective responsibilities,' he said. 'Others may well judge my decisions. I'm used to that. I'll make sure there is an inquiry into all aspects of the site visit, but that will have to wait. For now, my priority is to find Tom Kerr.'

A slight twitch of the mouth suggested that Terje Nordbo was displeased with this answer. 'Who decided to remove the leg irons?' he asked.

Wisting took little time answering. This had been a joint decision, but the final word had been left to Kittil Gram.

'It was rough ground,' he explained. 'Kerr had fallen twice. We thought it practical to take them off.'

'But who took the final decision?'

'Kittil Gram.'

'Wasn't it your suggestion?'

Wisting hesitated again. He was unsure what the exact words had been and who had said what. 'It was the lawyer who made the initial request,' was what he arrived at. 'He wanted us to remove both the handcuffs and the leg irons. I suggested that we could take off the leg irons only so that it would be easier for Kerr to walk, but it was Kittil Gram who was the operative leader. The final decision was his.'

'But you had appointed him, hadn't you?' Nordbo said. 'You were his superior officer. Would he have overruled you?'

'Yes,' Wisting replied firmly.

'You're ten years older than him,' Nordbo objected. 'You have seniority and authority on your side.'

'But Kittil Gram had the operative knowledge and experience,' Wisting answered. 'In any case, I believe it was absolutely the right decision and have no problem taking responsibility for it.'

They continued in this vein. Nordbo had several questions about the way Wisting had reacted and behaved after the explosion. 'Tell me about the electronic tracker,' he said.

'It's difficult for me to go into details,' Wisting replied. 'I wasn't aware that tracking devices had been planted on Kerr until after his escape. It was Stiller who had obtained the necessary permissions and took care of the practical details.'

'But that led you to believe that Tom Kerr was in the area the whole time?' Nordbo queried.

'He was traced to a summer cabin,' Wisting said. 'Observation posts were set up and preparations made for a raid.'

'Was immediate action considered?'

'Yes, but we reached the decision that it would be tactically wise to wait. It was obvious that Kerr had received help to escape. He would also need help to move on, and we decided to wait in order to arrest both of them.'

'So that you could apprehend the so-called Other One?'

'That was the opportunity we saw,' Wisting confirmed.

Terje Nordbo reshuffled his papers. 'The Other One has been a wanted man for five years,' he said. 'Could a potential arrest have impacted the grounds for your decision?'

'What do you mean?'

'Could the possibility of apprehending the accomplice have blinded you and caused you to make the wrong decision?'

'What wrong decision?'

'Well,' the Internal Affairs investigator began. 'Tom Kerr wasn't in the summer cabin after all. He had moved on immediately. The Other One never turned up. Deciding to wait for him simply gave Kerr an even longer head start.'

'From the information we had there and then, it wasn't a wrong decision,' Wisting insisted. 'Also, it wasn't my decision at all.'

'Who was it who took that decision?'

'The Chief of Police.'

'But you were the one who proposed this to her, were you not?'

Wisting nodded. Waiting for the Other One had been Stiller's idea. The fact that the site visit had culminated in an escape increasingly seemed like an alternative Stiller had envisaged and planned for. If anyone had been blinded by the possibility of arresting the Other One, then it was Stiller.

'Agnes Kiil is my Police Chief,' he replied, without mentioning Stiller's role. 'It was natural for it to be me who presented this possibility to her. She and the top brass considered it and they agreed to this plan of action.'

Nordbo sat in silence with his eyes fixed on his preparatory notes. Wisting could not resist the urge to check his watch. It was almost 6 p.m.

'I have an appointment in Asker in three quarters . . .' he began.

Nordbo raised his eyes. 'Do you think you could have done things differently?' he asked.

Wisting, not a fan of hindsight, shook his head. 'As I explained, there will be a reassessment of the entire incident,' he said.

Terje Nordbo nodded and returned to the circumstances Wisting had already outlined, posing the same questions in a different way. Half an hour later, he declared the interview over.

Wisting pushed his chair back from the table. Much had gone wrong with Tom Kerr's site visit, but that did not necessarily mean that there had been any misconduct involved. No one had behaved in a blameworthy fashion or against their better judgement. There were no grounds for an internal investigation, but Wisting got the picture. It was a kind of payback. Terje Nordbo had angled the case and initiated the Internal Affairs inquiry so that Wisting would be censured.

'You know, there's no need to create a scapegoat,' he said.

'You're right,' Nordbo replied as he switched off the camera. 'You've managed to do that all by yourself.'

39

The prearranged meeting place was the car park outside Billingstad School. Three uniformed officers and two plain-clothes detectives stood there when Wisting and Hammer arrived. It had stopped raining, but darkness was closing in.

Wisting checked his mobile before he got out. He had received a message from Line, a still from one of her videos. A screenshot. It was difficult to make out, but Wisting had seen it before. The picture showed a tree trunk with some of the bark scraped off.

Seen this? the message asked. *On the path, where Kerr tripped up.*

A man in jeans and a grey hoodie approached the car and Wisting stepped out, without responding to the message.

The man introduced himself as Tim Skage, leader of the local investigation. Wisting introduced Nils Hammer and apologized for being so late.

'No problem,' Skage replied. 'Nina and her people were also delayed, but we're ready now.'

A uniformed woman with cropped hair gave a brief nod and took out an iPad.

'This is Tallak Gleich,' she explained, showing them a picture from the photographic register of a bald man with dark eyes and a goatee. 'His previous convictions include GBH and breaking the gun laws.'

Making sure that everyone had seen the photograph, she dismissed it with a finger swipe and called up a satellite image of a house in an isolated spot at the end of a gravel driveway, surrounded by an expanse of open ground.

'He lives alone,' she explained. 'Most of us have been there before and know him.'

After glancing around at all the other uniformed officers, she gave a thorough run-through of the imminent action: 'Gleich is charged with supplying a gun and hand grenade to Chris Paust Backe shortly before he died. It's being investigated as a suspicious death. The gun and grenade may have been used in Tom Kerr's escape. We have permission to bear arms, but we're keeping a low profile. Make things simple and steady. Drive in with the Black Maria. Two men will get out and ring the doorbell. The rest will wait in the back of the van.'

She nodded towards the big black police vehicle. 'Questions?'

Her team all shook their heads.

'The rest of you wait behind this bend here,' she said, speaking to Skage and pointing at the map. 'Well out of sight.'

Five minutes later they were on their way, with Wisting and Hammer bringing up the rear. Darkness had settled around them. Wisting switched off the ignition to avoid their lights revealing their presence when they stopped at the appointed spot. Hammer rummaged in the centre console for mini binoculars before they left the car and joined Skage outside.

The lights of the Black Maria struck the house, which lay about two hundred metres ahead. It comprised two storeys with an entrance in the brick basement and backed on to a field beside a forest.

'Do you know whether he's at home?' Hammer asked, lifting the binoculars to his eyes.

Skage shook his head. 'We're going in regardless,' he replied.

As the police van drove to the front of the house, the brake lights came on and the vehicle drew to a halt, blocking their view of the entrance.

Hammer grunted with displeasure.

The van driver clambered out, skirted around the vehicle and disappeared out of sight.

Skage's police radio crackled into life. '*Ringing the doorbell,*' was the message.

Wisting was watching the windows, some of which were lit up, but there was no sign of movement.

Half a minute passed.

'*Trying again,*' a voice announced on the police radio.

A puff of wind rustled through the surrounding trees.

'He's doing a runner!' Hammer suddenly shouted, nudging Wisting on the chest with the binoculars before breaking into a sprint.

To the left of the house they spotted movement at the edge of the forest, out of sight of those standing in front of the building.

Wisting raised the binoculars to his eyes and saw the back of a man in a blue sweater disappearing into the trees.

Skage took hold of the police radio and called the operation leader. 'There's movement on the west side of the house,' he reported.

Although he received no reply, the side door of the Black Maria slid open and four police officers poured out.

Tim Skage swore aloud. 'She should have had someone at the back door,' he said.

The nearest police car started up and the gravel sprayed out as it sped off. Skage jumped in beside Wisting. When they reached the house, most of the team had been sent out to search the surrounding terrain.

The front door abruptly swung open – an officer had

unlocked it from the inside. 'The back door was open,' he explained.

Wisting waited outside until the house had been searched and declared empty before he entered alongside Skage.

The basement level contained five rooms, one of which was equipped with a bar. In another room, two mattresses were spread out on the floor, while the other rooms contained boxes and cases of items that seemed merely in storage.

The sound of voices drifted down from the upper floor. The TV in the living room was switched on, showing a programme about gold miners in Alaska. A can of cola and a half-eaten pizza sat on the coffee table, and the smell of cooking still pervaded the air.

A vacuum cleaner was set out, but had obviously not been used for a long time. Empty bottles, plates of leftover food and dirty washing were strewn around the room.

Over the police radio they could hear how the search for the weapons dealer was being organized. The team had followed a path through the forest and emerged into a residential area. Patrol cars were diverted to the locality and sniffer dogs requisitioned.

Hammer returned to the house. 'Useless,' he declared.

They split into teams to search the house. Room by room, they searched for guns, grenades or something to link Gleich to the dead Chris Paust Backe.

In a kitchen cupboard they found more than a hundred grams of amphetamines and equipment for weighing and packing. Smaller amounts of hash and various pills were seized as evidence, but it was Hammer who finally found what they were really looking for: a wooden packing case containing three hand grenades, stashed at the bottom of a wardrobe in the largest bedroom. Hammer had removed it and placed it on the bed.

'Excellent,' Skage said. 'We've found them. I'll get the bomb squad to make them safe.'

Wisting used his mobile phone to take a photo. The grenades appeared to match the fragments they had found at Eftang. These grenades were green with yellow writing. *Grenade Hand-Offensive MK3A2 – TNT.* Underneath, a printed lot number would enable them to trace where the grenades had been produced.

He sent the picture to Mortensen to find out whether he could confirm that these were the same type. It took only a few seconds for the crime scene technician to call back. 'Where are you?' he asked.

Wisting explained the situation. 'Is this the same type of grenade as the one that was used in the escape?' he asked.

'Yes,' Mortensen confirmed. 'Manufactured in America. We found part of a lot number on one of the fragments. It corresponds with what I can see on your photograph. In that case, the grenades most likely come from a break-in at a NATO warehouse in Trøndelag nearly four years ago.'

Wisting thanked him and wound up the conversation before turning to face Skage. Mortensen had given them a thread they would be able to follow.

'Any news of the runaway?' he asked, with a nod to the police radio on Skage's belt.

Skage shook his head. 'Not yet, but we'll find him.'

Wisting nodded. 'Let me know right away, then,' he said, heading for the door.

40

Maren Dokken's dissertation made interesting reading. *Malevolence: Evil as Motive.*

Line sat engrossed at the kitchen table. From there, she could see across the street to her father's house and keep track of when he came home.

The assignment was theoretical, based on existing knowledge and theories but containing personal reflection and excellent discussion. In addition, the material was well organized and the language easily assimilated.

The exposition was clearly defined. Some crimes could be so ruthless and ghastly that it was difficult to characterize them as anything other than pure evil, but the dissertation was not about such perpetrators. Instead it examined malevolence, the desire to practise evil, and the people who derived pleasure from inflicting pain and suffering on their victims.

This was material Line could use in her documentary project. In conclusion, it posed questions about whether malevolence was an animal instinct latent in all human beings. Whether this was what made a cat play with a mouse before finally taking its life, or why the bestial gladiator fights in their time could feed the enjoyment of the masses.

She stood up and cleared the supper plates and cups from the table. The light from a pair of car headlights spilled into the room and Line peered out through the window. It was her father, and she watched as he turned into his front yard, stepped out of the car and moved towards the house. Then, seeming to change his mind, he turned and walked down the street in her direction.

Line padded to the door to prevent him from ringing the doorbell. 'I saw you coming,' she said as she let him in.

'How are things?' he asked.

'Fine,' she answered without hesitation. 'Did you see the picture I sent you? Of the bark?'

He nodded. 'There's a similar mark further along the path,' he replied. 'Presumably where the gun was hidden.'

'Do you know anything more?' Line asked, though she did not have high hopes of learning anything from him.

'Nothing specific.'

She followed him into the living room. 'Would you like anything?'

'No, thanks. I was wondering if we could watch the film?'

'Then we'll have to go downstairs.' She gestured towards the basement door.

'Is there anything in particular you're looking for?' she asked, moving in front of him.

'I'd mainly like to listen,' her father replied. 'To hear who said what.'

She stopped at the foot of the stairs and gave him a questioning look.

'I've been referred to Internal Affairs,' he explained. 'They're speculating about who decided to remove the leg irons, among other things.'

Line had watched the footage several times now. She remembered a discussion between her father, Adrian Stiller and the leader of the operation, but not exactly what had been said.

'Can't they just watch the video for themselves?' she asked.

'They've probably done that,' her father answered. 'They believe it was my decision, but that's not how I remember it.'

They sat down at the desk and Line logged into her computer. She had made a note of the point at which Kerr wiped blood from the scratch on his cheek and licked his fingers clean. The leg irons had already been removed by then. She rewound two minutes back and started the playback.

Kerr and the rest of the entourage were walking alongside the old sheep fence, and came to a halt at the gate. '*We go down that way,*' Kerr said.

The camera turned slightly in the direction he indicated with his head. The terrain sloped down to a small stream and they could see the opening into the woods where Kerr had fled, the spot where the booby-trapped grenade had been placed.

'*That's far more difficult terrain than where we've been walking so far,*' they heard Claes Thancke say.

Kerr was back in the centre of the picture, beside his lawyer.

'*It's hardly advisable to head off down there with chains on,*' he continued. '*You're risking my client sustaining a serious injury.*'

Wisting leaned forward and turned his left ear to the loudspeaker. Line turned up the volume.

'*He does have a point,*' Wisting said.

'*We can support him,*' Gram suggested. '*One man taking each arm.*'

'*That's pretty awkward,*' Stiller commented.

Wisting turned to speak to Kittil Gram: '*Are you comfortable with us removing the leg irons?*'

Gram nodded and replied: '*As long as we keep the handcuffs.*'

'*Then we'll do as you both ask,*' Stiller said.

Kittil Gram produced the keys and asked Kerr to loosen his belt. Once the prisoner had complied, Gram unlocked the clamp around his ankle, pulled the chain up through his trouser leg and detached it from the handcuffs.

'*Move on!*' he said.

Tom Kerr began to walk.

Line stopped the recording and stole a glance at her father. 'Was that how you remembered it?' she asked.

He nodded. 'My suggestion, Kittil Gram's decision.'

'I think Stiller anticipated what happened,' Line said.

'That Kerr would do a runner?'

'At least that there would be an investigation if something like that did happen,' Line replied. 'He made sure he'd be in the clear.'

She rewound a little. The lawyer maintained that it was inadvisable for Kerr to walk down the slope and asked for the leg irons to be removed. Her father turned to the other two officers.

'*He does have a point,*' he said.

'*We can support him,*' Gram suggested. '*One man taking each arm.*'

'*That's pretty awkward,*' Stiller pointed out.

Line stopped the recording and jumped back five seconds.

'*That's pretty awkward,*' Stiller said again, though it was impossible to work out to what extent he was supporting Gram's suggestion or felt that it was best to remove the restraints.

Line and her father exchanged looks. He had drawn the same conclusion.

Gram was asked whether he was comfortable about removing the leg irons. '*As long as we keep the handcuffs,*' was his response.

Stiller raised his right hand slightly, as if in cautious warning.

'*Then we'll do as you both ask,*' he said, looking straight at the camera lens, as if he wanted to be sure that his abdication of responsibility had been recorded.

Line stopped the playback again. She did not entirely like what she had heard. It provided confirmation that Stiller was not to be relied upon, and she had to depend on him keeping his promises as far as the documentary project was concerned.

Her father ran his hand through his hair. She studied his worried expression.

'All the same, they can't blame you for Kerr's escape, surely?' she asked.

'Terje Nordbo has been handed the case,' he answered.

Line sighed. 'What on earth does he have against you?'

'An old grudge,' Wisting replied.

Line was familiar with the background. Nordbo had led the investigation at the time when her father had been hung out to dry on the front page of *VG* and accused of fabricating evidence in an old murder case. It had been an inquiry in which justice and honesty had been overshadowed by Nordbo's determination to win. To have her father condemned.

'Shouldn't someone else do it?' she asked.

Wisting shrugged. 'I can't go around thinking about that,' he said. 'I've got enough on my mind already.'

Line turned back to the screen. The playback was frozen on an image in which Maren Dokken was the person standing closest to Tom Kerr.

'Would you like to watch some more?'

Her father shook his head and was about to stand up.

'I visited Maren Dokken today,' Line told him, pointing at the screen.

'Did you?'

'I spoke to her a fair bit in the minibus on the journey from the prison. I wanted to find out how she was doing.'

'I should have been there,' her father said.

The corners of Line's mouth lifted in a smile. 'Some of

her workmates had already been to see her,' she said. 'You can't manage everything.'

'How was she?'

'She's damaged some tendons in her arm. She couldn't use it and I could see that it was painful, but I think she was struggling mainly with the idea that she had let Tom Kerr escape.'

'She can't be blamed for that,' her father broke in as he got to his feet. 'No one could have foreseen what happened.'

'I think it was preying on her mind all the same, what actually took place. I showed her the video footage. I think it did her good to see it.'

Something occurred to her. 'Wait a minute,' she said. 'I want to show you something.'

Wisting stayed on his feet as Line rewound to the point when Tom Kerr and his lawyer sat in the back seat of the lawyer's car.

'Maren says the lawyer showed him something on his mobile,' she explained. 'She saw it through the windscreen.'

Wisting grabbed the chair back with both hands and peered at the screen. 'Do you have a recording of that?' he asked.

Line shook her head. 'He didn't speak into it,' she rushed to clarify. 'The lawyer took out some papers from an envelope and showed him something on his mobile.'

She saw that this made her father pensive; he was dwelling on the possible significance.

'Do you think his lawyer can have been an accessory?' she asked. 'That he might have been passing information to Kerr?'

'I'll get Maren to write a report about it,' he replied.

It took a few minutes for Line to realize the implications of the possibility that had come to light. 'It would answer a lot of questions, wouldn't it?' she said. 'Communication in and out of the prison.'

'It could well have been completely legitimate, what took place in the car,' Wisting told her, removing his hands from the chair back. 'Thanks for letting me see it, though.'

He turned and walked to the stairs. She could see that she had given him something to think about, something that would keep him awake tonight.

41

Five people were gathered around the table for the morning meeting and a run-through of the case. Wisting had seated himself at the head of the table, and Nils Hammer, Torunn Borg, Christine Thiis and Espen Mortensen had assumed their usual places.

'Tore Bergstrand was in surgery yesterday,' Wisting began. 'A muscle in his leg has been badly torn. It's a complicated injury. He'll have to undergo several more operations, and there's still a danger that amputation might become necessary. Maren Dokken is on sick leave for a fortnight. The rest will be back at work by the end of the week. They'll be brought together for a debrief in the department tomorrow. Hammer and I will be there too.'

Hammer pushed his chair out from the table and squinted at the window before getting to his feet. 'The sun,' he grumbled as he skirted around the table to adjust one of the blinds.

Wisting gave a brief resumé of what had emerged in the course of the previous day. 'There's a lot of activity,' he concluded. 'But we still don't have anything concrete.'

There was a knock at the door and it swung open immediately, although no one had answered. Adrian Stiller put his head round it, as if to make sure he had come to the right room, before closing the door behind him.

'OK for me to join you?' he asked, pointing at an empty chair.

'We weren't expecting you here today,' Wisting said.

'I've a meeting with Internal Affairs at noon,' he explained as he sat down. 'In many ways, we at the Cold Cases Group were the ones who set all this in motion. Who bear the blame, in fact, so I'd like to follow things up. If there's anything we can contribute, I'd like to do that.'

'Do you have any results from the surveillance?' Hammer asked him.

He shook his head. 'Lone Mellberg had a visit from a female friend last night and had a late start at work today.'

'What about Floyd Thue?'

'He hasn't moved from his house. The only thing we've noticed is that he took delivery of a box of food at the door yesterday afternoon. He doesn't socialize much, but he's highly respected in financial circles. He's a kind of anonymous philanthropist – earns a fortune on the stock exchange, but also spends a lot on financing social entrepreneurship and donating substantial amounts to non-profit purposes.'

'His father was a paedophile,' Hammer broke in, taking out his snuffbox.

The others looked at him in astonishment.

'I've been doing a bit of digging too,' he explained. 'He was convicted several times. The first time for incest. Sexual abuse of his son.'

Stiller nodded in confirmation, but Wisting was unsure whether this meant he was in possession of the same details as Hammer.

'He died in Ila prison,' Hammer added. 'Hanged himself in one of the cells there.'

Stiller nodded again. 'We're taking a closer look at his movements in the last few days and trying to find someone who knows him who can tell us more.'

'He has a swimming pool in his basement,' Hammer cut in. 'Maybe Kerr has been there.'

'How do you know that?' Wisting queried.

'Google. There was an old prospectus on the Internet. He bought the house eight years ago. The estimated price then was nineteen million.'

'I'll take it up with Semmelmann,' Wisting said. 'Thue isn't listed as having any connection to Tom Kerr, but it's worth double-checking.'

He took up the thread again. 'This is a fragmented investigation that crosses several district boundaries,' he said. 'Our task is to find Tom Kerr. That intersects with Idar Semmelmann and Oslo Police's search for the Other One. The Øst police district suspect the accomplice in Nanna Thomle's murder, and Oslo Vest are dealing with the murder of Chris Paust Backe.'

'Who's that?' Stiller asked.

Wisting explained how they had discovered the origin of the grenade. 'According to a female friend of Backe, he got the grenade from a man on the drugs scene, Tallak Gleich,' he went on, giving an account of the previous evening's exploits. 'Gleich is a wanted man. We'll be notified as soon as he's arrested.'

Stiller drew the jug of water from the middle of the table and filled a glass.

'In parallel with this, Internal Affairs have initiated an internal inquiry,' Wisting continued, glancing around at his colleagues. 'In our department, this affects only Hammer and myself.'

Mortensen was given the floor. He had prepared a visual presentation of the work conducted at the crime scene and ran through the findings. However, none of this brought them any further forward.

Hammer had been busy examining the telephone traffic at Eftang but, to date, that had not produced any results.

'What about this Theo Dermann?' Wisting asked. 'Have you made any progress with him?'

'Only to find out that Dermann is a German surname from Westphalia.'

Torunn Borg had a list of tip-offs. A number of possible sightings of Tom Kerr had been followed up. 'We don't have any active assignments for the moment,' she told them. 'No tip-offs about possible hiding places.'

They spent the next ten minutes working on forward planning. Traditionally, investigation was a matter of searching for evidence that would lead in the end to a perpetrator. The task before them now was different. They all knew who Tom Kerr was and what he had done. It was simply a matter of finding him, but they did not have much to go on. Further progress would hinge upon tip-offs from the public – on Tom Kerr being spotted, or finding him via the Other One.

The meeting was now over and Wisting slid his chair out from the table. Turning to Stiller, he gave him an appraising look. 'You and I need to have a chat,' he said, 'in my office.'

42

Wisting hovered in his office doorway, waiting until Stiller was seated before he shut the door and sat down behind the desk.

'Could Claes Thancke have been involved?' he asked.

Stiller crossed his legs. He was wearing a suit today and his immaculate white shirt was freshly ironed.

'The lawyer?' he replied with a smile. 'What makes you think that?'

'The prison warden was in on it,' Wisting replied. 'The easiest way to send messages in or out of a closed prison is through a lawyer when he has meetings with his client.'

'But surely it was his girlfriend Kerr used to take letters out for him?' Stiller objected.

'That could just have been an attempt to mislead us,' Wisting said. 'There was no such address.'

Adrian Stiller looked preoccupied by his own thoughts.

'Thancke has visited Kerr in prison ten times in the past two months,' Wisting said, thumbing through the information received from the prison.

'Kerr was about to make a major decision,' Stiller pointed out. 'He was going to confess to another murder. They had a great deal to talk about.'

Wisting agreed. The visits had been frequent, both before and after Kerr had begun to spill the beans about the third murder to another inmate, but there was a valid explanation for them.

'And then I have this,' he went on. He pushed the report

he had asked Maren Dokken to write towards Stiller. It was more detailed than Line's account. Tom Kerr had received papers from a large envelope that Thancke had ripped open in the back seat of the lawyer's car.

Stiller frowned as he read it. 'Were you considering speaking to him?' he asked.

'Well, it would be the natural thing to do,' Wisting answered. 'After all, he's the one who has had most contact with Kerr recently.'

Stiller shook his head. 'It's all covered by lawyer–client confidentiality,' he said. 'He won't give you anything. This is Claes Thancke we're talking about.'

Wisting studied him, wondering whether he should confront him with what had been said and left unsaid when Tom Kerr's leg irons were removed, but came to the conclusion that he should let things lie. For the meantime.

'I've already requested a meeting,' Wisting explained. 'Sometimes it's a matter of listening to what's not said.'

'Then you'd better have a plan. A good one.'

'I do.'

'When are you going to meet him?'

'Eleven a.m., in his office.'

Stiller shook his arm to reveal a watch with a large face. 'Then we'll need to leave now,' he said.

'We?' Wisting repeated. 'Don't you have a meeting with Internal Affairs?'

'They can wait.'

43

The waiting room at the legal firm of Thancke & Co. was cool and quiet. The receptionist who had signed them in occasionally answered the phone. She passed inquiries on or promised to leave a message. Now and again her nails clattered on a keyboard. A few staff members came and went with folders tucked under their arms.

The receptionist had poured each of them a glass of water.

Stiller sipped at his. Ten minutes passed. The receptionist stood up, having obviously received a message on her screen.

'You can go in now,' she said, ushering them into an office at the far end of the corridor. Pushing the door open, she motioned with her hand to show them in.

It was a corner office lacking much of a view. All they could see were the roofs of surrounding buildings covered in generators and ventilation pipes. Claes Thancke sat behind a desk in the middle of the room. When they entered, he stood up and came forward to greet them.

'Any news?' he asked, shaking their hands in turn.

'I'm afraid we don't know where Tom Kerr is,' Wisting told him.

Thancke's lips tightened into a thoughtful expression. 'Extremely unfortunate, all of this,' he said, resuming his seat behind the desk. 'But I'm afraid there's very little I can do for you. Even if I did know something, I wouldn't be able to help you. I realize you have to come here, but it's my client we're talking about. The duty of confidentiality supersedes the duty to testify.'

Wisting and Stiller sat down. 'Does that mean you have provided Kerr with advice about his escape?' Wisting asked.

Thancke gave him a puzzled look. 'Of course not! How can you suggest anything of the kind?'

'The duty of confidentiality applies only to information you've received in connection with legal advice and assistance,' Wisting pointed out.

Claes Thancke shook his head as a sign that he disagreed. 'The information I become privy to must also be treated as confidential,' he said, glancing in the direction of the thick volume of Norwegian laws on his desk. 'All the same, it's not a problem. I don't have anything to tell you.'

The receptionist brought a tray of bottled water and glasses and deposited it on the desk. Wisting waited until she had left the room.

'You can't tell me what you were talking about in the back seat of your car, before we set off, then?' he asked.

'That would be completely wrong of me.'

'We have information that you gave Tom Kerr access to your mobile phone while you sat there,' Wisting went on.

Claes Thancke's Adam's apple bobbed up and down.

'You don't understand,' he said, attempting a smile. 'That had to do with a different case altogether. The whole conversation was about something else entirely.'

'Did you let Kerr use your phone?' Wisting asked.

Thancke placed his hands flat on the table. 'We had a camera filming the whole time,' Stiller interjected before the lawyer had a chance to answer. 'Even though we didn't have a mic on Kerr.'

Thancke shook his head gently, as if he did not really believe anything that had gone on in the back of the vehicle had been filmed.

'It came as a surprise to me,' he began, drawing one of the

glasses towards him. 'Kerr said he wanted to talk to me in private before we started walking, but it had nothing to do with the site visit or with Taran Norum.'

He poured some sparkling water into the glass and sat holding it in his hand.

'For a long time now I've been trying to arrive at a settlement with his insurance company,' he went on. 'The farm burned down at the time of his arrest. It was determined that the fire was a case of arson, and the insurance company insist that the claim is fraudulent. Kerr was already in custody when the fire started, but the company still weren't willing to cough up. Before we left the prison, I told him they'd approached me with an offer at last. That was what he wanted to talk about. I'd received an email and let him read it on my mobile.'

Wisting did not relinquish eye contact.

'Here,' Thancke said, producing his phone. 'I can show you.'

His forefinger slid across the screen. He opened his email, found the right one, and accessed an attachment. Wisting recognized the logo of the Gjensidige Forsikring insurance company, but the text was too small to read.

'I can obtain the traffic data from my phone company,' he offered. 'You'll see that my mobile wasn't used for calls or text messages.'

'That would be helpful,' Wisting replied.

'So, I was taken aback that Kerr was unperturbed about what we were about to embark upon, but you're on the wrong track there.'

Wisting's eyes did not move from Thancke. 'What about the envelope you handed him?'

Thancke put the glass to his mouth and drank until it was almost empty.

'That was about the same thing,' he replied. 'I'd had a lengthy conversation with him in prison on Tuesday morning, before you took him out in the minibus. It had little to do with the expedition. He was preoccupied with the compensation money. I told him I had a copy of the last letter I'd sent to the insurance company but that it was outside in my car along with the enclosures. He always wanted to have copies of all the correspondence. He was keen to see it before we set off. Both my letter to the company and the offer I'd received by email.'

The lawyer's explanation was in keeping with what Wisting had seen in Kerr's cell. He appeared obsessed with the insurance case and had copies and duplicates of the case documents. That could well have been what the conversation in the back seat had been about, but it could also be a well-prepared lie.

'Who is Theo Dermann?' he asked instead. He was prepared to receive no answer in response and concentrated instead on reading the lawyer's body language. A muscle at the corner of his eye twitched when Wisting mentioned the name.

Thancke was used to keeping a straight face. His countenance never betrayed his true thoughts when he stood in front of a camera talking about a client or an ongoing court case. For one fleeting second, however, his facial expression seemed about to crack and a genuine emotion to leak out. Some form of anxiety.

'Who?' he asked.

Wisting repeated the name and the lawyer shook his head. 'I can't help you,' he answered.

Stiller leaned forward. 'Is that because you haven't heard the name before, or are there other reasons you can't help us?' he asked.

'I don't know who Theo Dermann is,' the lawyer replied.

'But you've heard the name before?' Stiller insisted.

Claes Thancke evaded the question again. 'Where did you get it from?' he asked.

Wisting studied him closely. It was obvious that he recognized the name and, what's more, that it worried him to hear it.

'It's cropped up in connection with our investigation,' Stiller said.

'In what way?'

'It was someone Kerr had communicated with from prison,' Wisting answered, but refrained from giving any details.

Thancke pushed his chair away from the desk and stood up. He walked to the window and stood looking out. His eyes had grown distant, as if he was getting ready to say something important and had to weigh his words carefully.

'He's been here,' he said in the end, turning to face them.

His gaze was directed at the chair Wisting occupied. Neither of the two police officers said anything and instead simply waited for the lawyer to continue.

'It was four weeks ago, in the middle of August,' he said. 'He had taken Trude.'

'Who is Trude?'

Thancke sat down again. 'My niece . . .' he said, fingering the inside of his shirt collar.

Wisting sat up warily.

'My niece's cat disappeared during the summer,' Thancke explained. 'It was called Trude. Pathetic name for a cat, I know, but that was its name. My niece is called Nora. A man phoned and said he wanted a meeting. It had to do with Trude and Nora, he said. He was not sure if Trude was still alive, but he wanted to talk to me about it.'

He leafed through a desk diary. The pages were closely

written and finally he discovered that it must have taken place on Thursday 20 August.

'I had an uncomfortable feeling,' he went on. 'Really dreadful. Nora is only eight years old . . .' He shook his head. 'Two hours later, he turned up here.'

'What did he want?'

'He showed me a picture of the cat. It was dead. Mutilated. In the worst possible way.'

He paused before continuing: 'It was a threat of some sort, obviously. About what could happen to Nora. He wanted me to deliver a letter to Kerr in prison. It was sealed. I've no idea of the contents, but with the benefit of hindsight it's easy to imagine that it contained detailed instructions, maybe even photographs, to facilitate his escape.'

Wisting had no idea where to start. 'Theo Dermann is not a real name,' he said. 'No one in Norway is called that.'

'He didn't introduce himself to me, but that was the name he used when he signed in.'

'What did he look like?'

Claes Thancke gave a deep sigh. 'I don't really know,' he replied.

'You don't know?' Wisting reiterated. 'He sat in here, didn't he?'

'He was in his thirties and had a beard,' Thancke explained. 'But I think it was dyed. I also think it was something he had grown for the occasion. As camouflage. He had a number of sticking plasters on his face and glasses with yellow lenses. And he wore a cap on his head.'

'Had you seen him before?'

'Never.'

'How did he speak?'

'English. Broken English, but that was probably put on too.'

'How long was he here?'

'Not long. Five minutes, maybe. It was a short message.'

'Have you met him more than once?'

'Only the one time, but then another letter turned up. At my home this time, in my mailbox. An envelope inside an envelope with my name on the outside and Kerr's name on the envelope inside. The sender was given as Trude, a hint that I was meant to understand.'

'When was this?'

'Wednesday of last week. I delivered it the next day.'

Thancke straightened up. 'It's contrary to the guidelines in the Alternatives to Prison Act, but not strictly illegal,' he pointed out.

Wisting wanted to object and say that he had probably helped Kerr to escape, but decided to drop it.

'Did you speak to Kerr about this?'

'No. He took the letters, laid them aside and didn't open them while I was with him.'

'Did you receive a letter to take out of prison for him?'

'No, it was a one-way communication.'

'Did anyone else here see him or speak to him?'

'Janne.' He nodded towards the glasses and bottles his secretary had brought. 'Nearly everyone else was in court or out at meetings,' he added. 'Janne transferred the phone call and signed him in when he arrived. I've checked the phone log. He called from a social security office in Sagene, from a phone that job seekers are allowed to use. I even went up there. It's almost like an old-fashioned phone box. Anyone can go in and make a phone call from there. No supervision. No cameras.'

'Have you any kind of surveillance in here?' Stiller asked.

Claes Thancke shook his head. 'My clients aren't very keen on that sort of thing. We have cameras on the entry phone, but no recordings.'

'What about the letter in the car? Was that from Theo Dermann too?'

'No. That had to do with the insurance case.' The lawyer shook his head. 'I had no idea that he was going to run off during the site visit.'

'What do you think those letters contained?' Stiller asked. 'Who do you think they were from?'

'I assumed they were from the Other One.'

Stiller glanced across at Wisting and the chair he was sitting in. 'So you mean that the Other One was here? In your office?'

'It wasn't necessarily him,' Thancke replied. 'Not in person. Probably not. Most likely it was just a messenger, but the contents were from him. I think that Tom Kerr was telling the truth at his trial when he denied having anything to do with Taran Norum's murder. I believe he's innocent, but he realized that he had to bear the blame and confess in order to have any chance of getting out of the prison where he was being held. He had already been given the law's severest punishment. He had nothing to lose by confessing to another murder. On the contrary. Choosing to confess would show that he had changed, and in the long run that could lead to conditional release. But then he needed information. He would have to know how the Other One had killed Taran Norum and where he had buried the body. I assumed that the letters contained what Kerr needed in order to confess. I had landed in an almost impossible role as a defending lawyer, to be honest, since it would actually be in my client's best interests to give a false confession.'

Wisting let this line of reasoning sink in.

'Now everything seems to have been a pretence,' Thancke continued. 'Right from the start, when he began to talk to a fellow prisoner. But from then on things began to move fast. A bit too fast, probably. He asked me to get the site visit postponed. The correspondence requesting no armed police was part of that. The result was that he gained time to get hold of all the information he needed.'

'That suggests he initiated the correspondence with the Other One,' Stiller summed up. 'That he contacted his accomplice from inside the prison. How was that arranged, then?'

Thancke looked perplexed. 'I don't know. He has some regular visitors. A pen pal, for one thing. But that's mere speculation.'

'Have you any suggestions as to how we can identify and find this messenger?'

Thancke shook his head. 'I don't know any more than I've already told you,' he said. 'And some of that is just supposition.'

They ran through everything one more time, asked a few additional questions, received a more detailed statement about Theo Dermann's visit and discussed the possibility of a police artist drawing a sketch of him.

'You sat there with him in front of you,' Wisting said. 'Spoke to him. That's a good starting point for a witness sketch.'

'I've seen these sketches before,' Thancke replied. 'They're hardly ever useful, but of course I'm willing to give it a try.'

Wisting prepared to leave. 'Have you any ideas or theories about where Tom Kerr might be now?'

The lawyer pressed his lips tightly together again. 'No. I would honestly have chosen to tell you if I had.'

44

'I can't quite join the dots here,' Stiller said as they walked to the car. 'Thancke has smuggled letters in to Kerr, while Lone Mellberg has brought letters out.'

Wisting merely nodded. 'I'll get Semmelmann to make inquiries at the social security office in Sagene,' he said. 'That's the most tangible lead we have, the location he called from to make the appointment.'

'We must speak to his secretary as well,' Stiller said. 'Get her to confirm the statement and give us a description.'

They had reached the car. Wisting had registered the parking on an app on his phone and when he took it out to conclude the transaction he noticed two missed calls from Hammer while they had been in the meeting with the lawyer.

'I've just had an interesting snippet of information from the mail service,' he said when Wisting returned his calls.

'Theo Dermann?'

'They can't locate the given address either and said that any letters sent there would end up at the department for dead letters.'

'Dead letters?'

'Post that they can't deliver to the given address or return to sender is collected in the Østland terminal for tracing. That's where all the Christmas presents with wrong addresses wind up.'

Wisting got the picture. He had read an article somewhere about staff described as post detectives.

'In some cases the letters are opened to see if they can find the name of the sender inside.'

'So the letters to Theo Dermann may have landed there?' Wisting asked.

'The person I spoke to thought that likely, at any rate,' Hammer replied.

Wisting fired up the engine. 'Where is this terminal?'

'In Lørenskog,' Hammer told him.

'Then I'm only half an hour away,' Wisting said. 'Send me the address.'

As he hung up, he told Stiller what he had learned.

'I'm coming too,' Stiller volunteered.

They drove north, out of the city centre. After passing the Oslo boundary, they trailed behind a green articulated lorry from Bring. They followed it all the way into an industrial area all the way up in front of the post terminal building.

Stiller pushed open the door on his side of the car but Wisting remained seated with his hands on the steering wheel.

'What is it?' Stiller asked.

Wisting shook his head. A thought had struck him while they were driving, but it was so conspiratorial that he had to mull it over before he could put it into words. He stepped out and closed the door slowly as he collected his thoughts.

'He must have had a reason for doing it,' he said. 'For smuggling out letters to an address that doesn't exist.'

He lingered beside the car. 'Everything else has been well planned,' he continued. 'What if his plan was for the letters to end up here?'

Stiller stood staring at him before he understood what his colleague meant. 'That maybe he has someone in there helping him?' he said, gesturing towards the building before them. 'In the department for undelivered post?'

'I just wanted to mention it,' Wisting said, 'as a possibility.'

'Do you mean that the Other One might even work here?'

'Not necessarily, but someone willing to pass the letter on, at least, to where it's meant to go.'

'So what do we do?'

Wisting started walking. 'We go in as planned,' he answered. 'Find out if the letters are in there, for a start. Then we can make a list of the people who've had access to them, if they're not here.'

They reported to a front desk and were directed to a burly man who took responsibility for police inquiries. According to the sign on his door, he was the quality and security manager. Wisting explained that they were trying to trace two letters sent to the wrong address.

'Is this connected to Tom Kerr?' the man behind the desk asked. 'I saw you on the news.'

'It's just one of many leads we're following up,' Wisting replied. 'We're looking for two A4 envelopes, addressed to a street in Oslo that doesn't exist.'

'C4,' the stout man corrected him. 'Envelopes designed for A4 sheets are called C4.'

Wisting smiled. 'We'd like to investigate whether they've finished up in the dead letter department.'

'I see,' the man replied. He pulled out a drawer and began to search through a pile of papers.

'How long ago was this?'

'Ten days and four weeks ago respectively.'

'Then they may well have ended up here,' the man agreed, pushing the drawer in again. 'Have you filled out a search form?'

'It's urgent,' Wisting said. 'I want you to escort us to the department so that we can take this up with the staff working there. If we locate the letters, we want to take them with us today.'

The man responsible for security sat looking at him, as if considering whether Wisting's request was within the rules. Then he got to his feet.

'I see,' he said in the end. 'You can come with me, then.'

He accompanied them along a corridor, down a spiral staircase and through another corridor that ended at a grey, anonymous steel door. Inside were wall shelves filled with red boxes overflowing with parcels and letters.

A man and a woman sat at workstations at the far end of the rectangular room. The security manager waved the woman over and explained the situation.

Wisting remarked on the vast quantities of wrongly addressed post.

'The merger of various local authorities has presented us with challenges,' the woman explained. 'Many of the new large districts have reviewed their street names so that there is, for example, only one Storgate in each district. The intention is to make it easier for the post to reach its destination, but in the transition period it's confusing. People are not good at telling their contacts about changes of address.'

Wisting scanned the shelves of missing mail. In the nearest box there was a letter with illegible handwriting and a parcel that had no recipient's address. Both bore the same label: *Address Unknown*. The box had yellow Post-it notes attached with the date and something that must be an internal numbering scheme. The system seemed primitive and complex.

'We're looking for a letter addressed to Theo Dermann in Anton Brekkes vei in Oslo,' Wisting said. 'There's no such address, and there's no one by that name in the population register,' he added.

'It should be in the system somewhere,' the woman told

him as she walked back to her workstation, with the others following in her wake.

She sat down and opened a computer program. As Wisting spelled out the name, the colleague beside her watched inquisitively.

'I've got two results,' the woman said.

She turned to her colleague. 'You're the one who logged them in, Morgan.'

The man stood up. 'I can try to find them, then,' he offered.

The woman gave him a reference number for the first letter. The man limped across to a shelf, pulled out a box and began to riffle through the contents. Wisting and Stiller exchanged looks.

'A C4 envelope,' the security manager called out.

The male colleague pulled out a brown envelope and waved it at them.

'Here!'

The woman at the computer gave him another number, and the man located an identical envelope and brought it back to them. They were equally thick, and neither had been opened. The recipient's name and address were handwritten in sloping letters. An assortment of stamps was affixed to the top right-hand corner.

'Theo Dermann,' the man said, handing over the envelopes.

'We need a formal decision from the prosecutor's office in order to hand them over officially,' the security manager said.

Stiller began to argue that this could not possibly be necessary. Wisting took out his phone.

'I'll arrange it,' he said, dialling Christine Thiis's number. 'Anyway, we need a decision about opening them as well.'

The security manager carried the two letters while Wisting explained the situation to the police lawyer.

'Do you have a fax machine?' he asked.

The security manager shook his head. 'Only email.'

Wisting obtained the address and passed it on before sitting down. The letters lay on the desk between him and the security manager.

'It takes five to ten minutes,' Wisting said, nodding towards the computer.

'Can I offer you anything?' the manager asked. 'Coffee? Mineral water?'

Stiller said no thanks, but Wisting asked for a cup of coffee, mainly to get the security manager out of the room.

'Theo Dermann,' Wisting said, raising his voice. 'I think I know who it is.'

'Who, then?'

Wisting repeated the name. 'It sounds German, doesn't it?'

'Jewish, maybe,' Stiller agreed.

'What if it was English or American, though?' Wisting suggested. Stiller did not follow.

'How would you pronounce it in an American accent?' Wisting asked.

Stiller made an attempt, but it took a while longer before the penny dropped.

'The other man,' he said. 'The Other One!'

Wisting gestured towards the two envelopes on the desk. 'Either the contents of those letters are what we're looking for, or we've been conned. Again.'

'Conned? In what sense?'

'In the sense that it's a diversionary tactic, to make us look in a different direction.'

The security manager had returned with two cups of coffee. He placed one in front of Wisting and sat down with the other cup on his lap.

'So, who is this Theo Dermann?' he asked.

Wisting glanced at the time. 'Check your email,' he said.

The hefty man took a drink of his coffee, put it down on the desk and checked the computer screen.

'Here it is, yes . . .' He squinted at the screen as he read the contents of the formal decision. 'Everything's in order here,' he concluded, reaching for a letter opener on a shelf behind him.

'Excellent,' Wisting said. He stood up, picked up the two letters and headed for the door. 'Thanks for your help,' he added.

The chair legs scraped across the floor as Stiller followed his example.

Two minutes later they were sitting in the car and Wisting had the letters on his knee.

Stiller handed him a small pocketknife. 'Gloves?' he suggested.

Wisting nodded. It felt appropriate to handle the contents of the envelopes as potential evidence. He drew out two thin latex gloves from a packet in the door pocket and pulled them on. Then he checked the date stamps and ripped the first envelope open.

A bundle of lined sheets of paper was inside. He took them out and saw that they were blank.

Stiller groaned in the seat beside him. 'He's playing with us,' he said, and swore.

Wisting opened the second envelope. It too was full of blank sheets of paper.

45

'You haven't brought your camera?' asked the man behind the desk.

Line returned his smile. Elias Wallberg was one of two psychiatrists who had examined Tom Kerr. He was an over-weight man in his early fifties, with wrinkles on his face, grey hair sprouting from his ears and a glint in his eye. His external appearance exuded authority, suggesting experience and professional standing. He would make a convincing expert witness in a court case, and would also make the same impression in front of a camera.

'I thought I wouldn't record anything today,' she replied. 'It requires a good deal of preparation: equipment, lighting, and so on. But I'm really pleased that you could meet me at such short notice.'

She took out a folder filled with notes.

'In the work I've done so far, I've become very curious about your role, and what a forensic psychiatrist is capable of finding out.'

'You appreciate that I can't talk about Tom Kerr's specific case,' Wallberg warned her.

'I realize that,' Line said. 'What I need is a specialist who can tell me what evil is. Where it comes from and what it can lead to.'

Elias Wallberg leaned forward. 'Evil is the inner dark-ness,' he answered. 'An urge to inflict pain on other human beings.'

Line made notes. She was happy with what she was hearing.

The man's voice was gravelly and his words conjured images. It would make good TV.

'Where it comes from is more difficult to pin down,' the forensic psychiatrist continued. 'I've arrived at the idea that evil is something we can't understand and therefore are unable to guard against, control or prevent. Just like love.'

He gave a crooked smile and sat back in his chair again.

'It's not proven that evil is a psychological deviation,' he said. 'In fact, it may have its roots in physical processes inside the brain. Research shows that psychopaths have defects or deficiencies in the part of the brain where personality is created. Areas of the brain necessary for the ability to feel shame and demonstrate empathy are damaged. The required brain cells are quite simply missing.'

He raised his index finger to his own forehead. 'There's no cerebral matter where the emotional reaction to evil would give rise to regret, shame, guilt, anxiety and aversion.'

Line recognized some of these ideas from Maren Dokken's dissertation. 'But surely psychopaths understand the difference between right and wrong?' she asked.

'Psychopaths can adapt,' the psychiatrist said. 'Depending on how other people react, they can for instance appreciate that it is wrong to torment animals, but they can't connect that to their own understanding of the act. They do not feel guilt. It's an inborn lack. So they can't learn to become better people. They can be punished. We can put them in prison, but punishment has no educational impact, because they do not possess the brain cells that would normally lead them to regret and feel sorry for their actions. Psychopaths are unfeeling. Completely ignorant of notions of responsibility and guilt.'

'But psychopaths are not necessarily evil, surely?' Line said.

'No, the type of evil and sadism you're talking about is often executed by people with antisocial personality disorders. The conclusion I came to with regard to Tom Kerr was that he is a narcissistic psychopath.'

'What about the accomplice, the Other One?' Line asked. 'What sort of person is he?'

Elias Wallberg smiled. 'Of course I can't provide a definite diagnosis, but obviously he must be a person with the same sadistic and narcissistic traits as Kerr, but nevertheless different.'

'And has sneaked under the police's radar?'

'I'd think he'll feature in their papers somewhere. He's probably a well-respected person.'

'What makes you draw that conclusion?'

'Because he hasn't been caught. Most likely we're talking about a person who has created the illusion of altruism and modesty, someone expert at concealing his egotistical and egocentric motives and who appears for all the world to be honest, good-natured and even noble. So far, he has succeeded in passing himself off as a more likable version of himself and is well aware that if his true nature were to be revealed, he would not be able to retain the respect and status he has earned.'

'So the police should be looking for a man of high status?'

'Not necessarily,' Wallberg replied. 'The fact that he hasn't been exposed suggests that he has an extremely good capacity to adapt, but narcissists function best within frameworks characterized by control and predictability. In the police or the military, for example, where system and structure are key concepts.'

'Are you saying that the Other One may even be a policeman?' Line queried.

Elias Wallberg laughed. 'No, but it's not unthinkable. Typically, that's the kind of work a sadist would apply for. Sadism contains a fascination for the wielding of power and a desire to punish and control others. At the very least, it would be far more likely that the Other One is a care worker, for instance.'

He glanced at his watch. Line realized that it was time to round things off. She was given a few more reflections on the concept of evil before Wallberg got to his feet and accompanied her to the door.

'I've had many conversations with Kerr,' he said, with his hand on the doorknob. 'Certainly more than the investigators who worked with him. I believe him to be dangerous and erratic. An animal behaves according to impulses and instincts, whereas normal human beings behave in accordance with their conscience. Kerr has no conscience. In that domain, Tom Kerr is more like an animal than a human being.'

46

The empty coffee cup was still at the end of the conference table where Wisting had left it at the start of the day. He took it through to the kitchenette, rinsed it out and refilled it.

One by one, the other investigators entered the room and sat down in their usual places. The letters addressed to Theo Dermann were lying at Mortensen's place, each sealed in a transparent plastic evidence bag.

'Can you glean anything from them?' Wisting asked.

Mortensen shook his head glumly. 'Probably nothing useful,' he replied. 'It wouldn't be a surprise to find Tom Kerr's fingerprints and DNA on them.'

They all already knew the contents of the envelopes, but the bags were passed around the table so that they could scrutinize them.

'There is in fact one person who calls himself Theo Dermann,' Wisting informed them, and gave an account of the visit paid to Claes Thancke's office.

By now they had also interviewed the receptionist, who had confirmed how the appointment with Theo Dermann had come about, and described Dermann in identical terms as Thancke. She thought he must have distinctive scars on his face because of the sticking plasters.

The rest of the discussion led to nothing new and the meeting was short. They were treading water and were now in a position where they had nothing more to go on.

Wisting was last to leave the room. He headed for his

office to make a start on the stack of reports and messages. These were notes that Bjørg Karin from the admin office had delivered to him, and printouts of emails and text messages, mainly from journalists unable to reach him by phone. The last of these he had received during the recent meeting and was from a journalist at TV2 looking for a comment on the Internal Affairs investigation. He left it unanswered and was embarking on the next message when his phone rang. It was Tim Skage.

'Any news?' Wisting asked.

'Not as far as Tallak Gleich is concerned,' he answered. 'We've been to the address where he spent the night with a pal in the city centre, but haven't come any further than that. The grenades we found originate from a military warehouse, just as you thought. It's been confirmed.'

Wisting leaned back in his chair and ran his free hand over his forehead.

'Something else has turned up, something interesting,' Skage continued. 'I wanted to let you know.'

'What's that?'

Skage began in slightly long-winded fashion: 'You'll recall that for a long time we regarded the case as an accidental fire. It's only a day or two since anaesthetic substances were detected in Chris Paust Backe's blood and we drew the conclusion that the fire was deliberate. The homicide case has only been open for a couple of days now.'

It dawned on Wisting that they must have overlooked something important.

'Lots of criminals have a number of phones,' Skage continued. 'One phone for everyday use and another for business. Shady activity. One black and one white, if you like.'

'Yes?'

'Early on we obtained the telecomms data for Backe's white phone, but that didn't give us much, and it uncovered no conversations with Tallak Gleich.'

'How many mobiles did you find in the ruins after the fire?' Wisting asked.

'Two,' Skage replied. 'Or, to be more exact, five, but only two with links to a subscription. Now the technicians have finished with them. One of these we already had data for, and the other was registered to his grandmother. In that one, we found several conversations with Tallak Gleich, but the last person he called was Helene Norum.'

Wisting felt a tingle run down his spine. 'Norum,' he repeated.

'The mother of Tom Kerr's third victim,' Skage explained. 'Taran Norum.'

Wisting was well aware of who she was. Questions stacked up inside him. 'Are there any other conversations between them?' he demanded.

'Just the one. It took place about an hour before the fire was reported. They spoke for almost a minute.'

'Are they related in any way? Any kind of connection?'

'Not that we've been able to find. Not so far, at least.'

A pigeon landed on the window ledge outside. Wisting stood up and crossed to the window without scaring it off. He fixed his eye on the Svenner archipelago and the lighthouse far out on the fjord. What he had learned only added to his confusion. It did not fit, not in any way whatsoever, the idea that the man who had indirectly assisted in Kerr's escape had a connection to the mother of one of his victims.

'You'll have to talk to her,' he said.

'We'll try to gather some more information and then

we'll bring her in for interview tomorrow. I'll keep you posted.'

That brought the call to a close.

The pigeon flapped its wings and flew off. Wisting continued to stand there, contemplating the many threads they needed to reel in. But it felt as if someone else was also tugging them, someone with a will of his own.

47

'Thanks a million!'

Line was being served a cup of tea from Amalie's play kitchen. She put it to her lips and pretended to drink. Amalie beamed from ear to ear before toddling back to the little kitchen at the other end of the living room to stir a pot. Line put down the cup.

The TV was tuned to a children's channel, but Amalie was not watching.

'Mummy just needs to make a phone call.'

She turned down the volume on the TV and rang Maren Dokken.

'Oh, hi!' she answered in an affable tone.

'How are things?' Line asked.

'I'm on my way out,' Maren replied. 'I thought I'd go for a walk, to get some fresh air. Before it starts raining again.'

Line could hear echoing sounds and pictured Maren on her way down through the stairwell.

'I just wanted to tell you that I spoke to the psychiatrist today,' Line went on, though she had to laugh at herself. 'I mean, the one who helped you with your dissertation.'

'Elias Wallberg.'

'The very man. He seemed really good,' Line said. 'He's agreed to take part in the documentary.'

'That's great!'

'I just wanted to say thank you for pointing me in his direction.'

'I'm looking forward to seeing it when it's finished.'

Line heard a door slam. 'I've spoken to the producers,' she added. 'We'd really like to have you on board. So that you can tell your story about what happened on Tuesday.'

'I'm not sure . . .' Maren began.

'You don't need to decide right away,' Line rushed to add. 'But do think about it.'

'It's probably not just up to me,' Maren said. 'It would have to be cleared at work.'

'Of course,' Line said. 'But I can't imagine they'd have anything against it.'

'I'm going to a debrief at the station tomorrow morning at nine o'clock,' Maren told her. 'They've allocated an hour. We can have a chat after that. I'll give you a call.'

'Brilliant.' Line rang off, feeling upbeat.

Amalie came toddling across with a plate of make-believe food that Line then had to make-believe taste. She smacked her lips in satisfaction and changed channel on the TV to catch the news on TV2.

The broadcast began, and the first item showed Tom Kerr's face. The newsreader announced that TV2 could reveal exclusive images of what had happened when the brutal killer escaped. They then went on to relay footage of Tom Kerr running and the explosion that followed. Her images. Her recording.

She sat on the settee in disbelief. Three other news items were introduced before they returned to Tom Kerr. He had still not been caught and the police had not issued any new information, the studio journalist explained. After this, an item with archive pictures from the previous day was aired. A reporter restated the crimes of which Tom Kerr had been convicted and what had taken place since his escape. Then her images appeared again. The reporter repeated that TV2 had obtained access to exclusive footage. They knew how

Tom Kerr's leg irons had been removed, that he had walked down the steep slope and then suddenly broken into a sprint. The police stormed after him, and the clip ended with the explosion.

'What the fuck!' Line shouted.

The news item continued and her father's face appeared onscreen. It was from one of the press conferences, the one when he had been wearing a borrowed shirt. The reporter related that the police force's Internal Affairs section had launched an investigation into what had gone wrong when Tom Kerr escaped.

'Grandpa!' Amalie yelled.

She shot forward to stand in front of the TV. A chief inspector from Internal Affairs confirmed what the reporter had said but was unwilling to make any further comment.

The way the item was edited gave the impression that what had occurred had been her father's fault and implied that he was the officer under investigation.

Amalie grinned with delight as she clambered up on to the settee. 'Grandpa!' she shouted again.

The news item was over. Line turned down the sound again and phoned Stiller. She did not really have anything to do with how the police used her film footage. She had been paid for the job, and the recordings belonged to them, but she would have appreciated advance warning. Besides, it was totally unnecessary. The police had nothing to gain from releasing the images.

He replied almost immediately.

'I've seen the TV2 news,' Line said.

'Oh? I'm in my car, on my way back to Oslo.'

It sounded as if he knew nothing about it.

'Why have you given my film to TV2?' she asked.

'What do you mean?'

'TV2 have just shown the footage of Tom Kerr's escape,' Line explained.

Adrian Stiller cleared his throat. 'I know nothing about it.'

'Where would they get it from, then?'

'I've no idea. I'll have to look into this.'

'So it has to be a leak?' Line said. 'Who else has had access to the footage?'

'I'll have to look into it,' Stiller reiterated. 'But it's actually a positive development for you.'

'How can that be? Exclusivity's gone now.'

'Now it'll be easier for you to obtain permission to use the recordings. They're already in the public domain. There's no reason for the top brass to withhold them. There's no reason now to wait until the inquiry is done and dusted.'

Amalie was tired. She was snuggling up to Line's chest.

'Are you going to investigate it as a leak?' Line asked, stroking her daughter's head. 'Breach of confidentiality or something? I'd like to know where the leak came from.'

'In that case it would be Internal Affairs who'd need to delve into it,' Stiller replied. 'But it doesn't sound as if it's damaged the investigation. Maybe even the opposite. The more often Tom Kerr's face is splashed on TV screens, the greater the chance that someone will recognize him and report it.'

'I want to be there when you arrest him,' Line said.

'What do you mean?'

'I want you to let me know as soon as you have something specific,' Line said. 'When you know where he is. I want to be there and film it when you catch him.'

'Your father's in charge of the case,' Stiller protested.

'He's hopeless,' Line complained. 'Scared to death of confusing our roles. You were the one who set the ball rolling. You can fix it.'

There was silence at the other end. 'I'll see what I can do,' he said finally.

'Thanks.'

Stiller had another incoming call. 'I have to take this,' he said apologetically, and ended the conversation.

The TV news was now covering protests about new toll-road projects. Line rewound the decoder to watch the coverage of the escape once again. Someone in the police force had wanted these pictures to come out. She did not know who was on the distribution list, but the only person she could imagine to have any kind of motive was Adrian Stiller. He was right when he said that it would make the documentary project easier.

'Grandpa!' Amalie squealed, pointing at the TV screen again.

Line stopped the playback. Her father's face filled the screen.

Unless there was another motive, she thought. The use of the images was linked with the news that Internal Affairs were reviewing the case and had her father in their sights. The leak could be an attempt to allocate blame for Tom Kerr's escape.

48

It had started raining again.

The ventilation system in the police station switched off automatically in the afternoons when there were normally few people at work. Wisting had opened his office window for some fresh air. It could only be opened sideways, and now the rain was coming in, so he closed it.

The town lay like an amphitheatre below him, towering above the small arm of the fjord, encircling it and fanning outwards.

He had lived here all his life and had not really experienced much else of the world. He belonged here and felt like part of the town. Felt a responsibility to stand guard over it.

In an opening between two buildings he could see parts of Storgata, the main street. A car with flashing blue lights sped past without sounding its sirens. He could not make out what kind of emergency vehicle it was, but saw that it was heading west, and shortly afterwards the lights appeared again on the road that led to Stavern. It looked like a police car.

He returned to his desk. It had taken time to download Idar Semmelmann's data system on to his own computer. An enormous collection of information had been built up in the course of the hunt for the Other One. When Semmelmann had shown them the search functions on the relationship map and the possibilities they offered, it had seemed impressive. However, the actual manipulation features were complicated. He wanted to do a simple search for the name of Thea Polden's mother, but the response was an error message and a request to mark the basic data the search referred to in the settings. He couldn't make head or tail of it and had tried to ring Semmelmann for assistance, but received no reply. When he tried again, he ended up connected to his voicemail. He decided against leaving a message, but assumed that Semmelmann would call him back when he saw the missed calls.

Changing to another screen image, he began instead to read the case documents relating to Chris Paust Backe's murder. Normally, he liked to print out all reports and interviews in order to underline interesting aspects or scribble remarks in the margins. Now he contented himself with jotting down notes in a spiral notebook.

After half an hour, his phone rang: a call from the switchboard. 'We have an ongoing incident you might like to send an investigator to,' the operator said.

'What is it?'

'Our patrols are out searching for a white delivery van. A witness has reported seeing a woman being dragged into it.'

Wisting rose from his chair and moved to the window again. It was growing dark outside. 'When did this happen?'

'The report was logged here about three quarters of an hour ago, but it apparently happened some time before that.'

'Where is it?'

'Along Gamle Stavernsvei. We have a patrol car on the scene now with the witness. I don't know exactly what's going on as yet, but with what has happened in the past few days . . .'

Wisting was already making his way to the door. 'I'll see to it,' he said. 'I'm leaving now.'

He fumbled with one jacket sleeve as he rushed down to his car, jumped into the driver's seat and drove out into the rain.

The drive took no more than five minutes. In the middle of a long stretch of road two police patrol cars were parked at one side. A white tarpaulin was spread out between them.

Wisting drew up in front of the front vehicle, bonnet to bonnet. A man in a tracksuit was sitting in the passenger seat. The police officer at the wheel, with a laptop on his knee, acknowledged Wisting's arrival with a nod of the head.

Wisting stepped out and clambered into the back seat of the patrol car. He introduced himself briefly and asked the witness to relate what he had seen.

'I came running down here, on the opposite side of the road,' he explained, pointing to a spot about two hundred metres ahead. 'A girl was walking along the road; I could see her in the distance. Then the van arrived. It drove past me, swerved across the road and stopped. A van door slammed, and then it drove forward at full throttle, and the girl was gone.'

'She was taken away in the van?'

'I didn't see it actually happen. The van was between her and me. I just heard the side door close. The sound of a sliding door. There was no scream or anything like that, and it all happened so fast, but they must have taken her with them.'

'We've a description of the van, but not the reg number,' the man behind the wheel advised. 'It was a delivery van of some sort, a Citroën Berlingo or a Peugeot Partner, with no windows in the cargo space.'

The rain was pattering on the car roof and the fan was working overtime, but the inside of the side windows had misted up all the same. As a third police car drove past outside, the man in the tracksuit followed it with his eyes.

'I'm not certain that anything untoward happened,' he said. 'In fact, I'm not sure I would have phoned if it hadn't been for the shoe.'

'The shoe?'

'There was a hiking shoe, size 38, lying on the road,' the police officer volunteered. 'It's under the tarpaulin.'

The witness swivelled around in his seat. 'I didn't have my mobile with me, so I couldn't phone until I got home,' he said apologetically. 'By then, probably ten minutes or so had gone by. Maybe a bit more. I thought about it while I ran, that it had been strange, and thought it would be best to give you a call.'

Wisting ran his hand over the side window and peered out. There was little traffic on this road. Along one side was dense forest, and on the other nothing but fields. In the distance there were a few houses, but in this particular spot, no buildings. No witnesses.

As he tugged on the door handle and stepped out, his phone rang. It was Semmelmann: 'I see you've been trying to get through to me.'

'Yes,' Wisting said.

He strode forward and lifted the tarpaulin to see the shoe lying there: grey with a pink pattern.

'Has something cropped up?' Semmelmann asked.

Wisting replaced the tarpaulin. Rainwater was soaking his neck. 'It's happened again,' he replied.

49

The engine was running, and Wisting sat hunched over, resting his arms on the steering wheel. The thin dark stripes of falling rain were highlighted by the car's headlamps. Four police officers each lifted a corner of the tarpaulin while a fifth took a photograph of the shoe lying there. The harsh light of the flash cast sharp shadows along the asphalt.

'We should put out an all-points bulletin in the media for the van,' Wisting said, raising his head to the microphone on the hands-free set-up.

The police lawyer on duty disagreed. 'We've had a discussion about it in here,' she said. 'There are other things to take into consideration. We can't be sure about what has happened.'

'That's exactly why,' Wisting argued. 'We should announce that we're searching for the van and ask the girl who was walking along the road to contact us.'

'We'll wait until we have more information. It could all be just a misunderstanding. The witness could have got the wrong impression. The media is full of stuff about Tom Kerr's murders. That could well have influenced his judgement. He may have thought he saw something different from what actually took place. We need something specific before we make more of this.'

In front of the car, the shoe was being dropped into a brown paper bag and the tarpaulin was then folded up.

'What about the shoe, though?' Wisting asked.

'It may have been already lying there.'

'In exactly the same spot where the girl was picked up by a white van?'

The police lawyer gave a loud sigh. 'I've read the witness statement,' she said. 'He was two hundred metres away. He couldn't say with any certainty that the shoe was exactly where the van stopped. He only drew that conclusion when he spotted it.'

Leaning back, Wisting glanced at the tiny microphone in the roof. The police lawyer seemed determined to stand her ground. In all likelihood, she was simply defending a decision that had already been taken, and it would be a waste of time trying to counter her arguments.

She was called Stemstad, and her first name was either Gro or Gunn. From the sound of her voice, she was half Wisting's age. They had never met and did not know each other, but had conferred a few times on the phone in other cases. This impractical method of dealing with cases was the result of the reorganization and merger of police districts.

'Tom Kerr has been on the run for more than forty-eight hours,' the police lawyer continued. 'He must be far away by now. Why would he stay in your neck of the woods? It defies logic.'

Wisting had to admit she was right.

'We've had more than a hundred reports from members of the public who claim to have seen Tom Kerr,' Stemstad pointed out. 'Some of them insist they've spotted him in a white van. It's been checked out. People see what they want to see. It's important not to exaggerate this.'

The wipers cleared the rainwater from the front windscreen. By now the police officers had returned to their vehicles. One started up and drove off, with the others following shortly afterwards.

'So what do you suggest that we do?' Wisting asked.

'All patrols are keeping an eye out for the white van,' the police lawyer reminded him. 'We'll wait and see what comes of that. In the meantime, we'll keep the media out of it. You mustn't do anything to muddy the waters.'

Wisting stole a glance in the rear-view mirror and saw the sceptical frown on his face. 'What do you mean by that? Muddy the waters?'

'I'm just saying that everything that's going on right now is unnecessary. It could easily have been avoided. Tom Kerr should never have been given the chance to escape. He should never have been let loose into society again.'

After that, the conversation was abruptly terminated. Wisting was left staring at his reflection in the mirror. Was that how they all saw it? That it was his fault Tom Kerr was now at large?

He continued to sit there, dwelling on that thought. An unfamiliar sensation welled up inside him, a sense of guilt – an uncontrollable, relentless sense of guilt.

It was not unusual for him to feel a sense of inadequacy. Cases that dragged on or remained unsolved could weigh him down. He was appointed to lead investigations in major, complex cases and it was his responsibility to obtain results. This was a responsibility that he had become accustomed to with the passage of time, but feeling responsible was quite different from feeling guilty.

A car swept past. He looked ahead at the dry patch at the side of the road where the tarpaulin had been stretched out. The rain was steadily obliterating it. He hoped the police lawyer was right, because if a crime had been committed, it would be his fault.

50

There was nothing on the morning news to suggest that the police had made any progress in their pursuit of Tom Kerr. The coverage was characterized by criticism of the police. Line's father's name was not singled out, but he was the one who had been the face of the police to the outside world on the day Tom Kerr had run away, and this was the picture they continued to use.

Drinking the rest of her orange juice, Line put down her phone and glanced up at her father's house. He had not come home before she went to bed the previous night, and his car had been gone when she got up.

She cleared the table, helped Amalie to dress and packed her things for nursery.

Usually, they dawdled in the mornings, taking plenty of time, and were seldom in a rush for anything. Lately, it had been different. She hurried to get Amalie out of the house and on her way so that she could apply total concentration to the documentary project. Although it gave her a guilty conscience, she consoled herself with the thought that it was only temporary and, anyway, her daughter was happy at nursery.

Regarded in isolation, the life of a psychopath must be a simple one, she mused in the car after dropping off Amalie. No bad conscience, no regret, no feelings of guilt.

It was the same in the evenings. She sped through the housework while Amalie was still awake. Once her daughter had gone to bed, she could devote all her attention to the job in hand.

It was still raining and, actually, she should have gone out to look for new rainwear for Amalie, but that could wait until Saturday, when Amalie was not at nursery. Then she would be able to choose colours for herself and she could try things on.

Line descended to her office in the basement. She liked it down there: it was cosy between the old stone walls and there was little to distract her. Everything around her was job-related in some way or another, making it easier to gather her thoughts and forcing her to be focused and productive.

In her notes from the meeting with the psychiatrist she had accentuated one thing. That evil was like falling in love: no one knew where it came from.

Her immediate reaction had been that this was untrue. Love came from the heart, as something natural and genuine. But that was just a figure of speech. The heart really had no other function than to pump blood.

She made an effort to read up on other theories, to find other voices that could tell her something about the drive towards evil.

The head of the Norwegian Psychological Association had been interviewed about it in an article published a while back. His thoughts conflicted with what the forensic psychiatrist had said about psychopaths and narcissists. He felt that most of the evil in the world was inflicted by ordinary people who crossed the border from good to evil. It began with small instances and manifested itself in not showing concern. When you did not go to the bother of checking whether the man on the ground was sleeping off a drunken binge or was dying. When you let the taxi driver reel off racist jokes without telling him to stop. When you turned a blind eye to your neighbour's wife's bruises, or simply walked past when a down-and-out held out a begging hand. It could be tempting to stretch the truth or pass comment on the behaviour of others. To remain silent about what might place you in a bad light. Exaggerate a smidgen. Say something to protect yourself or your nearest and dearest. However, each time you lied or spoke disparagingly about other people was a step in the direction of evil.

A gust of wind flung a sheet of rain against the walls above. She had a fleeting urge to go upstairs for a coffee but was so engrossed that she read on instead.

It was a matter of apportioning responsibility. It was easier to take part in something when you did not have to take the punishment on your own. Then your sense of responsibility disintegrated, since you did not have to bear the burden of responsibility alone. Moral objections were eroded. A psychological experiment was shown in which a group of students was asked to play the roles of prisoners and prison guards in a jail. The experiment had to be aborted before the end of the first week, when it was found that the 'guards' were so blinded by their power and the punitive regime they humiliated the 'prisoners' to such an extent that several of them broke down completely. It was a case of 'us and them'. 'The others' were regarded as untrustworthy, dangerous and bad people who threatened our way of life.

The abuse of authority, subjugation and control, and domination of the will of others provided evil with fertile soil in which to flourish, and at the same time both blind obedience and uncritical loyalty to absolute rules were what could transform peaceful democracies into fascist dictatorships.

A great deal of what was asserted by the psychologist contained elements she recognized, but it remained difficult to understand how anyone could find satisfaction through mutilating and violating another human being. But evil undoubtedly existed. It was just as real as love.

A sudden noise caused her to lift her head to the ceiling. The wind must have picked up. What she heard was the bedroom window banging.

She got to her feet and brought her empty cup upstairs. Padding through to the kitchen, she fired up the coffee machine before moving to close the bedroom window. The rain had blown in and the floor was wet. She had to fetch a cloth.

The documentary project was starting to shift in a different direction, she thought as she wiped the floor. Taking on a new dimension. It was now not simply an account of the transgressions of Tom Kerr and his accomplice but also an exploration of what they stood for. For that, she also needed to find someone who could view their criminality from their point of view. Ideally, this would mean persuading Tom Kerr to appear. Alternatively, she could ask his lawyer to take part. Claes Thancke seemed to enjoy being in the media spotlight.

The coffee was ready and she checked the time. Half past ten, and she still had not heard from Maren Dokken. The debrief should be finished by now, but if she had to speak to someone about obtaining permission to take part in the documentary, then that could take longer.

All of a sudden she felt unsure of what their agreement had been, which one of them was meant to phone.

She sipped her coffee as she tapped in a text message, stretching the truth a little:

I'm in town. Can drop by if you've finished at work.

There was no answer. For some reason, that worried her.

51

The search had been scaled down around 11 p.m. and ended at midnight, and there had been no developments overnight. No one was reported missing. Wisting had to admit that the police lawyer had been right, and he felt some of his guilt ease off.

It had started raining when the incident took place. The witness had not heard anyone scream. More than likely, someone she knew had picked the girl up and offered her a lift home out of the rain. The shoe may have been dropped there earlier, fallen out of a sports bag on a bike or been set down on a car roof and forgotten when the owner drove off. He was unaccustomed to thinking up excuses instead of building a worst-case scenario and acting from that hypothesis. All the same, he was aware of the incident nagging at him. An annoying niggle he could have been spared if only they had made a public announcement and asked the girl and the van driver to contact the police.

Hammer appeared at his office door. 'They're about to start,' he said.

Wisting left his desk and they walked together up to the spacious conference room on the second floor, where they sat down at the very back beside the wall. Everyone involved in any way on the day Tom Kerr had escaped was assembled for a communal debrief. In addition to the police personnel, there were also a couple of paramedics in attendance.

It dawned on him that Line should have been included. He should have thought of that. More to the point, Stiller should have thought of that. He was the one who had engaged her services and, to make matters worse, she had no colleagues with whom to share the brutal experience.

Frank Kvastmo from the patrol section welcomed them all and led the proceedings. No direct evaluation was given, but the session was intended to reduce the level of mental stress, remove the revulsion and, not least, limit the after-effects of what had happened. Everyone who wanted to share feelings or say something was given the floor.

It was the vacuum that Wisting recalled best. What had occurred immediately after the explosion. The silence as all the oxygen was violently displaced, before the confusion broke out and everything was set in motion. It had lasted for only a fraction of a second, but in his memory the time was long drawn out. He saw everything in his mind's eye in iso-lated, spasmodic sequences, and in the midst of it all he glimpsed Line.

Wisting was given the opportunity to speak at the very end. He stood up, strode forward to the podium and sur-veyed his assembled colleagues. Some of the officers who had been in the procession were seated at the front. He could not see Maren Dokken among them, but nodded in recogni-tion to someone who sat with a bandage wrapped round his hand before he began.

He said nothing about his own experience but instead gave an account of the ongoing investigation. He held back the exchange of letters with Theo Dermann and the role Claes Thancke had played, but spoke in detail about the mur-der of Chris Paust Backe and the search for the man with the grenades.

His phone rang while he was speaking and as he took it out he saw that the call was from Line, so he turned it to silent mode before he continued.

When he had finished, Kvastmo led a round of questions before the official part of the debrief was concluded. Hot drinks and trays of open sandwiches were brought in and they were all encouraged to help themselves and stay for further, informal discussion.

Wisting checked his phone. Line had tried to phone him again. He moved into the corridor to return her call.

'Hi!' she said. 'Do you know if the debrief is finished yet?'

Wisting was taken aback by her question. 'It's just ended,' he replied. 'Why do you ask? Have you spoken to Stiller? Didn't he invite you to take part?'

'No, nothing like that. I wanted to meet up with Maren afterwards. She said it would take about an hour.'

Wisting checked his watch. It had taken almost two. 'It dragged on a bit,' he said. 'But Maren wasn't here.'

'She said she would be.'

'When did you speak to her?'

'Yesterday,' Line answered. 'She's not answering my messages, and I've tried to call her. Her phone's not switched on.'

Nils Hammer and Frank Kvastmo emerged into the corridor. Wisting asked Line to wait and lowered his phone. 'Have you heard from Maren Dokken today?' he asked.

Kvastmo shook his head. He was Maren's line manager and the one most likely to know something.

'She's on sick leave, but she did say she would come. I spoke to her yesterday.'

Kvastmo walked off, but Hammer stayed beside Wisting, who returned to his conversation with Line.

'She may be sleeping,' she suggested. 'She's taking pretty strong painkillers.'

'Maybe,' Wisting replied.

He was trained to believe that the worst had happened. Complications could have arisen in connection with the injuries she had sustained. Internal bleeding that had not been diagnosed at the hospital or had not occurred until now. Or something even more serious could have happened.

'I'm on my way into town now,' Line went on. 'I thought I'd call in at her apartment.'

'Then we'll see you there,' Wisting said, ending the conversation.

'What's going on?' Hammer asked.

Wisting apprised him of the situation.

'I'll get the car,' Hammer said firmly, heading for the basement stairs. 'I'll pick you up outside.'

Wisting paid a visit to his office to look up Maren Dokken's home address and found the name of the owner, a large property company with its own caretaker service. He made a note of the phone number and shrugged on his jacket.

In the corridor he bumped into Frank Kvastmo again.

'You were asking about Maren Dokken,' he said.

'Yes?'

'Her parents tried to phone me during the debrief. They're back from Singapore and are on their way here now. They've been trying to ring her but haven't been able to get hold of her at all.'

'We haven't either,' Wisting said, heading for the stairs. 'We're going there now,' he shouted back over his shoulder.

A camera team from TV2 stood outside the police station. There had been several journalists with video cameras hanging around the building in the past few days. Early this morning there had been no press presence, but now TV2 were back. Since their exclusive broadcast of Line's pictures, they were leading the media coverage and were keen to follow it up.

If it had still been raining, they would have sheltered in their vehicles and Wisting would have had no trouble reaching Hammer.

Now they were ready to pounce.

'Any news?' the reporter asked, even before the cameraman was ready.

Wisting just wanted to scurry past. It was no longer his job to answer press questions. That function had been passed to the police lawyer on duty in the prosecution section in Tønsberg. All the same, something made him stop. He waited until he was sure that the camera was ready and stated first that the police had no specific information to impart regarding Tom Kerr's whereabouts or who had helped him to escape. Then he gave an account of the large volume of tip-offs that had streamed in.

'Therefore I'd like to ask for the public's help in finding the owner of a white van that recently picked up a young woman.'

He gave the time and place, emphasizing that the circumstances were unclear, and repeated that the police were keen to make contact with both the van driver and the pedestrian.

The reporter asked a few follow-up questions about the new investigation into the murder of Taran Norum and the search for the Other One. Wisting gave a brief answer pointing out that he was unable to comment on these matters as the Kripos Cold Cases Group and Oslo Police District respectively were investigating these cases. He assured him that extensive coordination was in place, but stressed that his paramount task was to find Tom Kerr. He drew the conversation to an end with a nod of the head and rushed across to the car, where Nils Hammer was waiting.

'What did you say to them?' he asked.

Wisting brushed off the question with a wave of his hand. 'You'll have to watch the news,' he told him.

He would be criticized for the off-the-cuff interview. He had defied his superiors in the police hierarchy and followed his gut instincts as a police officer, doing what he thought was right, what they should have done the previous day.

He sat staring out of the side window. As Hammer swung out on to Storgata, Wisting caught a glimpse of his own reflection in the wing mirror and realized that something more lay behind his impulsive action. It was three days since Tom Kerr had run off. Criticism of the police was rising to a crescendo. Now he had given the media something else to chew on.

The traffic lights ahead changed to red. Hammer swore and switched on the blue flashing lights and sirens until he was on the other side.

'Take a right here,' Wisting said, pointing.

They spotted Line's car in the distance and Hammer drove up beside it. Wisting had the car door open even before the vehicle drew to a halt.

Line emerged from the apartment block. 'I've been up and rung the doorbell,' she said. 'She's not answering.'

Wisting phoned the caretaker service as he followed Line inside, explaining the situation as they climbed the stairs.

'He'll be here in about ten minutes,' he said, hanging up.

Hammer used his fists on the door, thumping three times, so hard that the adjacent walls shook. One of the residents on the floor below came out into the stairwell and stared up at them. Wisting took a couple of steps down towards her.

'We're from the police,' he said, flipping his police ID open. 'Have you seen the woman who lives here?'

'Maren?'

'Yes.'

'Not since yesterday.'

'When was that?'

'In the evening. She was on her way out.'

Hammer pounded on the door again. Wisting took another

couple of steps down the stairs. The neighbour looked about the same age as Maren Dokken.

'Did you speak to her?' he asked.

The woman shook her head. 'She was talking on her mobile.'

Line interrupted. 'When was that?'

'Some time after six o'clock,' the woman answered, after giving it some thought. 'About half past six.'

Line held her phone out to him. The log showed a call at 18.23.

'That was when I was speaking to her,' she said. 'She was going out for some fresh air.'

Wisting swallowed, unable to prevent himself from forming a theory of the very worst-case scenario. Nodding, he turned to the woman again.

'What was she wearing?'

'Wearing . . .' the woman repeated. 'I'm not sure . . .'

'Shoes,' Wisting clarified. 'Do you remember what kind of shoes she was wearing?'

The woman shook her head.

'What kind of shoes did she usually wear?' he repeated, his voice raised now. 'It's important!'

'I really don't know,' the woman repeated.

'Fuck this,' Hammer said.

Taking a step back, he raised one foot and delivered a mighty kick to the door. The frame gave at the first attempt, the door swung open and slammed against the wall inside.

'Maren!' Hammer shouted as he strode in.

Wisting remained on the landing with Line.

'What was that about her shoes?' she asked.

'Afterwards,' Wisting replied.

The apartment was not large. Hammer took no more than a minute to go through all of it.

'Not here,' he reported on his return.

Wisting crossed the threshold and lifted a sandal lying just inside the door. Size 38.

He put it down again.

The neighbour from the floor below had arrived at the door and was peering inquisitively into the apartment.

'You were asking about her shoes,' she said, holding out her phone. 'I've got this, if it's of any help.'

It was a photo, taken outside the apartment building, apparently during the summer, as the weather was fine and the leaves on the trees were green and fresh. Maren Dokken sat sideways on a bench with her legs pulled up to her chest, smiling at the camera. She was wearing a pair of grey hiking shoes with a pink pattern. Wisting recognized them at once. He had seen one of them before.

52

'What's the significance of the shoes?' Line asked.

Her father looked at her, then across to the woman from the floor below, and back again. His eyes were serious and worried.

'A shoe was found in the ditch at the side of the old Stavern road yesterday,' he said. 'A shoe identical to that. It was reported that a woman had been dragged into a van there.'

Line took a step back. It took a while for her to digest what he had said, and a feeling of horror surged inside her, making her feel dizzy. She had to take a few deep breaths to collect her thoughts.

'Tom Kerr?' she asked.

'Most likely,' her father agreed.

Descriptions of what the other victims had suffered whirled through Line's head. She gulped, squeezed her eyes tightly shut a couple of times and struggled to focus on something else.

The camera, it came to her. She had her camera down in her car. She should get it and document what was happening. All the same, she stood rooted to the spot, almost shocked by the cynical idea.

A phone rang – her father's. He took the call and gave a short, professional answer without taking his eyes off her. The expression in them had changed and they were now resolute, determined.

Line turned on her heel and took the stairs with increasing speed. Throwing open the door, she rushed to her car and took out her camera. It was not a matter of being cynical, she told herself, but of having something to hide behind: a role and function that allowed her to distance herself from the case in hand.

An electronic bleep indicated that the camera was ready. She aimed the lens at the apartment building, filming the entrance before locating the windows of Maren's apartment on the third floor. She could make out a shadow up there but could not tell whether it was her father or Hammer.

Her mobile rang. The sound could be edited out, she thought as she held the camera steady for another couple of seconds before she fished out her phone.

It was Adrian Stiller. She lowered the camera and answered.

'It's OK with us,' he said. 'I can have a chat with your father, but I'm sure it'll work out.'

Line had no idea what he meant.

'For a camera to follow the investigation,' Stiller explained. 'I've cleared it with the top brass here at Kripos, and I'll just have to have a word with your father.'

Line glanced up at the window on the third floor. 'Haven't you spoken to him?' she asked.

'Not yet.'

'About Maren Dokken, I mean.'

'What about her?'

'Tom Kerr has abducted her,' Line said. 'Dragged her into a van.'

She had to explain the little she knew one more time.

'When did this happen?'

'Yesterday evening. I spoke to her just before half past six. She was going out for a walk.'

Stiller cursed. 'The log,' he said, muttering something.

'What do you mean?' Line asked. 'What log?'

'I'll have to call you back,' Stiller said, and rang off before Line had a chance to say anything else.

53

It was Stemstad calling, the police lawyer from the previous evening. She was back on duty. Guro was her name, not Gro or Gunn. Her voice was sharp.

'What on earth is this?' she demanded. 'TV2 say that you've issued a statement.'

Wisting interrupted her. 'It's Maren,' he said, nudging the sandal on the floor with the toe of his shoe. 'Maren Dokken. He's taken her.'

'Who is Maren?'

Wisting had to explain. Anxiety churned unpleasantly inside him as he spoke. 'That's the explanation,' he said. 'That's why Tom Kerr came back here to strike again. He's taken one of us.'

Silence reigned at the other end of the phone. Wisting calculated the time that had passed. More than twelve hours – almost fourteen, in fact – had elapsed.

'We had no way to anticipate that,' the police lawyer replied. 'We did what we could.'

Wisting did not enter into discussion about what they could have done. They had to look ahead now.

'Get a statement out,' he said. 'An all-points bulletin, to all media.'

The police lawyer had nothing more to say. Wisting hung up and phoned Frank Kvastmo to bring him up to speed, speaking in short sentences about what they feared had happened.

'Her parents will be here at any minute,' Kvastmo said.

Wisting crossed to the window and peered down at the area in front of the apartment building where Line was standing with her camera.

'Can you see to that?' he asked. 'They'll have to be told before we go public with it.'

'I'll call them straight away,' he agreed, and disconnected the call.

Hammer was in the middle of another phone conversation. Wisting understood that he was organizing surveillance of Maren Dokken's mobile phone.

His own phone rang again, the Police Chief this time. The police lawyer must have informed her of the situation.

'How certain are you?' she asked.

'We're certain that Maren Dokken is missing,' he answered. 'Everything else is uncertain.'

'What personnel do you need? Resources?'

'Everything available,' Wisting replied. 'We have to make a monumental effort, and we don't have much time. All vehicles that fit the description will have to be traced. We'll have to check all vehicles that have passed through the toll stations, and all the speed cameras. All CCTV footage. It's going to demand a colossal input of manpower, and when this is made public we'll be flooded with tip-offs.'

'I'll make sure that everything else is set aside,' the Police Chief said. 'No one will work on anything other than this.'

Wisting heard another incoming call. 'Thanks,' he said. 'I'll get things moving at this end.'

'Just one thing,' the Police Chief added. 'You need to keep away from the press. Internal Affairs are investigating a possible charge of misconduct with regard to Tom Kerr's escape. It's under continual review whether you should have anything to do with the case at all.'

Wisting felt a prick of irritation. He had nothing against

avoiding contact with journalists, but the decision was tainted with mistrust. It was an indication that the media were correct in insinuating that what had happened was his responsibility. His fault.

'Fine,' was all he said, however. He rang off and answered the queued call, from Stiller.

'I should have been told about this yesterday,' he complained.

'You've heard about it already?' Wisting asked.

Stiller confirmed this. 'I may have something for you,' he said.

'What's that?'

'The surveillance log from Floyd Thue. At 23.34 last night, a Polish-registered grey Ford Transit Connect arrived at his house. It parked up for a moment before the garage doors were raised. Then it drove in and the doors came down. Five minutes later it drove off again.'

'Who was driving the car?'

'Difficult to see. A man. I'm waiting for a response from Poland with regard to the owner.'

'We need to go into that house,' Wisting decided.

'The grounds are a bit flimsy for a search,' Stiller objected.

'We need to go in,' Wisting insisted.

54

Hammer drove. Wisting sat in the passenger seat studying the pictures that Stiller had sent him. He had imagined that two detectives had been sitting in an unmarked car monitoring Floyd Thue's house, but the surveillance was electronic. Two police officers dressed as electricity workers had climbed up the nearest streetlights and fitted cameras. From an office in the Kripos building in Oslo, they could sit and control them, zooming in, panning out and tilting the cameras up or down. All the footage was saved, but each time a movement was registered it was also automatically captured as a still image.

The placement of the cameras meant they had a wide view of the house frontage, but the slanted angle made it impossible to see who was seated in the car.

A picture showed the vehicle on its way into the large garage underneath the house. Wisting used two fingers to zoom in on the small screen. He saw a pair of legs, as if Floyd Thue was standing inside, waiting.

In the next photograph, the driver had stepped out. The slanted angle meant that the camera took a picture only from the waist down, but it was obviously a man. The next three images showed the man skirting around the vehicle, as if to open the side door. In the last photo the doors were on their way down.

The picture was snatched away from the screen when the phone rang. This time the call was from the prosecution office. A different police lawyer this time, a different name.

Wisting had pleaded his case as soon as they had set off,

requesting permission to search the house. He had been told that the application would be considered.

'The conditions required for a search warrant have not been fulfilled,' he was told.

Wisting had been aware of that. That Floyd Thue had a connection to Tom Kerr, and that a delivery van had been spotted at his home, was insufficient to charge him with the abduction of Maren Dokken, but Wisting had hoped that the lawyers might be willing to stretch the rules for once. Now it would be up to him and Hammer.

They were approaching the house. Wisting knew the way and gave Hammer directions into the cul-de-sac. As the gate was open, they drove up and parked the car in the same place as on Wisting's previous visit.

'What do we do?' Hammer asked.

'Go in,' Wisting replied.

He marched up to the house and rang the doorbell. No reaction from inside. He was about to ring again when his mobile sounded. It was Adrian Stiller.

'There was a movement at the window when you arrived,' he said.

Wisting turned round and gazed up at the streetlights but was unable to spot any cameras. 'Are you sitting watching us?' he asked.

'Window 2-2,' Stiller added.

Wisting wheeled round again and took a step back. This was a military description that meant the upper floor, second window from the left. The curtains were drawn.

'He's only been out of the house to go to the mailbox and to accept food deliveries,' Stiller continued. 'He's still inside, unless he's sneaked out by the back door.'

Hammer rang the doorbell again. The sound of the chime inside reached as far as the front steps.

'Any news of the Polish vehicle?' Wisting asked.

'Registered to a Polish woman from Warsaw,' Stiller answered. 'They're making further inquiries.'

'Excellent,' Wisting replied. 'Thanks for the info.'

He dismissed the call and walked down the steps. A sign from a private security firm warned that the house was equipped with an alarm and that CCTV was installed. He could see no cameras but had no doubt that they existed. Floyd Thue was probably sitting at a desk watching on one of his computer screens.

'We'll go round the back,' he said.

A paved path ran round to the rear of the house. The luxuriant garden was well tended, with no weeds in sight and ramrod-straight edges between the lawn and flowerbeds. Three broad steps led up to a terrace of slate tiles and a substantial set of cast-iron outdoor furniture.

Wisting moved forward to the window and found a gap in the curtains. He peered into the room where they had met Floyd Thue. The room was in darkness, and all the computer screens were black.

Hammer whistled and waved to Wisting, pointing down to the basement wall on their left, where two rectangular windows were both fitted with metal bars.

'It's not long since those were installed,' Hammer commented.

Wisting descended from the terrace towards the flowerbed bordering the house. Hammer was right. Notches had been cut in the old basement wall and four steel bars had been fitted. The plaster around the brackets looked relatively new, maybe a year old.

He crouched down beside a bush to look inside. He could only see parts of an unfurnished room illuminated by a harsh, bright light. The walls were beige and completely bare and the floor was a darker colour. Directly across from the window he could see a grey door, without a handle, but with an inspection hatch on it. Like in a prison cell.

Hammer walked across to the other window. 'Bloody hell, there's someone lying down there,' he said.

A twig snapped as Wisting tramped on a bush. Hammer made room for him so that he could see. Someone in hospital-type pyjamas was lying on a padded bench, a strap wrapped around each ankle. Immediately above the knees, another strap was fastened. Wisting put his head close to the metal bars, but it was impossible to see the rest of the body from their position. It was also difficult to make out the sex and age of the body, or even whether the person was alive or dead.

Hammer was first to reach the terrace. He grabbed the door handle and shook it ferociously before banging the palm of his hand on the windowpane. The glass shook and vibrated, but no one appeared on the inside.

Wisting grabbed one of the garden chairs. The iron scraped and left tracks on the slate tiles as he dragged the chair behind him. He lifted it and, after a confirmatory nod from Hammer, smacked the legs against the glass door in one swift and sudden movement. He waited for an alarm to wail, but all that could be heard was the tinkling sound of shattering glass.

'Police!' Hammer shouted as he charged in.

Wisting followed close behind, into the next room and on into the hallway he had entered the last time he had been here. A staircase led down to the basement.

'Police!' Hammer called out again.

They followed a corridor and located the steel door. 'Locked,' Wisting said.

There was a loud bang as he slid the bolt on the inspection hatch. The strong stench of urine was immediately apparent.

The figure on the bench raised its head.

'It's him!' Wisting exclaimed, shouting his name: 'Floyd Thue!'

The head fell back again. Wisting began to suspect what was going on. 'Is everything all right, Thue?'

The answer was faint: 'Yes.'

'Do you know where the key is?'

No response. Wisting turned to face Hammer. 'Two-two,' he said, heading at top speed back to the stairs and to the upper floor.

He soon got his bearings and found the room where Stiller had spotted some movement. A woman backed away from the door when it burst open.

'We're from the police,' Wisting reassured her. 'Who are you?'

She looked hesitant but did not answer. Wisting checked that she was alone. The room resembled a hotel bedroom, with a TV and a small sitting area. He opened the door into an en suite bathroom. Empty.

'What's your name?' he asked her again.

'Regina,' she replied. 'Regina Babinski.'

In her mid-twenties, she was thin, had long black hair and wore a dressing gown. Her name could probably be found in a police report somewhere about sex workers.

'Polish?' he asked. 'Do you speak Norwegian?'

The woman nodded twice.

'What's going on here?' Hammer demanded.

'He wants this,' the woman replied. 'For twenty-four hours. I just look in on him, once every four hours.'

'Do you have a key?'

She glanced towards a little table by the door and they saw the key on it. Hammer grabbed it.

'When did you come here?' Wisting asked.

'Last night,' the woman stammered.

'How did you get here?'

She looked as if she did not understand.

'Who drove you here?'

'A friend.'

They persuaded the Polish woman to tell them how she had been driven there in a van and dropped off in the garage.

'Have you been here before? Done the same thing?'

She nodded.

'Does he pay you for this?' Hammer asked.

When the woman nodded again, Hammer shook his head in consternation.

'Stay here!' he said, pointing his finger at her.

They descended the stairs again.

'What kind of sick set-up is this?' Hammer mumbled.

Wisting repeated his previous conversation with Thue. About how being tied up had to be the optimal freedom. When you were unable to make any choices, and had no responsibility – all you could do was lie there, completely at the mercy of others.

Hammer grunted as he inserted the key in the lock and turned it round.

Floyd Thue raised his head as they entered. Hammer stepped forward and Wisting stood at the door.

'Leave me alone,' Thue said.

Hammer loosened the strap around one of his hands.

'We have to talk,' he said, unfastening some of the other straps. 'You have no choice.'

'Nothing illegal is going on here,' Thue assured them. 'Everything is voluntary. On both sides, her and me.'

Hammer undid the rest of the straps. 'Sit up!' he ordered.

Floyd Thue did as he was asked and sat on the bench with

his legs dangling. The thin pyjamas were soaked in urine that had begun to dry out.

'You don't understand,' he said, shaking his head. 'This is about meditation. Finding nothingness. Reaching the deeper layers of consciousness.'

'That's fine,' Hammer said. 'We're trying to find Tom Kerr. You're the person who has spoken most to him in the recent past. Have you any idea where he is?'

He placed his index finger on Thue's forehead. 'Somewhere deep down inside there?'

Floyd Thue twisted his head away. 'You're going to regret this,' he said, his voice bitter.

'The faster you tell us what we're looking for, the faster you can go back to your own business,' Hammer told him.

Thue directed his gaze at Wisting. 'I've already told you what I know about Kerr,' he said. 'We didn't have conversations of that nature. If his farm hadn't been burnt down, then he would probably have gone there. He had ideas of rebuilding it. But now I don't know. I think he'll just be enjoying his freedom.'

'In what way?'

'In the great outdoors.'

'Where?'

'On a high mountaintop or deep inside a dark forest. Far away from people.'

Wisting took a step towards him. 'Is that something you've talked about?'

Floyd Thue began to massage one of his wrists. 'To some degree,' he answered. 'Many of the conversations in prison are about the inmates wanting to be in a completely different place. Out in the open, for example.'

'Any particular mountain or forest?'

'No.'

'That doesn't help us much,' Hammer broke in.

'Sorry,' Thue said, swallowing loudly. 'I've told you before. I can't help you.'

Hammer put the keys for the home-made isolation cell down on the bench. 'You'll have to get hold of a glazier,' he said. 'Your terrace door is smashed.'

Thue nodded, without protest. Wisting had already left the room. They had wasted enough time.

55

A name Wisting had not seen for years popped up on his mobile screen. Holger Midthun. He had been the local policeman in Revetal before the reorganization, when his office had been closed down, but the number was still stored on his phone.

He pulled into the right lane and answered the call. As the retired officer introduced himself, the conversation was relayed over the loudspeakers in the car and Wisting let him know that Hammer was also listening in.

'I'll be brief,' Midthun said. 'You've probably got enough on your plate, but I've got something that might be of interest to you. People up here still get in touch with me if there's something going on.'

'Tell us about it.'

'I just received a phone call from a man who'd heard you were on the lookout for a white van. He was able to tell me about a sighting that might well fit, time wise.'

Wisting's interest grew. The former policeman explained that there was an old, disused welding workshop in the vicinity. About ten-thirty the previous night, a van of that description had turned up there. It had been driven into the workshop and the doors closed behind it. The witness lived further down the road but had been out fishing and was on his way home on foot.

'The workshop is fairly isolated, but the residents in the area are a bit more than normally observant. Things have happened before in that neck of the woods. Stripping cars for parts, that sort of thing. Two years ago, smuggled booze was stored in there.'

Wisting waited for him to continue.

'The workshop is at the end of a cul-de-sac,' Midthun explained. 'Just over an hour later, another car drove down the road. The witness saw it from his living-room window this time. He thought it must have come from the workshop.'

'So the van is still inside?'

'I don't know, but I was thinking of going up there to take a look.'

Wisting and Hammer exchanged glances, and Hammer nodded.

'We're not far away ourselves,' he said. 'We can meet you there in half an hour.'

'Then I'll wait,' Midthun replied.

He gave directions before disconnecting the call. Twenty minutes later they were parking outside the abandoned workshop, an ugly brick building with a flat roof situated beside a blasted rock face. Weeds grew wild along the walls and in the gravel yard.

A four-wheel-drive Subaru was parked at an angle in front of a shed that had been used as a store. The retired policeman stepped out. His paunch was larger and his beard thicker since they had last met.

All three shook hands. 'Any news of the missing girl?' Midthun asked.

'She's a colleague of ours,' Wisting told him, and went on to explain what had happened.

'Any leads?' Midthun asked, clearly shaken.

'Unfortunately, we've got nothing,' Wisting said. 'Her mobile has been traced, but it was switched off yesterday, about the same time and place as the abduction.'

Hammer moved towards the deserted workshop. 'Who owns the building?' he asked.

'An old acquaintance of mine,' the retired policeman replied. 'Peter Haugland. He ran a car workshop here, but it closed down nearly five years ago, just before I stepped down. We caught him with stolen cars. Since then it's really just been left empty. About two years ago he was arrested again, this time with 80,000 litres of smuggled liquor. He's in prison now.'

They approached the grey building. The windows in the double doors were blacked out.

'It's locked,' Midthun clarified. 'It's not possible to see in anywhere.'

'Can we get in somehow?'

Holger Midthun nodded. 'We dealt with a complaint while the former owner was running a welding workshop here,' he began. 'A few youngsters had gained access through the canteen window at the back. They had bored holes in the window frame, all the way through, at the top of the window, and used a steel wire to lift the handle inside. I went round and had a look. The hole's still there.'

They followed Midthun to the rear of the building. The window was not darkened like the ones that overlooked the workshop, and they could see a table inside with six upturned chairs stacked on top. Along one wall there was a kitchen worktop with a filter coffee machine, and a fridge stood in one corner.

The hole in the window frame was large enough to insert a ballpoint pen. Some insulation material and a wooden plug lay on the floor. The hole had obviously been re-plugged, and the retired policeman must have poked it out before they arrived.

'I brought this with me,' he said, taking out a long steel wire with a loop at one end.

Hammer grinned.

'It might be best if I do it,' Midthun suggested. 'Then you won't land in trouble.'

He threaded the steel wire through the hole and down on the inside of the window. After a couple of attempts, he succeeded in drawing the loop over the handle. He pulled the steel wire and released the catch and the window tilted open.

'Almost there,' Midthun commented.

Using an iron bar that he had probably found lying somewhere close by, he slipped it into the opening and used the bar to lift the security catch.

'There you go,' he said.

Hammer climbed in first and passed out a chair for the other two to stand on. Wisting clambered in next, while Holger Midthun returned to his car to fetch a flashlight.

'The electricity is cut off,' he explained.

The canteen door opened out directly into the workshop. It was virtually empty, with only a few car tyres piled up, one on top of the other.

The retired policeman was obviously disappointed.

'Wait a minute,' Hammer said, pointing. 'A paint shop.'

Further inside, against the back wall, there was an enormous container with ventilation pipes leading up through the roof and double doors closed with a padlock.

Hammer found an iron pipe and used it on the lock. Initially, it refused to budge, but after a few more strikes the shackle broke. Taking hold of one of the double doors, Wisting tugged at it and was immediately aware of the strong chemical smell of paint. When he opened the door wide, Midthun aimed the beam of light inside, and there it was: a white delivery van.

Wisting found a pair of latex gloves in his pocket. He pulled them on and stepped into the paint-shop container.

Midthun followed him with the flashlight. The cabin windows seemed to be covered on the inside.

He tried the driver's door and found it unlocked. Once it was open, it took him a few seconds to fathom what had happened. The entire cab area was coated in a layer of grey paint. A spray-paint gun was lying on the seat, and a coupling and several other parts lay on the floor beside the pedals.

Wisting had experience of cases in which fire extinguishers had been used to remove evidence in getaway vehicles after a robbery or another serious crime in which the perpetrators were reluctant to draw attention in the way that setting the vehicle alight would do. This was a more advanced approach. The tiny nozzle on the spray gun ensured that the fine spray of paint would achieve total coverage and leave a coating to make it almost impossible to find fingerprints or DNA traces.

'There's a compressor and a diesel generator out in the workshop,' Midthun told him.

They skirted around the van and he cautiously slid the side door open, unsure of what he would find.

The cargo space was empty, but it too was completely covered in paint.

The garage doors clattered behind them. Hammer had opened them from inside, and now daylight flooded in.

'I think this is the van we've been looking for,' Wisting said. 'We need to call out the technicians.'

56

There was nothing along the road to say how the attack on Maren had occurred.

Line held her camera low, directly above the white line, and filmed as a car drove past. Her body was tense, filled with anxiety. She had no other way to deal with it apart from keeping herself occupied and doing something practical.

She sat down again in the driver's seat and placed her camera on the passenger seat beside her. Her phone buzzed. A text message from Sofie, offering to pick up the children from nursery and keep the girls at her house.

Line thanked her with an emoji heart and then turned her car. The address was already stored in her GPS and it had been on her to-do list for a while now. She wanted to visit the place where Tom Kerr had held his victims captive: his smallholding in Østmarka.

It was a relatively long drive, into Oslo, through the city and out into the forested area beyond, but she would be home again in good time for Amalie's bedtime.

On the road she caught two news broadcasts on the radio. In the first she heard that the police were keen for the driver of a white delivery van and his female passenger to get in touch. The next one stated that a twenty-seven-year-old woman had been reported missing, and linked this to a witness account of a woman being picked up by a van driver the previous evening.

She drove past the turn-off twice. It was nothing but a gravel track with grass growing in the middle and dense vegetation along the verges. After a few hundred metres, the track divided in two, with the one on the right closed off by a steel wire secured to two trees. A sign was attached to the wire: *Private*.

Line took out her camera, filmed the sign and the track that continued on in between the trees.

As the wire was held with a simple carabiner hook, Line unhitched it and laid it down at the side of the track. Then she drove a couple of metres along the track, hopped out of the car and reattached the wire.

The track ahead was no more than two wheel ruts. The grass in the middle was higher here, but in some places it was flat, as if a car had driven down here not so long ago.

Before she had left home, she had entertained the idea that Tom Kerr might have come back here, but she had dismissed the notion. There was nothing to come back to. It was more likely that someone had been here on a mission similar to hers, a journalist keen to recount his story, or someone simply being nosy. All the same, she locked her car doors.

She drove over the cattle grid that had been removed in the past, hindering the fire brigade from accessing the blaze at the time when the farm had gone up in flames. She stopped and left the car again to do more filming.

Two hundred metres further on, the forest opened out into a clearing. Line had gained the impression that the entire smallholding had burned down, but two small buildings were still standing. One was a red-painted annexe, directly behind where the farmhouse had been situated, the other an outhouse on the fringes of the forest.

The place was completely derelict and the sky above the trees was dark and gloomy. Heavy, plump clouds, tinged a deep grey-blue, would look suitably atmospheric on film.

The door locks sprang open when she touched the handle, and she took out her camera as she stood surveying the scene. A car had been here recently. The yard between the ruins left by the fire had been covered in gravel, but the entire expanse was being reclaimed by nature. There were puddles of rainwater and tyre tracks left by a vehicle.

A rough, bare-brick chimney was all that remained of the farmhouse. Charred beams and shattered roof tiles lay inside the perimeter of the foundation walls. Nettles and other weeds had sprouted all over it, and a few trees that had taken root in the ruins had now grown to a height of a metre or so. An overgrown bush with white flowers was twined around the few remnants of the framework in the far corner.

The barn was equally devastated. A rusty, burnt-out tractor stood inside it, with only the metal threads of the steel cables left of the large rubber tyres.

One part of the barn was equipped with a cellar, and Line moved up to the edge of it to look down. Two black birds took off and flew away.

A variety of plants had taken root in the ashes and a broad-leaved bush climbed up the brick wall. An opening in the wall led out to the back, where there had once been a door. Line skirted around it to the rear of the barn. She had to negotiate her way through a thorny thicket and cover her head with her arms to avoid being scratched.

She walked through the cellar and into an adjacent, smaller room, where she saw a bathtub in the middle of the floor, with no plumbing attached. It was the old type, the kind sometimes used on farms to hold water for horses or cows. In several places, patches of enamel had flaked off, and it was full of withered leaves.

Beside the wall a steel worktop was blackened with soot and chains hung from a number of hooks. In the corner she saw an upturned chair with four tubular metal legs but no seat or back.

Line stepped back and an involuntary shiver ran through her body when she realized that this could be the room in which Tom Kerr had dismembered and steeped his victims in chlorine before burying them in the woods. For a while she stood paralysed before she managed to raise her camera and take some film. She shot from several angles before going up again and filming down through the opening in the floor.

She decided she needed some overview pictures too and drove the car away to make sure it was not caught in her film. She parked on the track with the bonnet pointing forward, ready to drive home.

Viewing this place had a powerful effect on her. It brought her up close and gave her the intimacy she hoped to convey in her film.

She manually adjusted the aperture to obtain greater depth of field. The dark clouds and the dense forest in the background of this deserted place reinforced the bleak impression.

On the right-hand side of the barn's imprint she could see a trail through the tall grass that was now, from a distance, easier to discern. She doubted whether animals had made it. There was a distinct track leading to the outhouse, as if someone had walked repeatedly to and fro.

She lifted her camera and zoomed in on the outhouse. The timber was grey and weather-beaten and on the side facing her there was a lattice window and a door that looked barred and bolted.

A gust of wind soughed through the trees, making the leaves rustle. Line shivered. She was lightly dressed in only a sweater and jeans and, though she had a jacket in the car, she had not thought to bring it with her. Walking up to the fire-damaged ruins again, she followed the trail of around thirty metres back to the outhouse.

One of the small panes of glass was broken. She peered in, but it was difficult to make out anything in the darkness. Resolutely, she pulled back the bolt on the door and heard the hinges protest as she opened it wide.

The outhouse was piled high with old beehives and bee-keeping equipment and the floorboards creaked as she moved inside. Dust swirled up and the air she sniffed was dry and stuffy.

She looked around for signs that might tell her why some-one had been here, but as she could see nothing she turned to step outside again.

Right inside the door a spade was propped up, with crumbs of earth on the floor in front of it. She carried it with her out into the light and realized it could not be long since it had been used, as dark, damp earth still clung to the blade.

Line felt her chest tighten. The path she had followed ran on alongside the outhouse and into the forest, towards the place where the bodies of Thea Polden and Salwa Haddad had been unearthed.

57

This did not bode well. The Police Chief's secretary had phoned to tell him, and Hammer, to attend a meeting in her office. Being summoned in this way only ever meant bad news. Wisting had been given a dressing-down a couple of times before, including the last time that Terje Nordbo and Internal Affairs had placed him under investigation. On that occasion he had been informed that he was suspended from duty.

They drove from the workshop as soon as the crime scene technicians had arrived to take over. Hammer had discovered that the white van was registered to a building firm in Asker.

'The plates have been reported stolen,' he said, without looking up from his phone.

'Stolen and attached to a similar vehicle,' Wisting commented.

Hammer agreed. 'The same happened when Thea Polden and Salwa Haddad were abducted.'

Wisting turned into the town centre streets of Tønsberg. A few journalists were hovering outside the main entrance of the large police station.

Hammer swore under his breath. 'We haven't got time for this,' he said.

Wisting was of the same opinion, but didn't say anything. The van and workshop could represent the breakthrough they had been waiting for. There were several balls to start rolling, and in all honesty they had no time to lose.

None of the reserved parking places outside the police

station was vacant and he was forced to park a block away. A couple of photographers took pictures as they entered.

Immediately inside the doors, no expense had been spared on furnishing a room where the police could meet the press, including specially installed fibre-optic cables for TV transmissions, suitable lighting and a back wall emblazoned with the police logo. The door stood open and glasses and carafes of water were laid out.

The lift took them to the top floor and the receptionist stood up when they arrived.

'Kiil is expecting you,' she said, moving towards the door, where she knocked, opened it and then ushered them inside.

They each took a seat.

'You've found the van, I hear,' the Police Chief said, motioning in the direction of the computer screen.

'Most likely,' Wisting answered. 'We've just come from there.'

Nodding, the Police Chief changed the subject. 'We've found it necessary to make some changes in the organization of work,' she said. 'It's less than helpful, having an investigation led from a number of directions.'

Wisting agreed, appreciating what she meant. A total of five different investigation teams were involved in these intersecting cases and, in addition, Adrian Stiller and the Cold Cases Group at Kripos still retained an interest.

'The most pressing aspect is Maren Dokken, though,' Hammer pointed out.

'I've discussed the case with the other chiefs and public prosecutors in the relevant districts,' she continued. 'We've agreed that the work needs to be coordinated in a different, more effective fashion. Therefore we've decided to create a separate investigation group, cutting across the various districts.'

She fixed her eyes on Wisting. 'It would be customary to appoint you to lead and coordinate the work but, unfortunately, you're currently under investigation by Internal Affairs.'

'That's just a formality, surely,' Hammer broke in.

'Unfortunately, another issue has cropped up too,' the Police Chief added. 'A lawyer called Henden has been in touch in connection with a complaint by Floyd Thue. It concerns unwarranted access to his house, in addition to misconduct.'

'The measures taken were completely warranted,' Hammer protested, launching into an explanation.

The Police Chief cut him off.

'He has sent us footage from his CCTV system,' she said. 'It's entirely possible that you acted in good faith, but breaking a window to gain access seems somewhat precipitate. Anyway, the complaint has been sent to Internal Affairs and it will be up to them to judge whether your actions were reprehensible.'

Hammer groaned. Wisting sat forward, perching on the edge of his chair.

'Who will lead the investigation?' he asked.

'Idar Semmelmann,' the Police Chief replied.

'Semmelmann?' Hammer repeated. 'He's been searching for the accomplice for five years now. To no avail. All he's achieved are forms and databases.'

'He's the one who knows the case best,' the Police Chief said firmly. 'He's been involved from the very start.'

'Has he been informed?' Wisting asked.

The Police Chief nodded. 'I said I would let you know.'

Shuffling some papers on her desk, she glanced at the clock. 'The prosecutor responsible on our side will be Guro Stemstad,' she went on. 'I'll announce the reorganization at a press conference in thirty minutes, at the same time as we announce that the missing woman is Police Constable Maren Dokken.'

'What will we do now?' Hammer asked. 'Where do we fit into this reorganization?'

'You are both relieved of your duties,' the Police Chief said.

'What do you mean? That we've been taken off the case?'

Agnes Kiil placed one hand on top of the other. 'A problem of impartiality has come up,' she answered. 'In addition to you both being under investigation by Internal Affairs, you're both emotionally involved. The actions you took at Floyd Thue's residence clearly demonstrate that. It's especially important that the rules of criminal procedure are followed to the letter when it applies to one of our own.'

Hammer stood up. 'You mean that we have to sit on our hands while one of our colleagues has been abducted?'

'You're relieved of duty on this case,' she repeated. 'You've worked a great deal of overtime in the last few days. I suggest you take some time off, with effect from today.'

Wisting also rose from his seat. Inside, a tumult of thoughts and emotions was raging and he had to get a strong grip on himself to avoid betraying his feelings.

'Was that all?' he asked. The Police Chief gave him a brief nod.

58

Several journalists had arrived outside the police station and stood huddled in small groups, chatting, anticipating being let in at any moment. A man with a TV2 logo on his jacket elevated his camera and pointed it at them. One of the reporters standing nearest the door addressed himself to Wisting, asking if there had been any developments.

'There's a press conference at 4 p.m.,' Wisting replied, transferring all his attention to his mobile phone.

He had missed two calls while they were meeting the Police Chief. Both were from Line. He returned her call as soon as they were out of earshot.

'I'm at Lerketvedt,' Line told him. 'Tom Kerr's smallholding in Østmarka.'

Wisting immediately felt a sense of disquiet. 'What on earth are you doing there?'

'Filming,' she replied. 'Mainly doing a recce and some research for my documentary.'

They had reached the car by now.

'Someone else has been here recently,' Line went on.

Wisting clambered into the driver's seat. 'Oh?' he said.

'It's a bit . . . suspicious,' Line added. 'Someone's been digging out here.'

'Digging?'

'The spade was in the shed,' Line explained. 'There's mud on it. I followed a track into the trees at the back and found a spot some distance into the woods. It's covered over with twigs and brash, but it looks like someone's buried something there.'

'Are you sure?'

'I can send you a photo.'

'Do that,' Wisting replied as he started the car.

'I phoned Stiller when you didn't answer,' Line added. The conversation had now switched to hands-free. 'He's on his way here.'

His thoughts were racing. He had been removed from the case, but this was an offshoot of the investigation and also concerned his daughter. No one could deny him the chance to help her.

'Hammer and I are on our way too,' he said as he shifted into gear.

59

The engine was ticking loudly after the strain of the fast journey and the heat made the bonnet vibrate.

Wisting jumped out and rushed towards Line and Stiller, who were waiting beside the ruins of the barn.

'Should you actually be here?' Stiller asked. He had obviously been informed of the restructuring of the investigation team.

'We're taking time off,' Hammer replied.

'It's OK with me,' Stiller said, shrugging. 'Kiil's not my Chief of Police.'

'Have you spoken to Semmelmann?' Wisting inquired.

'I've tried to phone him. He's not answering.'

'The press conference probably hasn't finished yet,' Hammer told him.

Opening the boot of his car, Stiller took out two spades and handed one to Hammer.

'We should've had a technician with us, or at least someone who could document what we're doing,' Wisting pointed out.

'Line can do that,' Stiller suggested. 'She's worked for us before.'

After he had brought a tarpaulin, gloves and white overalls from the car, they followed Line as she led them off into the woods.

The long grass was well trodden. Once grazing land, it was all now overgrown and the forest was slowly making inroads, creeping in at the edges. Wisting brought up the rear. There was a distinct trail, as Line had said. He did not know how many times she had walked back and forth, but it was clear that a path was being formed between the trees.

Line led them about two hundred metres in, to a marshy area. They followed a stream for the last thirty metres, all the way to a backwater.

The grave was easier to see in reality than it had been in the photograph. Three of the branches covering it had been lifted off. The top layer of turf had been dug up in a chequerboard pattern and then replaced. The leftover earth had probably been tossed into the stream. In a few weeks' time, it would barely be possible to see that there had been anything here.

'Was this the spot where the others were found?' Hammer asked.

Stiller shook his head. 'No, that was further in, but otherwise very similar. Soft earth with no roots or any other obstacles. A blanket of twigs.'

Line was busy with her camera as Hammer and Stiller pulled on protective suits and gloves. No one spoke as they set to work. The remaining twigs were lifted off and heaped up. Then they started to dig. First the turf squares, then the loose soil.

About half a metre down, they caught sight of something, and Stiller gave the order to stop. Hammer drew the back of his hand over his forehead to wipe away the perspiration, and Line moved in closer with her camera.

'Black plastic bag,' Stiller noted.

He brought out the tarpaulin that Wisting had carried, a thick, white plastic sheet measuring two square metres. He unfolded it on the ground beside the hole.

Earth rained down from the sides as he lifted the bag and deposited it in the middle of the plastic sheet. Wisting managed to make out that there was more black plastic down in the pit. Glancing across at Line, he gazed straight into the camera lens and wished her a hundred miles away. They all knew what they were about to find, and he fervently wished she were not here to see it.

The bag was tied with a simple knot and barely a quarter full.

'We need a knife,' Hammer said.

No one had anything they could use to cut the bag open. In the end, Stiller used his car key to tear the plastic and his fingers to pull it apart.

Hammer swore. Wisting moved closer and saw what was inside: a leg and a foot.

60

'Right,' Adrian Stiller said, straightening up. 'We need to let the crime scene technicians take over now.'

'You'll have to let Semmelmann know too,' Hammer said.

Line held the camera steady. Pale toes protruded from the opening in the black bag. A grey earthworm wriggled over the tarpaulin. She waited until it was out of the picture and zoomed in until the tear in the plastic filled the whole shot.

Stiller drew back and began to speak into his mobile. Line tilted her head to one side of the camera to see without her view being filtered through the lens.

She saw the foot and parts of the leg. The florid skin was covered in pale blisters. However, what struck her was the size of the foot. It was long and broad.

'It's a man?' she said, a hesitant question in her voice.

Her father nodded. As Line moved to find a different angle a whiff of chlorine made her nostrils flare.

'He hasn't been here long,' Hammer commented. 'No more than twenty-four hours. Those are caustic burns, not decomposition.'

'But who is it?' Line asked.

Her father opened his mouth to answer but decided against it, as if reluctant to share his thoughts with her or in front of the camera.

'It can only be one of two people,' Hammer insisted. 'Either Tom Kerr or his accomplice.'

Line lowered the camera, struggling to imagine what had happened. How it all fitted together.

'You mean one of them has killed the other?' she asked.

Hammer agreed. 'Well, that's the most likely explanation, in my humble opinion.'

Stiller's phone conversation had ended. 'The technicians will be here in an hour,' he said. 'There's probably a head somewhere down there as well. Hands with fingerprints too. We should have an answer as to the identity by this evening.'

Line checked her battery capacity. Just over an hour left, and she had another fully charged battery pack in her car.

However, she still felt confused. Had Tom Kerr murdered his accomplice, the person who had helped him to escape, or had his accomplice taken Kerr's life?

'It's Tom Kerr,' Wisting said, gesturing towards the hole in the ground. 'That's the only plausible explanation.'

Line pointed the camera at him. 'Why do you say that?' she asked.

Her father refused to elaborate. Line tried to follow the same line of reasoning. Tom Kerr was the only person who could expose the Other One. Kerr had indicated that he was willing to make a confession, to put all his cards on the table in the hope of avoiding a lifetime in custody. It had probably been a ruse. An impression he wanted to give in order to create an opportunity to escape. But the police knew his identity. The likelihood was strong that he would be recaptured sooner or later. Would he then remain silent about the identity of his accomplice, or would he spill the beans so that he would receive a reduced sentence? As long as Tom Kerr was alive, he would pose a risk to his sidekick.

She was unable to make all her thoughts stack up, but the most significant aspect at present, as far as she was concerned, was that the body they had found did not belong to Maren Dokken.

Her father walked to the edge of the hole they had dug and hunkered down, resting his elbows on his knees and folding his hands. He stayed like that for some time before turning his head up to the other two policemen.

'How deep is it likely to be?' he asked.

'Why do you ask?' Stiller replied.

'I'm wondering how many bags are lying down there,' Wisting answered, getting to his feet. 'And whether we have one or two bodies.'

61

Wisting's mobile had started to ring while Hammer and Stiller were digging. He had turned off the sound but had continued to feel the steady vibration in his pocket. When he checked the phone, he had thirteen missed calls, from the press and various numbers he did not have stored. Only one of the people who had tried to get hold of him had left a voicemail. When he played it, he heard that it was from Terje Nordbo of Internal Affairs, leaving a brief message for Wisting to get in touch.

Leaning back on the car bonnet, he stole a glance at the trail into the woods and went on to check the online newspapers, starting with *VG*, where he saw a photo of Maren Dokken in police uniform. She was reported missing without trace. The story also included a picture of Idar Semmelmann, taken at the press conference. Described as leader of the co-ordinated investigation, he had taken over responsibility for the hunt for Tom Kerr, which after three days had proved pretty ineffectual.

Semmelmann had stated that they had now traced the grenade used when Kerr escaped to a theft from a military weapons warehouse. In connection with that, the police were also searching for thirty-two-year-old Tallak Gleich. A photo of him had also been released, the same image from police records he had been shown before they raided his house. A bald man with a goatee, easy to recognize if you came across him.

Further into the story, he found his own name and picture

and the explanation for all those missed calls. He read that he had been removed from the case and was under investigation by Internal Affairs, suspected of official misconduct that had enabled Kerr to escape. It was certainly true that he had not responded to the newspaper's request for a statement. Guro Stemstad, the police prosecutor in charge, declined to answer when asked if he had been suspended from duty.

As he put his phone back in his pocket, his thoughts returned to the events when Tom Kerr had cut and run. He had spent a lot of time thinking about it, trying to pinpoint something he should have done, said, or thought differently, but all this had led to was self-reproach. Normally robust in his dismissal of negative circular thinking, Wisting was aware that this particular situation was taking its toll on him.

The noise of several vehicles made him move from his perch on the car bonnet. A police patrol car rounded the bend, followed by the capacious van used by the Kripos crime scene technicians.

Stiller greeted them and introduced Line. Wisting and Hammer simply nodded to the new arrivals.

Equipment was unloaded and carried into the woods, and it was growing dark by the time they were ready to continue digging. A tent had been erected and floodlights set up. The bright lamps cast a harsh light on the hole in the ground, and conversations among the technicians were drowned out by the loud drone of the generator.

There was a single flash, followed by a salvo of bright lights. The black plastic bag that had already been lifted out was transferred to a cardboard box, marked and set aside. The next bag was lifted out and photographed. One of the technicians used a carpet knife to cut an incision in it and an arm was revealed.

The technicians continued with their laborious task.

Everything they did was documented by photographs. In addition, they had Line's camera directed straight at them.

The third bag, heavier than the others, had a shape that suggested it might be the torso, devoid of arms and legs.

One of the technicians slit it open to confirm the suspicion.

Someone with a flashlight came walking along the track towards them: Semmelmann, accompanied by two other detectives Wisting had not met before. The technicians took a break while Stiller brought them up to speed. Once they were apprised of the situation, Semmelmann turned to face Wisting.

'Sorry things worked out as they did,' he said, referring to the change of command. 'I've full confidence in you. The decision was made over my head.'

He looked directly at Hammer before turning back to Wisting. 'You've both been taken off the case,' he reminded them. 'You shouldn't really be here.'

'We're staying until we know what's lying in that grave,' Wisting said, gesturing towards the technicians and the hole in the ground.

It seemed for a moment that Semmelmann was about to make a comment, but he dropped the idea. 'What have you got for us so far?' he asked instead as he approached the three boxes.

'One leg, one arm and a torso,' Stiller replied.

Semmelmann lifted a lid and used a pen to extend the opening in the plastic to see with his own eyes.

'They need to go to the lab for examination and analysis,' one of the technicians warned him.

Semmelmann did not appear to catch the mild rebuke. 'Can't you scan the fingers here and now?' he asked. 'Then search the fingerprint records and get an immediate answer?'

'We're taking all the bags out first,' the senior technician said.

'I see,' Semmelmann replied with a nod.

He replaced the lid of the evidence box and motioned for them to continue. One of the technicians jumped down into the pit again and drew out another bag. The shape suggested that this was the head.

'There's only one bag left,' he said, hoisting it up.

This information caused Wisting's shoulders to relax. Only one body.

The plastic bag was photographed from various angles before it was opened. All Wisting saw was hair. Long, black hair. The technician opened out the incision in the bag and turned the head to one side so that the face came into view. It was covered in blisters and burns caused by a corrosive liquid. The eyes were closed and the contorted mouth gaped crookedly, but there was no doubt about the identity of the corpse. Tom Kerr was dead.

62

Wisting turned the car into the driveway and drove slowly up to the house. He sat with his hands on the wheel as the headlights bathed the house façade and entrance in harsh light. The door needed a coat of varnish. He could not remember the last time he had painted it.

The thought passed. He turned off the ignition and was enveloped in darkness.

This had not happened before. He had never left a job unfinished. There were cases that had to be shelved when they were unable to make any further progress, but he had never stepped aside from an active investigation. The feeling of resignation made him restless.

Stepping out into the cool of the evening, he glanced down at Line's house before letting himself in and switching on the exterior light.

The house was dark and silent and the emptiness tugged at him, reinforcing the deep sense of powerlessness that engulfed him. Reminiscent of hunger, it gnawed at him and wore him down.

He headed for the kitchen, where he opened the fridge and took out a half-full carton of potato salad and some cold meat. He ate half of it before pushing his plate aside and taking out his work laptop.

The discovery of the body in Østmarka was all over the news. There was a picture of Tom Kerr with the headline reporting that he had been found dead.

Within the text of the story, Idar Semmelmann was depicted

in the bright light of a camera flash. It was only a few hours since he had taken over responsibility for the investigation and already he was able to show results.

Wisting did not bother to read the story but agreed with the decision to publicize the fact that Tom Kerr was dead. The idea of him on the loose had generated fear and there was no reason to withhold the information.

He changed the screen image and logged into the case-management program. On searching for the Tom Kerr case, he saw that he no longer had access to it. The folder was now emblazoned with a red 'forbidden' sign. When he moved the cursor over it, a dialogue box popped up saying that the case files were restricted. Guro Stemstad or Idar Semmelmann had administration rights and could be contacted if anyone had a professional reason for access.

He searched out the missing-person case concerning Maren Dokken and found that it was similarly marked.

His position and professional work meant that he had more extensive user rights than his other colleagues. Normally, he had access to all cases, including those he was not involved in, and cases containing sensitive information that were protected to avoid leaks. Now he was completely cut off.

The computer system had a direct-message function in which employees could send short messages to each other outside the email system. It was blinking, indicating that someone had sent him a DM. He opened it and saw that it was from Tim Skage, the Oslo Vest investigator. The message was brief. Just a name, Helene Norum, and a link to a video interview of her.

He clicked on the link and accessed an image of a sterile room in which two women were seated on opposite sides of a table. The woman on the right was formally dressed and sat with a case folder in front of her, whereas the woman on the left had a round, slightly quizzical face and shiny black hair. This was Helene Norum, the mother of the third victim, the one who had never been found.

The time in the right-hand corner showed that this was a short interview, only twenty-four minutes long.

Wisting pressed play and watched as the investigator ran through a few formalities. She announced the time and place and explained that this was a witness interview in connection with the investigation into the death of Chris Paust Backe, without letting the woman opposite her know that it was probably Backe who had delivered the hand grenade to whoever had helped Tom Kerr to escape, or that the death was being investigated as a murder.

'How did you know Chris Paust Backe?' the interviewer began.

This was a proactive approach, suggesting that the police had already come to the conclusion that they were acquainted, and made it difficult for the interviewee to deny a connection between them.

However, Helene Norum shook her head. 'I don't know who that is,' was her response.

The plain-clothed policewoman nodded and thumbed through her notepad, as if switching to an alternative plan. 'What kind of phone do you have?' she asked.

'An iPhone.'

The policewoman read out the number and Helene Norum confirmed that it was hers. 'Is there anyone else who uses your phone?'

'No.'

'Could anyone else have access to it?'

'In what way?'

'Do you always carry it with you, or do you sometimes

leave it at home so that someone else could answer it for you?'

'I usually have it with me,' Helene Norum said. 'I live alone.'

The policewoman nodded. 'On Tuesday 25 August at 21.53, Chris Paust Backe phoned you,' she explained. 'What did you talk about?'

Helene Norum shook her head. 'That has to be a mistake,' she said. 'I have an unlisted number. It must have been a wrong number. I don't know anyone of that name.'

'Does that sometimes happen? That people phone you by mistake?'

'It has happened.'

The policewoman pushed a sheet of paper across the table. 'This conversation lasted almost a minute,' she said, her index finger firmly attached to the paper. 'That's a long time for a wrong number.'

Helene Norum studied the paper without saying a word. She seemed bewildered. Her response did not seem faked in any way, but as if she was searching for an explanation or an answer that eluded her.

'Do you remember who called you?' the policewoman asked.

'No . . .' Helene Norum took out her phone, obviously checking the call log.

'It doesn't go as far back as that,' she said.

The policewoman repeated the date of the call. 'Can you remember where you were that evening?'

The woman checked her calendar and shook her head vehemently when she could not find an entry.

The interview now took a different direction. 'Do you have any contact with your ex-husband?' the policewoman inquired.

'We've been divorced for twenty years,' Helene Norum replied.

'You still have the same surname, though?'

'It's my maiden name. He took it when we got married in an attempt to start a new life. I wasn't aware of it at that time, but his name had a lot of baggage.'

'In what way?'

'You must have it in your papers, surely?' Helene Norum asked. 'He's been inside. Before we met, he was accused of a number of assaults in the place where he came from. I knew nothing about it. Later he was convicted of the same kind of thing. After we separated. We were only married for three years.'

'Did you have contact with him when Taran disappeared?'

Helene Norum nodded. 'We had to,' she answered. 'After all, we had her together. Neither of us had any other children. He took it hard, even though Taran refused to have anything to do with him in the last few years. He had been in prison for rape, you see.'

A tense expression came over her, as if a vague idea had begun to take shape. She raised her head and stared at the ceiling. The policewoman must have understood this. She remained silent to avoid disturbing her train of thought.

'There *was* a strange phone call,' she finally said. 'I thought maybe it had something to do with Johannes.'

'When was this?'

'It must have been three or four weeks ago. It was late one evening, from a withheld number – you know, the kind that doesn't register when it calls you.'

She put her finger on the sheet of paper with the print-out of calls: 'That must have been him. It was a man. He phoned and said that he had got hold of the goods we wanted.'

Wisting craned forward, concentrating hard in order to hear more clearly.

'What goods?' the policewoman asked.

'That's what I asked him too,' Helene Norum replied. 'But I didn't get any explanation. He just repeated that he had arranged for what we wanted. I thought he must have called the wrong number, but he insisted he hadn't.'

'No?'

'No, he asked whether he had reached the Norums, and read out my number. It was the right one.'

'How did the conversation progress?'

'There was no further conversation. I asked who was calling and he asked me to wait for a minute. I heard a few noises at the other end, as if he was putting down the phone while he was checking some papers or something. After half a minute he came back and apologized, and then the connection was cut. As if he realized that he had phoned the wrong number and just hung up.'

'Why did you think it had something to do with your ex-husband?'

'I think he mentioned that. He referred to "you and your husband". He talked about the goods that you – plural – wanted.'

The policewoman ploughed on for a while longer to extract as many specifics as possible about what had been said during the phone conversation, before she began to summarize the content of the woman's statement.

Wisting leaned back. Something jarred here. He had no reason to doubt what Helene Norum had said, but all the same he could not get it to add up.

Only an hour after this phone conversation with Helene Norum, Chris Paust Backe had been killed and his apartment set on fire. Wisting outlined various scenarios. He

291

would have liked someone to discuss this with, but he had been taken off the case. The information that had emerged from the interview was not meant for his eyes and ears. Anyway, it was too late to phone Tim Skage, as it was well past midnight now.

The onscreen interview had ended and the screen turned black before the media-player program shut down.

There was another file in the folder to which he had been sent a link, the interview with Tallak Gleich. It had been conducted only half an hour ago. He must have been arrested some time this evening.

Wisting double-clicked on the icon and the media player reopened automatically. It had taken place in the same interview room. This time, Tim Skage was seated on the right of the table. The man opposite was bald but had no goatee. There was also a third person in the room, wearing a well-cut grey suit with an open-necked shirt, leafing through a bundle of case documents. A defence lawyer.

Tallak Gleich gave his name and address. The investigator explained that he was charged with the possession of narcotics and breach of the gun laws. He acquainted Gleich with the information that during the search of his premises, 123 grams of amphetamines and 28 grams of hash, as well as various prescription drugs, had been found, in addition to three hand grenades.

'The drugs are mine,' Tallak Gleich admitted of his own accord. 'But I don't know anything about the hand grenades. Someone must have left them at my place. Someone who was visiting me.'

'They were in a cupboard in your bedroom,' Skage pointed out. 'Your fingerprints are on them.'

Tallak Gleich shrugged. 'I've no idea where they came from,' he insisted.

'They came from a theft at a military weapons store,' Skage said. 'But you're not being charged with that. That's not what this is all about.'

Gleich looked across at his defence lawyer.

'What is this about, then?' the lawyer asked.

'I think you've both worked that out for yourselves,' Skage answered. 'These grenades are packed in sets of four in a box. There were three left in the box we found in your house. We have information that you gave the fourth grenade to Chris Paust Backe. What we want to know is whether he told you what he intended to do with it.'

The lawyer leafed through the documents and leaned forward. 'What does Backe himself say about it?' he asked.

His client answered this before Skage had a chance to say anything. 'He's dead,' he said tersely. 'Burned to death in a fire.'

Tim Skage nodded. 'Chris Paust Backe died three weeks ago,' he confirmed. 'When was the last time you spoke to him?'

Tallak Gleich hesitated. Wisting's mouth felt parched. He looked around for something to drink but could not bear to leave the screen.

'Listen,' Skage went on. 'I'm trying to put all my cards on the table here. In the days before Backe died, he asked a few folk whether they could get him a hand grenade. We have reason to believe that the grenade was used when Tom Kerr escaped. That means he had probably met the Other One.'

Tallak Gleich was about to say something but was interrupted by his lawyer.

'Wait a minute,' he said, raising his hand. 'How did Backe die? In a fire?'

'It's being investigated as a suspicious death,' Skage replied.

'Homicide?' the lawyer queried.

'That's our main hypothesis,' Skage verified.

The lawyer glanced across at his client. 'Can we take a break here?' he asked. 'We need to have a discussion.'

Skage gave the exact time and announced a suspension of the interview. The screen went black. Wisting paused play. He got to his feet, made for the kitchen worktop and filled a glass with water. Draining it in one gulp, he refilled it before going back to collect his laptop and take it through to the living room, where he could sit more comfortably.

The break was over. When the interview resumed, the lawyer spoke first.

'My client admits he delivered a hand grenade and a gun to Chris Paust Backe, but he had no knowledge of what they were to be used for.'

'Did he say anything about who wanted them?' Skage asked.

Tallak Gleich shook his head.

'Only that he didn't want them for himself. They were for another guy. Chris was a fixer, someone who could get hold of anything. The kind of person you went to if you needed something.'

'When was this?'

'A week before he died.'

Skage encouraged Tallak Gleich to give more details about how Backe had made contact and to describe the specifics of the handover.

'I spoke to him after he'd delivered the goods,' he said. 'He was stressed out. Really nervous.'

'Why was that?'

'Maybe it was more that he was confused, as if he regretted something he'd started. He was different, anyway, and it wasn't just his beard. He seemed paranoid. Couldn't even sit still. He was looking around all the time, as if he thought someone was following him.'

Wisting paused the recording again. Something in what Tallak had said was tugging at him. He went back and played it one more time.

'*He was different, anyway, and it wasn't just his beard . . .*'

The statement might suggest that Chris Paust Backe had adopted a beard and changed his appearance. It was a fragment of information that corresponded with another one. The man who had pretended to be Theo Dermann had sported a beard. Claes Thancke had thought it was some kind of disguise. That he had grown the beard before he visited the lawyer's office with the letter that Thancke had been forced to take into the prison.

He restarted the playback and waited for Tim Skage to follow this up, to ask about the beard, but Skage lacked Wisting's reference points and so had no reason to attach any importance to these words. The interview simply rolled on.

'When was this?' he asked.

'A couple of days later. I got my money. That was the last time I saw him.'

Tim Skage leaned forward as if seeking clarity. 'So you spoke to him again, after he had delivered the hand grenade and gun?' he asked.

'Yes.'

'That means a few days before he died?'

Tallak Gleich nodded.

'And you're certain he had delivered those items?'

'Yes. If not, I wouldn't have got my money.'

Out of the corner of his eye, Wisting noticed the headlights of a car out in the street. He craned his neck and saw it draw up outside Line's house. It was nearly 2 a.m.

Onscreen, Tim Skage and Tallak Gleich had reached the

conclusion that he must have delivered the hand grenade and gun at least three days before Backe died.

He understood why Skage was preoccupied with the exact timing. It did not match the phone call to Helene Norum. Wisting had also assumed that the *goods* Backe had said he had obtained referred to the hand grenade and the gun.

He drank from his glass and sat holding it in his hand until Skage announced that it was now 23.17 and declared the interview over. Wisting sat back with a feeling that there was something that did not add up. The information was only a few hours old. He needed some time to take it in and analyse it all. Strictly speaking, it was no longer his role or assignment, but he just could not let go.

63

Wisting had fallen asleep in the chair and was roused by the phone ringing. It was quarter to seven and light was dawning outside.

The call was from Hammer. 'I've come across something interesting,' he said.

Wisting cleared his throat.

'I couldn't sleep and I've been sitting here poring over the case documents all night,' Hammer went on.

'Haven't you been denied access?'

'Yes, but this is in Semmelmann's database. We can still get into that.'

'The relationship chart?'

'The telecomms data,' Hammer replied. 'Are you at home?'

'Yes.'

'Then I'll come over and show it to you.'

Wisting took a quick shower and brewed a pot of coffee before Hammer arrived.

They sat down together at the kitchen table. Hammer had brought his own laptop, in which he had systematically sorted the raw data gathered from the various telecomms companies. All mobile-phone conversations and text messages within the coverage area of Tom Kerr's smallholding during the time before it burned down. There were over a million results, spread over a period of three months. The smallholding was in an isolated spot but within the same coverage area as the E6 main motorway and the eastern suburbs of Oslo.

'He and his accomplice must have communicated somehow,'

Hammer began. 'Semmelmann and his team have checked out everyone Tom Kerr has been in contact with by phone, without finding anything.'

Wisting nodded.

'Meaning that he – or both of them, for that matter – must have used mobiles that were not registered to them while they were talking to each other.'

'A needle in a haystack,' Wisting commented.

'Semmelmann's group have also mapped out Tom Kerr's movements in the time period prior to his arrest five years ago. They know where he was working, for instance. Sometimes he was away from home for days on end. For example, he was involved in building a new swimming-pool complex in Mosjøen. He was up there for a fortnight. I've weeded out all the numbers that were active during the time we know Tom Kerr was *not* at home and deleted them completely from the data.'

'Wasn't that done before?'

Hammer picked up a mug and held it up while Wisting poured in some coffee.

'Well, all I know is that there's no reworked list in the material we've received from Semmelmann,' he said.

He raised the mug to his mouth and drank. 'That still leaves a lot of conversations and messages, but most of the others who live in that vicinity or regularly frequent the area have been eliminated. The remaining material is much easier to deal with.'

'What have you found?' Wisting asked.

'My starting point was the idea that the Other One also had previous convictions. I've sorted out all the phones registered to criminals.'

'Semmelmann's group had also looked at that,' Wisting objected.

'That's right, but I thought it would be interesting to take a closer look at them all the same. Borrowed phones often go walkabout in the criminal fraternity.'

Nodding, Wisting drank from his mug.

'We're talking about 122 different phones registered to people with criminal records,' Hammer went on, 'thirty-four of them convicted of sexual assaults.'

He turned his computer screen to face Wisting. 'These two are the interesting ones,' he said, pointing.

It was an overview of the communication between two numbers. Conversations and messages listed in chronological order, accompanied by date and time.

'Steffen Skjeberg and Tormod Jahren,' Wisting read aloud. 'Who are they?'

'Jailed for sexual offences,' Hammer replied. 'Steffen Skjeberg was convicted of an assault and rape in Tøyen Park. Tormod Jahren for incest and the distribution of child pornography.'

Wisting could see from his expression that there was more to come. Hammer jabbed his index finger on the date column on the screen.

'The point is that they were both in prison at that point in time,' he said, 'Skjeberg in Ullersmo and Jahren in Ila. They got long sentences. Steffen Skjeberg died two years ago, at the age of sixty-two. Jahren is twenty-nine and was released last year. He has a different mobile number now. They come from different parts of the city and there's nothing to suggest they even knew each other.'

'Someone must have been paying for the phone use?' Wisting queried.

'They could be automatic direct debits that continue until the subscription is cancelled,' Hammer said. 'Or SIM-only deals topped up with a pre-paid card you can buy in any shop. Anyone can do that.'

Wisting understood. At the time when these SIM-only subscriptions had been entered into there had been no need to register personal details, although the rules had been tightened up more recently. If you wanted to continue your pay-as-you-go subscription or take out a new one, you now had to show ID. As long as the subscription was not blocked, in principle, anyone whatsoever could pay the running costs without being traced.

'This was more than five years ago,' Hammer continued. 'All the other user data on the subscriptions have been deleted. We only have what was gathered in at the time to map out the phone use around Tom Kerr's smallholding.'

He scrolled down through the spreadsheet before he went on. 'The last time the phones were in contact with each other was eight hours before they tried to abduct Freja Bengtson,' he said. 'Before everything went wrong for them and Tom Kerr was arrested.'

'You've found their contact point,' Wisting said.

They were really homing in on something now, some-thing that could represent a meaningful breakthrough. At the same time, Wisting's feeling of disquiet had returned, the gnawing sense that there was something here that did not add up. It had accompanied him into his sleep the night before. Now it was back with a vengeance, with increased intensity. There was something seriously wrong here.

Hammer pulled his laptop back. 'We have to draw this to Semmelmann's attention,' he said.

Wisting stood up and crossed to the window. Line's car was still in front of her house. 'I think we should keep this to ourselves,' he said.

'What do you mean?'

Wisting turned to face him. 'Where do the phones come

from?' he asked, but then reframed the question. 'Where are phones kept when the owner is arrested?'

Wisting could see that Hammer realized what he was getting at. Phones were taken as evidence, especially in the case of sexual offences. Photos and other contents were combed through in a search for documentation of crimes. Thereafter, they were stored in the police warehouse for impounded material. If they had been used in connection with a criminal act, they were confiscated and destroyed. Some phones were signed out to family members or sent to prison along with other personal effects, where they were stored until the owner was released, but most phones were left in the hands of the police.

64

It was light in the room when Line woke. She had forgotten to pull down the roller blind when she went to bed last night. The sky outside was dark grey, the clouds fat with impending rain.

Reaching out her hand for her phone on the bedside table, she tugged it out of the charger. It was seven forty-nine. No messages. The online newspapers had little news to impart. The articles had different headings but were uniform in presentation. They retold what had happened when Tom Kerr had made his escape, and described it as a police blunder that was currently under investigation. Pictures of her father from the time when he had given a press briefing out at Eftang were used to illustrate this.

TV2 was the only media outlet that had succeeded in obtaining a comment from Claes Thancke. The defence lawyer was taciturn, simply confirming that he had been informed that his client had been found dead and that he had no wish to speculate. The article was accompanied by a still from her video taken at the time of Tom Kerr's escape, but the image was not credited either to her or the police.

Idar Semmelmann had refused further comment following the impromptu press conference he had held the previous evening.

The way the police had now organized the investigation, his role was pivotal in the narrative of what had happened. If the case were to be solved, then he would be the hero of the hour. At the same time, she would probably need to angle the story in a negative fashion with reference to the preparations made by the police for the site visit during which Tom Kerr had escaped. Her father would then be portrayed in a bad light.

At the moment, what had happened still seemed unreal and difficult to grasp. She felt at a loss because of the uncertainty surrounding Maren Dokken.

Throwing the quilt aside, she sat up, struggling to push away the thoughts of what the policewoman might have experienced and been subjected to. When she rushed into the bathroom and into the shower, she left the water running for a long time and tried to concentrate on her work. It was not all that different from covering an ongoing news story. The difference was simply that it would be a long time before she could present the material she had gathered.

She would have to try to persuade Claes Thancke to speak to her, she thought. He was almost duty-bound to appear. Now that his client was dead, he would be the only one able to speak up on his behalf.

The water had begun to cool. She finished up, wrapped a towel around herself and tucked it in under her armpits before heading for the kitchen. She sat down and found the number for Thancke's legal office, but the call went straight to an answering machine, and it dawned on her that this was Saturday. The office was closed and she was given a number to call in case of emergency.

On the webpage, there was no direct number provided for the firm's lawyers. She could probably obtain Thancke's personal number from her father or from Stiller, but she'd hardly be the only one trying to call him today.

Instead she wrote an email in which she introduced herself and her project, referring to the fact that they had met during the site visit and asking for a meeting without obligation. She did not really expect to hear anything back from him. He would probably be inundated with media inquiries, but an initial approach would make it easier to follow up later.

Extricating herself from the wet towel, she returned to her bedroom to get dressed. The phone buzzed to indicate an incoming text message, but she left it until she was dressed and ready. It was from Sofie, wondering if Line could take the girls while she attended to some business.

It didn't really suit her. She had too much on her mind, but she could hardly refuse.

65

The fridge motor started up, a faint humming noise.

Wisting and Hammer were sitting on opposite sides of the kitchen table. Neither spoke. They were both considering the implications of the discovery they had just made.

'Black phones,' Wisting said. 'It wouldn't be the first time.'

This was a practice with roots in the investigation of drugs crimes and the handling of informants. It had become an expression they used. A black phone was a phone that had been seized in evidence in connection with an investigation but which the narcotics investigators misappropriated from the police store and used to keep in touch with their informants. In this way, they reduced the risk that associates on the drugs scene would expose a source. Their conversations could not be traced back to the police, but seemingly the calls were made to other criminals. It was a practice that teetered on the extreme edge of the law. Items used in connection with criminal activity were forfeit, confiscated for the benefit of the public purse. A smuggled vehicle could be sold at a used-car auction. A used phone had no significant resale value and was destroyed if the owner did not have the right to have it returned.

'We'll need to look at these cases before we can do anything further,' Hammer said. 'Find out if the phones were seized as evidence. See if they were signed out or impounded.'

'The cases don't belong to our district, though,' Wisting said. 'We don't have access to them.'

He drew his laptop towards him and searched for them in

the data system all the same, managing to locate the case numbers, but if he wanted to read the electronic documents, someone would have to transfer them across. The data system had limited capacity. Each individual investigator had reader access only to cases in their own police district. In addition, these particular cases were more than five years old and probably stored in the electronic archives. The IT service would most likely have to be brought into the picture if they wanted to extract these.

'Stiller,' Hammer suggested. 'The people in the Cold Cases Group lift cases from the archives all the time.'

'But these cases are not unsolved,' Wisting pointed out.

'But he must have countrywide user access,' Hammer said. 'He can get hold of them with a few keystrokes. Phone him!'

Wisting picked up his phone and found the number. 'Where are you?' he asked when Stiller answered.

'At home,' Stiller replied. 'Is there news?'

'To some extent. We need your help with something.' He explained what they had discovered and what they needed.

'Give me twenty minutes,' Stiller said.

Eighteen minutes passed before he called back. 'You're right,' he said. 'There are a number of points: in interview, Steffen Skjeberg and Tormod Jahren gave the phone numbers you've found. They were both in prison when the phones were used in Østmarka, but then you already knew that.'

'Were the phones taken in evidence?' Wisting asked.

'Yes. They were examined by the computer-crime centre but not confiscated.'

In sexual crimes, phones were routinely checked with the intention of finding compromising material. The fact that the phones were not seized meant that neither of the accused had photos or films related to their crimes on their phones.

'They're listed as having been returned to their owners,' Stiller told him.

Wisting shook his head. That could not be.

'The SIM cards may have been taken out,' Hammer suggested. 'Used in another phone.'

Stiller had not finished: 'Neither Skjeberg nor Jahren has signed for them,' he added.

This was not unusual. Once a sentence was pronounced, all material evidence had to be sorted out before the case could be archived. This usually ended up with personal effects being placed in an envelope and, unless cash was involved, or jewellery or other valuables, this was sent out in the post. The investigator who finalized the evidence procedure was the only person who signed the declaration.

'Who signed it out?' Wisting asked.

'Skjeberg's phone was squared up along with a bunch of keys,' Stiller replied. 'It was dealt with by Lina Streif; she's in charge of Sexual Crimes now.'

He paused for a moment before continuing. 'Tormod Jahren's phone was signed for by Chief Inspector Idar Semmelmann. That happened five days before it was used.'

66

Silence reigned in the corridors of the police station. The investigation had been moved to Oslo, but the large conference room was still set up to lead the search for Tom Kerr. Semmelmann's relationship map hung on the wall and the ring binders crammed with tip-offs were laid out on the table.

Stiller had arrived from Oslo. Hammer closed and locked the door behind him.

'We should go to the Police Chief,' Wisting said.

Stiller sat down at the end of the conference table and took out his laptop. 'You've been taken off the case,' he said. 'I've a meeting with her at 4 p.m. We need to compile the facts so we can put them to her then.'

Wisting wanted to ask him what kind of meeting he had planned with the Chief of Police but left his thoughts unspoken.

'Where do we start?' Hammer began.

'We have to find some point of intersection,' Stiller replied. 'A starting point. Tom Kerr was convicted three times, but earlier in the noughties Claes Thancke got him off on a rape charge. It was due to a technical error, bad police work.'

He called up the case on his laptop screen. The documents were listed by number, description and name of the detective who had written the report. One name recurred constantly: Idar Semmelmann.

Hammer grabbed a marker pen he saw lying on the table. Flipping off the red cap, he got to his feet and strode up to the relationship chart on the wall.

'It's incomplete,' he declared.

It was intended as an overview of all the people who in some way or another were linked to Tom Kerr. People with whom he had had various dealings. Close and distant connections. However, there were no police officers listed.

The marker pen squeaked as Hammer drew a new ring around Tom Kerr's inner circle. He hesitated to write anything and ended by leaving the ring empty. None of them had voiced aloud the idea that one of their own could be the Other One.

'Helene Norum has a withheld phone number,' Wisting said in support of the unspoken theory. 'She said so at her interview. Someone called her the night Chris Paust Backe died. Someone who had access to her number.'

Another detail surfaced. 'The beard,' he said. 'I must phone Tim Skage.'

Without any further explanation, he took out his phone and called the Oslo Vest investigator.

Skage launched into a lengthy apology about how the investigation was now organized. 'It's just crap, all of it,' he said. 'And of all people, they've appointed Semmelmann to lead it.'

'You managed to get hold of Tallak Gleich,' Wisting commented.

'Yes, I sent you a link to the video of the interviews with him and Helene Norum,' Skage said. 'Not much came of them, right enough, but I was left with the distinct impression that Chris Paust Backe was involved in something that had somehow got out of control.'

'I've watched the interview,' Wisting said. 'He mentions something about a beard. Did Backe have a beard?'

'Not normally, and not when he died. He'd shaved it off by

then, I suppose, but we've been monitoring his movements and have some video footage of him with a beard.'

Wisting asked him for further details.

'It had to do with his card use,' Skage explained. 'We've a list of all the places where he used his bank card.'

Wisting understood. This was routine procedure in every major investigation.

'We've also gathered in video footage from the customer cashpoints with CCTV,' Skage went on. 'Virtually all of them, in fact.'

'Can you send that to me?' Wisting asked.

'You're no longer on the case, though, are you?'

'I've a rookie officer who's gone missing,' Wisting answered. 'I'm not letting this go until she's found.'

'I'll put it in a folder and send you a link,' Skage said. 'But there's nothing there. He's on his own on every occasion.'

'Thanks, anyway,' Wisting replied.

Skage grunted something incomprehensible. 'Semmel-mann should never have been put in charge,' he repeated. 'They moved him just to get rid of him. He should never have been given that kind of responsibility.'

'Who wanted to get rid of him?'

'The top brass,' Skage replied. 'He'd worked for years in Sexual Crimes, you see. Worked his way up to the post of chief inspector and head of section, but that became a prob-lem after a while.'

'What do you mean?'

'Only rumour, but people thought he was a pervert him-self. It was said that he took too long going through the material seized in evidence. He took it upon himself to ana-lyse the worst of the sexual-abuse films. It was also said that he liked to get sexual-assault victims to describe what they had been subjected to. Down to the smallest detail. There

310

were a few complaints, but they never managed to catch him out in anything. When Tom Kerr was arrested, they moved him sideways and appointed him to lead a group tasked with trying to find the accomplice. Five years he's been doing that. Maybe he'll succeed now, but I have my doubts. I've said it before and will say it again – he should never have been given that job.'

67

It had started raining again. Wisting walked to the window, opened the blinds a crack and peered out. A man with a red umbrella was hurrying across the street.

The computer gave a signal. Tim Skage had sent him Chris Paust Backe's bank account printout and the pictures from the cashpoint cameras. Stiller and Hammer stood on either side of him as he opened each image. They saw Backe in front of the cash machine in various shops, wearing a number of outfits. His beard grew longer and fuller in each picture and eventually covered the whole lower part of his face.

In one of the last images, he also had a sticking plaster on his right cheek and under his left eye. The date stamp indicated that this was taken on 20 August at 14.37.

'Where was that?' Stiller asked.

Wisting checked the file name. 'Deli de Luca in Akersgata,' he read off. 'Oslo city centre, just a stone's throw from Claes Thancke's office.'

'He's the one who went there, without a doubt,' Stiller said. 'He's Theo Dermann.'

'He's nothing but a message boy,' Hammer broke in. 'A pawn who was used. Someone who could get hold of guns and run errands.'

'Someone he had to get rid of, more to the point,' Stiller added. 'A forgotten frying pan on the hotplate. All policemen have been to fires like that. It's one of the first things the technicians look for. They rarely do any further investigation after that.'

Standing up again, Wisting returned to the window and opened it slightly. The air that wafted in was fresh but damp. 'We need more,' he said.

'We can't wait,' Hammer insisted. 'If he has Maren Dokken, then every hour counts. Every minute, in fact.'

Stiller had found Semmelmann's address. 'He's divorced and lives alone. No children.'

'He must have a place he uses,' Hammer said. 'Somewhere that's not his own but that he has free access to. Much the same as knowing that the welding workshop where we found the van was lying empty.'

'Can we put surveillance on him?' Wisting asked.

Stiller shook his head. 'I can't send out a team without telling them what they're doing.'

'Where is he now?' Hammer inquired.

'Probably at work,' Stiller replied. 'In his office. I can find out. Come up with an excuse to phone him.'

'You could ask if he's investigated the social security office in Sagene,' Wisting suggested. 'The call to Claes Thancke came from a jobseeker phone in there. He should check it out, check whether anyone remembers a man with a beard on 20 August.'

Hammer grew impatient. 'We could follow him,' he said. 'Use our own cars. No more than forty hours or so have gone by since Maren disappeared. He held the others for at least three days. He might well lead us to her.'

'He's an experienced investigator,' Wisting reminded him. 'He'd recognize our cars and easily cotton on to being followed.'

'I can get a tracker placed if we find his car,' Stiller said. 'That way we can keep our distance.'

Hammer, with his jacket in his hand, glanced at Wisting. 'Are you with me?' he asked.

There was something over-hasty about the suggestion, but at the same time it contained a simple logic. 'Yes, I'm with you,' Wisting agreed.

He was last to drive out of the back yard at the police station and had lost sight of Hammer even before he reached the motorway. Squalls of rain lashed the windscreen, reducing visibility.

After an hour at the wheel, Stiller phoned. He connected all three vehicles in the conference call. 'I've spoken to him. He was at the office. We've made a deal. I'm going to go in. He's found a link between Chris Paust Backe and Johannes Norum. They served time in prison in Oslo together. The phone call to his ex-wife on the night Backe was killed suggests that he might be involved.'

'That's part of the pretence,' Hammer said. 'The call to Helene Norum was a smokescreen, a diversion in case an investigation was instigated.'

'I'm going to see him for a run-through,' Stiller said. 'They're working on the theory that it was some kind of revenge attack.'

Wisting turned off the road into a petrol station. 'That gives us some time, then,' he said, addressing himself to Hammer: 'Do you have an address for Tormod Jahren? We need to talk to him about the phone that was confiscated.'

'It's in Stovner,' Hammer answered. 'I'll send you the address and his new phone number.'

Wisting drew up in front of the petrol pumps, waited until the conference call had ended and stepped out to fill his tank. Then he drove on, turned off on the Ring 3 ring road and followed the directions to the blocks of flats that surrounded Stovner town centre. The rain was beating on the car roof. He stayed in his car in the huge car park, found Hammer's message and called the number he had been given. Not really expecting an answer, he was taken aback when Tormod Jahren answered at once and introduced himself by his full name.

Wisting gave his name and explained that he was from the police. 'I'm doing some investigation into suspected misappropriation of goods from the police evidence warehouse,' he began. 'There's something I'd like to speak to you about.'

'What kind of investigation?' Jahren asked. 'It's a long time since I had anything to do with the police.'

The scepticism in his voice was obvious.

'I'm in Stovner at the moment,' Wisting continued. 'Could we meet?'

'I'm not at home,' Jahren replied hurriedly.

Wisting looked up at the blocks of flats in front of him. He had no idea exactly where Jahren lived but imagined that he might well be at home.

'To be more specific, it's suspected that a police officer may have stolen items seized in evidence,' he said. 'There are some personal effects we can't account for. I'd hoped you could help me to clear up a few details.'

'Can't we do it over the phone?' Jahren asked.

Normally, Wisting would have made more of an effort to have the opportunity to speak to the man face to face, but he decided against it this time. 'You were arrested six and a half years ago,' he began. 'Among the belongings the police confiscated from you were your computer equipment and your mobile phone.'

The man at the other end remained silent.

'Can you remember what kind of phone you had then?'

'A Sony Xperia. I have one now as well, but the latest model.'

'Do you recall the phone number?'

Tormod Jahren hesitated. He began to recite a number but then realized that he did not remember it after all.

'Do you recollect what kind of subscription it was?'

'Pay-as-you-go, a top-up card.'

Wisting nodded. 'Do you know where that phone is now?'

'No idea.'

Wisting appreciated that he had framed the question badly. 'Did you get it back?'

'Yes, but I haven't a clue what became of it. It became so outdated while I was behind bars. I think I just threw it away and bought a new one.'

'So you definitely got it back?'

'It was among my things when I was released. I think it had been in the prison storeroom the whole time, along with the other personal belongings I didn't need or wasn't allowed to have with me in my cell.'

'So you definitely received it when you were released?'

'That, my wallet and my keys, even though I no longer had that apartment. There were a few other things too – memory sticks and CDs. There was nothing missing when I got out. I don't think I can help you.'

However, Wisting was not ready to end the conversation. 'So while you served time, your possessions were transferred from the police to the prison?'

'I assume so. At least, they were there when I checked out.'

'Do you know when that happened?'

'Not a scooby. You'd have to ask at the prison.'

The answers he received from Tormod Jahren were not as unambiguous as he had hoped, but they prompted an unexpected reaction. 'You were in Ila?' Wisting asked him.

'At the beginning I was. For the final year I was banged up in Berg in Vestfold district. That was where I was given my

things when I got out, but they had probably just been transferred when I was moved.'

'Who was your contact warden at Ila?' Wisting probed
further.

'I had several,' Jahren answered. 'Some of them left or
were replaced.'

He mentioned a couple of names. 'And then there was
somebody called Molander,' he added.

Wisting's eyebrows shot up as he pictured the arrogant
prison guard in a crumpled uniform shirt who had stood
guard while they ransacked Tom Kerr's cell.

'Fredrik Molander?' he asked.

'Yes, but he applied to work in the detention centre and
started work in there.'

Wisting tilted his head and peered out of the side window.
Something began to dawn on him, just a narrow, modest
crack of light at first, but it opened out to reveal a possibility.
The possibility of an alternative explanation. It could not be
more difficult for a prison employee to misappropriate a
phone than it was for a detective. Quite the opposite. He was
not familiar with the system or routines, but access would, if
anything, be easier and the risk less.

He rounded off the conversation. The wipers swept over
the windscreen and cleared away the rain. He sat for a few
minutes longer before moving off and calling Hammer.

'Stiller's in the police station now,' Hammer told him. 'I'm
sitting outside waiting. It could take quite a while. Have you
spoken to Jahren?'

Wisting recounted the conversation with Tormod Jahren
but refrained from sharing the thoughts he was left with
about what had emerged.

'I'm going to pay a visit to Ila,' he concluded. 'I want to
know when the phone arrived there.'

They knew when the police had signed for the phone. That had been three weeks before Tom Kerr and his accomplice had abducted their first victim. But they did not know when the phone had been handed in to the prison. The time was the crux of the matter, pointing to where their suspicions might lead.

68

The huge prison building was bathed in grey mist. A woman with two small children, a girl and a boy, both around ten years old, stood in front of the visitors' entrance. Wisting produced his police ID and followed them in through the metal security door when it swung open.

They knew he was coming. He had phoned in advance and told them what he wanted. The prison governor was not on duty that day, but a senior warden welcomed him into a cramped office. Broad-shouldered, he sat leaning forward with his forearms on the desk and his hands folded in front of him.

Wisting explained that he had been there three days earlier and had searched Tom Kerr's cell. 'We spoke to his contact warden,' he said. 'Fredrik Molander. Is he here today?'

The senior warden shook his head. 'No, sorry. He's taking time off in lieu,' he said. 'It suited us for him to do that now that Kerr's not in the section.'

'He'd been off sick earlier, though?' Wisting recalled.

'Yes. He came back just after Kerr escaped.' The senior warden shifted in his seat. 'But I understood that this was about something else. A previous inmate? Tormod Jahren?'

'Yes,' Wisting confirmed, realizing that he would have to give an explanation for why he wanted to see this folder. 'It looks as if the Oslo police made a mistake in handling the evidence in his case,' he said, to make sure the warden understood that he did not suspect the prison staff of doing anything worthy of criticism. 'A mix-up,' he added. 'It wasn't discovered until now.'

The warden looked far from convinced but made no comment. Turning to the right, he picked up a folder and pushed it across the desk.

It bore Tormod Jahren's name and prisoner number.

'Where are the prisoners' personal effects stored while they serve their time?' Wisting asked.

'In the effects store,' the warden replied, without any further explanation of where this was or who had access.

Wisting opened the folder. The papers on top were from the transfer to Berg prison. They contained a list of valuables and belongings that the carrier had delivered to the new prison. An employee had signed for receipt of the effects. The name was barely legible. The list itself was a computer printout with a precise record of DVD films, CDs, books and magazines mentioned by title. Various memory sticks with approximate storage capacity. Shoes, boots, trousers, jackets and other articles of clothing listed by brand name. A wallet with no cash, but a precise overview of bank cards and ID papers, a bunch of keys with the exact number stated and a Sony Xperia mobile phone.

At the very back of the folder was a shorter list from the time when Jahren had started his prison term. There were fewer films, books and CDs, and no keys, memory sticks or phone listed. Jahren himself had signed for the items he had handed over for storage. The highly detailed description of each item was a practical device to avoid inmates later claiming that something was missing.

Wisting leafed through the papers. Each time Jahren had exchanged CDs or clothes the transaction had been recorded in the form of a new document that was numbered and dated. It looked as if the contact warden had responsibility for the list. Fredrik Molander's name repeatedly appeared in the receipt field.

After Christmas, the list grew longer. Several DVD films, CDs and books. Wisting browsed through them until he found what he was looking for. His eyes skimmed the text more than once as a sensation began to build inside his chest.

Three items. Wallet, keys and mobile phone. *Transferred from the police* was what Fredrik Molander had written. The three items had been signed for six days after Tom Kerr's arrest.

'Have you found what you're looking for?' the warden asked.

When Wisting glanced up, he realized this was the second time the warden had asked. 'Yes,' he replied, withdrawing the sheet of paper. 'This date, is it automatically generated?'

He pointed at the field on the right and the warden craned forward. 'Yes,' he answered.

Wisting had detected a hesitation. 'But?' he asked.

'It can be overwritten,' the warden added. 'The effects can often be left lying for a while in the duty room before they're moved down to the storeroom. The record can be back-dated so that it matches what's factually correct.'

'The police system works in the same way,' Wisting said, to avoid giving the impression that he was assigning blame.

He waved the page in the air. 'Could I have a copy of this, please?'

The warden appeared sceptical, as if he had already gone too far by allowing the police to inspect these records without a warrant. However, he stood up and took the page away with him. A short time later he came back, handed Wisting a copy and placed the original back in the folder. Wisting had to look at it one more time to be sure that it was as he had thought. That he had read it correctly. Then he folded the sheet of paper in two and tucked it into his inside pocket. He was keen to leave, but a sudden thought detained him.

'Could you check one more thing for me?' he asked.

69

There were several missed calls on the phone when it was returned to Wisting after his prison visit, two of them from Internal Affairs. They probably wanted him to come in for another interview. By this stage, they had most likely changed his status from that of witness to suspect.

He had not had a chance to check the other calls when Stiller phoned.

'Hold the line,' Wisting asked, 'so that I can bring in Hammer too.'

Wisting jumped into his car and had turned out into the road before the call resumed. 'They've decided to bring Johannes Norum in for interview,' Stiller said.

'They'll make him a scapegoat,' Hammer surmised.

'It's possible they can cobble something together that will make it look as if he helped Tom Kerr to escape so that he could get his revenge on him, but they won't be able to make him into the accomplice,' Stiller replied.

'There's no logic to it,' Hammer declared. 'Why would he kill Tom Kerr before he had shown us the burial site? Tom Kerr was supposed to tell us where Norum's daughter was and what had happened.'

'Did you manage to attach the tracker?' Wisting asked.

'In his laptop bag,' Stiller answered. 'I'll get a message if he moves it more than ten metres.'

'Any other news?' Hammer asked.

'The technicians are finished with the van you found in the welding workshop in Revetal,' Stiller replied. 'The vehicle was originally registered in Sweden, and was reported stolen there six months ago. The plates were taken from a similar van in Asker.'

Wisting nodded. He already knew about the number plates.

'Basically, it's the same manoeuvre as when Tom Kerr and his sidekick took the other girls,' Stiller went on. 'Our hypothesis is that the workshop was to be set on fire some-time later, when it would no longer be natural to link the fire to the abduction of Maren Dokken.'

Wisting moved out to the centre of the road and overtook a moped. 'Any news of Maren?' he asked.

'No,' Stiller answered. 'They believe Tom Kerr was killed and dismembered at the workshop and that it happened before Maren was taken.'

Wisting asked for a more detailed explanation.

'It took place inside the paint shop,' Stiller clarified. 'All traces were painted over afterwards. There's a whole new layer of paint on the walls and floor. The technicians have found large quantities of blood beneath it. It's been typed but not yet analysed for DNA. All we know in the mean-time is that it's Tom Kerr's blood type, and not Maren Dokken's.'

'How can they know for sure that Tom Kerr was killed before Maren was taken?' Hammer queried.

'It has to do with the hardening of the paint,' was Stiller's response. 'The paint inside the van was not as old as the paint in the paint-shop container. That makes them believe that Kerr was killed there as early as the first night he was on the run. The witness mentioned by the former local police-man has been formally interviewed. He confirms that there was someone on the premises then.'

'That explains why she didn't raise the alarm,' Hammer

said. 'So he was alone when he took Maren Dokken. He was a familiar face to her. Someone she trusted.'

Wisting pictured in his mind's eye how Maren Dokken would begin to struggle when a hand holding a rag soaked in anaesthetic fluid was placed over her face.

'What about the post-mortem?' he asked. 'Does that say anything about the time of the killing?'

'The post-mortem on Tom Kerr is taking place right now,' Stiller replied. 'I don't know how they examine a dismembered body that's been bathed in chlorine, but I think it'll be difficult to establish a precise time of death.'

'Where did that happen?' Wisting asked. 'The chlorine bath, I mean?'

'In the workshop,' Stiller answered. 'There's a tub inside the paint shop that's been spray-painted.'

Wisting tried to re-create the chronology: 'So Tom Kerr was murdered, dismembered and packed into bags. Then he was driven a hundred kilometres and buried on his property in Østmarka before the Other One returned and spray-painted the crime scene.'

'They believe he used the van to transport the body,' Stiller said. 'The registration number was picked up by toll stations along that route. They drove through Oslo about two o'clock in the morning and back again two hours later.'

'He could have dug the hole in advance, of course,' Hammer suggested.

Wisting began to think aloud: 'How does that fit with Semmelmann's movements? I spoke to him on the phone around three o'clock, four hours after Kerr had escaped. He got here about half past six.'

'He could have had time to pick up Kerr from Ringshaugstranda before that, where the boat was found,' Hammer broke in. 'Then driven him to the welding workshop and

324

used it as a safe house, or else killed him straight away. And gone back again after he checked into the hotel.'

'He left the police station and went to the hotel about midnight,' Wisting recalled. 'He was back again for the morning meeting, at the back of eight.'

'He could have managed all of it,' Hammer concluded. 'Without a problem. We're going to –'

Stiller cut him off abruptly. 'Movement,' he reported. His voice was sharp and the words clipped. 'Idar Semmelmann's on the move.'

70

The girls were playing in the living room with a toy kitchen and some dolls. Line sat in her workspace in the basement, indexing her video recordings from the previous day. She had left the door at the top of the stairs open and was able to hear the constant stream of voices from their role-play games.

Onscreen, Idar Semmelmann arrived at the discovery site. Her father screwed up his eyes when the flashlight beam struck his face. In the bright light, his wrinkles appeared deeper and the shadows under his eyes became more distinct. His hair was sticking out in every direction, and his jacket hung lopsidedly over his shoulders. He looked old and tense, and for the first time ever it dawned on her that one day he would no longer be a policeman. His job as an investigator would be subject to age limits. She wondered what effect that would have on him. These days, he had no interaction with anyone apart from his fellow workers, no hobbies or leisure interests. Hardly any family. She could not envisage him in another job, such as a fraud investigator in an insurance company, where many retired detectives ended up.

Semmelmann pointed out that her father and Hammer had been taken off the case. Her father's reply was indistinct, and Line adjusted the sound. Stiller explained what they had found while the technicians took a break. It was a thorough run-through and would function as a good summary, but she had only used the built-in microphone in the camera and the sound quality was less than adequate.

The camera focused on Semmelmann. His thick, grey hair looked recently cut. He seemed under stress and wore an irritated expression, as if he was unhappy about the situation.

Lifting the lid of one of the boxes in which the body parts had been placed, he took a pen from his inside pocket and used it to move and unfold the black plastic to get a better view, uncovering a hand.

One of the technicians warned him that they had not finished examining the contents. Ignoring him, Semmelmann cocked his head and asked if they could check the fingerprints. The answer he received was that it would have to wait, and then he fumbled with the lid again and threw a glance at the camera before straightening up.

Line scrolled back to the point where Semmelmann arrived at the discovery site and placed an index mark so that it would be easy to find it again later.

A message in the top right-hand corner of the screen told her that she had received a reply to the email she had sent to Claes Thancke. He wrote that he was at his cabin in Holmestrand for the weekend, doing preparatory work for a forthcoming court case, but that he could meet her there.

Line turned around and darted a glance upstairs. Maja would be picked up in an hour. She could hardly ask Sofie to watch Amalie again. Instead, she would take her along.

71

They followed Semmelmann out of Oslo, on the E18 towards Vestfold. Wisting was at the back; Semmelmann's car was out of sight for him. The phone was linked up to the others, but no one was saying anything. All that could be heard was the hissing of the open phone line and the swishing sound of the tyres on the wet asphalt. His thoughts drifted in all directions, without restriction. He considered concrete facts, sensible arguments and alternative interpretations. Struggled to let go of deep-rooted assumptions. Reshuffled suppositions and used other inferences as his starting point. Sought confirmation and fresh answers.

A small lorry moved up beside him and drove past. Wisting checked his speedometer and realized that he had fallen behind.

'Turning off at Tønsberg,' Stiller reported.

Wisting was almost ten minutes behind now. Accelerating, he drove past the lorry that had overtaken him and swung off from the motorway just as Stiller advised that he was heading for the town centre.

'He's going to the police station,' Hammer decided. 'Some meeting or other.'

'My meeting,' Stiller said. 'I've an appointment with the Police Chief in twenty minutes. It would be understandable for her to have invited Semmelmann to be present.'

'What kind of meeting are we talking about here?' Hammer asked.

Stiller refrained from answering but instead announced

that Semmelmann was parking in one of the reserved spaces outside the police station.

Wisting turned into a bus bay, swivelled round to the back seat and reached out for his laptop. 'Don't start the meeting without me,' he said.

Stiller hesitated. 'The meeting is about the internal investigation,' he said. 'It's about you.'

Wisting ignored him. His thoughts were racing. Ever since he had left the prison he had pushed and pulled at his deadlocked theories, struggling to find space for new ideas. He needed more time, but was well on his way to opening up an undreamed-of possibility.

'I'll be there at four o'clock,' he said, and ended the call.

72

Hammer waited outside the Police Chief's office. It was Saturday and no one else was in the waiting room. The clock on the wall behind the empty desk indicated it was 4 p.m.

'They've gone in,' Hammer said, motioning towards the solid oak door.

Wisting knocked but did not wait for an answer before he opened the door and slipped inside.

They were seated around the conference table immediately inside the door. Agnes Kiil, in mid-sentence, stopped and looked quizzically at Stiller. Idar Semmelmann, who sat with his back to Wisting, turned round with an expression of annoyance.

Wisting walked straight in and pulled out a vacant chair. The Police Chief half rose from her seat. She seemed to be searching for words.

'Do we have an appointment?' she ended up saying.

'I have new and important information,' Wisting replied.

'Can't it wait?' Semmelmann asked.

Wisting shook his head. 'We know who the Other One is,' he said, using his hand to gesture towards Hammer, who had followed him into the room.

'It's no longer your case,' Semmelmann protested. 'You're under investigation.'

The Police Chief subsided into her seat again. 'Let me hear what you have to say,' she said.

Wisting sat down and waited until Hammer had also taken a place at the table.

'Theo Dermann,' Wisting began. 'There's something about his visit to Claes Thancke I've kept coming back to.'

Semmelmann interrupted him. 'It was Chris Paust Backe,' he said. 'The lawyer's secretary recognized him in the pictures we showed her.'

Nodding, Wisting glanced across at Stiller. They had already drawn that conclusion, but there was something else that had constantly tugged at his subconscious.

'The first approach came from a jobseeker telephone at the social security office in Sagene, Oslo,' he continued. 'But Chris Paust Backe lived in Asker. He had no affiliation to Sagene. Besides, he'd been receiving disability benefit for eight years.'

'Johannes Norum is out of work,' Semmelmann interjected. 'He belongs to Sagene. That's something we're looking at now. He's coming in for interview this evening.'

Wisting disregarded his comments. 'The same phone was used in another case,' he explained. 'In a blackmail case four years ago. I couldn't remember the details and had to spend some time looking it up. A prison warden was tempted into a honey trap and ended up in a hotel room with a young girl. It was secretly filmed and the video used in an attempt to persuade him to help an inmate to escape. The blackmailer made contact via the jobseeker phone in Sagene. The prison warden was married, but a break-up was already on the cards. He went to management and an operation was set in motion. A Yugoslavian was arrested and convicted. The case didn't reach the media, but it was presented at a seminar on corruption and its influence on public employees.'

'A well-known method, of course,' Semmelmann said. 'What's the relevance?'

Neither Hammer nor Stiller seemed to understand the connection either.

'I'm coming to that,' Wisting replied.

He let Hammer give an account of the phones Tom Kerr and his accomplice had used to communicate prior to Tom Kerr's arrest.

'Tormod Jahren was convicted of incest and the distribution of child porn,' he rounded off, now addressing himself to Semmelmann. 'You had responsibility for that investigation.'

Semmelmann gave a tentative nod, as if he vaguely recollected the case.

'What did you do with the phone when it was removed from the evidence store?' Wisting asked.

Semmelmann shook his head. 'That was years ago,' he answered. 'I've dealt with a lot of cases.'

'What's the protocol?'

'If it's not seized as evidence, then it's handed back to the owner.'

'That's right,' Wisting agreed. 'But that's not what you did. You handed it over to the defence lawyer. He didn't hand it into the prison until several months later.'

'Claes Thancke!' Semmelmann exclaimed. 'I remember it now. His lawyer was Claes Thancke. I gave him the phone.'

The Police Chief leaned forward. 'What does this mean?' she asked. 'Did Claes Thancke let Tom Kerr use another client's phone?'

Wisting shook his head. 'No. It means that Claes Thancke is the Other One,' he replied.

73

The Chief of Police slumped back into her chair. 'That's an assertion you'll have to substantiate in greater detail,' she said.

Stiller was also keen to say something, but he seemed lost for words. The conversation had veered off in a direction that had taken him completely by surprise.

'What about the other phone from the police storeroom?' he asked.

'Steffen Skjeberg was represented by a junior lawyer from Thancke's law firm,' Wisting replied. 'But it was Thancke himself who returned it to the prison.'

He produced copies of the records from the effects store at Ila and Oslo District Prison. The latter printout he had obtained with the help of the senior warden at Ila. It had been photocopied and sent across by fax. On both of them, Claes Thancke's name was given as the person who had handed in the phones.

Wisting turned to face Semmelmann. 'Where would you place Thancke on your relationship chart?' he asked.

'He's not in the database,' Semmelmann answered.

'But what index rating would you give him? Where would you place him in relation to Tom Kerr?'

'Closest of all,' Semmelmann admitted.

'That's not good enough,' the Police Chief objected.

'Thancke also defended Chris Paust Backe in a case three years ago. Backe was accused of threatening someone with a gun. He was the right person to approach to ask him to get a hand grenade.'

'Risky, though,' Stiller said. 'He visited the office. Other employees might have recognized him.'

'The lawyer's secretary has worked there for only six months,' Wisting explained. 'Her predecessor had to leave after making complaints about sexual harassment. The meeting was arranged for a day when most of the others in the office were busy in court or else away. There was no one about who would be able to recognize him.'

'All the same, he had to get rid of him once the job was over and done with,' Hammer said.

Wisting took up the thread: 'The blackmailer who used the jobseeker phone at Sagene – Claes Thancke was his lawyer too. As for sticking plasters on his face, in 2013 Thancke defended a rapist who had camouflaged himself with sunglasses and sticking plasters just before he attacked his victims. Easy to put on and easy to remove – and these were details that lingered in the victims' memories. For the first few weeks, the police were searching for a perpetrator with cuts on his face.'

'But what was the point of this arrangement?' the Police Chief asked. 'Why devise a situation in which he ends up having to admit that he had smuggled messages into the jail?'

'As a back-up,' Wisting replied. 'In case suspicion was aimed in his direction. A sheer diversionary tactic of the kind he has used in court many times. When his clients confess to something less serious, it seems more convincing when they later tell a lie. And it worked. We never doubted what he told us.'

The Police Chief nodded in response.

Wisting had more to say, however. 'The phone call to Helene Norum. Claes Thancke had access to her number from the case documents. The man who owns the welding workshop where Tom Kerr was killed is a client at Claes Thancke's legal firm. He knew that it lay empty and in all likelihood had access to a key. In 2010 he defended a vehicle painter who was accused of picking up sex workers and raping them in the back of his van. Before the police arrested him, he had spray-painted the cargo space and removed every trace of evidence.'

'He fits the profile,' Semmelmann admitted. 'Strategic and creative, high level of intelligence, ability to think far ahead and anticipate consequences. A well-respected person who's established an image of himself as unselfish and appears to be honest, kind-hearted and self-sacrificing.'

The description had been there the whole time, but no one had recognized him.

'Claes Thancke is like a chess player,' Wisting added. 'He thinks several moves ahead. If we find his DNA or fingerprints in the welding workshop or some other place, he's already covered that up by having a different, legitimate reason to be in that place. He's constantly aware of the placing of the pieces in relation to one another. This has made him a competent defence counsel but also a calculating criminal. His experience means that he knows how the police think and can anticipate our actions, such as when he knew we would remove Kerr's leg irons if he told him to stumble.'

'That conversation in his car.' Hammer had a sudden thought. 'He must have been giving Kerr his final instructions, maybe even showing him pictures of where the grenade and gun were hidden.'

'I've tried to turn it upside down,' Wisting said. 'To see everything from a different angle and avoid this particular line of thought, but the conclusion remains the same no matter what. Everything in this case points to Claes Thancke.'

The Police Chief raised her right hand and lifted her finger as a sign that she had a question: 'Where is Claes Thancke now?'

74

The mist hung motionless in the air. Most of the boats in the marina had been taken in for the season and were lined up on land, covered in tarpaulins. Gentle waves lapped at the shore and two seagulls took off from an old marine crane.

Claes Thancke stood beside the steering console of a large, open boat as it glided slowly into the cove. Line raised her hand in greeting. Thancke returned a similar salute and manoeuvred in towards the jetty. He was wearing a sporty leisure outfit and cap and looked very different from when she had seen him before.

Line zipped up Amalie's jacket and looked up at the low-ering clouds. Neither she nor Amalie was suitably dressed for a jaunt across the sea, and there were not many hours of daylight left. She could have suggested meeting the lawyer another day, in another place. Alone. There was no rush to discuss the documentary film project with him, but there was really another reason for her being here. Maren Dokken. Claes Thancke was the person who had been closest to Tom Kerr in recent years, the person most able to have some idea of where he might have a hiding place where Maren Dokken could be held captive.

Approaching the edge of the jetty, she grabbed the boat as Thancke moved alongside. 'I had to bring my daughter,' Line explained. 'I'm on my own with her. It's not easy to get a babysitter at such short notice.'

A twitch in one corner of Thancke's mouth betrayed that

he was far from pleased. 'I don't have a life jacket in a child's size,' he said.

'I brought one with me,' Line replied with a smile.

Claes Thancke nodded. 'What's her name?'

'Amalie.'

'Jump aboard, then!'

Line hoisted her bag of camera equipment. She had no plans to do any filming but had decided to bring it with her anyway.

'Can I leave it parked there?' she asked, pointing at her car.

Apart from Thancke's Mercedes, there were no other cars in the gravelled yard.

'It'll be fine,' the lawyer replied.

Line helped Amalie to clamber aboard and put on her flotation vest. Thancke pushed the boat off from the jetty.

'It only takes ten minutes,' he said, gesturing in the direction of a group of islands out on the misty horizon.

As the boat ploughed through the dark water Line hugged Amalie close and licked salt seawater from her lips. The breeze caught Thancke's cap and he used one hand to keep hold of it. His hair was grey at the temples and it took Line a few seconds to realize that this was paint. He had flecks of the same colour on the hand clutching the tiller.

'Have you been doing some painting out there?' she asked.

'Eh?'

Line nodded at the paint stains on his hand. 'Are you doing some renovating?'

He gave a fleeting smile. 'It's car paint,' he corrected her, without going into any further detail.

She returned his smile. 'Thanks for taking the time to see me.'

Claes Thancke answered with a brief nod. Line went on to tell him about her plans for a series of programmes.

'You were the one who found him, I believe,' Thancke said, without taking his eyes from the water in front of them. 'What made you travel out to Østmarka?'

'I wanted to see what it looks like out there now and take some footage.'

'It's not so long since I was there myself,' Thancke told her. 'Wasn't the track closed off?'

'There was a wire across it down by the crossroads,' Line replied. 'When were you there, then?'

'Last week, I think it was. The insurance from the fire hasn't been settled yet and I had to take a trip down there in connection with that.'

'There was a track into the woods, behind the shed,' Line explained.

Thancke nodded but said nothing for a few minutes. Then he told her: 'All I found was a dead crow. It was lying on the stone slabs in front of the shed and I used a spade to toss it into the bushes.'

They were out of the cove now and, as Thancke changed course, the boat scudded through the waves. 'Were you present when the crime scene technicians were working?' Thancke asked.

'Yes. They didn't finish up until about two o'clock in the morning,' Line told him.

'Did they find anything?' Thancke persisted.

'What kind of thing do you mean?'

'Any leads? Anything to say what had happened? Who was behind it?'

'I don't think so. After all, everything has to be examined more closely. They probably went back in daylight.'

There were no other boats on the water. Thancke was heading towards an island covered in deciduous trees that grew all the way down to the water's edge.

'There used to be sheep here,' Thancke explained. 'Now it's all become overgrown. It's almost impossible to see the cabin from the water.'

They were approaching a jetty. From there, a broad footpath led up to a white-painted house almost hidden by trees. Thancke had been clearing the path, and there were branches and twigs cut and gathered into bundles, some of which had been chopped up in a garden shredder and turned into woodchips, which lay piled up.

'Are you the only one who stays here?' she asked.

Claes Thancke nodded his head. 'My family have owned this island since before the war. I can have complete peace and quiet. No one else ever docks here.'

Line had read up on his background. He was the third generation of defence lawyers, but the line would probably stop with him as he was unmarried and had no children. Neither of his parents was alive. The only remaining member of his family was a brother who worked in shipping.

They drew alongside and Thancke tied up the boat. Line moved forward and lifted Amalie on to the shore before grabbing hold of her bag to jump after her. While she did that, the boat slid away from the jetty, the mooring rope tightened and she got her foot caught in it. As she stumbled, she realized that she was about to come a cropper and managed to throw her bag of camera equipment on to the jetty, but then her shoulder struck the edge, followed by her hip as she plunged into the water. She succeeded in grabbing a rope with one hand and held tight to prevent her head from going under.

Claes Thancke arrived and knelt down to grasp her arm. Kicking out, Line was able to haul herself up on one of the jetty posts.

Amalie watched her in alarm. Line couldn't give her a

reassuring hug because she was dripping wet. Instead she smiled and burst out laughing to avoid scaring her.

'Do you have a change of clothes with you?' Thancke asked, glancing at her bag.

'No, I . . .'

'You can't walk about like that,' Thancke said firmly. 'I've got some clothes in the cabin. You can get changed. I've got an airing cupboard too. Maybe we'll be able to get your clothes dried before I take you back.'

Most of all, Line felt embarrassed. She patted her pockets and took out her mobile phone. It was still working, but the screen was discoloured.

'Is it waterproof?' Thancke asked.

'Yes, but there's a crack in the glass,' Line answered. 'I don't know how long it will last.'

He reached out his hand to take a look at it. 'I never use my phone when I'm out here,' he said. 'I switch it off, but I check my emails now and again.'

Seawater poured out when he turned the phone over. 'We'll put it in a bowl of rice,' he suggested, removing it from its cover. 'That draws out the moisture. I've got some in the cabin.'

They started walking, with Line holding Amalie by the hand and Thancke carrying the bag. He showed them the way to the bathroom and then commandeered Line's mobile phone and went to find some clothes.

Line took off her shoes, socks, jacket and sweater, reassuring Amalie all the while and telling her that everything was all right.

Thancke returned with a pair of checked pyjama trousers, a T-shirt, woollen socks and a thick sweater.

'I don't think the trousers have been worn,' he said, handing her the bundle of clothes.

Line thanked him and closed the door when he left. She stripped off the rest of her clothes and wondered if she could keep her bra on, but it was sodden as well.

She stood naked in front of the large mirror, twisting and turning her head and body to examine her injuries. Her left hip and thigh were sore, and she was going to have an enormous bruise there.

Goose pimples formed on her skin as she stood there. She looked around for something to use to dry herself.

'There are towels in the cupboard under the basin,' Thancke called out from the other side of the door, as if he had read her thoughts.

'Thanks!' she shouted back.

The salty seawater had made her skin sticky.

'You can take a shower, too, if you like,' Thancke suggested.

She cast a glance into the tiled shower cabinet. It would have been welcome, but she decided to wait until she got home. She dressed and gathered up her wet clothing. Thancke was standing just outside the door when she opened it.

'I can take these,' he said, taking charge of the bundle of wet clothes. 'The airing cupboard is in the utility room.'

He opened the door of a room immediately across the hallway and connected an electric plug so that the fan heater in the cupboard began to whir.

'Maybe you'd prefer to do it yourself,' he suggested, handing back the clothes.

Line nodded and hung up her trousers before looping her bra on a hook. Amalie watched, filled with curiosity. Thancke disappeared and returned with her shoes. He waited until she had finished before placing them on a grille at the bottom of the cupboard.

'Do you have your car keys?' he asked.

She had put her keys in her back pocket. When she checked, she found that they were still there. She took them out and placed them between her shoes to make sure she would not forget them.

Thancke closed the door and flicked a switch so that the airing cupboard was at full heat. 'We'll go through to the kitchen,' he said.

On the way, he stopped at a door and looked down at Amalie. 'I might have something for you in here,' he said.

The key was on the outside of the door. He turned it and opened the door wide. It was a bedroom, and the curtains were drawn. He turned on the light switch. At the end of the bed there was a collection of colourful plastic horse figures with all the paraphernalia that goes with them.

'My Little Pony,' Line said, smiling.

Amalie had some at home. Line took Amalie by the hand and walked in with her. She chose a pony with a long, lilac mane and sat down on the floor with it.

'My niece,' Thancke explained. 'She's grown out of them now. She hasn't been here for years.'

'Mummy will be in here,' Line said to her daughter, pointing out the location of the kitchen.

Thancke put on the kettle. 'Do you have water plumbed in?' Line asked. 'On the island?'

'There's a well further in, with its own pump,' Thancke explained. 'And my own septic tank down at the jetty. The archipelago service empties it every autumn. Electricity comes via an undersea cable.'

He took out a bowl and filled it with rice to dry out her phone.

'It was the Germans who installed it all during the war,' he went on. 'They had an artillery base out here.'

A thumping noise suddenly sounded, as if someone had

fallen on the floor. Line turned round and looked along the hallway to the guest bedroom where Amalie was playing.

Thancke switched on the radio. The kettle was boiling. He took out cups and teabags. 'Earl Grey?' he asked.

Line nodded.

'Sugar? Sweetener?'

'Two sweeteners, please.'

The tea was left to brew on the kitchen worktop as Thancke took out a packet of chocolate-chip biscuits. He poured them out on a dish, placed it on the table and set out the cups.

'What's your impression of Tom Kerr?' Line asked, curling her hands around the large cup.

'Client confidentiality between Kerr and me still applies,' Thancke warned her. 'Even though he's dead. If I'm to take part in this documentary series, you have to understand that I must pay attention to his presumed interests and intentions.'

'Evil intent,' Line let slip.

'What do you mean?'

'That's how the psychiatrist describes him,' Line said. 'With an inner need to inflict pain on others.'

She drew the cup towards her and took a sip. The tea tasted bitter.

Claes Thancke's face had taken on a thoughtful expression. He rotated the cup slowly between his chubby fingers. His eyes seemed distant, but his gaze was directed at her, fixed at chest level.

As Line pushed her shoulders forward, it crossed her mind that she should have taken a shower. She still felt cold.

It was the Police Chief herself who finally took the decision that Claes Thancke should be arrested. She signed the formal document and pushed it across the desk.

'Do it as discreetly as possible,' she said. 'No uniforms, blue lights or sirens.'

The sheet of paper was left lying for a moment or two. Semmelmann leaned forward and pushed it towards Wisting. The Police Chief gave him a nod before he drew it closer to him. He was the one who would lead this operation.

They divided into two groups. Semmelmann and Stiller went to the lawyer's office in the city centre, while Hammer and Wisting drove out to his house in the west end of the city.

Hammer was rounding off a phone conversation when they turned off from the motorway. 'His phone can't be traced,' he said.

'What does that mean?'

'That it's not in use. Either switched off or outside the coverage area.'

Wisting tightened his grip on the steering wheel as he tacked his way through the quiet residential streets of Frogner. Two patrol cars were positioned at an intersection. Wisting waved to them as they passed, and Hammer called them up on the assigned channel and asked them to stand by.

They parked in the street outside the address. A dense hedge inside a high wrought-iron fence blocked their view into the property. The gate was locked and bore a sign warning that the place had CCTV. The rain had left puddles in the gravel in front of the house and there were no cars parked there. Green ivy climbed up the stone façade, twining around empty, dark windows.

Hammer tried the doorbell on the gatepost. They waited for a few minutes before he climbed the fence, swung himself over the top and squeezed his way through the hedge.

Wisting followed suit. They strode up to the door and tried the knocker, but no one came.

'Alarm,' Wisting commented, pointing at a sticker.

Hammer called the alarm company and asked them to make a verification call back via the police switchboard. They skirted around the house while he explained where they were and that they intended to enter the property. The guard at the security firm's switchboard remotely deactivated the alarm.

They chose a verandah door with small windowpanes at the rear of the house. Hammer smashed the glass nearest the handle, thrust his arm in and opened it.

Wisting stepped over the shards of glass and looked around. The living room was full of heavy, expensive furnishings and the carpet was thick and soft.

'Police!' Hammer shouted into the house. All that came back was an echoing silence.

They searched the house room by room. Two floors and a basement. It took them ten minutes to ascertain that the house was empty. All the interior furnishings were old and imposing. There were high ceilings, chandeliers and huge windows. Paintings with broad, carved frames. The spacious villa had probably been inherited, just like the legal practice.

In one part of the house there was a workroom with a separate entrance. The walls were covered with integral bookcases. The books were thick tomes with the author's name and the title in gilt lettering on the spines. By the window, there was a desk with no computer on which everything seemed to have a specific place, including a brass table lamp with a rectangular shade of green glass. In the centre of the room, a solid three-piece suite of antique leather with deep armchairs and a well-polished coffee table in mahogany or teak. Behind this were four antique wooden filing cabinets. One of the tambour doors was half open, and Wisting walked across and pulled the handle. The shutter rolled smoothly up and he saw that the cabinet contained timeworn client folders stored in alphabetical order from S to Å. Hammer drew up the adjacent shutter. The contents were the same, but this time the folders ran from K to R. The third was A to J. The cabinet on the far left was locked.

Semmelmann phoned. Wisting crossed to the desk and answered. 'Was he at home?' he asked.

Wisting pulled out a drawer and rummaged through some papers. 'No. We're inside now. No sign of him.'

'Same here,' Semmelmann reported. 'His secretary let us in. We picked her up from her home. She thinks he may be at his cabin. He's been there a lot recently, she says.'

Wisting glanced across at Hammer. They had checked this out. Thancke did not have a summer cabin.

'It's registered to the company,' Semmelmann explained. 'It's situated just past Holmestrand.'.

Wisting checked the time. It would take just under an hour by car, but they would have to leave now. He shut the drawer forcefully. The movement was so abrupt that a pen bounced up and landed in the gap between the drawer and the desk. He pulled the drawer half open again and was about to push it back when he spotted a key.

'The cabin is on an island,' Semmelmann continued.

'Stiller is taking an unmarked car from the nearest police station to see if he might be there. A helicopter is out of the question because of the fog, but they're requisitioning a boat and monitoring the area until we get there.'

'Good,' Wisting replied.

He took out the key and examined it. It looked like a key for an old chest.

'We've found something else of interest,' Semmelmann went on. 'A property transfer. Thancke established a company to purchase Tom Kerr's smallholding in Østmarka, including all outstanding debts. This means that if he reaches an agreement with the insurance company, the settlement will come to him. We're talking about a sum in the region of five million. It's probably an arrangement that was entered into in order to avoid the insurance settlement being paid into the compensation sum Kerr was ordered by the court to pay to the families of the girls he killed, but it also gives Thancke a financial motive.'

Wisting shot a glance at the fourth cabinet on the wall. The key might fit that.

'We're leaving here now,' Semmelmann concluded. 'Heading for Holmestrand.'

'We'll soon be finished too,' Wisting said, dismissing the call.

He walked around the desk and across to the row of filing cabinets. The key slid into the lock of the one on the far left and turned easily.

76

Hammer pulled up the tambour shutter. The contents appeared to be the same as in the other filing cabinets, but not in alphabetical order this time. There were only bundles of case documents and folders. Wisting extracted one of them. A name and date were written on it in ballpoint pen. *Tanner 2012.* The folder was worn and dog-eared, as if it had been taken out repeatedly.

He opened it and saw a photo of a naked woman tied to a bed with a pillowcase over her head. There were a number of photographs in the folder, of the same woman, taken from various angles. Further back there was a close-up of burn marks on her breasts being made by a cigarette. Her body was tensing and writhing in pain. Other pictures showed her skin being slashed with a knife, and her vagina and anus being penetrated, first with fingers, and then with a variety of objects. The final photos showed the wounded, bloodied body of the woman lying in a puddle of urine.

'What the fuck . . .' Hammer groaned.

Wisting took out another folder. *Krüger 1998.* These pictures were of poorer quality but showed the same sort of thing. A woman tied to a tree in the woods, a rope tight across her breasts and around her stomach, digging into the soft skin. Her legs were spread with a metal contraption, and she had a ball in her mouth held fast with a strap around her head. In the next photos she had red whip marks on her body and in others she was being brutalized with wooden sticks. Blood was running down her legs.

The next folder was thicker than the others and marked *Loch-Hansen 2014*. A naked woman was stretched out on a settee, obviously unconscious. On a table in front of her were half-full glasses, ashtrays and empty bottles. Her clothes were piled up beside her. The next photograph was staged. This time she was sitting with her legs on the table, spread out in front of her. Her head hung back, over the back of the settee. Several photos showed different objects penetrating her. An erect penis was forced into her mouth, held open with two fingers. The last of the pictures showed her face smeared with semen, and her attacker using a spoon to scrape it off her lips and cheek before dribbling it into her open mouth.

Other photographs in the same folder were taken in the same living room, with the same settee, but with different women. Their ages varied, but they were all being abused in the same way.

'Fredrick Loch-Hansen,' Wisting said. 'He was convicted of drugging and abusing more than ten women. He administered sleeping pills in the drink he gave them. None of them had any memory of what had happened. Claes Thancke was his defence counsel. This is some of the evidence material. Pictures from Loch-Hansen's mobile phone. Some of the girls were never identified.'

Hammer lifted out another folder and riffled through pictures of two naked children. 'These are from his cases,' he concluded. 'They go back a long time.'

He handed the folder to Wisting and took out another one. This one contained photos of sexual abuse that one of Thancke's clients must have downloaded from the Internet.

Wisting took a step back and paused for some time to digest all of this.

Outwardly, Thancke had appeared to be an unconventional

defence lawyer. One who regarded it as his duty to society to take on unpopular cases and who stood up for people who were otherwise shunned. In reality, he had sought out such cases in order to satisfy his own lust, his own desires. By defending perverted attackers and rapists he had built up a large portfolio of deviant photographs, kindling his personal fantasies. Then he had met Tom Kerr, and these fantasies began to be played out in real life. He was no longer an observer. He became the accomplice, the Other One.

77

'You're freezing,' Thancke said, catching her eye. 'We'll go into the living room. I can light the fire.'

He pushed his chair out from the table and Line got up too. She heard that noise again, a series of faint thumps.

'I'll just go and see to Amalie,' she said.

'Do you think she'd like something to drink?'

Line shook her head. 'I can bring her a couple of biscuits, though,' she said, helping herself from the plate.

Amalie was in the middle of a game. She was lying on her stomach with a little horse in each hand, conducting a conversation between them.

'Are you OK?' Line asked, handing her the biscuits.

Amalie glanced up at her and took the biscuits. 'You're wearing strange clothes,' she said.

Line smiled, gave her a hug and went out to the living room. It was a gas fire, and the flames were already licking up the glass. On the walls, various awards and diplomas were on display, along with a number of framed photographs of Thancke with politicians and other VIPs.

Two picture windows faced south. The mist had turned into fog, but they could still make out the sea. Just outside, there was a paved terrace and a small swimming pool with a glass roof. The steam from the hot pool formed beads of condensation inside the glass.

The planks on a trapdoor in the floor creaked when she moved to the window to take a better look. In summer this must be idyllic, but on a day like today it just seemed cold and bleak.

'Beautiful,' she commented all the same.

Thancke came up beside her and used his foot to push a rag rug back in place.

'It's a salt-water pool,' he said, smiling. 'So I don't have to add chlorine.'

Thancke had carried the teacups through. Line sat down where he had put hers, nearest to the fire.

'Can't you give me some idea of what Kerr was like?' she asked.

Thancke brushed some fluff from his trouser leg. 'Well, he was more than the sum of his actions,' he answered. 'In my experience, he was in many ways an energetic and resourceful person. A man of many interests.'

'You've a lot of clients of that kind,' Line pointed out.

'What kind do you mean?'

'Sexual criminals. Rapists and deviants. What is it like to defend such people?'

Thancke cleared his throat. 'I've never defended, and never will defend, their crimes. I defend my clients' rights. I understand very well that people become outraged by the cases I bring to court, but it's my task to go in and examine the evidence and check if it is sufficient. To make sure that where there is an element of doubt, it is to the benefit of the accused. I've never had any problem with that. I don't engage my personal feelings in my role as a defence counsel, but I put effort and commitment into every case.'

He was an excellent interviewee, Line thought. His answers were well expressed and wide-ranging, but these were of course questions that had been put to him many times before – the answers were well rehearsed. Nevertheless, he appeared to be an altruistic and reflective man.

'Doesn't it have an impact on you?' she asked.

'Does it dull my senses – is that what you're thinking?' He shook his head. 'In this job you can't be deterred by how awful something is. The same applies to doctors, of course. It's my task to see past what is distressing and sad and concentrate on my work of defence. I have to put all the rest out of my mind.'

'So you don't give a thought to the victims of the men you defend?'

It looked as if he did not entirely comprehend the question. 'It gets easier after a while,' he replied. 'You grow hardened over the years. What seemed strong meat at the beginning eventually becomes a daily occurrence. I don't think it means that I've become emotionally stunted.'

The noise was back. Three regular, dull thumps.

'What's that noise?' she asked.

'What noise?'

'The thumping.'

'Oh,' he said with a smile. 'It's the filtration plant for the pool. There's air in the pipes. I'm so used to it that I don't notice it at all.'

Line looked past him. A bird had landed on the swimming-pool roof.

'Did you have no inkling that he intended to escape?' she queried.

Thancke shook his head. 'I thought he had come to an understanding with himself,' he replied. 'That he wanted to confess and move on. I was tricked. He fooled everybody.'

'Where could he have hidden? Until the time when he was killed.'

'We don't know when he was killed,' Thancke replied.

'I'm thinking of Maren Dokken,' Line said. 'Where she might be hidden.'

The thumping noise from the water pipes was almost inaudible, but the vibration they caused was making circles form in her cup. With every thump, there was a tremble in the hot tea, as if a big, heavy animal was stomping about.

'They're assuming that it was Tom Kerr who abducted Maren Dokken,' the lawyer objected. 'We know nothing about it, really. It hasn't been proven in any way at all.'

'In a sense, you're the one who knows most about him,' Line said. 'If he had a hiding place, how would we go about finding it? I realize it may not be in your client's best interests, but Maren Dokken is still missing. It could be a matter of life or death. That must surely override your duty of confidentiality?'

'Isn't that a side issue with regard to the subject of your documentary series?' Thancke asked.

Line put her hands around the teacup again and stared down into it.

'Sorry,' she said. 'But I met her the day Kerr escaped. I spoke to her on board the minibus. The thought of what she's going through . . .'

Thumps. Circles in the teacup. They were coming in a regular rhythm now. First three short ones with spaces in between, then three long ones, and then three short ones again before there was a pause.

'I met her too,' Claes Thancke said. 'I spoke to her and, if I had known what had happened to her, then of course I would have passed that on. But I'm just as much in the dark as the police.'

Line did not move her eyes from the teacup. She concentrated hard on listening. Three short thumps, three long ones and three short again. SOS. These intervals were not random. Someone was trying to send a signal.

She glanced across at the cellar trapdoor by the window.

Heard three more thumps. Someone was banging on the water pipes below the cabin.

'You've hardly touched your tea,' Thancke said. 'Is something wrong?'

'No, of course not,' Line replied.

She forced a smile and drank from the cup, and at the same time an unpleasant possibility opened up inside her head. The pieces fell into place. The communication in and out of the prison, the planning, the preparation: Claes' Thancke was the person who would have least difficulty helping Kerr to escape. He fitted the psychiatrist's profile of the perpetrator in every respect.

Her tea was no longer hot, but she forced it down.

'How did you come into contact with Tom Kerr?' she asked. 'For the first time, I mean.'

'We go back a long time,' Thancke answered. 'I took over the legal practice from my father. He had defended Tom Kerr's father. The first time Tom Kerr needed legal assistance, it was natural for him to apply to my office.'

'What had his father done?'

Thancke gave her a condescending smile. 'You can probably find out for yourself, but it's not right for me to be the one to tell you.'

She took another gulp of tea, simply to fill the silence. Her thoughts were racing and she could not collect them at all.

'I'll just go and see to Amalie,' she excused herself, and set her cup down on the table.

Walking through the kitchen and out into the hallway, she could hear Amalie playing. She wondered if she should snatch her up and flee, but there was nowhere to go. The boat was locked and tied up and, anyway, she had no shoes.

Through the window beside the front door she could see down to the jetty. The boat was only tied up by the rear mooring, and if the sea grew rougher or the wind changed direction it could easily come adrift. Thancke must have forgotten the other mooring or not finished tying it up when she fell into the water.

She shouted to him. 'The boat's not tied up properly,' she said, darting a look down at the jetty.

Thancke muttered something she did not catch as he grabbed his jacket and stormed out.

Line rushed back to the living room. The rag rug now covered the trapdoor on the floor. Pushing it aside, she opened the hatch and peered inside. There was a light on down there. A steep staircase led to a room with a concrete floor. She glanced towards the kitchen and hallway before clambering down.

78

She probably had no more than a couple of minutes, maybe not even that.

The room was empty. Two doors led into other rooms, but they too were empty. At the other end, there was an opening into the hillside, like a miner's shaft. Something from the war, perhaps, when the Nazis had occupied the island.

A cable ran from one dome light to the next and hung in a loop under the ceiling. Parallel with the power supply were two metal pipes. Line reached out and grasped one of these with her hand as she stood waiting for a vibration. She was just about to let go when three thumps came in rapid succession. The sound was clearer down here and came from somewhere in front of her.

She followed the path. After ten metres, it ran down ninety degrees to the right and ended at a door, locked and bolted, built into the hillside.

She grabbed one of the metal pipes again and waited for the next series of thumps, but none came. She wanted to shout but held back. Instead she scratched a stone loose from the rock wall and tapped it three times on the pipe to send a signal to whoever was on the other side of the door.

The response came immediately. Three rapid thumps and a muffled shout.

She felt a tingle of panic, spreading like a warm wave from her diaphragm up to the top of her head, making it difficult for her to breathe.

She took a few fumbling steps back and tripped over something but managed to keep her balance. Then she turned around, dashed back, scuttling up the stairs, and looked around, expecting to find Claes Thancke in the room, but she was still alone. She dropped the hatch back in place and covered it with the rag rug. Then she rushed out to the kitchen, up to the worktop and plunged her hand into the bowl of rice. She dug down, looking for her phone. The grains of rice spilled out over the worktop and on to the floor. It was not there. He must have taken it.

When she heard a noise at the front door she scooped some of the rice back into the bowl and struggled to control her breathing. Forcing herself to breathe slowly out, and slowly in again, she finally found a rhythm and walked forward to meet him.

'I think it might be best if Amalie and I go home now,' she said. 'It's her bedtime in an hour.'

Thancke stood in the hallway, positioned between her and the room where Amalie was playing. 'But your clothes aren't dry,' he objected.

'That can't be helped.'

He looked past her into the kitchen. 'You haven't even finished your tea,' he said.

'That doesn't matter.'

He took a step back and one hand fumbled for the door to the guest bedroom. In one speedy move he pulled it shut, turned the key and removed it from the lock.

79

Confirmation came before they were halfway there. Claes Thancke's car was parked at the marina. He was at the cabin.

A low-slung sports car moved aside for the blue lights and sirens. The Police Chief had requested discretion, but that had been while there remained room for doubt that they had the right man. That doubt was gone now.

'We must summon some manpower,' Wisting said. 'Officers closer than us.'

'They're on their way,' Hammer assured him. 'But they probably won't get there any sooner than we do.'

The fog thickened as they approached the sea. The road narrowed and grew more tortuous, ending up at a small private marina. Three police cars were already parked there. Uniformed officers were preparing to embark on a boat with a large outboard motor.

Wisting lingered behind the wheel, his eyes trained on a fourth vehicle. A clammy fear took hold of him as the wipers swept across his windscreen. It was Line's car.

He struggled to deny the thoughts that rose to the surface, but it slowly dawned on him what this meant.

Stiller and Semmelmann's car drew up alongside his. Wisting opened his door and planted one foot on the ground. The boat was ready to set out and the policeman standing with the mooring rope called out to them.

'Are you coming?' Stiller asked.

'Line's out there,' Wisting said. He slammed the car door and strode across to her car. It was locked.

'Phone her!' Hammer suggested.

Wisting already had his phone out. He tried her number but could not get through.

The man with the mooring rope shouted again. Hammer pulled Wisting away and he finally found a place at the front of the boat. As it hurtled away from shore with a jolt, the headwind ruffled his wiry hair. The sea breeze around him was heavy with fog and salt water. He wiped a drop from the side of his nose and lowered his eyes.

80

'Now you're going to do exactly as I say.'

Claes Thancke tucked the key into his pocket. From the other side of the door, Amalie screamed for her mummy.

Line kicked Thancke in the groin. He made a noise and doubled up in pain. It would have been more effective if she had been wearing shoes.

She pushed past him towards the exit, but he grabbed her round the waist, knocking her off balance and hurling her against the wall.

She managed to hold back a shriek but crumpled and gasped for breath. Thancke grappled with her again and brutally slammed her against the wall. Her head was propelled backwards, hitting the wood and bouncing back. His voice rang in her ears, but she could not make out what he was saying. Her arms flailed blindly as she used her legs, her knees. It was his strength and size versus her desperation. He pressed his whole body weight against her, squeezing her left forearm against her throat with one hand and seizing her wrist with the other. His forehead made contact with hers and she could feel his hot breath on her cheek. Twisting her face away, she dropped her head on his shoulder and gave him a vicious bite. Her teeth pierced his skin and she could taste blood.

Claes Thancke screamed. He let go and lashed out at her. The blow struck her on the side of the face and threw her into the wall again. He caught her by the hair, whirled her round and flung her to the floor. She managed to struggle up and stagger to her feet, trying to move towards the front door, but he pounced once more and hauled her back. Another blow caught her on the cheekbone, just under her right eye. She spun round and hammered into the door of the utility room. It sprang open and Line toppled in, landing on her back. She managed to sit up and slide into a corner, knocking over a bucket and catching hold of a sweeping brush as it fell. She brandished it as a weapon, but Thancke snatched it out of her hands, tossed it aside and launched himself at her. He had both hands around her throat now and pounded her head against the tiled floor over and over again. Line wildly thrashed her arms about, trying to scratch him, but she was met with nothing but thin air, and she could feel Thancke tighten his grip around her larynx, using his thumbs to increase the pressure.

Line resisted with the whole of her body, but she was aware of a burning pain behind her eyes as the room lurched around her. She heard herself make gurgling noises while she tried in vain to force his fingers away so that she could get some air. His grip only grew harder, tighter. Everything began to swim before her eyes. She succeeded in planting one hand under his left eye, her nails puncturing his face in a desperate attempt to push him away. Her other arm was flapping madly at one side of her body, and she caught hold of something and used it to whack Thancke in the side. She caught a glimpse of what she had picked up: a blue spray bottle.

Changing her grip, she placed two fingers on the pump and aimed the nozzle straight at his face. Nothing happened when she depressed the button, just a jet of air. She tried again and this time the resistance was greater. A sudden spray hit Thancke on the chin. The stinging smell of chlorine spread immediately. She pressed the button again and sent another squirt, this time smack into his right eye. The reaction was instantaneous. Thancke released her, with a loud yell of pain, and shoved aside the arm with the spray bottle.

Line scrambled up as Thancke rubbed his eyes. She lurched along the hallway to the door where Amalie was and tugged frantically at the handle.

Thancke came staggering after her. One eye was swollen and glued shut. He roared and Line tottered backwards. They stumbled into the kitchen and the struggle continued there. Line caught hold of his head, clawing at his face and pulling his hair. He forced her on into the living room and pushed her up against the wall.

She waved her arms and grabbed a framed diploma, swinging it towards him and smashing the frame into his face. The glass broke and slashed across his cheek. A large flap of skin hung loosely from his mouth, fluttering each time he breathed.

Line drew back towards the terrace door, fumbling with the handle. Thancke grabbed hold of a wooden chair, swung it round and slammed it into her side. She could feel her ribs crack. He lifted the chair for another blow, and this time it was so forceful that one of the chair legs broke. She collapsed, falling to her knees. Blood was dripping on to the rug in front of her. Her strength was draining away. He had the upper hand and knew it.

Tossing the rag rug aside, he flipped up the cellar trapdoor. Line gritted her teeth with exertion, desperately struggling to gather her strength. If he managed to get her down there, she would probably never come back up again. Not alive, at least. And never back to Amalie.

81

The fenders scraped against the edge of the jetty as the boat drew alongside. Wisting was among the first to leap ashore. The uniformed officers spread out as they advanced towards the cabin on all sides, weapons drawn. Wisting took the shortest route, with Hammer by his side.

They could hear noises from inside, indistinct noises. Disquieting noises.

They approached the front door and looked through the side window. The doormat in the hallway was curled up and a framed picture lay smashed on the floor. Bloodstains led into the cabin.

Wisting wrenched the door handle, but it was locked.

They stormed round the cabin to a terrace with an outdoor swimming pool and two huge picture windows. Line was kneeling on the floor inside the living room, with blood on her face and hair. Thancke was moving towards her, about to grab hold of her again, when he stopped and turned to face them. One eye was glued shut, and his mouth was crooked. His expression was incredulous.

A uniformed policeman moved up beside Wisting and aimed his gun at Thancke.

Line struggled to her feet, without noticing what was going on outside. She had a wooden chair leg in her hands and raised it like a club. The swinging blow struck Thancke on the side of his neck and brought him to his knees. Wisting had reached the door but was shoved aside and held back. A police officer used the butt of his machine pistol to break the glass, and they rushed in. Forcing Claes Thancke to the floor, they dragged him to the middle of the room and clapped handcuffs on him.

Wisting took Line by the arms, holding her up and hugging her close. He felt her trembling.

'Amalie,' she whispered. 'Amalie's in the bedroom.'

He pushed her away very slightly and looked at her as she repeated this. 'He's got the key in his pocket,' she told him, gesturing towards Thancke.

Wisting let her go.

'Wait,' she said. 'I'll get her. You must . . . Maren . . .'

Line turned her head away and focused on the open trap-door to the cellar. 'Maren Dokken is down there,' she whispered.

'Alive?' Wisting asked.

'I think so.'

He shouted to Hammer and clambered down the opening in the floor. Hammer brought one of the uniformed officers with him.

'Tools!' Wisting shouted from beside the locked door. 'We need tools.'

Hammer ran back and relayed the message up into the living room. The room above them sprang to life, filled with activity. Doors opened and cupboards slammed. Stiller came down with what they had found: a crowbar and a hammer. Wisting used the crowbar and tore the bolts out of the wall. Lumps of plaster and concrete dropped to the floor. The crossbeam fixings loosened, and Hammer tossed it aside as Wisting pushed the door open.

The room was poorly lit and at an angle. The walls and ceiling were padded with foam rubber and it stank of mould and damp. The beam of the flashlight held by one of the police officers flitted around, running along the floor, highlighting grey fluff and dust.

They jostled one another as they moved through the door. When they turned a corner they found her, lying on a bed beside the wall. Naked. Her arms were raised and outspread, chained to each bedpost with two handcuffs.

Her ankles were tied with rope. One of the ties had loosened, so that one foot was free. Bloodstains told of the effort she had made to kick the pipe on the wall.

She lifted her head and squinted in the glare from the flashlight. A broad length of plastic tape covered her mouth and was wound twice around her head. Her eyes rolled back before they closed completely.

82

Darkness was overtaking the chill grey fog. Line stood on the jetty with a blanket round her shoulders, gazing up at the cabin. Both Maren Dokken and Claes Thancke were still inside. A rescue vessel had been summoned and the crew were now down in the cellar, preparing to bring Maren out.

Amalie had fallen asleep between her and Wisting on the bed in the guest room. He had carried her on board the rescue vessel and was sitting with her in the wheelhouse. She had been shielded from seeing much of the attack, but Line was going to have to spend a lot of time talking to her and explaining what had happened.

The cabin door opened. Stiller emerged and walked down towards her. He was carrying her bag of camera equipment.

'They're bringing him out now,' he said, handing her the bag.

Line did not at first understand what he meant. 'They're bringing him out now,' Stiller repeated, motioning towards the cabin. 'Claes Thancke. They want him out of the way before they take Maren out.'

Line took her bag and put it down on the jetty. Pain shot through her ribs as she bent over and took out her camera. She polished the lens with a corner of the blanket, attached the flashgun and moved a few metres up the path before switching it on.

As the cabin door opened again Line checked the display and adjusted the focus. A police officer stepped out first, followed by Claes Thancke, with two policemen immediately behind who moved forward and grabbed an arm each as soon as they were through the door.

Thancke was walking with his head bowed. He was dragging his feet, and his hands were behind his back, in handcuffs. He came closer, into the camera light. Line was struggling to hold the camera steady. The officers escorting him held back a little and Thancke raised his head. He had a square bandage on one eye. The deep cut on his lip was closed with butterfly stitches. Some of the blood had been wiped from his face, but his clothes were blood-stained and his hair was tangled with dried residue from the struggle.

He passed her at a distance of one metre, one eye staring at her through the lens. His eyes were so dark that Line could not make out the transition between the iris and the pupil, as if they could not contain or reflect light. Then he turned his head away and was led on board the waiting boat.

83

'They're bringing him out as we speak.'

Stiller ended a phone conversation and gestured towards the hotel entrance. Wisting leaned forward between the front seats as Line picked up her camera and stepped out of the car.

A few minutes passed and then the doors slid open. The Internal Affairs investigator came out, escorted by two plain-clothes officers from Stiller's Cold Cases Group at Kripos.

Line moved further forward.

They did not have handcuffs on him, but the photographs would leave no doubt about the situation. Terje Nordbo was led to a waiting car with tinted windows. The two officers had a tight grip on each arm. One of them opened the door to the rear seat and raised his hand to protect Nordbo's head as he moved inside. He caught sight of Line and stood bent at the waist in the opening before putting an arm in front of his face and turning away from the camera.

Wisting felt the reaction was overly dramatic and that an arrest was unnecessary.

'It's about far more than a leak,' Stiller told him. 'We're not just talking about a breach of confidentiality. He has misled his superiors in order to support a false accusation against you and actively contributed to over-hasty condemnation in the press.'

Wisting sat with the photographic evidence in his lap. They were screenshots from TV2's news broadcasts. Several of the pictures were of him and had been used in articles critical of the police operation when Tom Kerr escaped, stating that Wisting was under investigation and had been removed from the case.

Stiller had distributed four copies of Line's video footage of Kerr's site visit. One to his own senior officers at Kripos, one to Chief of Police Agnes Kiil and her colleagues, and another to Wisting and his investigation group. In addition he had made a copy at the request of Internal Affairs. Each copy had been marked. He had inserted a barely visible watermark on each film. At the far edge of the photograph, Wisting could make out the contours of the letter I, for Internal Affairs. The recordings shown on TV2 could only have come from one source, from one man.

The doors on the unmarked police car were slammed shut. One of the investigators sat at the back with the arrestee. The other was in the driver's seat.

'The case against you will be dropped before the day is out,' Stiller said. 'I'll make sure TV2 reports that and that it gets more than a minor mention.'

Wisting nodded. The outcome of the internal investigation had not worried him. He had faced this before, but this time it had been different all the same. He would continue to believe that the trip with Tom Kerr could have been handled differently. The preparations could have been more meticulous, and the operation itself could have been less compromising. The escape and what happened in the wake of that could have been avoided entirely. At the same time, that would not have yielded the answers they now had. The Other One would still have been out there, still at large.

84

There was snow in the air. The thin flakes melted as they drifted to the ground, but the frost soon followed.

Wisting stood with his jacket lapels turned up. The search was being led by Maren Dokken. Three months had elapsed and she was back on duty. The shoulder injuries she had received in the grenade explosion would never heal completely. She would never be able to return to the patrol section but had been appointed instead to the criminal investigation department. Her body had suffered other damage too, but the mental trauma had been the most serious.

A car arrived. It swung out on to the withered grass of the summer meadow, turned around and parked. Adrian Stiller clambered out, along with Idar Semmelmann. They nodded to Wisting and Hammer and stood beside them in the lee of the old sawmill.

Three police officers stood ready with spades. They had also been present on the day of Tom Kerr's escape. Line filmed the scene as they began to dig in the heap of old, grey sawdust. Espen Mortensen had donned a pair of white overalls and was standing at a distance, ready to take over if any significant finds were made.

Nils Hammer tucked a sachet of snuff under his lip. 'The cadaver dogs should have picked up a scent when we were here with them in September,' he said.

Wisting was not so sure. It had been a number of years since Taran Norum had disappeared.

'The Gjervan case,' Stiller commented.

It was almost twenty years old. A farmer had raped and killed a young stable girl. The corpse was finally found in a woodchip bin. The dogs had not reacted because the sawdust had insulated the smell.

'Claes Thancke was his lawyer,' Stiller added. 'He may have picked up the idea from there.'

'Tom Kerr was familiar with this area,' Semmelmann added. 'Almost every second summer cabin out here has a hot tub or a swimming pool.'

The top layer was shovelled off. Underneath, the sawdust had turned to compost, dark, granular and moist.

The excavation work proceeded rapidly. There were no stones, roots or any other impediments. When they had dug down to a depth of half a metre, Maren Dokken ordered a halt. Wisting went over to the edge, along with the others. A piece of black plastic was jutting out from the earth.

Mortensen moved forward with his camera. 'He shouldn't have used plastic,' he commented.

'Practical for transportation, though,' Hammer pointed out.

Maren took over one of the spades and scooped off some more earth. She located the knot at one end of the bag and lifted it out after the go-ahead from Mortensen.

A white tarpaulin had been laid out, and Maren Dokken placed the plastic bag on top. Mortensen handed her a carpet knife. Slicing carefully with the blade to make a circle, beneath the knot, she cut another opening in it.

A few small bones fell out, followed by a couple of larger ones. Maren Dokken lined them up on the sheet of plastic, removed a few more parts of the skeleton and laid them down so that, together, they formed an upper arm, forearm, hand and fingers.

Somewhere in the vicinity, a dog barked. Maren Dokken stood up and gazed fleetingly straight into Line's camera lens. Then she turned her gaze to Wisting and the corners of her mouth stretched a little. It was not a smile but an expression of satisfaction. He managed to return her look before she took hold of the spade and continued.

She would be fine, he thought. She was marked for life, but she would be able to get over it. She had a strong will and was going to do well in life. He looked around at the other investigators, Hammer, Stiller, Mortensen and Semmelmann. They needed people like her. There were still a few more out there. A few others.

LOVE *WISTING*?

A
QUESTION
OF
GUILT

COMING 2021

I

A fly landed on the rim of his water glass. Swatting it away, Wisting sat down in the shade of the parasol. After drinking half the water, he checked the total number of steps on his phone app – almost four thousand, and it was not yet noon. Most of them had registered as he walked back and forth across the grass with the lawnmower. His aim was to walk ten thousand steps every day during his holidays, but the daily average was down below eight.

Some years before Ingrid died, they had each received a step counter for Christmas from Thomas – a small digital device that had to be attached to a belt or waistband just above the hip, recording movements in the pelvic area as steps. For the first few days he and Ingrid had competed to see who walked most. Eventually, however, the step counters were left lying in a drawer. But he always had his phone with him.

Squinting at the screen, he opened his browser. The latest news was of Agnete Roll, who had disappeared the same day Wisting had gone on holiday, though she had not been reported missing until two days later. The first articles to appear had described the search for her, but with each subsequent update the story had looked less and less like an ordinary disappearance. It had begun to resemble something different, something Wisting had witnessed before.

Now the leader of the search party no longer explained which areas had been fine-combed. The case had stepped up a gear and Nils Hammer was acting as spokesperson. Three separate references in the article by the local journalist described Nils Hammer as being acting head of the Criminal Investigation Department.

The press coverage actually contained nothing new. Agnete Roll, thirty-two years old, had been in town with her husband when an argument sparked and she had left for home before him. Half an hour later, he told his friends he was heading home too. According to the online newspaper, the missing woman had last been seen when she left the pub in Stavern town centre just before midnight. That had been four days ago.

Each time Wisting picked up his tablet, he expected one of two things to have happened: that Agnete Roll's body had been found, or that her husband had been arrested and charged.

He put down his iPad and took another gulp from the glass. Stretching out his legs, he leaned his head back and watched as a seagull wheeled above him.

He still thought there was something special about a physical newspaper, but nowadays it was too long to wait until the next day for a news update. Especially if something was unfolding. He liked having access to the latest news, whenever and wherever he wanted. Besides, it was reassuring to know that he had mastered the latest technology and new methods of acquiring knowledge and information.

He was unaccustomed to following a potential murder case from the sidelines without playing an active part in the ongoing investigation. From the facts he had gleaned from the media, a great deal jarred. Agnete Roll's husband was not named, but Wisting had found him on social media. Erik Roll, who was one year older and worked in a local IT company, had waited nearly forty-eight hours to report her missing. A pattern was taking shape.

Missing person cases were always difficult, but he had already worked out how he would organize the investigation. The approach had to be both wide-ranging and in-depth. Wide-ranging in order to cover everything, and in-depth in order to focus on whatever stood out and might point the investigation in a particular direction.

He knew that Hammer and the others would be knuckling down and that Erik Roll would be a person of interest about whom they would make intensive inquiries.

The iPad on the table allowed him to log into the police computer system and read the case documents, but he had consciously refrained from doing that. Being on the outside was something he would soon have to get used to, as before too long his age would oblige him to leave the police station for good.

All the same he felt curiosity tugging at him. The key to missing person cases was almost always to be found in words and incidents from the days before someone went missing.

A sudden noise made him open his eyes wide. The lid of the mailbox slammed shut out in the street on the other side of the house.

He remained seated until he heard the postman drive on. Only then did he get to his feet, walk through the house and exit on the opposite side. A smoky-grey cat, lying in the shade beside the garage, leapt up and darted out into the street, disappearing into a neighbour's garden.

Wisting cast a glance down towards his daughter's house. He had promised to take in her post, and she had now been away from home for five days.

Approaching his mailbox, he removed the contents: a collection of advertising leaflets but also one letter, a white envelope with his name and address written in neat capital letters. He turned it over, but no sender's details were marked on it.

Line's box contained nothing but the same junk mail. He dropped it all straight into the recycling bin and made his way home, curious about the letter he had received.

Only rarely did he receive letters these days, at least of this kind. He hardly ever received bills either, as most of them were paid by direct debit. The black handwriting on the envelope was unusual and almost looked professionally printed. The 'W's in William and Wisting were virtually identical and made him think that this must be some kind of personally addressed advertising material, while the 'i's were slightly different and gave the impression that it really was handwritten.

Taking a sharp knife from the kitchen drawer, he sliced the envelope open and removed the contents: a plain sheet of paper that had been folded twice. It looked as if it had been crumpled up and then smoothed out again. In the middle of the sheet there was only a series of numbers: 12-1569/99.

These numbers were written in a similar style to the address on the envelope. Precise and painstaking, stiff and straight.

He hovered in the kitchen with the paper in his hand, aware of what he was looking at, but baffled nonetheless.

It was a case number, labelled in the way cases had been organized when he began in the police. These days, new criminal cases were allocated eight-digit reference numbers, but in the past the case number was designated in such a fashion that it was possible to decipher it. The last segment, after the slash, was the year, 1999. The two initial numbers indicated which police district the case belonged to, with 12 signifying the former police station in Porsgrunn. 1569 was the actual case number, a sequential number given to new cases in chronological order.

It made no sense.

He laid the paper down on the kitchen table and stood gazing at it.

Police district 12 also encompassed the local station in Bamble, a neighbouring district, but Wisting had never worked there. In size it was similar to his home district, with around 50,000 inhabitants. They had approximately the same number of criminal cases per year, around 3,000. Case 1569 should therefore be a case from the summer of 1999.

This was so long ago that the case had probably been deleted from the electronic records. He would not be able to find it in any computer system, but the files should still be held in an archive somewhere.

He tried to cast his mind back, wondering if there had been any special events in the summer of 1999, but could not think of anything. Line and Thomas had turned sixteen in the June of that year and were about to start upper high school that autumn. He could not recall having gone on any summer holidays. Line had had a summer job at an ice cream kiosk in Stavern, or had that been the following year? He did remember that Thomas had been working at the marina.

He left the letter and headed out on to the terrace again, where he sat down with his iPad to look up the year 1999. By then major newspapers already had their own web pages but it was difficult to retrieve individual coverage. However, there were Internet pages listing the most significant milestones of each year. The notorious triple murder at Orderud Farm in Akershus took place on 23 May. In Russia, Boris Yeltsin's government resigned and 15,000 lost their lives in a Turkish earthquake. There had been local council elections in Norway and Bill Clinton had paid a visit to Oslo.

Having conducted a search for Porsgrunn combined with the year number, he ended up with an incomprehensible list of results. Some of these were police matters, but there was nothing at all that made sense.

Case 1569 had not necessarily received media coverage, but the anonymous sender must have a particular reason for sending him that number. It must be a case to which he had some kind of connection.

Or not.

As a detective, he had received any number of anonymous letters, normally lengthy, full of conspiratorial thoughts and disconnected allegations. Some were directed at him personally and concerned cases on which he had worked, while others had simply found their way to him in his capacity as a criminal investigator.

Moving inside again, he studied the unusual formation of the individual letters. A black felt tip pen must have been used. The strokes were approximately one millimetre in breadth. There was a stamp on the envelope, which had been postmarked the previous day, but that failed to reveal where the letter had been posted.

It felt intrusive to receive such a letter in his mailbox at home. No threat seemed to be involved, but it was unpleasant all the same. Disquieting, as if it contained a warning of more to come.

Opening a kitchen drawer, he took out a roll of plastic freezer bags, tore off two and used a fork to prod the letter into one bag, the envelope into the other.

This entire business had begun to irritate him. It was not something he could ignore. He felt compelled to track down the case.

There was no longer a police station in Porsgrunn, but if he were lucky the case may have been included in the boxes moved to the new police headquarters in Skien. He might then be able to get an answer as early as today. In the worst-case scenario, if the case files had ended up in the national archives, it could take a few days.

He rang Bjørg Karin in the records office. A civilian employee, her work was nevertheless one of the most important elements in the force's daily operations. She had been employed in the police longer than he had, was familiar with all its labyrinths and was his go-to person when he needed to decide where to turn within the system. In all likelihood, she would know who to phone to request a search in the archives of a neighbouring district.

Before he came to the point, he had to tell her how his holiday had gone so far, give a few observations on the weather and outline his plans for the rest of the summer.

He omitted mention of the anonymous letter and simply said that his inquiry had to do with an old case in an adjacent district.

'Can you requisition it for me?'

Bjørg Karin asked no questions. 'I'll phone Eli,' she answered. 'And then it'll be here by the time you come back.'

Wisting assumed Eli worked in a similar post to Bjørg Karin.

'I'd really like to have it sent over as soon as possible,' he said.

'I see,' Bjørg Karin replied, though it did not sound as if she genuinely did. 'We get the internal mail tomorrow around noon.'

'That would be fine.'

They were about to round off the conversation.

'One more thing,' Wisting said, glancing again at the letter. 'Can you ask Eli to check what kind of case it is and let me know?'

He understood from Bjørg Karin's response that she found it strange for him to be asking to have such an unknown quantity sent over, but she made no comment and merely promised to comply with his request.

Wisting moved out on to the terrace again and sat down to read the online newspapers. Half an hour later, Bjørg Karin called back.

'I've spoken to Eli,' she said, holding back a little: 'Could this have to do with a murder case?'

'I expect so,' Wisting replied. 'I only have a case number.'

'She's sending it over,' Bjørg Karin continued. 'It'll arrive here around lunchtime tomorrow.'

'Excellent,' Wisting said.

Getting to his feet, he walked to the railings and gazed across the town spread out below him.

'Who was murdered?' he asked

'Tone Vaterland,' Bjørg Karin told him.

The name meant nothing to him. He repeated it to himself but it held no associations.

'Then I'll see you tomorrow?' Bjørg Karin asked. 'You'll drop into the office?'

'See you then,' Wisting confirmed.